The Gl

Also by Jenny Hall in this series

On the Dragon's Breath – a tale of Merlin
(Published 2003)

Comments from some people who have read

ON THE DRAGON'S BREATH – A TALE OF MERLIN

I have just finished reading Jenny Hall's fantastic book about a boy from the 20th Century drawn back into the Dark Ages of Merlin, Arthur and his dog Cabal. The author's ability to draw you into this magical world is excellent and the pace of the narrative and characters etc is first class. I can't wait to find out what happens next in the sequel. *Joe Delaney – Hailsham*

A bewitching story full of heroic deeds and scary adventures. Jenny Hall kept me turning the pages with her weave of magic, comedy and romance - well done! I am looking forward to the publication of her next book entitled "The Glaston Giant" with great anticipation. *Anna Pieri - London*

Wow! This book has got to be one of my all time favourites because of its mix of adventure, magic, comedy and ingeniously scripted characters. Jenny Hall manages to keep you turning page after page with this never tiring story - an epic adventure of Jack and Cabal! This book is a must read for everyone young and old alike, and can be enjoyed on different levels to suit. I hope you all enjoy it as much as I did. *Pete Watts – Chelmsford*

Leo . M

The Glaston Giant

... a tale of Merlin

SN8 3ea
Whiltshire

Jenny Hall

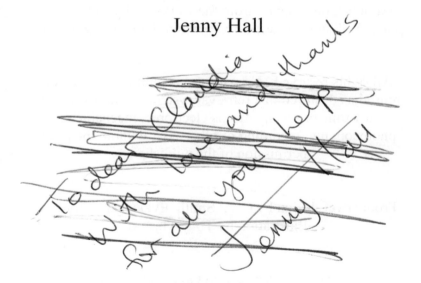

To dear Claudia
With love and thanks
for all your help
Jenny Hall

Theophilus Books

Published by
Theophilus Books
13 Eastwood Road
East Sussex
England

A catalogue record for this book
is available from the British Library

10 digits ISBN 0-9545423-1-2
13 digits ISBN 978-09545423-1-7

The famous short one-liners that appear in this novel are
extracted, once again, from the works of that celebrated
bard, William Shakespeare, to whom I am very grateful.

Front cover design by Cecil Smith, EVERGREEN*Graphics*
Illustration by Tony Masero

Printed and bound in Great Britain by
Antony Rowe Limited, Chippenham

For my granddaughter, Lauren,
with love

Acknowledgments

I am much indebted, once again, to Claudia Holness, Jacqui Barnes and Alex Hall for all their hard work and patience in reading and re-reading my work and correcting those typos and errors that seem to creep in unawares. I also very much appreciate Jim Hutchinson's help with his IT expertise. Again, I have drawn on many fond memories of my old dog, Sandy – her character and sense of fun appearing, once more, in my hero's hound, Cabal.

The Glaston Giant – a tale of Merlin

I haven't the foggiest idea how I got there that day, but I found myself, once more, sitting on the clifftop overlooking Tintagel Island. It was one of those rare and glorious golden autumn days, still and warm, and as I looked down I could see a thousand suns winking back at me with millions of sparkling eyes from that crystal sea and the island itself was resplendent - an emerald jewel waltzing upon it. As I said, I had been there before, when we used to go on our special days out as children, but I had never seen it look as beautiful as it did that day. In fact, I don't think I could have kept myself from exploring it even if I'd tried; I was drawn - the proverbial moth to a flame.

It took a while to make my way down the cliff face; it's always been very dangerous – steep with crumbling sides. But then as soon as my foot landed on the beach the darkness closed in as though I'd triggered a switch - the day suddenly disappeared, sucked up an invisible chimney – whoosh, it was gone! I knew it couldn't be far past noon, as I'd only recently eaten some of the food my mum had packed for me 'and at that time, like you two,' Jack said directing this comment to his grandsons as they sprawled on the floor listening to his tale, 'I reckon I could always tell the time by my stomach!'

Staring back at the flames that leapt in his fireplace, Jack's eyes took on that familiar faraway stare he always had when he reminisced on those long ago days.

Gingerly, I crossed the narrow bay that led to the island. The sun, although high above, was now becoming obscured by the slowly rising mist – a watery yellow balloon floating in a hazy sky. It had become eerily quiet; I couldn't hear the seagulls any more and the sea didn't break on the shore but made hissing noises, like the sound you hear when you put a seashell up to your ear – far away - mind it could have been the warning noise from a snake, or would that be serpent?

Also, I was getting quite disorientated and couldn't tell from which direction the noises were coming. When it first started to get dark I thought I'd better hurry back across the causeway as I wasn't sure how far the sea would come up – but, peering this way and that, I began to get panicked by the enveloping mist and lost my way.

It had now got very chilly, with dread clutching around my head like a vice. If I went in the wrong direction I could end up being blocked in when the sea rose - I could remember that some of the sides of the rockface on the mainland were sheer - and then I might drown. It continued to get even darker and it was then that the huge monster materialised unexpectedly in front of and over me - a huge, open-mouthed ogre with sunken eyes and arms raised ready to make a grab at me. I froze but it was drawing me inexorably towards it, the tentacles from its arms reaching down to drag me towards its gaping mouth. I held my breath – literally too frightened to breathe. The mist slithered around my legs – the serpents were back, their mouths ready to strike at me or perhaps wrap their bodies around me in an iron grip to strangle me or drag me away - that scared me almost as much as the monster. I could feel the moisture from the mist starting to drip off my hair and down my neck and my clothes were becoming clammy and cold where they clung to my burning body; but my mouth was bone dry, my tongue almost sticking to the roof of my mouth with fear.

Starting to shiver and shake, I realised I had to get away from the monster and serpents and try to find my way out of the bay or I might never be seen again. The monster was by now preparing to strike – it leaned forward and then back as it gathered momentum to launch itself at me when, as the swirling mist cleared unexpectedly for a moment, I could see that the dark shape was not, in fact, a monster at all but a huge rock protruding above the entrance to one of the caves on the island itself. Of course it was! I knew that all the time!

2

Letting out my breath with a silent "phew", I took a step forward and peered into the mouth of the cave and, straining my eyes to search ahead, saw that the mist inside rose no more than knee high. I stood peering in for what seemed an eternity, but which could only have been a half-minute or so.

Making a life changing decision, I slowly edged my way into and around the inside of the cave, my eyes gradually becoming accustomed to the dimness, and I saw that, inside, the walls were not as black as they had at first appeared, there being a dark green luminosity to the walls which bounced around and gave back some light.

The dripping sound I had heard before was louder inside the cave, echoing around it like water falling from a great height into a deep well or someone throwing a pebble into a quiet, still pool of deep water, except it was always behind me and whenever I turned around I heard it again, yet again behind me; I couldn't tell from which direction it came. After spinning around a few times to see who might be there, I got so dizzy I started to panic again. My heart was banging inside my rib-cage and I could feel the blood rushing through my ears. I put my hands over them and told myself to stop it. It was getting harder by the second to keep myself from completely losing control.

I turned to run out of the cave but as I did so I could see that the mist outside had grown as thick as a curtain and also the tide, which now sounded a lot louder, was coming in fast; looking down I was shocked to find that the water was starting to slosh around my shoes as the sea rose.

I had never been over to the island on my own before and was now obviously beginning to regret that I'd done so. What if the sea filled the whole of the cave! The sides were too smooth to climb and there didn't appear to be a foothold anywhere so how could I get above the waterline if it did rise? Oh, I wished I knew just how high the water would come up. I didn't know what to do. I couldn't go outside again, at least not until the mist cleared, in case I walked straight into the sea. That, then, would be the end of me! But was this going to be the end of me? Was this where I was going to die?

I leaned against the damp wall and tried to think but in the grip of this mist I felt myself becoming colder and colder until eventually I started to drift into some sort of dream world. I could hear the condensation dripping from the roof of the cave and echo around inside it but it seemed like a million miles away. I shook my head to try and clear it and thought I had better start moving, more, at that moment, to keep my circulation going than in the hope of finding a miraculous way out, so I continued to explore the cave as best I could in the dimness, in the hope of escape. Groping around in the semi-darkness, I eventually found a small ledge about shoulder height and decided to climb up. I skinned my knee in a few places in my struggle to haul myself up, slipping back down the sheer sides more than once, but finally I made it. I huddled as far back on the ledge as I could and, with my back leaning against the wall, hugged my knees to my chest to try to keep as warm as possible. Dropping my head onto my arms I tried to think of something I should do to try and get away.

I don't know how long I sat like that but I believe the mist and the hissing of the sea (if it was the sea) made my mind drift again and I fell into a trance-like sleep, even chilled to the bone as I was – or could it have been the beginning of hypothermia? I'd heard about that at school but I was, by then, too worn out to try to do anything about it or even care.

'Ah, there you are, Percy,' said a very melodious voice and I awoke with a start. I could still see the inside of the cave and the mist but it appeared to be on the other side of the now apparently see-through rockface. It was as if I had fallen backwards through the rock wall itself and was looking back out to the cave through a distorted glass window. I was extremely disorientated and, as I was still quite cold, after

4

half-heartedly trying to feel that crystal wall, felt myself drifting away again.

'No, no, no! No time for that now,' said the voice, all businesslike; 'you've found the doorway. Come, quick, let us get out before it closes. I didn't think it would take you this long to find me! Still, you've finally made it, so let's go!'

I turned around and saw the strangest sight ever. A very tall man stood there. Very, very poised and absolutely in control of himself! I was amazed as I looked at him and not a little anxious as I thought I might be hallucinating. From his head to his feet he was dressed as no one I had ever seen before in my life.

He wore a midnight blue cap, which fitted very close to his head – a bit like a swimming cap, I thought. It covered his hair - that is, if he had any hair. Looking back, I never saw him without that cap, so I never found out if he had hair or not. However, if he did have hair it would have been very dark due to the fact that his eyebrows were black - eyebrows that almost always had a quizzical look to them. Stitched - I believe it was stitched - onto the cap was a silver plate fashioned into the shape of a falcon's head whose eyes were made of the most magnificent rubies that glowed and flashed as he moved. He wore a long robe, also in midnight blue. I would have thought that it should have impeded his walk but it appeared not to hinder him in the slightest. He always walked with very long strides and I can remember that at that time - and when I think of it even when I was fully-grown - I almost always had to run to keep up with him.

He nearly always held a staff in his hand, which was about six-and-a-half feet long, when he was out and about. He used it for countless things, even as a weapon.

I once saw him point it at a man who was running toward him to hack at him with an axe. Now I, personally, would have turned and run like the clappers – in fact, looking back again, I believe I did. The man, who was huge and wild, looked completely off his head – mad as a hatter. He was dressed in a bear-skin, which probably made him look even bigger, tied around with a thick leather belt, and half his face was smeared in blue woad. His face was contorted with rage or madness and he was screeching and howling like a banshee as he ran at us but, as I said, as soon as the staff was raised at him, the man dropped dead in his tracks! One minute he had been a positive steam engine hurtling toward us at full throttle, the next, not even a puff of wind! Dropped dead on the spot. Whump – gone! Amazing! That was something, I can tell you!

I have also seen him use it to hit a fish on the head in a stream for his supper. It had many uses, and one day I shall tell you more as to what they were, but mainly it was used for walking.

The staff was made of what appeared to be wood, but it was almost black in colour and had very intricate designs, like hieroglyphics, carved into it. He must have known what they all meant but every time I asked him he always said something like, 'Not now, Percy, I shall tell you when we have more time.'

I don't think he ever found the time to tell me, now I come to think of it. The staff was extremely tough, as at one time a knight tried to knock it away with his sword and the sword was the thing that broke! That was a laugh, I can tell you! You should have seen the knight's face. It, too, was topped with a silver falcon's head, complete with rubies; it was obviously much smaller but it matched his cap.

He was strikingly handsome, with piercing black eyes and, I believe, could have been any age. Over the time of knowing him, at different times he could look anything between 35 to 135 years old. At this time, however, he looked fairly young – late 30s, I would say.

I was very bewildered and thought I was dreaming. 'How did I get here?'

'How did you get here? How did you get here? Percy, you are having fun with me, are you not? No! No, I cannot believe you are unaware of what's what. Like me, you must have slept a long time, much too long. But you must know something?' he queried, raising one eyebrow and holding his forefinger across his lips. 'Hmm, I hope it's not too late! Anyway, to the present, come, quickly, take my hand.' I was quite dubious about doing that but had no choice as he grabbed me by the wrist and pulled me forward. 'We have very little time. If we don't get out now, we will both be trapped in this crystal prison, perhaps forever.'

At that, he yanked at my hand and, pulling me with him, we stepped forward – well, we fought forward: it was like being suctioned through rather than stepping through - out of the glass rock, out of the cave, out of the darkness and mist and, as I was very soon to discover, out of the 20th Century.

'That was very close! I can still feel the pull. I shall tell you another time how I came to be trapped in there. But now, we must hurry.'

He started to walk, with those his very long strides of his, from the mouth of the cave. Holding on to my elbow, he was almost dragging me along. 'Wait, wait!' I yelled. 'Where are you taking me? What is going on? Who are you?' I thought I was being abducted.

He stopped and peered at me with those piercing black eyes of his; eyes that could change from black to golden brown like a hawk - or should I say "a merlin"? - as they reflected his temperament.

'Percy, Percy, my dear boy, you couldn't forget me could you? Don't you remember me?'

I looked up at him and there was a vague stirring in my memory but I just couldn't grasp it.

I hate those times when a remembrance enters your head and then, before you can grab hold of it, it rushes right out or down one of the corridors inside your brain. I've spent hours in the past trying to backtrack through my mind to find what had just jumped in and then out of it just before I could grab hold of it; opening doors inside my head and still not finding what I was looking for – it's extremely frustrating! Or, sometimes, when I've been chatting away, someone interrupts me or something happens and I completely forget what I've been talking about and no matter how much I try and think, I just can't remember what it was. I look at who I've been talking to and can tell by their face that they think I'm mad.

Anyhow - to continue: I carried on staring at him, mouth most probably hanging open like a moron; so, on reflection, he must have thought me a complete half wit.

'It's Myrddin! Myrddin! He looked at me expectantly, nodding as if I knew who he was and would respond, and then, quizzically, 'Surely you must remember? We spent a whole year together. No? Do you not remember Arthur? Or Sir Ector? You must remember Cabal! And surely you haven't forgotten Rhianne! Do you not remember your quest? You must remember that! How I sent you off? How you went? You must remember, as you've come back the same way. You must remember that I needed you to learn more and grow more before we go after the giant!'

That was it! I was now getting very nervous indeed, thinking I'd met someone from the local lunatic asylum. My mum had repeatedly warned me about these men and had told me to always give them a wide berth. I didn't really have a chance to escape this one, did I? Well, perhaps if I hadn't come to Tintagel in the first place I might have escaped. But I had and that was that. However, I had never experienced anyone as crazy as this man before in my life, let alone one dressed in such a fashion. Although he hadn't attempted to harm me I must admit that I was ready to run – and I was a pretty fast sprinter then. But, where would I run to? The cliffs and land looked so different now than when I had sat on the grass yesterday; or was it yesterday? The mist had gone!

8

Taking my courage in my hands, I looked at this man and stated, 'I do *not* remember any quest or know how I came here, so how could I remember how I was sent, if you say I was sent? And my name is *Jack*! You've got me in a muddle with someone who must look like me – this, er, Percy!' I felt completely bemused by everything and not a little scared. It was weird as well, as my family name is Percival and my friends at school called me "Percy". I was trying very hard not to cry and, being the youngest in the family, I had always used tears as my best form of defence – and whinging - but I could see that that wasn't going to do me any favours here. Also now, as I thought about it, I had better stop using the waterworks; well, I mean, I was going to be twelve quite soon!

'Jack, Percy, it's all one to me! Keep quiet, you are making much too much noise and keep still, Percy, I do not want the enemy to see you or hear you and I suppose I had better try and refresh your memory before we go much further.' Sighing, he sat on the sand and leaned back against the rock at the mouth of the cave and, drawing a dragon in the sand with his staff, said 'You came here on the dragon's breath!' He started nodding at me, again raising his eyebrows in expectation of my agreeing with him. Mad!

The hair on the back of my neck stood out at this and I felt as if a million spiders were dancing up and down my spine making me shiver. I had heard this dragon stuff talked about in the village but I thought it was just a story to keep children safe indoors when the mist started rolling in off the moors. I had heard how people had wandered for days out there and been attacked or killed by wild animals - or was it the dragon or this giant he had mentioned? But this man - Myrddin? - spoke as though the dragon existed. And it wasn't just as though he believed it but as he spoke I began to believe it too, even though I didn't want to or even know why!

9

'I sent you out on the dragon's breath, into the future, to find out how our battles would progress. What the Picts and Scots were up to. Where the Saxons and Angles would encamp. How many there were in their respective armies? Who were their leaders? Who were loyal and who would prove false. Would they fulfil their quests? How did Arthur fare?' Did you find this out for me?

'What year did I send you to?' He suddenly stopped speaking and turned to me, staring intently at me with those piercing black eyes before continuing. I felt myself being drawn into them and I don't believe, for one minute, that I could have lied to him to save my own life! Then, more softly, 'Come, lad, tell me, what year is it now?'

'1951. I was born in 1939. I don't believe in dragons. I don't know anything about any battles. I was only a small boy during the war.'

'1951! 1951! Well, my spell seems to have been a wee bit more powerful than I intended. 1951 indeed!' He rubbed his chin and drew his brows together as he strode up and down, mulling this over. Eventually, 'No wonder I was so weak that that witch managed to entomb me in that cave! Tell me what you do know about the battle! Was Arthur in it? You do remember Arthur? You know, Arthur, Chief Dragon, or Pendragon as he is known, son of Uther?'

'Do you mean King Arthur?' I laughed, yes I actually laughed. 'But he's only a legend. He's not real. He never was! I always thought he might be but everyone tells me he's just a story, made up by someone. I've read about him - lots. Everyone says he's only a myth. And, it wasn't a battle, it was a war, World War II. Everyone knows that.'

'Well, not everyone knows that because I don't know that!' He spoke in a very acerbic way to me. 'But a king, yes, that I do know! The greatest king! Well, you do have some intelligence, though I was beginning to doubt it. Yes, Percy, I do mean King Arthur and he is no myth: he is real.

10

What else do you know? Apart from a world war, that is.'
He snorted. 'No war could cover the whole world – there
aren't enough arrows for that, nor swords for that matter.'
The man turned to me. 'What have you got to tell me, Percy?
Lots, eh? You've been gone so long.'

'So, you don't know everything, then, do you?' I was
getting a bit too cheeky now. 'The war *was* over the whole
world ... and don't keep calling me Percy? My name is Jack!
And I do *not* know who you are! I have never heard of
Myrddin. I don't know what is going on. I don't know where
I am. I don't know how I got here. *And* I don't know who
you are,' I repeated. 'I want to go home'. I was, by now, on
the verge of tears.

'Hush! I don't know this and I don't know that. You do
go on! I sent you off to find out so much for me and now you
come back with all these "I don't know this or I don't know
that". And keep your voice down. We cannot warn them,' he
said. 'Not now that I have had to wait this long. Well, we
have a few hours before morning. So I suppose I had better
answer some of your questions. Start then', he ordered.

I sat staring at him. This strange man stood there waiting
to answer questions that I didn't even know I wanted to ask. I
was completely mystified and in the back of my mind felt
sure I was dreaming - or going mad. Like all dreams or, I'm
sure, madness, they have to take their course, so I just kept
looking at him (and pinching myself, just in case I was asleep
- I wasn't. Well, I didn't think I was but, then again, I could
be pinching myself in a dream, in which case I wouldn't wake
up, would I?) and waiting for the next thing to happen (or,
alternatively, waiting to wake up – I didn't – I already was)!

'Oh, well, if you won't start, I will. Perhaps then, *you*
might get motivated. Don't keep looking at me as though
you've lost all your wits, lad, and please shut your mouth.
Try to concentrate on what I am saying instead of looking like
an absolute dolt. Hmmm, it's possible you did lose your

11

mind whilst travelling on the dragon's breath! It has been known. Well, that is I chance I had to take. Let me see if I can answer your silent questions.

'I call you Percy, because that is your given name. You came to me, as I said, on the dragon's breath, as someone with the gift of the Old Way. There are only a few of us left - more's the pity. I gave you the name Percy, an honourable name, as you must have some royal or Druid blood in you somewhere, like me, otherwise you would not know as much as you do - or did, at any rate,' he mused, screwing up his lips. He frowned a little before continuing, 'If it's been slightly changed to that of Jack …'.

'*Slightly!*' I thought, '*It's nothing like it!*'

'Well, maybe it's not,' he appeared to react to my thought! How did he know what I was thinking?

'Even, so, 'he responded, 'well, so be it! Things change, things move on! Ah, yes, if I remember correctly, my name was changed slightly too - Merlin, yes that's what they called me in later years, Merlin! Something to do with the French mocking my other name! The Romans, however, called me Merlinus Ambrosius! Sounds grand, doesn't it? Yes - Merlin's my name!'

He could see that the blood had drained from my face and that my eyes now stood out of their sockets – those proverbial organ stops!

Yes! Now I understood! Everything came crashing back into my memory, almost knocking me off my feet!

His eyes lit up as he exclaimed, 'By the Sword, you know! I can see it written on your face! So, tell me, what did you find out in these fifteen hundred years?' He sat down, placed his elbows on his knees, the tips of his fingers together and, staring over the tops of them, waited for my answer.

At the mention of the name of Merlin it all came flooding back – Arthur, Cabal, Mad Mab and (blushing) Rhianne. I looked up at Merlin and saw him smile. He did not smile

12

often. His work and his quest were too serious for that. But when he smiled, the sun shone, the violins started up and the angels sang, and I would have followed him to the ends of the earth. Some might say I was hypnotised or mesmerised! No, that was not it. It was his quest and, after I had met Arthur, it became my quest, too! It was contagious! He knew many things, exciting things. At times I believed he knew everything that was going on in the whole world. But he took me under his wing. He taught me many things about the Old Way – a way he said that came from the beginning of time. A way that people had lost, as they grew more "sophisticated" or more evil. A good way - a way that led to adventure. As some of those past adventures rushed into my mind a flight of moths began dancing in my stomach. Yes, from whichever year I had last met him, I realised how much I had missed him. The yearning for all that Merlin did and was grew back in my heart and my ambition again was to follow him once more into the adventures, which, I believed, only he could create.'

TWO

It had been almost two years since I had last laid eyes on Arthur. He was now nearly fourteen years old and I must have shown my surprise at how he had grown when I came into the room, he jumping up and giving me the biggest bear hug I have ever had. He had grown as tall as Sir Kay but where Sir Kay was slim Arthur had filled out – broad of shoulder and chest – and one could see that when he was full grown – and he wasn't far off that now - he would be a mountain of a man, like Sir Ector, and a mighty warrior to boot.

'Heaven's above, Percy, where have you sprung from? Man, I've missed you! But you have grown!' he exclaimed, laughing, as he spun me around and thumped me on the back. 'The family are all out at the moment but they will be thrilled when they see you. Merlin, old friend, well met!' He turned and also gave the druid a bear hug, which, I could see, delighted him. Looking back, when I had first seen Arthur who was then aged eleven, the comparison with then and now was like a million years; then he had cuddled the "old man" as Merlin had addressed himself; now it was the gesture of a friend on an equal footing.

Arthur, who had been honing a short sword, went over to the far table and poured two tankards brim full with a frothing beer. After handing one to each of us he returned and poured one for himself. Walking over, he raised his arm and wished us good health. Now, I had not, up till that moment, ever had anything more alcoholic than wine gums and I wondered what would happen should I drink it. On the other hand, would I offend Arthur if I refused to drink everyone's health, as he had proposed? Then again, my mother's voice echoed into my thoughts with, "If I ever catch you sneaking your father's whisky, you won't be able to sit down for a week!"

These thoughts had hardly had time to start working themselves out in my brain when, tankard to my lips, the solution hit me like a bullet - literally! I was hurled over to the other side of the room - crashing into and almost breaking a couple of quivers full of arrows which were leaning up against the wall, beer flying everywhere - by a deliriously excited and completely uncontrollable hound. Up till now I don't think I'd said more than a couple of mumbled words as, seeing how Arthur had grown, I had been overcome by a bashfulness that I never knew I had. But now, my old friend Cabal had totally melted any ice that may have existed as mayhem reigned for the next few minutes.

I kept trying to get up, only to be knocked back down again by the over-excited dog, while Arthur tried to catch him, calling him to heel but being ignored, only to be cheated of catching him as Cabal feinted to either his left or right – a feat not easily achieved by so great an animal as a wolfhound. Merlin just stood and grinned at the scene.

Eventually order was restored - Cabal had managed to accomplish what our reticence could not – we were once again best of friends, as though the two years' separation had never existed.

Cabal later explained that he had been out hunting in the forest when he'd picked up not just the scent of Merlin and me but had also managed to tune in to some of our thoughts as we re-entered his world. He told me that his excitement had known no bounds. He had been about two miles away and had started there and then to run as fast as he could – even though he had just about filled his stomach with hare. At this point I had frowned at him and he had apologised – almost! There was always a bit of tongue in cheek with his contrition.

It took me a while, but when I had recovered my breath, which had been fair knocked out of me, and could manage to get Cabby to stop licking my face, I felt free to ask some of the questions which had begun to run riot inside my head. 'What's been happening since I've been away?' I asked Arthur. 'Merlin came to me and said that I should come back and spend some time with you again. You can't imagine how happy I am to do so, but as to what's been going on since I've been away, well, that, I am afraid, he has left for you to tell.'

Arthur's face aged as it took on a more serious expression. 'Yes, and well he might! I am afraid that there has been quite a lot happening in the last couple of years. The king of this part of Britain – you know, the one that Kay went to serve for a time – was slain by his own cousin, who had been in the pay of another king from the north. Apparently, a few minor kings from that part of the country have formed a coalition to try and take over the rest of the country. They are even considering making an alliance with the Saxons. We know that there is a prophesy that there will be one High King of all the Britons one day; well these men have taken it into their heads to kill off all the other kings and take that particular title for themselves. I don't think they could have fully thought it through, though, because once they have killed all the other kings – and that will never happen, of course - they will then have to fight to try and kill off one another until there is only one high king left! Anyway, how they managed to get a man to kill his own cousin, well, I cannot start to imagine! We are living in evil days, Percy!'

His face fell and I noticed that he had started his pacing – hands rubbing together in front of him as he walked, slightly bent forward as he did so, and then clutched behind his back, walking tall and straight – his eyes showing that his thoughts were a million miles away. I knew better than to interrupt these ruminations of his. Merlin just leaned against the wall and waited – patient as ever.

Arthur's mind finally returned to the present and he stood looking at me. 'My father - Sir Ector, and Sir Kay have been scouring the countryside for some of the men who went out to

16

battle with him many summers ago. We have a force of about six score men – though most are getting on a bit in years I am afraid. However, they are strong and true and will fight alongside my father to the death. We have all been training for a twelvemonth and it seems that we are virtually ready for battle.' He turned with a strange light in his eyes as he exclaimed, 'Percy, it will be my first battle. I can become a true warrior at last.' Eyes flashing as he said this, he almost grew another couple of inches.

'My boy,' Merlin interrupted. We had almost forgotten that he was there. 'I do not believe it is Sir Ector's intention for you to go with him this time.'

Arthur spun around and faced Merlin, a look not only of incredulity but also of growing anger on his face. 'Not take me? But why? I am as able and strong, if not stronger, than the next man!' he declared. 'They need all the men they can get and I can wield a sword and shoot an arrow with exceptional ability. Everyone around here knows my aptitude with the sword and also with the bow, I never miss my target. No, you must be mistaken Merlin – Sir Ector will take me with him.'

'Sir Ector will take you where?' said the man himself as he strode into the room. He walked up to Merlin and almost crushed him in welcome and then, turning, thumped me so hard on the back I almost fell over. 'Well met, Merlin; well met young Percy,' he laughed as he pulled off his riding gloves and stood with his back to the fire, lifting his jerkin as he did so to warm his "nether regions" as he put it. He stood for a while waiting for the warmth to penetrate his leggings, then, 'Well, Arthur, and where am I going to take you?'

'To battle,' he replied, chin jutting forward as he pulled himself to his full height.

'And what battle might that be?'

'Ah, you know, sir. We go to fight the marauders from the north.'

17

'*We* go nowhere,' he emphasised the 'we' as he frowned at Arthur. 'I am still lord of this place and I still make the decisions.' Sir Kay entered as he was speaking. Like his father he, too, was very happy to see us and was very welcoming toward Merlin and me, clasping Merlin's arms with his hands and, again, I got slapped on the back. *'One day,'* I thought, *'it'll be me doing all the slapping!'*

Both Merlin and Cabal looked at me – Merlin with an enquiring raise of his eyebrows and Cabal with a single wag of his tail. *'Oops,'* I thought – now putting up my mind barrier, *'I'd forgotten about the mind speaking bit.'*

Sir Ector was still speaking. 'If you were to go with me I would be breaking the promise I made about you and, as you know, I am a man not to break his word.'

'What promise? I know of no such promise?' said Arthur, getting very red in the face and finding it extremely hard to keep his temper in check.

'And you will continue in that state of ignorance, young man, because the promise was not only made to someone else but it was also made in confidence. Only the person who extracted that promise from me and I know what it was and it will remain that way. The person who extracted the promise will one day reveal what it is all about. I am not at liberty to do so. Until then, it is in God's hands. No, no more,' he held up his hand as Arthur opened his mouth to interrupt. 'That is the end of the matter.'

Arthur could be seen to battle with his emotions, will and mouth, but then thought better of it – for now.

The atmosphere, which had been charged for the last few minutes, took a subtle change as the door opened and the ladies entered. The first lady through the door was Sir Ector's wife, Lady Elise who, when she caught sight of me, rushed over and hugged me – a nice change, I had to admit, from being thumped on the back, but still having the effect of making me squirm with embarrassment. As she did so I saw, over her shoulder, her daughter, Rhianne. Wow, had she grown up! She had been very pretty the last time I'd seen her but now, well – she was beautiful! Here we go again, I thought, as my face blushed crimson. I remembered, when I had stayed with Sir Ector before, how I would blush as I caught sight of Rhianne and how I would then look over at Cabal, who, fortunately, seemed to be the only one that noticed. Cabal, of course, noticed again now but, as luck would have it, Lady Elise took the credit as she apologised for discomfiting me.

'Well,' said Sir Ector rubbing his nether regions as he walked away from the fire, 'let us go and satisfy our hunger. I assume that everyone needs to be fed? Good company and good food will put us all in a better humour,' he stated as he moved over to the door. 'Come, Merlin; come, Percy,' and he ushered us through to the main hall where another fire blazed in the enormous fireplace, fresh rushes were strewn across the floor and a table groaned with all manner of fare. I had not realised just how hungry I was but then, as luck would have it, what did they do? They had to go and seat me directly opposite Rhianne. My appetite vanished – unlike the redness in my face, which did not.

She hadn't changed too much in the two years since I had last seen her and yet she had, in subtle ways. She must be coming up to fifteen by now but I noticed that where once she had been taller than me, I now slightly had the edge on her. She was still very slim but her face – and her figure - had lost some of its childish plumpness and was now more defined; her high cheekbones made her violet eyes look even more beautiful, if that were possible, as they were certainly stunning before.

I suddenly realised that I was again thinking too much about her and shot a swift glance at Cabal. He appeared to be dozing, with his head on his forepaws, but as I glanced over at him he opened one eye, looked straight at me and thumped

19

his tail – just once - then closed it again. He never misses a trick!

'Come, Percy, eat!' ordered Sir Kay as he grabbed a huge beef bone from the platter in front of him. Holding it at both ends and breaking it at the joint he made a great display of his strength. Passing half of it to me he chuckled, 'If you are going to start your training again with Arthur, well, you will certainly need to put some muscle onto those flabby arms and that chest of yours. Otherwise I shall personally take great delight in turning your flesh black and blue!'

With that, and remembering the pastings I had taken in the past, I tucked in with a will. Supper seemed to go on forever, but I didn't mind. Rhianne was less self-conscious than I in that she asked me lots of questions about where had I been and what had I been doing over the last couple of years. I glanced up at Merlin who, although seemingly deep in conversation with Sir Ector, spoke swiftly into my mind to *'take care not to let anything slip!'*

I told her how I had helped on my uncle's farm and had learned a bit more about smithying. I spoke of my older brother James and mentioned his girlfriend. She was a little confused at the term "girlfriend" and so I told her it was a colloquialism meaning "intended" – she seemed satisfied with that. I felt, after a few close shaves, that I should turn the conversation and, when Arthur joined us, asked them to bring me up to date with what had been happening over the last two years. I also wanted to speak to Merlin, when I could get him on his own, about the remark he'd made of "no wonder I was so weak that that witch managed to entomb me in that cave". Did he mean Mad Mab? I was surprised that I remembered her name, seeing as how I had forgotten so much before Merlin had reminded me of his name. I suppose that now I had dropped back into the past so completely, everything seemed as if it carried on from where I last left it off – except for the missing two years that is. But then, news didn't travel as swiftly in the fourth and fifth centuries as it did in the twentieth!

Arthur launched into the story first. 'Today is the first time we've seen Merlin since you both disappeared two years ago. We wondered what had happened to him because he has never been gone so long in the past. He usually showed up some time in the spring – we joked that he hibernated like the bears and when he wakes up he's as hungry as one and would always comes to us as we have such a good table!' We all laughed and looked over at Merlin as he said this. Merlin, himself, appeared not to have heard, as he was still deep in conversation with Sir Ector and Sir Kay, though I knew he didn't miss a thing!

We seemed to be in two different camps in that room as the older men were on one side of the huge fire, talking about whatever it is that older men talk about and we were on the other side, talking about something else – or were we? Lady Elise was busy, in and out of the room, directing servants to replenish the beer, mead and small foods on the side tables and to clear the large table of the remnants of our meal, setting new, large candles into the candelabrum at its centre – experience must have told her this would be a long evening. Cabal and his brother Griff were snuffling about under the tables to see what had been or might be dropped for them; Griff had managed to secure one of the large beef bones and was happily grinding away at it at the back of the room. Cabal appeared to be vacuuming up everything else.

Arthur continued his story. 'We needed to know what was going on, so far as Merlin could advise us, because, after the king had been murdered, there were lots of to-ings and fro-ings between all the lords of the lands hereabouts and many were very worried indeed. More than one lord packed up his wife and daughters and sent them far away just to keep them safe. My father has reinforced the compound walls here and has made sure that there is always a guard on duty. He

21

has also sent a rider to my mother's family in Wales to send for reinforcements and I understand that we are to expect quite a large contingent to arrive in the middle of next month. So, Percy, you can see just how serious things have become.'

Rhianne then took up the story. 'Although father has strengthened our defences, there is something a little closer to home that has been worrying us – well my mother and I, at any rate! The men – well, my father and brothers - think that we are being fanciful – being women that is – and that we have been imagining things.'

Arthur sat well back in his chair, crossing his arms and shaking his head as if to confirm this.

'Go, on,' I prompted, ignoring him. I was intrigued.

'Over the summer months, usually at full moon, both my mother and I have been woken up by a shaking coming up from the earth. No-one else has noticed it and my mother said that by the time she was able to wake up Sir Ector it had stopped, so he thought she'd been having a nightmare. We spoke about it some time later and then realised that we had both been experiencing the same rumbling sensations at full moon - for at least three out of the last twelve months. And, Percy, I am sure that Cabal has felt it too!' she raised a conspiratorial eyebrow at me.

As we looked over at Cabby, now lying in his favourite place before the huge fire - and I wonder how he didn't ever set himself alight, he was that close – Arthur scoffed at the idea. 'How on earth can you know what a dog feels, Rhianne? No wonder the men think you're being fanciful and imagining things!' She looked slightly abashed but I could sense that she would not be turned from what she knew she had experienced.

I began to think, then, about what could possibly be happening. I was determined to get out of Cabby what I could, when I could. It looked very much like it was going to be tomorrow as the only time I could have a good conversation with the hound was when we went off hunting as we'd done in the past during the late afternoons while Arthur met with one of the monks for religious instruction. I glanced out of the window and could see how dark it had now become. Yes, I would have to be patient.

'Come, children; hmm you are not so much children now are you?' said Lady Elise as she returned once more, followed by two strong lads carrying large trays groaning with more food and beer for the men. 'It is time you retired and left the men to their business without further interruption.' With that she ushered us out of the hall and sent Arthur and I one way while she and Rhianne went to their respective rooms.

I was once again sharing a room with Arthur, just as though I had never been away. We chatted for a while as we readied ourselves for bed, but, both being tired, we lay down on our separate pallets and very soon I could hear the even breathing of someone fast asleep. As I settled down to sleep that night I had much to ponder. It looked as though there was going to be a battle, if not a war! How awful that a king should be murdered – and by his own kin! I wonder what the earth shaking that Rhianne had talked about meant.

'Sleep, Percy! We'll go out tomorrow and get you up to date with my contribution.' Cabby lay across the doorway to Arthur's room – completely faithful as always. I smiled, remembering how he would doze but stay alert at the same time, and, thus comforted, settled myself down to sleep.

'OK Cab; let's hope it's a fine day.'

'Oh, it will be a fine day! Now sleep!'

THREE

The next day, as we prepared ourselves for the physical training that took up most of the morning, Arthur, his face still showing the dejection that his disappointment of the day before had produced, turned to me and announced that he'd decided he'd be going on a pilgrimage to Hinton St. Mary in Dorset.

'One of the monks has been there and has told me all about the pilgrims that have started to visit the place. A holy man has had a mosaic of Christ laid in a small building there and the people that have visited have said that they have certainly felt His presence as they have prayed and some have even experienced healing. So, as I cannot go to war, I shall go to peace!' He stuck out his chin, as he took up once more his - peculiar to him - striding backwards and forwards across our room. 'I shall ask Sir Ector of course, but I cannot see that he will have any objection. You will come with me Percy?' It was more a demand than a request and, as I knew that I, also, would not be allowed to go to war, I acceded to his "request". I thought it would be great fun to see some of the sights of an England so many years younger – and possibly cleaner - than it was in my day. I decided to have a word with Merlin as soon as I could, just to be sure.

We broke our fast and strode off into the practise yard. It had changed little since I had last been there, although there were now straw "men" stuck onto poles for spears and bows and arrows' practise that had not been there before and the walls surrounding the compound had been strengthened and made taller with six feet high thick tree trunks bound together and secured around the top of the stone walls.

First, then, one of the older warriors took us through our paces with the practise swords. I had not realised how out of practise I was. Over the next few days I did manage to

24

improve as I remembered the different ways of dodging the weapons aimed at me but every night, when I undressed to fall – literally – into bed, my body was covered with bruises of different hues from ugly purple, through to lilac, red and yellow. It created a huge amount of ribbing from Arthur who, being stronger, older and more adept than I, thought it hysterical. 'Your body looks more like a rainbow than skin!' and he would fall about laughing. He really had the weirdest sense of humour at times.

'Oh, ha ha,' I can remember saying to him, in quite a caustic manner, which only sent him off into more fits of laughter. It's funny how different times and different places have different senses of humour. Arthur obviously didn't notice the sarcasm in my tone, or perhaps he did and just laughed at it all the more.

Over the next few days I got better with the sword - I had to, for my own sense of self-worth let alone self-preservation, otherwise I wouldn't have been fit for anything; however, I was still much better with the bow and arrow and sling.

We took up our academic studies again during the early afternoons and both Arthur and I had improved very considerably during our two-year separation. In fact our tutor was so pleased with us that we managed to get out of our lessons much earlier than we should have – most days. I suppose in a way that made us try to improve even more, as the times out of the schoolroom were preferable to the ones stuck inside it – especially on a gloriously sunny day like that first full day back.

Late afternoons were again a time of separation as Arthur sat with his religious teacher. I would look over at him, head bent in concentration, as he and the monk sat under one of the apple trees and studied the scrolls but I soon forgot everything as Cabal and I ran off into the forest, the warning of 'Don't go too far!' dropping out of my mind as soon as it entered.

That first day, as Cabby and I took off down one of the forest paths, was heavenly. We ran and wrestled while I laughed and he sneezed until we were both breathless – me leaning over with my hands on my knees, trying to catch my breath, while Cabal stood, tongue lolling out of his mouth as he, too, tried to catch his. After sitting for a few minutes we eventually started a more leisurely walk through the trees and caught up with what had been happening since we had last seen each other.

'Where have you been for the last two years? I kept looking for you and calling for you but it was as though you had completed disappeared. I had begun to fear that you were dead!'

'I did warn you that I would be going away for some time. To tell you the truth, I have missed you too.' I looked at Cabal and ruffled the top of his head as I thought how little he had changed.

'Well, you've changed,' he responded to my thoughts. *'You've got much taller and have filled out a lot, too – and I can see you still like Rhianne,'* he said, raising one eyebrow. Then continuing, *'How old are you now?'*

I had forgotten all the facets of mind speaking and that anyone with that particular gifting of the Old Way could tune in, whether they were being spoken to in the mind or just being thought about in the mind. I needed to remember to put up a barrier so that he, or whoever – and especially Rhianne - couldn't read everything that was going on in my brain. Before Cabby had interrupted I had almost gone on to think about the fact that I thought he might not have still been alive! I think he would have been really offended by that one. Needless to say, I thought all this with my barriers up!

Getting back to his question I responded with, *'Eleven and a half.'*

'A half? A half what?

'Eleven and one half years,' I responded.

'Well, that's still eleven isn't it, whether you say "half" or not? You're not twelve, are you?'

I shook my head.

He harrumphed!

I continued to hide my thoughts from him as I thought how important that half year was to me, especially at school where almost everyone in my class was the same age in years, but it was really essential to be just that bit older than the next boy; the pecking order at school was measured not only in years but also in months – academia didn't come into it at all. Obviously, to Cabal at any rate, it was something that was not important at all.

Changing the subject, I asked him where Salazar and Jasmine were, as I hadn't seen them since I had returned.

'After we returned from the Tor, Salazar helped Merlin, well, that is until you both disappeared, at any rate. They worked on various concoctions and spells, studying scrolls and the moon and stars and things until, one day, he told Lady Elise that he and Jasmine would be leaving us for a while as he felt drawn to visit the standing stones that stood at various points in Britain. Over a period of about two moons they sat and studied charts and Merlin's little book of languages until the next sickle moon appeared and then Salazar and Jasmine left. There was a fabulous feast in the great hall the night before they went which was a jolly time but tinged with regret as everyone had grown to respect and even love the unusual couple and they would be sorely missed. Salazar had a great way with herbs and potions and many a person had been cured of some illness or other and one of the men, who had fallen off his horse and cracked his skull – he was not expected to live through the night, you know – was ministered to by him and made an almost complete recovery. I say almost because he had a foul temper before and would kick anyone who got in his way – me, once, so I kept away from him after that – and when he recovered

27

he became the gentlest soul you could ever meet. Absolutely amazing!'

I laughed aloud at that because I thought I could recall the man that Cabal was talking about – a brute of a man that we all had kept well away from.

He continued, *'Also, you may remember, Jasmine had a rare gift of being able to know what was going to happen up to one day before it actually did and more than once we were able to fight off raiders or horse thieves because we were ready for them and, as we haven't seen Merlin or you now since Salazar and Jasmine went away, we've been at a loss to know what is happening to anyone!'* Cabal turned and nudged my hand with his muzzle and squinted up at me as the sun, which was now quite low on the horizon, glinted in his beautiful eyes. *'I'm so glad you are back Percy.'*

'And so am I,' I said as I crouched down and hugged the hound round his neck. How could I have forgotten the best friend I had ever had. *'Carry on, Cab; tell me what's been going on up at the Hall and I especially want to know what Rhianne was talking about when she said the ground shook.'*

'Ah, yes! Well, whatever the men might have said about it being women's fancy, I know that it was not. The ground did shake – but not for long. I would say that it lasted less than half a minute but it rattled windows and doors and the floor certainly did vibrate. I have to admit – and it shames me to do so – that it had almost the same effect on me as a storm. I crept up to Arthur's bed and tried to get under his cover. Fortunately he didn't wake up and so, when I thought it was safe, I crept back to the doorway. Stop laughing!'

I couldn't help it. To look at Cabal – wolfhound extraordinaire who was almost the size of a pony – being fazed by an earth tremor, let alone thunder, was absurd. But then I had to admit that I was slightly concerned when I saw a spider, even a very small spider – he thought that just as ludicrous as he could either completely ignore it or, if it was just in front of him, step on it and squash it and give it no more thought – well he wouldn't have given it another thought before we'd met the Faerie King. We both began to respect all creatures but realised we still have our phobias!

As these thoughts shot through my head, I eventually stopped laughing and apologised to a very affronted hound. I wiped the tears from my face with the back of my hand, and urged him, *'Carry on, Cab,'* as I followed him down the forest pathway. He had stalked off – nose in the air and tail straight out behind him. I had to apologise to him a few times before he let me catch up with him. But, like most dogs, he was and is a very forgiving hound.

'OK, as you well know, I sleep very lightly and as soon as the ground started to shake I was wide awake. This happened on three occasions only. The first time the ground shook, it began from the eastern side of our hill and moved west; the second time it was the other way round – west to east; the last time, nearly three weeks ago, it was east to west again. Weird!'

'I'm going to see if I can have a word with Merlin about this to see if he knows what's going on. I'm sure he won't say that it's anything to do with women's fancies.' I looked around at a darkening forest; the sun had slipped down behind the horizon and I was not quite sure how far we were from the compound.

'Don't worry, Percy; it's not far. We'll be home before supper.'

Setting off at quite a fast pace, true to his word, we entered the compound as the moon, short of its fullness by about three days, rose over the tops of the trees. Cabby and I entered the enclosure and made our way round to the kitchens. I had not realised how hungry I was until my nose twitched at the delicious aroma of one of Old Molly's pies. Cabal pushed the door open with his nose and loped into the room. Molly turned and admonished him with the wooden spoon, telling him he would feel the full force of it if he dared even think about stealing any of the food. We both looked guilty – although for the life of me I cannot think why - as we carried on through the kitchens and into the main hall.

Almost all the family were milling around and talking as they waited for the rest of us to join them before starting the meal. As I entered from the kitchens, Arthur and Sir Kay entered through the opposite doorway. Merlin and Sir Ector beamed as they made their way to the table. Sir Ector, a giant of a man, obviously loved his food and now that we were all present he was happy as now he could eat.

'Come, be seated all of you.' He clapped his hands and the servants entered with trays of meats – a huge boar's head on a platter with an apple in its mouth, some beef, a ham, and mounds of bread and vegetables. Three huge pies proved to contain game, hare and chicken. After all of this we were served with a large, very ripe cheese and blackberry and apple pie or apples, apricots and hazelnuts. Merlin always took as many hazelnuts as he could "for future consumption," he would say although I knew he used them in a lot of his magic.

We certainly didn't go hungry. The dogs prowled around again, waiting to pounce on whatever fell or was thrown from the table – the prize, of course, always being the shinbone from the joint of beef.

While dinner progressed, the talk drifted up and down the table and ranged from the more mundane matters of the Hall to the more serious subject of the murder and the accompanying uneasiness felt in all of the surrounding districts.

Before long Sir Ector turned to address Arthur. 'Now, young Arthur, I hope you've got all that nonsense out of your head about joining us in battle!'

'I have, sir,' he responded, straightening. 'I go on a pilgrimage instead – to Hinton St. Mary in Dorset.' He lifted his chin and waited for the rebuff.

Sir Ector appeared quite surprised at this but raised no objection. He stared at the young man for quite some time considering his plan and then asked, 'When do you intend this expedition to take place?'

'I had not thought too long about dates but I think that I should arrive there on All Saints Day – a propitious time do you not think? I should like to spend a good few days there – time enough to give thanks to our Lord for his goodness to us all - and then return home in time for the celebrations to be held at the Christ's Mass.'

'An excellent plan, Arthur. I shall help you organise it.'

Arthur's face fell a bit at that, as he would have liked to have organised the whole thing himself. However, he told me afterwards that he intended to make all the necessary decisions. If he didn't like any suggestions, he would not take them on board. Who would know if they weren't there?

I was not so sure that Sir Ector would allow him to go if he was not satisfied that all the necessary precautions and arrangements were to his liking.

'We will discuss it on the morrow. For now, Merlin,' Sir Ector said, turning to the man, 'a song, if you will.'

'*Oh no,*' I thought, remembering, '*He's got a terrible singing voice!*' Oops! I had forgotten to put up my barriers as I thought this blasphemy. He turned to me and stared for, oh such a long time. I felt my face suffuse with colour as I prayed for the floor to open up and swallow me.

'Certainly, sir,' he replied with his eyes still fixed upon me. 'Percy, go get my harp, if you would be so kind,' this said sweetly and much too over the top, although I believe I was the only one who felt the barb.

Oh dear, it would be a cold day in hell before he would let me forget that one! Cabal followed me out to the entrance to the Hall and gave his equivalent of a '*tut tut*'. I wasn't very polite to him either, as I told him that if he didn't have anything constructive to say to shut up. He stalked off back into the main hall and I was left to feel bad about him as well. Why does everything always seem to go wrong at once? I returned to the Hall with Merlin's harp and had some idea of what it feels like to be a dog that has been admonished by its beloved master. If I'd had one, my tail would surely be down between my legs.

Merlin was very gracious as he took the small harp from my outstretched arms. Thanking me in over-polite tones, he walked over to the fireplace and spent a few moments strengthening the strings and tuning them. Before long he was ready and we all sat around expectantly. I glanced about me at the assembled party and each one of them had a look of excitement on their faces as though something momentous was about to happen. All I could think of to expect was the awful noise he made when he hummed – I remembered to veil these irreverent thoughts from absolutely everyone who could possibly tune in to my brain!

Before too much longer Merlin began. He sat on the edge of one of the benches he had pulled away from the wall and closer to the fire. He started plucking at the strings. I soon began to understand why they had asked him to "sing". As his hands moved over the strings of the harp, I felt a shiver run up my spine. The sounds it made were quite otherworldly. I heard music that could be the tinkle of a faerie waterfall, miniature stars being thrown into the air to cascade down and around us - aglitter as they fell, our spirits soaring into the sky to dance with the planets – the moon, the stars. I was mesmerised.

Afterwards I would remember the faces and demeanour of the others in the room, almost as if in a dream, as they listened – transported to another world and time. Then, as he spoke, his voice thrilled. I seemed to recall, somewhere in the back of my mind, that I had heard it said that although he couldn't sing as such, his voice had so wonderful a resonance that it was, in itself, melodic.

He began by recounting the story of a gallant king and one or two knights who accompanied him to a battle – one of the knights I recognised as Sir Ector - who looked extremely pleased to be mentioned in a song – and of their heroics, the charge of the horses and the thunder of their hooves. We were all on the edge of our seats as he started to narrate this, apparently, well known tale. As he continued with the story, I could see the effects it had on all those gathered – they clapped and roared encouragement when it recounted brave and illustrious deeds; they wept when they heard again of many of the valiant warriors who had lost their lives in fighting for their loved ones. But mostly they sat, breath held, hanging on to every word that Merlin said as he recounted the familiar tale in a new and breathtaking way.

The "song" lasted almost half an hour and was shown its appreciation by a thunderous applause and shouts of "encore" and "more".

'A short respite, if you please,' he laughed as he lifted his tankard of ale to his lips. 'This is very thirsty work!'

However, he was hardly two minutes into the recounting of another tale when he stopped so suddenly that the room became eerily quiet and still. The fire stopped crackling and seemed to hold its breath and even the candles and torches in their brackets stopped flickering in case they missed something. We were all looking at Merlin in any event but now as we stared at him there was an amazing change – he glowed – a golden man!

It was like seeing a person whose substance had gone and which had been replaced by a shimmering apparition. We could still see him but it seemed that we could also see through him as though all the elements were combining to show us that there was absolutely nothing false to be found in him at all. His voice changed as he lifted up his head and brought forth a prophetic utterance:

33

"He is well known in Gaul.
In Britain he is a household name.
He keeps a home in Camelot.
A dwelling place in Avalon - in readiness.
He has broken all the warriors' arrows as kindling for
the fire.
All the weapons of war he has melted down to make
into instruments of praise.
Oh how bright he shines, his face reflected in the
bonfires that burn his loot.
The warriors raging against him have been made
powerless.
They are no more. Their conceit and arrogance have
come to naught.
The horse and rider have abandoned their posts - melted
into the mists.
Furious is he and awesome.
Britain falls to her knees and, trembling, holds her
breath.
But in righteousness he hands out judgment.
In fairness he rules the land.
He brings all Britain together and makes it whole.
He saves the wretched from the foe.
To the foe, if he bows the knee, he shows mercy.
Bring garlands and offerings to the high king who
brings peace.
Bring garlands and offerings to the high king's
High King, the maker of peace."

Merlin stopped, gripping the mantelpiece for support, with
head bowed as he panted for breath. The glow faded from his
body and he was, once more, the solid but exhausted Merlin
we all knew; the silence was complete and lasted many
minutes. A soft weeping – Lady Elise dabbed at her eyes.

Sir Ector looked fierce; Arthur entranced - it was he who spoke first. 'Oh to be such a man as that. To bring peace and harmony, mercy, compassion and safety to a land that is in such dire need of it. Who, Merlin? Who is this man? Who is this high king?'

Merlin looked up, a dazed expression on his face. He suddenly appeared old and very tired. He, also, had been weeping. 'I saw such beauty,' he whispered. Everyone had to turn their ear to catch his words. 'A land at peace where a man does not fear his neighbour. A High King of all the Britons who rules regally and in fairness. A man raised in honesty and integrity. I saw many falling in at his side, happy and honoured to share his fortunes and misfortunes alike. Then I saw the other side of the coin – those who hated this just king - jealousy, envy, evil, war, death …peace will come – but only at a price.'

'Yes, Merlin, go on,' Sir Ector prompted after a silence.

'And who is he?' Arthur begged again.

A few moments more and Merlin, shaking his head as if to clear it, turned and looked at all of us gathered there. He seemed bemused and then, recalling what he had said, made a determined effort to shake off the melancholy that threatened to overwhelm him. 'Ah, but that is the question; and am I at liberty to say, young Arthur?'

Putting a guard on my thoughts I could feel my heart hammering inside my chest, as I knew that Merlin was and was not answering the question at one and the same time. I knew that Arthur would one day be high king as surely as I knew who would be reigning in the 20th Century. I wondered if anyone else had caught on to what Merlin had said.

After Merlin's prophesy, as if by some silent agreement, exhausted, everyone drifted off to their bedchambers. No-one seemed to be in the mood for any more entertainment and no-one wanted to talk - just think. I was relieved, therefore, when I heard Arthur's first gentle snore.

35

FOUR

Merlin was gone!

Sir Ector said that he had made his excuses the night before, saying that he would leave long before dawn as he had need of solitude and strengthening. His experience of the previous evening had drained him more than he would have liked to admit. He would return, but he knew not when.

I felt quite put out! I had slept badly, knowing that I would need to apologise for my rude "thoughts" the night before regarding Merlin's "singing". Now I would suffer, knowing this was something that couldn't be forgotten – or forgiven - until I had actually been able to say I was sorry; I would now have to carry my guilt around with me until I saw him again and as I had a feeling that that was going to be a long time off, I felt the burden of my sorrow growing heavier upon my shoulders by the minute. My only consolation was the thought that, well, he couldn't sing – never had been able to so far as I could judge. But, at that time, that thought gave me little comfort.

It was in this state of melancholy that Rhianne found me. All my defences were down and she heard my thoughts as clear as day. I must remember to keep a guard on them – you never know who might be listening in!

'Percy, don't fret so. Merlin loves you as a son and those that a father loves, he disciplines! He just wants you to grow up into the sort of man that you were destined to be. He will not hold against you what you thought of him. He knows that by feeling his displeasure, you will start bringing your thoughts – and thus your actions - under control. It's for your good.'

'Rhianne, I am so sorry ...' I started to say. Blushing again as I thought of my negative thinking towards Merlin's singing, especially as not only he but Cabal and Rhianne had obviously picked up on them. I'd thought that I had just dropped back into the scheme of things in those far off days, but I obviously had not. I really needed to sit down and have a good think through. Someone had mentioned that old witch and I must admit that I had jumped when they did so. I hadn't thought about her for so long that she had almost completely slipped out of my thinking. Now, that was someone I would need to be wary of; although she wasn't that good at mind-speaking conversations - this being something that was quite difficult to develop in those who were less than good – and she was positively evil, but she could pick up the odd word here and there and, more particularly, as she held grudges she would definitely be out to get me if she knew I was around again. She'd tried to get me once, when she managed to travel to the 20th Century, but, well, that was a long time ago. However, Merlin had told me she never forgot things like that and she would always try to get her own back. I shivered! Again, returning to the "present" (wherever that might be!), I noticed that Rhianne had been following most of my muddled thoughts. *'Blast!'* I thought, remembering in time to put up my guard before that expletive.

'Percy, you will make yourself ill if you keep worrying about all these things. Trust Merlin. Remember how he looked after us the last time.' She touched my arm as she tried to reassure me, bringing the inevitable rush of blood to my face. How I wished I could control that particular problem; I even looked around to see if Cabal was watching me but this time he must have been off somewhere with Arthur. Small relief! As I thought, with my barriers securely in place, of how much I felt about Rhianne, I did wonder how I could have forgotten about her so completely over the last couple of years. Perhaps it was something that Merlin did. One of his mysterious concoctions, no doubt.

'Sorry, Rhianne. I suppose that with what happened last time and the fact that there is such a lot of evil in the world –

'and it hasn't changed much since those days,' I thought, again to myself – 'it's hard not to worry. But, like you say, I shall try to trust to the good and not contemplate the evil.' She smiled, but this time my blushes were spared as we both turned to see Arthur and Cabal striding across the compound towards us.

'Good news, Percy. There will be a party of us going on pilgrimage! Brother Geraint has been thinking of journeying to Dorset for some time and Brother Aebbe has given permission for him to join our company. Shake Spear will also be coming along as my father has said he would probably cause complete chaos on the battlefield! Tailor – you remember, Percy – he received a broken arm when fighting with the Cyclops – well, his arm never properly healed but he is still strong and will help to guard us and the wagons. Wite and Brosc are also coming and a few others. There will be no-one left at the Hall except a few farmers and servants and so Sir Ector has given permission for Old Molly to come along and cook for us. So we'll hardly be deprived of any luxuries, eh!' He grinned at this as Old Molly was reputed to be the best cook in Christendom.

'What do you mean, Arthur?' Rhianne enquired. 'Who will take care of mother and me?'

'Why, didn't I say, Rhianne? You and mother are coming too!'

Her eyes lit up as she contemplated the adventure opening up before her. 'I can't believe that mother wants to leave her comforts, especially at this inclement time of year!' she exclaimed.

'Oh but she does! She said that she has waited too long to make pilgrimage and to thank the Lord in a fitting way for returning her precious daughter to her.' Arthur held her hands and spun her around, laughing and whooping.

The rest of the day passed in a blaze of happiness and anticipation as we all, in our own ways, considered the adventure that was almost upon us. I did, in the recesses of my mind, wonder what Arthur – or any of them, come to that – would say if I mentioned that in my day we could get there and back well within a day and that a couple of cheese sandwiches and some apples would suffice! Talking of sandwiches, they never ever made any in those days and laughed at me when I stuck a lump of cheese between two chunks of bread. They copied me a couple of times but then gave up when the large chunks of cheese they used kept falling out of the bread - they thought it barbaric. Different times – different customs! Hey-ho, I had best put these thoughts out of my head as I was not 'in my day' - I was as far removed from it as I possibly could be - and I was determined to enjoy what lay ahead – every minute of it!

We had weeks to plan and sort out all that needed to be packed, filled, made, pickled, stored, mended - not only for ourselves but for Sir Ector and his warriors, as well as instructions to be given to the very few staff and workers left at the Hall. Sir Ector had told us that the force sent by his father-in-law, a high noble in Wales, would arrive some time in September and that we would all probably go our different ways about the same time. Those weeks seemed to drag and yet go swiftly at the same time. Funny, that!

My job for that day was to pick whatever late apples were still on the trees in the orchard, take an inventory of the apple store and check how much other foodstuffs were available for our trip. Arthur was doing the same but his task was aimed at supplying the troops going off to war. We bumped into one another as the day progressed but didn't have much time to talk other than when we stopped for lunch. Meanwhile, Cabby spent part of the day with him or me, but mostly in the forest.

Lady Elise was getting quite excited as she would be meeting her brothers for the first time in many years and she had the house in a fluster getting it cleaned and polished, rooms being prepared for her family and barns, pens and outhouses being emptied for the men and animals that would soon be arriving.

Rhianne passed her time stitching, either repairing or replacing her father's emblem on his coat of arms, making good his or Sir Kay's jerkins or leggings or helping the maidservants with banners, tents and blankets.

So, all in all, there was much to do, and we were a very busy party of people. I did notice, however, that now the time was drawing close, most of us kept off the topic of the impending battles. Many of the men spent time at the Hall or on the farmsteads, gathering in the rest of the harvest before the winter set in and before they went off to war. When they weren't doing that, they were sparring with one another in the practise yard.

You could see the worry on the faces of their wives when they thought they were unobserved, as they, too, came and went from the Hall on their various errands, and it could be heard in the brittle laugher that erupted from the men as they tried not to think of whether they would return and see their loved ones again.

However, it was brought home to us late one evening when an exhausted rider and steaming horse arrived, shouting to be let in and proclaiming that the Lady Elise's brothers and their men would arrive early on the morrow.

There was a flurry of activity well into the night and from early morning until noon as rooms and outhouses were made ready to house the army; ground was cleared for the men to pitch their tents if they had them or make some sort of shelter while they readied themselves and got to know Sir Ector's men. Early next morning some of the children from north of the Hall came skipping in to say that they had seen the army approaching.

We ran up to the battlements and, yes, way off into the distance we could see, first of all, a cloud of dust, later, pennants could be seen fluttering in the breeze and, finally, a band of men moving our way. We shaded our eyes and waited as the army grew nearer until individual characters could be discerned. The sun, meanwhile, gathering herself up in her robe, looked over her shoulder and gave us all a farewell wink as she slipped beneath a blanket of black cloud. Then staring up at the sky as it filled with more swollen, dark grey clouds, which galloped across the sky like stampeding horses hurrying to join up with the main thrust, we wondered which would arrive first, the men or the impending deluge.

I thought of Cabal, as the sky boded ill for him. Storm clouds were thickening and he just hated thunder. He and Griff had run off into the forest at early light and had still not returned. I tried to call him through my mind but there was no response. Well, I couldn't concern myself with him just now. There were too many other things to worry about.

FIVE

The men dismounted as the first drops of rain began to fall. It was, unfortunately, the beginning of a torrent that would take up residence over the next five days. The persistent rain over those days seemed gradually to dampen the spirits of most of us. However, to begin with, Mistress Elise was overjoyed to see her one younger and two older brothers. She had been in an anticipation of excitement since the first runner had arrived to inform them of their imminent arrival but now, at that initial meeting, she was all aflutter, calling for refreshments, sending the servants scurrying hither and thither, hugging her kin, crying, laughing and sometimes breaking off into a strange tongue that made us all, rather rudely, stop and stare.

Eventually Sir Ector could see that chaos would soon reign if he didn't take control so, after sitting his lady wife down by the fire with her three brothers, he directed the small army to the barns, fields, storerooms, stables and kitchens.

A distant rumble of thunder preceded a very fast-moving couple of hounds into the Hall. Griff, a little braver where storms were concerned, nosed around the newcomers and then proceeded to search for scraps, even though it could be seen from his distended belly that he had dined sufficiently of whatever he'd caught in the forest, whereas Cabal shot between Mistress Elise's chair's legs and settled himself under it until such time as he felt it safe to come out. I stared at him and mentally *"tut-tutted"* but he ignored me.

After a while, and several dabs at her eyes with a completely insufficient handkerchief, Mistress Elise got herself enough under control to make introductions to those of us in the Hall. She almost broke down again as she introduced her youngest brother; he had been a mere child of seven summers when she had married Sir Ector and travelled with him to Devon. They all looked very alike, with brown

42

hair and blue eyes, although her older brother's hair now had more grey in it than brown and he had brought his eldest son with him – Culhwch - who had nineteen summers to his name. For the short time he was at the Hall, both Arthur and Percy thoroughly enjoyed his company. He had spent the previous summer at the Hall with Arthur, so it was good to meet up again. They were a jolly crowd and it was interesting listening to their lilting voices – very different to the slower and broader dialect I had grown used to in the West Country.

We feasted like kings – Sir Ector always had a well-stocked larder and a groaning table. Many times he replenished the food and the wine, and, being the man that he was, didn't forget to send out and make sure that his in-laws' men were also well fed and watered.

That first evening was a very happy time – the prime reason for their journey to Devon, at that time at any rate, deliberately not being touched upon - and it was thus extremely late when we all turned in for the night.

The storm had passed as the evening progressed, although we could all still hear the beat of the rain against the sides of the building – a sound that would truly get on our nerves over the days ahead.

Eventually the sun made up her mind by graciously showing us some sympathy – and what a grand entrance she made: rising majestically through the morning mists in mid-September she spread her glistening robe all around, reflecting back her glory in miniature rainbows of colour from trillions of drops of water hanging from every tree and blade of grass – all of which had grown a great deal over the last week of rain, although the trees had not done so well in the wind, losing a lot of their foliage. Now that she had deigned to show us her favour, we, too, could not help but show our pleasure in being honoured by her visit.

Once she had dispersed the mist, we were blessed with a gloriously warm Indian summer's day. All changed!

43

Everything possible was laid out to dry, the horses were rubbed down and brushed; spits and cauldrons were hung over cooking fires, all now allowed to blaze with vigour, which let off aromas, some of which were new to me; and soldiers cheerfully took up all the other tasks that had had to wait during the dismally wet days of the past week.

Cabal and Griff loped off into the forest and were not seen for the best part of that day. Cabal did turn and wink at me as he sped ahead of his brother but it could be seen by the set of his head and tail that he intended to catch up on the amount of fresh meat he had had to forego while the storm had been raging. I grimaced.

Sir Ector and his brothers-in-law were taken up that day with a morning spent going over maps and in deep discussion, followed by an afternoon inspecting the troops. Their faces were grim and their demeanour tense as they finally entered the Hall at suppertime.

Lady Elise and Rhianne put down their stitching as they turned to look up at the men entering the room and we jumped up from our lounging by the fire to hear their decisions.

'We are prepared, My Lady,' declared Sir Ector, 'and will be setting off on Michaelmas Day. I have sent riders to the other lords hereabouts and it has been decided that we shall all be meeting up at Bath; it is a large town that should be able to accommodate all of our men and horses. From there we shall head for Londinium, joining with the other lords on the way and then we'll advance north.'

I whispered to Arthur, 'What day is that?'

'Michaelmas? It's the twenty-ninth day of September. We have four days before they go. I think they are virtually ready but there is still much to do. Let's hope it doesn't rain any more!'

The Lady Elise looked pale but she managed to hold her head high: she knew that what her husband and brothers were

44

going to do was the only thing possible; if these men did not strive for peace, then the whole of Albion (that is what she always called Britain) would be in chaos.

We were a sombre lot that evening. Even Cabal, who had a terrific sense of fun, dozed by the fire and hardly bothered to look my way – even when I happened to be talking to Rhianne! Knowing I nearly always blushed scarlet when we conversed, he didn't even raise an eyebrow this evening. Before he let the melancholy take hold completely, Sir Ector ordered us all to bed, adding that it would be early mornings and late nights for the next few days, making all ready for the impending departure. So, with heavy hearts, we all said our good nights and made our way to bed.

Arthur and I talked long into the night – well, Arthur did all the talking, really, and I just added a "yes" or a "no" as was required. It had really been too early to go to bed and, as I lay there, I wondered how many others were doing the same as me and just staring at the ceiling or were chatting away to whoever they might be sharing a room with. Cabal, obviously fed up with being kept awake by our chatter, let out a few heavy sighs as if to wish us asleep, and it was with very great surprise that I found myself waking up.

When had I actually fallen asleep? I lay there for a while thinking that sleep was a very peculiar thing indeed. We lay in bed, which is where we mostly sleep, waiting for sleep to "happen". But – how does it happen? It's as if we are lying there and then we wake up and, somehow, sleep has happened somewhere between the laying down and the getting up! Hours gone in the twinkling of an eye! Very peculiar indeed! How do those hours disappear? I know we sometimes have dreams, which we invariably forget as soon as waking time takes over, but they mostly don't make sense! Nightmares are another thing! I can remember nightmares from years ago as though I had dreamed them only the night before. However, although I can remember them very well, they, too,

45

don't make much sense! Oh well, that's another of life's peculiarities.

Cabal had disappeared. By the amount of light coming in through the window, and the delicious smells creeping up the stairs, I gathered that breakfast was well and truly in full swing – I hoped I hadn't missed it; I was feeling quite hungry. Arthur had awoken as I sat up in my bed and together we quickly dressed and descended the stairs to the kitchens. All was hustle and bustle. Old Molly shouted directions to the maids and men who were serving the soldiers. We took our places at one of the long tables and ate our fill and then spent the rest of the day helping and watching the army prepare itself for departure. Those four days went like lightening.

We celebrated St Michaelmas Eve in the traditional fashion and a great time was had by all. Bonfires were lit around the gates of the main compound and there was much laughter and many games as we celebrated this saint's day.

Spits had been erected during the afternoon, some of the younger servants spending the day turning them and gradually roasting at least six whole lambs for the feast that evening.

Other foods had been cooked in the kitchens under the watchful eye of Old Molly – we often heard her yelling at someone or other who'd somehow got it wrong - and boars' heads, chickens by the score, savoury and fruit pies and cheeses and creams were, together with huge baskets of apples, pears and nuts paraded through the inner and outer courtyards. Not to be outdone by Molly's efforts, Sir Ector made sure that his barrels of mead and beer didn't run dry. There were definitely going to be some bad heads tomorrow!

We all set to with a will. It was a very happy time and everyone present was determined to enjoy it, resolute in not thinking about the morrow.

SIX

Michaelmas Day arrived. Before dawn's light, the sound of jingling harnesses and the grating of cartwheels could be heard alongside the snorts of the horses and stamping of their hooves, together with the more subdued sound of the men talking with one another.

Lady Elise and Rhianne stood holding on to one another as Sir Ector hugged them both and said his goodbyes. This time Lady Elise could not hold back the tears as her eyes searched his face and that of her brothers, most probably believing that this might be the last time she would ever see them again and wanting to make sure she would always remember what they looked like. Oh, it was a very sad time for all of us who'd be left, but I couldn't help but notice the gleam in Sir Ector's eyes at the thought of the impending conflict. I only caught a quick glimpse of Sir Kay, who was busy organising the goods wagons at the rear of the cavalcade but I expect he, too, was very excited about their adventure. Griff went too, trotting happily alongside Sir Ector's horse.

All too soon, they were gone! The ladies had stood for as long as they could, waving their scarves even after the convoy could no longer be seen, finally disappearing to their rooms as the last of the dust raised by the horses had settled, dabbing at their eyes with those same scarves. Arthur and I were left alone in the courtyard wondering how soon we should start organising our own journey to Hinton St. Mary. Arthur said he would think on this and talk it over with Brother Geraint when he came to see him later that day but thought that St. Selevan's Day would be the most auspicious day to start their pilgrimage; they could then be almost certain of arriving on St. Crispin's Day, weather permitting.

Another set of saints' days! Why does everything hinge on saints' days out here in early Britain?

I asked Arthur – a bit ungraciously, I must admit - if he would tell me more about those saints' days.

He smiled at me. 'Percy, the common calendar is always run on saints' days. St Michaelmas, which is the day that Sir Ector set off on his venture, is the day that marks the end of the harvest and, thus, farmers are able to calculate how much feed they have for their animals during winter. If they have too many animals to feed, they'd sell them or slaughter them and salt them for provision for the winter. It is also a quarter day and so everyone's finances need to be looked to and rents paid. As the harvest is in and some farm labourers would have no work, they go off and search for employment for the winter months – there is always work to be done, like repairing properties, clearing woodlands – you know, things that can't be done during the rest of the year.

'St. Crispin's day is 25th October. St Crispin is the patron saint of shoemakers. It is customary on that day for the rich to give their old shoes to the poor. Now, that makes sense as it is getting near winter and the poor cannot afford new shoes, so as their old ones are wearing out – the ones they were probably given the previous year - they get some more which will keep their feet shod through another year – until the next St Crispin's Day. Obviously, it is also the day that rich people get new shoes!

'Also, for instance, St. James' Day - this is when oysters are eaten, as it marks the opening of the time they are ready to be harvested. The poor eat many as they are easy to collect and are free. This is on the fifth day of August. On the twenty-fourth day of June, which is Midsummer Day and St. John the Baptist's Day, we celebrate by dressing our wells and our homes with flowers and branches. This is always a happy festival, with bonfires and jugglers and, sometimes, a travelling fayre. Men jump through hoops of flames as this is supposed to bring good luck – not so good, though, if he caught himself alight, eh!' Arthur fell about laughing.

48

Again I was amazed at his peculiar sense of humour. For the life of me I couldn't imagine that anyone running about in flames, in peril of losing his life, or at least being badly disfigured, should be the subject of such hilarity. But, there you are, each of us comes under the influence of his own wit.

He was just about to start on yet another saint's day, when I interrupted, a bit ungraciously I must admit, and said that I believed I'd got the idea. If he'd have gone on for much longer in this vein, he might be at it all day! I, for one, had had enough of saints' days!

'Well, it's not so much giving everything a saint's day – and there are hundreds of them you know –it's simply that as most of the population can't read or write, they have to be able to judge their calendars another way. So, they are reminded, Sunday by Sunday by monks or one of the brothers, as to which saint's day is coming up, and then they are able to judge what they should be doing or celebrating. Easy!'

I personally thought that it would be easier to say "24th June" rather than try and remember which saint's day it was, but thought better of it, as Arthur was bound to launch into further saints' days, and my head was spinning by now anyway.

As it was, we had glorious weather to prepare everything for our adventure and would eventually start our pilgrimage on Old St. Michaelmas Day – 10th October – a full five days early.

But for now, Brother Geraint arrived at around 3 o'clock after Arthur and I had had an hour's late sparring in the practise yard. We got washed up and he and the monk went off to the Hall to discuss the Bible, while I found Cabal and, with the sun lowering herself gracefully towards the hill and an hour-and-a-half's daylight left, went off to the woods.

A decision I was to wonder about for many a day to come!

SEVEN

Hearing a commotion from the roadway, Jack stopped chopping the pile of logs into kindling. He grinned as he watched his two now not so young grandsons racing one another up the incline towards his smallholding. Each tried to cut-up the other on his bicycle, whooping and shouting as they did so. Cabal rushed to the gate, barking and wagging his tail at them, ready to join in the fun. They threw their bikes against the hedge, the race forgotten, as they strode over to their grandfather.

'Hello granddad,' Daniel was first to greet him, swiftly followed by Ben's, 'Can we help?'

'Sure you can. You can start by putting your bikes in the barn. It's going to rain pretty soon and also it'll save you from doing it later. Has your mother left yet?' he asked, as he thought of his daughter, Kate.

'Yes.' Ben was striding back, rolling up his sleeves as he did so. 'She said to tell you that the course is going to last only two weeks, instead of three, so she should be home on the twenty-ninth of September.'

'And she said thanks for looking after us,' added Danny.

'The pleasure is all mine,' laughed Jack as he directed their proffered help, 'and looking at the size of you two now, I reckon you will soon be looking after me! Let's stack the logs by the fireplace before it rains and then we'll go and get your stuff from home.' Then, a slight sense of unease disrupted the otherwise peaceful afternoon as a whisper from the past reminded Jack that the twenty-ninth of September was St Michaelmas Day – the day they had all started on their various adventures all those centuries ago, when Sir Ector and the men went off to war – days of fear and trepidation.

Shrugging off those morbid thoughts, Jack organised the rest of the afternoon which the boys spent in collecting their

50

clothes, school books and games from their house in the village, preparing their room upstairs in the old cottage, and getting themselves settled in. Jack knew it wouldn't be long before they'd get him to continue telling them more of his adventures in the Dark Ages, but that would have to wait for now. Cabal, meanwhile, would trot along with them or lie by the fire and keep watch – just like any faithful hound would do.

The next day brought some of September's very inclement weather, where the wind gusted and rain lashed on and off for the best part of it.

After breakfast, Jack gave up on any outdoor work that morning and picked up where he'd left off his tale. He was, of course, happy to recall those days when he had travelled back "on the dragon's breath" to the days of Merlin and Arthur and was even more delighted that his grandsons were still eager to hear those tales.

His mind recalled the time he had told them about his adventures when they first came to live with him, which must be about six years ago now, and they still never tired of listening to him - quite often correcting him!

'*Well, I'm happy to remember them, too*', he thought, looking over at Cabal as he did so.

Cabby merely wagged his tail.

Clearing away the dishes from the table after their breakfast, they stood in the doorway watching the rain lash down in torrential sheets and sparking up from the cobbled yard. They realised that there would be no outside work done at all that day and thus settled down in front of a log fire to hear about what happened next in the story of the Glaston Giant, Danny prompting his granddad that he had got to the bit where he and Cabby had gone off into the woods.

Cabby and I decided that we would spend the last part of the day discussing what we would do whilst on this pilgrimage to

51

Hinton St. Mary. It was obviously going to take a very long time to get there as we would be travelling at a snail's pace with only a few ponies and some wagons for the ladies and everything we would need for camping and sustenance, tools and weaponry and a handful of men on foot. It would be hard work and tiring. However, even going that slowly, we must make it an adventure.

It was with these thoughts and discussions in our minds as we conversed with each other in the forest that we came upon a miniature waterfall we'd never noticed before. The waterfall fell down the face of a smooth rock, making a pool at its base, before disappearing into the earth a few feet away. As we watched, the last rays of the sun glowed brightly on the face of the rock, turning the water to molten gold. Both Cabal and I were spellbound and just stared at this phenomenon. I don't know how long we stood there – I believe it was merely seconds – when I noticed a soft whining coming from the hound. I glanced at him and then back at the waterfall, as that was where he, also, was looking, and then noticed what I thought was a sad face – distorted by the running water – staring back at me. The face didn't appear to be behind the waterfall or in front of it, but seemed to be made up of the water itself and, as it was continuously flowing, it was very misshapen. Thus, it took a while for me to recognise the face but once I did my heart leapt into my throat! Merlin! I ran my hand through the water to reach out for him and the face disappeared, only to re-appear once again when the water was running freely without my interruption.

'Percy?'

I jumped and looked around. I could hear a faraway voice calling me. I finally looked back at the face in the water and then, when it realised I was concentrating on it, it called me again. 'Percy?' it croaked faintly.

'Merlin!' I was shaking. 'Merlin, is that you? It's me, Percy! Is that you in the waterfall?'

'Percy, listen with care. I am so weak. That mad woman … Percy, watch out for Sir Kay.'

I waited for so long for him to speak again that I thought he slept or something. 'Merlin, what about Sir Kay? Please, Merlin, what am I to do?'

'Sir Kay is not …'. As the sun disappeared behind the horizon, he faded, rallied but, with a final gush of the waterfall, disappeared, his face sliding downwards in slivers like shards of broken glass into the pool beneath. The cascade was drying up as though it had never been.

'Merlin!' I was almost screaming by now. His voice had faded as though it travelled lightly away, enveloped within the miasma that was, even now, rapidly disappearing. 'Merlin, come back! Where are you? Please come back! What am I do to?'

But he had gone.

Or had he been there in the first place?

'Percy, come. Let's go back. I don't think we should speak about this to anyone. Perhaps Merlin will try to contact us again. I think that mad witch has something to do with this. Come, come, Percy.'

I looked down at Cabal and, shaking my head to try to clear it and understand what had just happened, absentmindedly tousled his head and turned to walk back with him, my mind in a whirl of confusion.

'I wasn't dreaming, was I? I asked the hound. *'What do you think he meant when he said, "Sir Kay is not" Cabal?'*

'I really have no idea! Until we've any news of him or see him again, I reckon we will not even begin to understand what he is or is not. It's really not something we should worry about. I expect we'll know one day. Although we have obviously got to be on our guard, otherwise he would not have bothered to try to contact us to warn us but as to what we need to be on our guard about, I haven't the slightest inkling!'

53

I was still shaking when I arrived back at the Caer and Lady Elise sent me straight to bed in case I had the ague. She wanted me well, as we would be travelling within the next sennight and she wanted me fit enough to go. Thus it was I was found, lying wide awake, when Arthur came up to bed.

'Well, Percival, I thought you would be well asleep by now! Or, at least, tossing in a fever, but you appear to be fine. What ailed you?'

I had no intention of telling Arthur about my vision in the forest; he had always thought me overly fanciful since our adventure at the mad witch's castle, and I didn't want him to start lecturing me again with regard to getting a grip on an understanding between reality and romanticism. He could get very serious at times and my mind at the moment was over-exercised as it was, without him spouting off. So, I just told him it must have been something I ate, but that I was alright now.

He seemed happy enough with that and so we spent the next half hour or so chatting happily about our forthcoming pilgrimage before he settled down. Once in bed, he was asleep within minutes but I lay staring at the ceiling for ages pondering why Merlin had tried to contact me. I had also forgotten just how uncomfortable these fifth century stuffed mattresses were and spent the time between my thoughts pummelling and thumping the lumps out of my bed when, after Cabal had harrumphed for the third time, I concentrated on trying to get to sleep, a hard task, as my puffy eyes bore witness to the next morning. Still, it gave support to the lie that I had been sick the day before.

The day arrived for the start of our expedition. The sun shone, the birds sang and the world looked young and new as we all bustled about in high spirits, impatient to get going. Of course, there is always the last minute this or the last minute that, as first one and then another remembered something that just had to be retrieved from the Hall as it would be impossible to live without it for so many weeks. Thus, one or two others started to get short tempered and impatient and the ponies, also fretting to get under way, were chomping at the bit and pawing their hooves, before we were finally all ready to depart. And so, we were on our way, becoming an extremely cheerful party as we headed due east toward Wheddon Cross, our first resting place, situated in the lee of the Brendon Hills.

Initially, Arthur took his place at the head of our party, with Wite just behind him holding Sir Ector's banner so that everyone would know it was an important party that was travelling. I was happy watching the pennant flutter in the gentle breeze at the head, as I took my place at the rear. In the beginning, Cabal ran wide, enjoying the freedom of pastures and smells new – and, most probably, hare and mice – but would return at intervals to keep me informed of all that was happening in the fields and forests around - we did not want to be surprised by anything that might be harmful to our little band, especially as we had the ladies with us.

All went well - at first - with balmy days and nights free from frost. We had organised our course so that there would at least be a forester's cottage for the ladies to use overnight and maybe a barn for Arthur and I, if not an inn, which would provide much better accommodation. Funny, though - no-one ever considered the men, though they seemed quite happy to make do with whatever shelter they could find or make for themselves and didn't even think that they should be looked after, let alone thought about. How times change!

After we'd been travelling for a almost a week, the weather took an unfortunate turn for the worse; it had deteriorated as we travelled further east, with a few squally showers suddenly soaking us to the skin. Lady Elise, who had ridden far ahead with Arthur, got soaked by a sudden downpour and had been taken with a severe chill that had held up our party for two days.

We had by now travelled the length of the Brendon Hills and then south-east through what is now called Bishops Lydeard. It was during our short time at Kingston St. Mary, that her Ladyship had been drenched and thus had taken to her bed in the nearest inn.

Cabby and I decided to explore!

The trees, at this time of the year, still held on modestly to their covering of leaves, shuddering now and then as a chill wind nipped at their limbs causing them to lose their grip on a leaf or two and consider the fact that in the not too distant future they would not only be unclothed, their nakedness thus on show to the whole world, but that they would also be extremely cold – best to close their eyes and sleep for a few months until they could grow some new clothes! However, at the moment they were arrayed in a display of the most gloriously changing colours. It was while I was looking at them, thinking just how much cleaner and brighter they appeared in the fifth century as opposed to what they looked like in the twentieth, that Cabby came crashing through the undergrowth toward me, tongue lolling and ears flapping.

'See who I've found!' he spoke into my mind.

My eyes searched all around but could see no-one.

'On my back, Percy!'

'Ogwin!' I exclaimed as I stared goggle eyed at the very small Faerie King; then a whisper from home as a thought from my mother bounced off the insides of my skull, *'Manners, Jack!'* I corrected myself, 'King Ogwin, Your Majesty.' I still felt very awkward about doing it, not ever having had to do so in my other life, but knew I had to make my obeisance. I stuck my left leg forward, removed my cap and made my bow. Thank goodness, he didn't appear to notice my rudeness and, as I looked up at him, I could see he was delighted. He was sitting astride Cabal, almost lost in and holding on to the coarse hair at the back of the hound's neck.

'Well, young man,' he responded, 'you *are* far from home! Are you and this hound alone? I must say, when I caught sight of him, I was in two minds as to whether I should stand or run when I recalled the last extremely damp experience I'd had with him! Well, I mean, he might not remember me, even though I remembered him!' He gave me a thorough, fierce and disapproving stare, as he checked me over from head to foot. He always had a way of making me feel very uncomfortable, silently accusing me of mistreating spiders – if I remembered correctly.

I was finding it extremely hard not to squirm on the one hand or laugh on the other but managed to keep myself under sufficient control, deciding neither an appropriate reaction; this very small man *was* a king and he might take offence. As to Cabal not remembering him, well, he obviously didn't know what a fantastic memory this particular hound had.

'Your Majesty, we travel with a party. Arthur is with us as well as several of the men you met the last time. We also have Rhianne in our party as well as her mother, the Lady Elise. Rhianne, you may recall, is the sister of Arthur whom we were on our way to rescue when we inadvertently strayed into your faerie circle.

'However, we're at a standstill at the moment due to the Lady Elise having caught a chill. She is laid up at the inn in the village of Kingston St. Mary and it is by chance that Cabal and I are out hunting and have met you.

'Where are your people? Can you come and meet with Arthur and our party? We are on pilgrimage to Hinton St. Mary to thank God for Rhianne's safe rescue from that mad witch, Mab.'

'Ah, the Mighty Smell!'

57

'What! Do you mean Mad Mab? Is that what you meant the last time we met when you said to beware the mighty smell?'

'Of course it was. Well, it must have been. I mean, we only knew her by her smell and as soon as one or other of us smells it, we're off and running like the clappers; didn't know her by a name at that time. Goodness me,' he said, turning to me, 'you humans aren't very bright are you? Did you let yourselves get caught by her after my warning?'

I felt the blood rush to my face, more with anger than embarrassment, but, of course, I couldn't argue with a king, could I? However, the tiny king didn't seem aware of my discomfiture.

He carried on talking, seeming to be completely at ease on the back of his unusual mount. Cabby, too, didn't seem to mind him sitting there either. *'Should have been a horse,'* I thought, recalling, too late, to block it. Very sheepishly, I looked over at him, to see one quizzically raised eyebrow and a haughty angle to his lower jaw. Remembering to put up my barrier this time, I just thought *'Oops!'*

I now felt rather despondent. When one makes mistakes, I don't believe our reactions to them come in isolation. All I could now remember was that I had made myself look an idiot in front of a king, had upset my friend into the bargain and then recalled that I still had to make my apologies to Merlin. And – as to that - where on earth *is* Merlin? Oh, I wished he were here.

'I said, I should like to meet Arthur again,' Ogwin was saying, as I tuned in again to him. 'Are you listening to me, or have you completely lost your wits? I must say that I'm not used to being treated so scurvily. Pull yourself together.'

This time, Cabal was staring at me with a very amused glance. Right, by now I had had enough and, so, throwing caution to the winds, I just turned and ordered them to follow me.

58

I walked in front of them, stiff backed and head held high all the way back to the inn, where I handed the king over to Arthur. However, during that time Cabal had great fun in trying to make me respond to his taunts. Sometimes that hound has a nasty twist to his character, I believe. If the king hadn't been there, I reckon I would have said other things that I would have regretted – something more to add to the burden I already carried. Perhaps it was as well he *was* there.

After greeting each other warmly, Arthur and Ogwin took up a place near the fire and chatted as easily as people that had known one another for years, instead of the fact that they had met only once before. I could have joined them but in some perverse way – probably making myself suffer for the way I was feeling – decided to sulk on my own. It was still light, so I went off into the forest to kick whatever might be in my way. Oh, how I wish I'd been more even-tempered and less sulky. Apart from making myself look foolish, I might never have put myself and all the others in such a dangerous situation as was awaiting me among the trees. I was so caught up in my bad temper and feeling so sorry for myself that I was completely off guard. Bad move that!

'I suppose you are going to stop the story there, granddad, aren't you?' said Danny, as Jack got up to let Cabby out of the cottage.

'I'm afraid so, Danny,' he responded as he walked back toward the fire. 'You must admit, it is late!'

'OK,' he sighed. 'I know it's no good trying to get you to go on once you've made up your mind, but, tell me one thing - is Mab going to be in this story?'

'Mab? Oh, yes! Oh my, yes!'

EIGHT

Early the next morning Daniel and Ben hitched the horse to the cart and made their way into the village with a huge load of logs and kindling. There was always plenty of bartering going on between local farmers and shopkeepers. Jack, still a fit man despite his 50-odd years, managed to keep a lot of the villagers supplied with wood for their winter fires and, in turn, was rewarded with eggs, bread, chickens, milk, flour, butter, cheese, meat, vegetables and even newspapers. The boys, now almost full-grown themselves, had been entrusted to make these deliveries and bring back whatever goods they received in exchange. Of course, there were a few of the older folk, friends of Jacks, to whom he sent his logs free of charge. These folk, in days when they had been younger and more able-bodied, had helped Jack out in many and various ways and he would no more think of charging them anything than he would think of stopping their delivery of logs. 'No,' he would say, 'you don't take aught from your friends!'

By the time they returned from their morning's work, they were ready for lunch and a break. Under Jack's directions, they stored the goods, unhitched the horse and made him comfortable with a drink of water and some oats as a treat, before finally letting him loose into the paddock.

Sitting round the big wooden table for lunch, Jack continued with his tale.

We knew that the next part of our journey would continue to take us in a somewhat south-easterly direction toward Hinton St. Mary but little did Cabby and I, or anyone else, for that matter, have any idea on that chilly morning in mid-October, that the adventure was about to take a completely different turn - through the southernmost passes between the Quantock Hills, north-east toward Glastonbury! But not for me!

However, I wasn't thinking about our journey right at that moment, as, still in a huff, I walked quickly out of the inn and took off into the forest. I half expected Cabal to catch up with me but he must have decided that I needed to be on my own for a while to sort out my bad temper. I must admit, I missed him and it added to my ill humour that he didn't follow me. After kicking a few tree stumps and whipping some ferns with a switch I'd made, I sat down against a tree and started pulling the seeded heads off some rye grass. I was thus engrossed when I heard that first peculiar sound.

Plop!

I looked up, expecting to see Cabal but he wasn't there.

Plop! Plop!

There it was again. I jumped up and searched all around but could see nothing.

Plop!

This time it was right behind me and, spinning around, I saw a pathway – well, more of a track – leading between high trees that rose cathedral-like and fell sheer to the edge of the forest. The trees were very wet and it was the water dripping from their ceiling that was making the plopping sounds as it fell into ever increasing puddles. I wondered, rather absent-mindedly, why this track was here, when there was a perfectly good road that ran beside the inn but I didn't stop to work it out logically. I set off, quite gingerly at first, down this very wet and slippery path, not meaning to travel more than a few feet – just sort of peering about to see what might be there before going back. But I gradually picked up speed until I was running, though I don't know why - it seemed to take hold of me, drawing me forward.

Then I noticed the man standing at the far end of the roadway and my heart flipped inside my chest. It was Merlin! He waved at me and beckoned me to him. I didn't think twice but immediately took off again, running towards him at first at a cracking pace; slipping now and then before moving more carefully. Looking back, I can't believe that I could have been such a complete twerp.

After slipping over a couple more times I decided it was best if I didn't go quite so fast. I had to keep looking down to make sure I didn't fall over anything or lose my footing and each time I took my eyes off him – even for a second, I noticed that when I glanced up again Merlin would be either turning a bend or would be walking on again just as far away from me as he had been at the beginning, beckoning me over his shoulder to follow. I just didn't seem to get any nearer to him. I don't know how long we travelled this way but soon my legs started to shake and wobble as they got very tired; the sweat started to stand out on my forehead and my heart began to pound in my chest. I kept calling to him to wait but he either didn't hear or ignored me and I still didn't seem to get any closer to him. This went on for ages and then I really did start to suffer: my breath was rasping through a very dry mouth, my legs were turning to jelly and my heart felt like it would burst out of my chest. If I didn't catch up with him soon, I thought I would pass out. I stopped to take a drink from one of the pools of water I'd seen here and there and was surprised to find that they had all dried up. I was still in this cathedral-like tunnel of trees but the rain or whatever it was had stopped. I hadn't noticed that it had and wondered how long ago it had happened.

The ground beneath my feet began to rise and fall as though I was on a roller coaster, while the trees began rushing past me like they did when I went on the back of my brother James' motorbike. I was now being overcome by dizziness, with bile starting to rise in my throat. I couldn't go on any longer and, dropping to my knees, closed my eyes to shut everything out. My breath gradually returned to normal and I took the chance to look back; I'd decided to retrace my steps but, to my horror, found that the trees had closed in behind me where the path had once been, effectively cutting off my retreat. I tried to break through the trees but to no avail and of the path that I had been traveling, there was no sign! I must be going mad! I turned back wearily to see if I had got any nearer to Merlin. Surely he'd wait for me now.

The sweat was running into my eyes, which made the figure of Merlin indistinct in the distance: I had still not got any closer to him. Nearing exhaustion, I fell to my knees and lay down, too weary even to weep.

I couldn't sleep and lay there for I know not how long but eventually decided that I needed to go on. The pathway before me was still visible, though dusk was rapidly approaching. I could see Merlin waiting patiently for me at the end of the roadway and, making a huge effort, I managed to get myself to my feet. As I peered at him he beckoned me on again. I must admit I'd hardly any strength left in me at all. I tried to run but all I could manage was a dragging walk. I told myself not to look at anything except Merlin and that in doing this I should catch up with him; surely he couldn't move far away from me again if I did that. But then he turned a corner and was gone. I groaned inwardly but kept going.

The road came to an end!

Well, the road out in the open came to an end. It ended at the mouth of a cave. I looked up and the cathedral of trees came to rest at the face of the cliff. I looked behind me and the trees had closed in on me once again. There was nowhere else to go except into the cave. I stooped down and stuck my head in to see if I could see Merlin or if I could see anything, for that matter. Merlin I could not see. Where had he gone? There was, however, a luminous path that meandered through and sloped upward inside the cave. I stepped through and stood upright, glancing around to see if there was anything else or any other pathway. Nothing!

Then I heard the entrance slam shut behind me. Spinning around I tried to find the opening to get back outside but of a doorway or boulder there was no sign. It was as if a solid inside wall had been there all the time. I started to sweat again – this time with fear.

Well, there was only one thing to do, wasn't there? I had to go up this luminous pathway. I moved along with narrowing walls at the sides; sometimes I had to squeeze through the slimmest of gaps to get to through but, somehow, I managed it. After a while the walls widened and I was travelling along a fairly open area. This was a lot more comfortable and made me feel a little better. But that wasn't to last for long, though.

The whispering started while I was in this open area and I found myself searching about for what might be hiding there. I called out to see who might answer me, thinking it was Merlin, but all that happened was that my "hello" echoed backwards and forwards, bouncing off every possible rockface that was inside that cave, some loud echoes seeming to whip past my face, making me duck. I had to pull myself together. It was pretty dark everywhere except upon the luminous path and I began to imagine the most awful things waiting to pounce out on me from the gloom. The path got narrower and, as it did so it rose into the air, the edges beginning to fall away sheer on either side. I felt like I was walking on a tightrope in places. I had to keep my eyes in front of me to see where the next bit of the path was going and at the same time stop my feet from slipping off it.

The first thing leaped at me from my right side and almost sent me over the edge to my left as I jumped right out of my skin. It was horrible! To this day I'm not sure what it was. It looked a bit like a hyena but was covered with eyes on the end of stalks that were searching for me and shifting about all over the place as they moved. It didn't manage to get me and slid back down the side again. While I stood still with fright another of these things jumped up from the left side and stood in front of me, opening its mouth wide as it did so. Its eyes were swivelling all over the place and then, not having too good a grip, it slipped off and vanished down the side again. They had been making weird noises and it was the one that had stood in front of me that made it clear what that noise was: it was lip-smacking – the sort of noise someone or something makes when it is contemplating a nice meal.

Two things came to mind: the first was that I was most probably the nice meal they were contemplating and the other thing was that there must have been scores of them by the amount of lip-smacking that was going on.

I had to get out of there and fast; that is, if there was a way out.

Trying to ignore the noise and the occasional leap from these beings, I determined to move along the narrow ledge as quickly as I could but with every step I took those bug-eyed monsters would be there; every time my foot landed, a sharp mouth would launch itself at my ankle. I was now having to move very fast and fright was giving me wings. But it was not the only thing that had been given wings!

No sooner had I started to move on again, trying to dodge those creatures or kick them out of the way, than something huge swooped down at me from above. I ducked, and only just in time I think, although I was extremely lucky not to fall off my precarious perch. The road had narrowed to only about ten inches across, with sheer and precipitous sides falling away to I knew not where. Hanging on to the sides of the exceptionally narrow pathway and lying on my belly, I crawled and pulled myself forward. 'Why?' I asked myself several times; I didn't know where I was going and it might be worse up ahead than it was behind. All that I knew was that every time I had tried to go back the way was barred. So, moving on, I tried to still the pounding of my heart whilst trying to determine my new attacker's identity. I didn't have to wait long as another of those many-eyed beings, this time with huge wings, swooped down and, piercing my leather jerkin with its talons as it grabbed me, swept me off my ledge, whilst another of the monsters on the ground made a grab at my leg. As I was swept into the air I could feel one set of teeth struggling to keep hold of my foot while the needle-like talons from the one above chafed at my shoulder. It flew higher and higher, smacking its lips as it rose, leaving me just enough time to wonder which part of me it was going to eat first. As I struggled I tried to prise open the talons from above whilst kicking the monster below with my free leg. I suddenly felt my jerkin begin to slip. Now, what was going to be worse – being taken up to some monstrous eagle's (if it was some sort of eagle) eyrie and being torn by its huge beak to be fed bit by bit to its young or falling into the claws of the many-eyed, lip-smacking monsters below? Fear once again gripped me as I imagined both scenarios. However, I didn't have long to wait to find out which one it was going to be as, with a mighty ripping noise, my jerkin finally gave way and I began to fall - down, down, down …

The last thing I remember was the bird flying away with my flapping jerkin still held in its claws and the other creature finally letting go of my leg and falling down alongside me, both of us staring at one another with completely perplexed expressions on our faces as we fell ever downwards, although he looked worse than me as his confusion was reflected back at me through all of his eyes whereas mine was just from two.

NINE

Twilight was falling at around five o'clock and Cabal, who had finally decided it was time to see what I was up to, came back into the inn, bringing in a swish of leaves with him as he pushed open the door. Brosc, jumping up to close it before it let in too much cold, scolded the dog, before he, in turn, was told off by Arthur for doing so.

'He's only a dog, Brosc! Do you expect him to knock on the door and ask leave to enter or, perhaps, make a bow to you as he comes in, let alone close the door behind him?'

'Sorry.'

Arthur just nodded at him. He was fretting at not being able to go on with his pilgrimage. 'Well,' he had said earlier, 'it was *I* that wanted to go in the first place and now it seems the whole household needs to go. Why not ask the whole neighbourhood? It's seeming to take forever to get there, what with one hold up after another! I should have just packed up and gone on my own.'

'Arthur,' Rhianne checked him. 'Be fair! It cannot be helped that mother is sick. I know the pilgrimage is important to you but mother should be important as well! Hopefully, she should be well soon and we will then be able to get on our way. It's only a couple of days' delay and we should still be there for All Saints Day.'

'I'm sorry Rhianne, and to you Brosc. I'm just frustrated that we cannot continue our journey. Just sitting around, doing nothing, is making me fretful. I forgot how irritated I had become whilst Ogwin was here but now that he's gone I am feeling very restless. However, I shall try to learn patience. Forgive my impoliteness – and, of course, I do care about mother.

'I shall rise early tomorrow and put in some practise. Yes! We shall sharpen up our weapons and make a morning of it. We need to keep ourselves ready and prepared for all eventualities.

'We'll cast lots to see who will practise with whom. Percy, get pen and paper and … where *is* Percy?'

'Haven't seen him all afternoon,' Shake Spear responded. 'He went off into the forest late morning and hasn't come back.'

Rhianne looked over with an enquiring eye at Cabal and, upon his response of "*Outside*", followed him into the yard.

'Cabal, what is it?'

'*Speak to me in your mind! You never know who might be listening.*'

'*Sorry, Cabal. Where is Percy? What do you know?*'

'*For a start, I don't like this place! Too many people are losing their tempers. First, Percy this morning took umbrage at silly things and, when we returned to the inn, flounced off on his own into the woods. That's not like him. I wish now that I had gone with him but I thought that he needed time to think things through and get his temper back in check. So, regretfully, I didn't go with him. Secondly, Arthur, too, is getting short tempered and is chafing at the bit to go on with our journey. Now Brosc has just shouted at me and that is not like him either. He is usually the most even-tempered of all the men. I believe we should move on from here as soon as we can or, at least, as soon as Lady Elise is able to travel.*'

'*Yes, Cabal, but what has happened to Percy?*'

'*I don't know! I followed his trail out into the forest. I came across the place where he sat against a tree and shredded some foliage. I could smell where he got up and walked over to a small clearing and, unless he retraced his steps, it seems that he just disappeared. There is no sign of him having moved off in any other direction. He just seems to have vanished into thin air! He couldn't have retraced his steps as he would have come back to the inn and, as he hasn't, I am fearful as to what may have happened to him.*'

68

Rhianne, during this discourse, had turned quite pale. She took in what Cabal had said and, coming to no conclusion whatsoever, asked him again if he had any ideas as to what they could do.

'Well, obviously I can't say anything but I think you should go back to the inn and voice your concern about him. Say that you have already been outside with me and we have searched but as I was just going round in circles it is clear that the trail has gone cold. Perhaps the men could search. The thing that really worries me, Rhianne, is that no-one could just vanish into thin air! I checked to see if there were signs of wolves or bears that might have snatched him up and run off with him but there were no suspicious smells. I have a sneaking notion that evil is involved here and the only person that comes to mind is that mad witch!'

'Mad Mab?'

'Quiet! Don't even think her name let alone say it out loud. That might be all that is needed to bring her here!'

'Oh, I'm so sorry, Cabal. The shock of the thought that she might be involved with us again is more than I can bear. I shall try to keep my thoughts to myself. Oh, I do hope it isn't so. I don't think I could stand coming into contact with her again.' She began shivering as she thought of her.

'Me neither,' he thought – with his barrier up against Rhianne, sneezing at the memory of her awful smell attacking his finely tuned and delicate nostrils.

They turned back into the common room at the inn and Rhianne, sitting down next to Arthur, voiced her concern with regard to my whereabouts.

'We have just been talking about him and the men have gone to search the inn and stables. There is no-one in the barn as most of the men have been sleeping in there and would have noticed if he'd gone in. We'll have to wait and see if he returns or if anyone can find him.'

But, of course, nobody did!

69

After searching well into the evening and finding not one clue, everyone took to their beds; there was no laughter that night and Arthur's bad mood seemed to invade everyone's being. It was a sorry lot that awoke the next morning.

How strange we are at times. Arthur had been straining at the leash to continue his journey and then, conversely, wanted to wait at the inn for me to return or, at least, to try and find me. Rhianne, who had by now agreed with Cabal that I had been whisked away and that everyone should remove themselves from this weird place, managed, after much arguing, to get them to agree to travel.

With instructions to Wite and Shake Spear to stay behind and scour the countryside, Arthur prepared to move on as soon as possible.

They wrapped up their still very unwell mother and made her as comfortable as possible in the wagon, moving at a gentle pace towards their next stopping place – Thornfalcon, south of the river. Rhianne stayed with her mother all the time they were travelling, only leaving her side to take a little exercise when they stopped to eat and then only if Arthur or Old Molly stayed with her and promised not to leave her side till she returned. The poor woman had been delirious with fever ever since taking to her bed. The chill had worsened and there was no sign of it abating.

King Ogwin had said he would send a dandelion draft to lower her fever. Rhianne wondered if he would be able to find them now that they were on the move but, then again, the birds and insects of the forest would send him word, she was sure.

During these breaks, she caught up with any news there might be from both man and dog. But of me there was no report!

TEN

I awoke, I know not how many hours later, and it was completely dark. Of Merlin there was no sign – how could he do this to me? I felt around myself and could find no bits missing. I strained my ears to hear any noises. I heard no lips smacking or wings flapping. That was a relief I can tell you. Looking up and down and around I strained my eyes to find the illuminated roadway, but there was nothing; it was completely dark. I was still shivering with fatigue and cold and not a little fear. Pulling my shirt around me for comfort I sat for an age before my shakings stilled. However, my mouth was extremely dry and no matter how many times I tried to make some spit to wet it, it stayed dry and would do so, I thought, until I got something to drink. I hoped I wasn't dehydrating which made me start to panic thinking I was, as I had come so far and had had no refreshment whatsoever. I got up onto my feet and tried to control my legs, which were still very wobbly from so much use. I couldn't see a thing and had no idea where I was. I tried to reach out to Cabal and Merlin with my mind but there was nothing. Was I in a dungeon – or a tomb? Maybe I was being stored for later consumption! I started to panic before I managed to convince myself that that would be very, very unwise indeed.

Walking gingerly and feeling each step with a carefully positioned toe, I started to explore. I wondered why Merlin had been so mean in not waiting for me but then thought that he would let me know why when we met again. The floor over which I was travelling - ever so slowly - was, after I leaned down and felt it, made of stone; it was cold, but dry. I was still trying to wet my mouth and throat but what with all that sweating and, of course, the ever-present fear that was creeping up my spine, I was quite unsuccessful. I had almost given up and was about to sit down again and feel sorry for

71

myself – and also wait and see what would happen next – when my foot came into contact with something soft that started to move and groan as it was disturbed.

I jumped back, thinking it might be one of those many-eyed monsters or a rat or something but with hindsight - well any sight would be helpful at the moment as I couldn't see a thing – it would have had to be an extremely big rat as my foot couldn't move it very far!

I nudged it again but apart from being able to lift it a little, it didn't move. Kneeling down, I was cautious as I felt the moaning object and discovered that there was another body sharing my space. I hoped it was not dead – but that was a ridiculous thought as it had just moaned. I shook my head to try and make it start working sensibly again and carefully reached out and touched him with my hands. It was definitely a man, I thought, as I felt his face and was relieved to feel his breath on the back of my hand. At least I hope for his sake he was a man as he definitely had a prickly chin – probably in need of a shave, I thought. I felt around and eventually came across his chest, which was moving, thank God. The man was either semi-conscious or asleep. He was dressed in a heavy weave shirt and thick cloth leggings, similar to almost everyone in those days. He had no weapons that I could discover and, like me, did not appear to be harmed in any way or be trussed up. Perhaps he was as exhausted as I was. I shook him but there was no response.

Well, I supposed that if we were not in a dungeon we must still be in the thick of the forest in the night and as there were no stars or moon we would just have to wait until morning before we could see or do anything. I was still extremely tired and before long must have just curled up and gone off to sleep.

I awoke with a start, I know not how much later, by being shaken awake quite violently by the person I had discovered the night before.

I eventually made it known to this other person that I was by now quite awake and he could cease from shaking whatever wits I still might have left.

'Oh, thank goodness,' he moaned, 'I thought at first that you were dead.'

'Well, that's what I thought about you but I am glad to see – well, if I *could* see, that is – that you are alive as well.'

'Percy! Percy, is that you?'

'Yes, I am Percy, but who are you?' I enquired

'It's me, Kay! What are you doing here? How did we both get here?'

I jumped up, absolutely astounded. 'Kay! Merlin brought me here! But, what are you doing here? I thought you had gone with Sir Ector. You did go with Sir Ector! How come you are here? And what's wrong with your voice?'

'Oh, Percy, it's a very long story but I very stupidly got hurt. We were jousting and I fell off my horse and injured my foot. I could kick myself – it was such a stupid thing to do. Well, it got steadily worse and my father told me to come home and get well. I have had a bit of a limp now for a week or so but it's gradually getting better. I didn't want to stay at the Caer on my own and so I travelled on to meet up with you all on the pilgrimage to Hinton St. Mary. But now we are here, wherever here is! And I am so thirsty!'

'Kay – can you see anything? I can't see a thing and I am a bit scared that I've gone blind.'

'No. I think we must be in a dungeon or something like it as I can't see anything either. I don't think any harm is meant us – well, not yet anyway – because if they, whoever they are, wanted to dispose of us, they would have done it by now. So, I reckon we'll just have to wait and see what happens. By the way, are you hurt in any way?'

'No.'

'That's good. Have you got any food on you?' he asked. 'I am mightily hungry!'

73

'No. I'm hungry, too. Or I feel sick - one or the other. Sometimes I can't tell the difference – I expect it's something to do with the stomach being in knots.'

We agreed to get up and make a search of our surroundings. I was still moving on wobbly legs whilst holding my arms straight out in front of me as I cautiously felt my way forward. We kept up a conversation, more to make sure that we were both still there than anything else, and spent a good few minutes searching. I felt nothing! I came up against no walls, trees, ditches, tables or anything. I wondered if we were in something like the peculiar pathway I had gone along whilst following Merlin or inside that awful cave. Merlin! Now where was he?

'Kay, how did you get here? Did you follow Merlin? I followed him but wasn't able to catch up with him. And where *is* Merlin?'

'I don't know anything about Merlin, but let me tell you what happened before I ended up here. I know that I was riding through the forest on my horse when I think I was knocked off him by riding into the branch of a tree. I had been following your trail and asking at various inns and farmsteads where you'd been staying to see if they knew in which direction you were travelling. I was extremely keen to catch up with you now that I had decided to join you. I suppose I wasn't concentrating enough and ran straight into the branch. The next thing I remember is waking up here with you.'

'Have I asked you if you have any water on you? I am extremely thirsty.' I think I must have been getting delirious.

'Sorry, Percy. Don't have any of that either.'

We both then fell silent, lost in our own thoughts and despondencies. The next thing I remember – I must have fallen asleep again - is being shaken awake by Kay! It was daylight; in fact it was broad daylight and we were perched on top of a very high mountain, the top of which was about the size of half a football pitch. It was cloudy – hence the darkness, I supposed, but there was no rain and so it was dry. My mouth, which had been parched to start off with, had now, with fear, become even dryer as I recalled that I'd tried to find the "edge" of our dungeon a few hours ago and thanked whoever was obviously looking after me that I hadn't! Phew, if we had taken one step too many we would have fallen off and down the side of this mountain to our deaths. After walking round the edge and peering over, it confirmed that all the sides were sheer. In fact it was so high that in some places we couldn't even see the ground.

Then the thought occurred to me, how on earth had we both got here?

ELEVEN

I turned to Sir Kay with a completely bemused look on my face. He had moved into the middle of the flat-topped mountain and sat there, beckoning me over to him.

'We could have been killed here last night!' he whispered. 'Who or what brought us up here?' He was obviously afraid of heights and I thought that if I'd had a tape measure I would find that he would most probably be sitting right in the centre of the mountain's crest. He certainly looked a peculiar colour.

I just couldn't speak. Not only was I still spit-less, but at that moment I was so scared, I just couldn't have said a word if you'd paid me. My mind was grinding slowly and thoughts and fears plodded through my brain, slow marching behind one another before being dismissed as fanciful, completely absurd or absolutely genuine. Although my fears were beginning to run riot, the only thought that kept returning to me was, *'where was Merlin and why had he done this?'*

Very gradually the clouds started to disperse and a weak autumn sun began to break through. I walked around the edge of our plateau again – but not too near the edge – to see what I could actually make out below. We were extremely high up and everything below us, until the sun could disperse it, was shrouded in mist. I could find no way down and so after a while I gave up and went to sit with Kay. We sat for the next few hours, resting against one another's backs, staring out into space, each lost in his own thoughts.

And thus it was, that she found us.

First we heard a sound, both of us jumping up at the same time. It was faint to begin with - the flapping wings of some huge bird, and then, getting louder as a swift shadow flew across the face of the sun making us blink. As it got louder I

76

became aware of a smell, just a whiff of unpleasantness which then disappeared. It was vaguely familiar but there was so much going on I dismissed it. We waited with, in my case at any rate, bated breath. Then, as if it ran up the sheer sides of the mountain, blocking out the rays of the sun as it did so and temporarily blinding us by its shadow, Hellion rose high above us.

I recognised the white dragon immediately. After its confrontation with Moon Song - Merlin's beautiful red dragon - it could never be forgotten. Its huge, leonine features filled the sky as its piercing eyes glared down at us while smoke shot out of its nostrils. *'Oh Merlin, where are you?'*

'Ha!' she shouted. 'If it isn't my little friend Percival and his friend's brother, Sir Kane.'

'It's Sir Kay, actually,' he responded.

'Kane, Kay, it doesn't matter,' she spluttered, her temper ever ready to fray. 'You won't need a name soon, as no-one will see you again, and no-one will hear you! And you, certainly, won't hear or see them! Now, can you deduce why? Of course you can because you will no longer exist – either of you! But you will stay alive long enough - at least until I get what I want from you. So how long that is is completely up to you. Mind, now I come to think of it, the longer you live means the longer you experience suffering.' She stopped, grinning. 'But at least, then, you will still be alive! How kind I can be at times!'

She had, unfortunately by then, jumped down from the back of the dragon and had come exceedingly close to us, almost knocking me over by the power of her very unwholesome stench. If she wasn't careful, she'd kill us with her bad breath before she had time to devise anything worse – hmm, could anything be worse? Sir Kay, it must be said, must be made of stronger stuff than me, as it didn't seem to have the same effect on him.

All the while, Hellion was pacing around us, shaking the ground with his huge talons and breathing out gusts of red smoke that was threatening to turn to fire.

'Well, now,' she rubbed her hands together as she spoke, 'I expect you are both hungry and thirsty and ready for a nice warm bed. Is that so?'

Neither of us moved or deigned to answer her; we knew her generosity was virtually non-existent.

'Come now,' she purred, 'I am not so awful as to leave you here forever. I know I threaten and growl, but I am not so bad.' She sounded almost human as she pranced and turned on her heels and, in fact, I think she almost believed it herself. I, though, knew better. She might try and deceive herself into thinking she was sane and reasonable but she certainly wouldn't fool me.

We were in a quandary, though, and, whatever was going to happen, two things came to mind. First, we would not get off this mountain without some help and, secondly, with that awful dragon at her command we would certainly have to do as she said. So, using what little strength of character I had left and speaking through my very dry mouth, croaked, 'Alright, Mab, we are at your command. I, for one, must admit that I am terribly thirsty and could do with a little food. So, what do you want us to do?'

She grinned at me – and yes, she had lost two or three more of those brownish, wobbly teeth since I had last seen her. It certainly wasn't a good idea for her to smile. Not her worst feature, I thought, but certainly not her best!

'I hope you don't think that by being so agreeable I will forgive you for what you did to me before.'

She stared at me until I thought I might own up to the sins of the universe instead of just the ones I had committed with regard to her – although I don't believe for one minute they were sins on my part but I expect in her book they were. I looked away.

78

'Percival,' she called me, making me look back at her. 'Did you enjoy your journey here?'

'What do you mean?'

'Did you enjoy following Merlin?' She was trying to hold herself in check; her mouth was twitching furiously as the laughter tried to erupt from it.

'How did you know that ...?' I started to ask, stopping as I suddenly realised what she was about to tell me.

Off she went again into one of her awful laughing fits as she realised I knew what she was about to tell me. This time she did fall over; well she fell backwards and landed on her backside. It didn't stop her laughing, though, and I just stood there, mouth clamped tightly, waiting for her to stop.

'You know!' she gasped, trying to get her breath. 'Yes, you really do! I am so wonderful! You thought it was Merlin, didn't you? It was me! All the time, it was me and you followed like a little lamb to the slaughter. I could have killed you, you know. I could have thrown you off that pathway but I wanted to have some fun. And fun I had! Did you like the little monsters? I'll let you into a secret.' She pulled herself up from the floor, cackling as she did so, and stooped to whisper, in a very conspiratorial way, 'They don't exist! I put them into your mind. It was great fun watching you duck and dive and when you started falling – or thought you did – that was hilarious! Your arms and legs were thrashing about like windmills.'

'Then how did I get out?'

'Hellion got you out and placed you on the mountain. You didn't see him because you only saw what I let you see; and what you saw were monsters. Great fun! Fantastic!'

Still laughing – or coughing with the effort of it - Mab pranced back and forth before us and then, clicking her fingers, called the dragon over. Before stooping to allow us to alight, he circled around us, licking his lips and snorting out flame-filled smoke. I shivered – if Mab wasn't around I believed he would fry us rather than fly us and not even say grace before he ate us.

She made us climb up between the folds on its back and we then took off. This flight was not like the one I had experienced with Moon Song. Where she was sleek and silken, this dragon was podgy and damp and had a very unfortunate odour – not like Mab, but irritating nonetheless. Regardless of all of this, I felt rather more comfortable than I had done on top of the mountain. At least we were now on our way to terra firma but I blanked off my mind as to what might be awaiting us when we got there. I looked over at Kay and must say that my regard for him went up a few notches; not only did he not seem to be scared but he had actually gone to sleep. Sleep for me, though, was a long way into the future.

I knew I would need to keep all my wits about me so far as this mad woman was concerned and so, feigning sleep – now was that what Kay was also doing? – I watched her through lowered eyelashes. She, however, took not the slightest bit of notice of me, merely straining her eyes forward as we travelled due south. After a while I relaxed a little. It would be soon enough when we landed for the witch to start on Kay and me and that was something I didn't want to even start thinking about.

As I lay back in the folds of the dragon's scales, I studied this peculiar excuse for a woman. First, I don't believe she had washed at all since I had last seen her and, naturally, the smell was overpowering, especially as she was perched upwind of us on the dragon's back. Secondly, I reckoned she was wearing the same dress, although I couldn't be sure, as there was such an accumulation of spillage all down it that the real material just didn't show through. Perhaps I might get an opportunity to pick off a crust of dirt and check the pattern. No, I didn't want to get that close! If I remembered correctly, the dress should be blue! Her hair was much the same as it had been – mostly plastered to her head by grease with wild frizz at the ends. As she held on to the fan around Hellion's neck, her sleeve fell away from her arm showing just how far the dirt had travelled, from grimy dirt filled nails to crusty tide-marked elbows. I had to turn away as I was starting to feel sick.

'Ah, poor lamb,' she said sarcastically as she looked over her shoulder at me. 'Air sick, are we? Don't like being so high?'

She had no idea, had she? I thought.

I rapidly put up my barriers. I had completely forgotten that she could read my thoughts, albeit poorly. I hope she hadn't read too much as I knew that she always got her own back on anyone and everyone that put her down, and she already had a score to settle with me – no point making it worse, though whatever she did to anyone to get her own back was always the worse thing she could think of. So, I really must remember to use my gift of mind-speaking, listening and barrier adjusting wisely!

As the sun was setting to our right, an extremely large castle came into view. It was not dissimilar to the one in which Mab had had Rhianne incarcerated but this one was a great deal bigger.

We flew around it a few times before gliding down over the moat and gates and landing gently on the lawn inside the walls. As we descended I noted just how huge this place was. The gates were enormous and, I suppose to save keep opening them every time just one person wanted to come in or go out, they had placed a smaller door within – but, then, how on earth were the big ones opened? It must surely take about a dozen men to move just one and then they'd be straining their muscles to do so.

I was still trying to puzzle this out as we were ushered, rather unceremoniously, into the keep – something else that was overly huge.

Mab was watching me closely as we entered. Funny though, I perceived somewhere in the back of my brain, as we walked through, that she didn't seem to take much notice of Kay. Looking at him - and I must admit, he was acting very peculiarly - I decided that he must have had a slight concussion when he had fallen from his horse or maybe his wound had festered and given him a bit of a fever which might give him trouble with his memory, although, he didn't seem unwell, just not quite with it.

Anyway, going back to what I was saying, Mab was staring at me with narrowed eyes and an uncontrollable twitch to her mouth as I entered the keep and, finally, I found out why!

My heart did a somersault in my rib cage as I stared, goggle-eyed at what was in front of me. Sound asleep beside the fire and snoring fit to burst was a monstrosity of a man. He was gigantic! My knees buckled and I almost fell down with fright. I could feel the blood drain from my face and thought for a moment or two that my bowels might let me down; I would have fainted if it hadn't been for Sir Kay - the stars had already joined hands and were starting to dance the conga before my eyes and the throbbing in my ears was beating to their rhythm. He grabbed me by the arm as I swayed against him and, keeping me upright, whispered to me to be brave.

Several seconds had gone by before I could pull myself together and then Mab, who had been watching my every move, started howling with laughter.

'Stop,' I thought, 'you'll wake him up?'

She slapped her thigh and rocked backwards and forwards so violently that I thought she would fall over. I secretly hoped she would. However, remembering her twitchings and spasms from the past, I reckoned she must know her limits and, before long, she managed to stop, wiping her streaming eyes and running nose with the hem of her dress, thus displaying an extremely grimy leg- yeuk! And yes, you've guessed it, after wiping away her tears she left slightly cleaner track marks down her otherwise grimy face and a glistening wet, snail-like trail from one nostril to her ear.

Well, her high-pitched laughter had the desired effect and after a few grunts, the giant jumped to his feet. He looked down at the three of us standing there and in a flash had raised his foot to crush us. Just in time, Mab called out and he stood, foot still raised for several seconds, obviously trying to wake himself up, remember who she was and deciding who we might be, before he finally removed his foot from above us and replaced it on the floor. We all let out our breath at the same time – fortunately Mab was facing away from me!

She threw back her head and, raising her voice, called up to the giant. 'Ysbaddaden, please let me introduce Sir Kay, brother to Arthur who are cousins to your enemy, Culhwch, and Percival, friend of Arthur.

The giant peered down at me with his deep-set eyes, the lids almost drooping over them.

'Percival, Sir Kay,' she raised her hand and pointed to the giant, 'Ysbaddaden – the Glaston Giant. The trap is now set – soon I get Arthur and you get Culhwch.'

They grinned at one another and then, without trying to control themselves, gave vent to their mirth. The ground shook as Ysbaddaden laughed – he not only made the loudest sound which started deep in his belly and exploded out through his extremely big mouth but, at the same time continually thumped his foot on the floor and banged the wall with his fist. I held my hands over my ears and closed my eyes but the noise still reverberated through my brain which I thought might explode or, if that didn't happen, the building must surely collapse on top of us and crush us, as was evidenced by dried dust and mortar being loosed and falling down around us. They eventually got themselves under control and Kay and I were able to relax – well as much as

83

anyone could in the presence of two such intimidating personages.

With the noise from those two mad people still echoing throughout the castle, I found the courage to stare upwards in awe - and consternation I must admit - at the giant. He stood well over nine and a half feet tall –nearer ten feet, I guessed, and legend had it that he came from a long line of giants. In fact, I understand that he, himself, had at some time boasted that his line went all the way back to Goliath of Gath. Well, who was going to argue with him? It was certainly not going to be me. History might repeat itself if I, like King David of old, had an opportunity to attack him; I was pretty good at slingshot but my sling and shot were still in my satchel back at the inn so I reckoned he was quite safe for the moment!

   Starting from his head and moving down – well, you couldn't move up, could you? – he had blue-black hair, masses of it, like an electrified haystack! It stuck out and moved in all directions as though the wind was howling through it, with huge, bushy eyebrows to match. He had a swarthy complexion and small, deep-set, rheumy eyes – one being dark blue and the other light green, both floating in a sea of bloodshot white. Well, they looked odd enough like that anyway but as they were also out of alignment – and one couldn't tell who he might be looking at at any one time – he looked frightening. It was said that many a time someone had made the mistake of thinking he was staring in the other direction when, after a huge roar and being knocked almost senseless by the giant's mutton of a fist, he realised that he was the one being watched all along. His nose, I reckon his most redeeming feature, was neat and just the right size for his face – being not too big and not too small. His teeth, however, flashed white from a very wide mouth but, because he had too many, were broken or twisted and, as was noticed by the lacerations on his lips – the bottom one being much to large and flopped over sideways, reaching halfway down his chin - seemed as though they caused him quite a bit of pain.

The rest of the giant's body was really just what one would consider a giant's body to look like – thick muscular arms, a huge chest and obviously a huge stomach, as everyone knows that giants eat a lot – although at that moment I didn't really want to think about just what (or even who!) they ate! He also had thick legs and huge feet, which made the earth shake as he walked along and, much to my surprise – as I expected a "fee fi fo fum" – spoke just like Sir Ector's men – only louder. So, all in all, what with his odd eyes, bushy hair and eyebrows, flashing teeth and great height, he was, as you will no doubt agree, someone not to be messed with – and not easily missed – that is, unless he was asleep! I did recall the fact that Merlin had said he was invisible when asleep, although he had been asleep but visible when we had come in. Hmm, I expect Merlin must have meant hibernating rather than sleeping but I wasn't going to think about that just now as he was now not asleep and was, obviously, larger than life.

'Have them taken away, Ysbaddaden, while you and I talk.'

The giant clapped his hands together – another explosion of sound for my poor, pounding head to cope with - and two very peculiar people entered. They were almost identical; in fact they were identical except that one was white with black tattoos all over what could be seen of his body and the other was his negative copy, black with patterned white tattoos - a negative mirror-image of the first! Paisley, yes, that was the pattern of the tattoos. They wore knee-length breeches and not much else. Apart from the fact that they looked dead scary in any event, the white one had a familiar shock of bright red hair! *'No,'* I thought, *'It couldn't be!'* as I remembered the two thugs from that farmstead of a couple of years ago. Pushing that thought aside, I told myself that I had to keep my wits and try not to let my imagination get the better of me or I might end up in a worse predicament than the one I seemed to be in at the moment. Fat chance! How was I to get out of this one, eh? The two tattooed men bowed low to the giant and to Mab and then ushered Kay and I from the room, Positive in the lead and Negative following behind us. I never did find out what their real names were but as one looked like a photographic negative of the other, well those were the names that jumped into my head, and those were the names that were going to stick – well, Pos and Neg at any rate.

As we were ushered across the grounds to a round tower in the far corner, I tried, once again, to call in my mind to my friend Cabal and even Merlin but there was still no response. I wondered if I might even be in a different time zone – but I had to dismiss that thought as Mab and Kay were with me and I knew that even though Mab had trouble time travelling, for Kay it would be impossible. I would just have to keep on trying – they must be able to hear me at some time or other.

When we arrived at the far corner of the castle grounds, Pos produced an enormous key, undid a gigantic lock and pushed back the huge wooden door. Holding the door open they gestured for me to enter and, as I did so, before Kay could also follow, the door was pulled back in place behind me.

'Hey, hold on,' I called, 'Kay, what's going on?' But by then, the door had clanged shut and I was, once again, in the dark. I called again to Kay but my voice just bounced back at me from my prison walls. Panic started to climb up my spine and threatened to overwhelm me as my mind suggested all the awful things that were waiting to pounce upon me. I squeezed my eyes shut and open a few times to see if I could see anything. At first, nothing – pitch black! Eventually, my eyes grew accustomed to the darkness and, looking up, I saw a glimmer of light immediately and far above my head and, gradually, as my eyes could take in more as they adapted to the dimness, a circular staircase leading toward it.

My ears suddenly twitched as I heard a scraping noise to my right. I spun around when I realised it was getting closer and peered at the hole behind the stairwell. The noise started to change; whatever it was I believe that it must have been startled awake by the outside door opening and clanging shut. There was first a snuffling, then a whine and finally a low and angry growl.

When I first heard it I froze but as it got closer my fear forced me into action. I searched about for an escape route but there wasn't anything except that huge staircase so there was nothing for it but to climb up. Have you ever wondered whether there is the slightest chance of you ever taking control of your life or whether it might have already been mapped out for you? Well, I firmly believe that there are choices to be made but, sometimes, the options are very slim indeed. And this, unfortunately, was one of them.

I managed to haul myself up the first step, noticing movement out of the corner of my eye as I did so and, looking over my shoulder to see what it was, almost jumped out of my skin - this place was becoming more bizarre and scary by the minute. Can you remember when I told you about the little green man that assisted Merlin in his cave? Well, this was just like him in every sense except his head. He was similar to what I believe is called a chimera – a fantastical creature made up of two or more different animals – in this case, the body of a dwarf topped by a two-faced head! The thing that was looking at me at that particular moment had the face of cat but as I turned to haul myself up the step its head swivelled round and its other face stared up at me: this one was the face of a very angry dog, lips curled, teeth bared and saliva dripping from the corners of its mouth. You just can't imagine how thankful I was that this "thing" could not get up the stairs. He, or it, ran at me snapping at my heels. He grabbed at me with one of his long-fingered hands and caught hold of the end of my leggings. He was exceptionally strong and we had quite a struggle. He would have dragged me into its mouth if fear hadn't given me wings. He had a grip on me that was not going to let go and I could feel the sweat starting to run down my back in my panic. Almost without thinking - I believe some sort of primitive survival instinct had taken over – I raised my other foot and brought my heavy shoe down on the hand that had hold of me. I still feel sick when I think of it now, as I am not a violent person, but when I crashed my foot down on his hand I felt as well as heard the crunching of many bones. He let out a terrible howl and a hiss as he pulled his hand away, but not before I'd noticed that I was a split second away from being attacked by those terrible teeth as he lunged at me with his huge mouth. Giving one last look over my shoulder before I moved out of its range, I saw it staring at me with angry red eyes and then, after rubbing its injured hand with the good one, swivelled its head round again and the cat face gently started licking its wounds. My deprived mouth was getting dryer by the minute.

With some difficulty, I climbed to the top of the staircase. It took forever as it had obviously been made for the giant. My poor abused legs now did not feel as though they belonged to me at all. When I arrived at the top of the tower I walked through the open door and collapsed in a heap against the inside wall until I could feel the blood circulating through me again. Puffing as though I'd run a marathon, I lay as still as I could until my breath evened out.

Finally, looking around, my eye was caught by a wooden tray upon which was laid out, almost like a feast I thought, a chunk of bread, some apples and – "nectar" - a jug of water. I lunged at it and soon my parched throat was soaking up the precious liquid. I lay back, wallowing in quiet and grateful thankfulness before attempting to eat any of the food.

'Who's there?'

I jumped out of my skin.

'Come on, I'm not scared of you! Show yourself!'

I'd stood up and was peering into the corner where, in the twilight, I thought I had seen only a bundle of rags. I hadn't thought that there was anyone in the tower but me and, as the room was only lit by archers' arrow slits in the walls, I had not been able to see too clearly. Oh dear, had I eaten whoever it was' food? I had to clear my throat a good many times before I was able to speak properly. 'Who are you?' I croaked.

For a few seconds there was silence and, then, 'Percy! Percy, that's you isn't it?'

Now the voice sounded slightly familiar because of its intonations but there was something wrong with it – it was course and flat, whereas, as I was soon to find out, the person whose voice it was supposed to be usually had a happy lilt to it. I was very cautious when I answered, as I didn't want to give anything away or put myself in any predicament. 'Er, yes, I am Percy,' I replied.

'Oh, thank God,' he said on a sob. 'Are you here to rescue me? Is Arthur with you? And the men?'

'I'm sorry,' I responded, 'but I am not quite sure who you are.'

Well, if things were weird before, they now took a decidedly bizarre turn for the worse.

'Eh? Percy, it is I, Kay!'

I know my mouth dropped open when he said this and I got a kind of peculiar buzzing in my ears – the sort of feeling you get when you are about to pass out or when you have that awful gas they use at the dentists to knock you out before you have a tooth out. How could this be? He couldn't possibly be inside and outside this tower at the same time! If his claim to be Kay was strange, you can imagine how I felt when he stood up and, with the light from the window shining full on his face, showed him to be none other than Arthur's and my archenemy Mordred!

If ever I wished to have a sword or naiad root or, better, Merlin's dragon's droppings with me, it was most certainly then.

TWELVE

Standing up to stretch, Jack followed Cabal over to the door to let him out; then, leaning in the doorway, watched the hound lope off past the barn and into the trees. Ben slid past him and went off to the outhouse while Danny, throwing a couple of logs onto the fire, looked over at his grandfather and asked if the witch had done something to him or, perhaps, the water had been drugged.

'No, Danny, I was perfectly *compos mentis* and she had certainly not drugged me while I was in the keep as we hadn't been given any food or drink. There might have been something in the water in the tower but I don't think so.'

Ben came back and Danny went to take his turn in the outhouse.

It was almost time for bed and, unusually, Jack felt that it might be one of those nights that sleep would elude him and, if and when it did come, would be unwelcome anyway. He shook his head and mentally berated himself for being fanciful. Nothing was going to happen, he told himself, and even if it did, he and Cabby were always ready, especially after their last episode with that evil duo. Nevertheless, when Cabal returned, he would make sure that all the fastenings were secure on door and window alike.

After a very restless night, Jack awoke to a perfectly normal, sunny morning but feeling the effects of a disturbed night. *'What an idiot I am,'* he said to himself.

'Hmm,' Cabal responded, giving his tail a quick wag.

'Less of that!' he retorted with a self-deprecatory grin as he turned to watch the boys descending the stairs.

'Hey, granddad,' Ben complained, 'I didn't sleep too well last night. Tossed and turned a lot and only really went off just as it was getting light and the birds started singing. Was it something I ate?'

'I doubt it; it was probably the atmosphere – it feels as thought we might be going to have another storm. So, perhaps we had better get on with our work before it hits.'

The rest of the morning and most of the afternoon was spent tidying up Jack's smallholding, clearing the ground and storing away the last of the hay in the large barn's loft and sorting and laying up the late vegetables and fruit before winter hit home. It was hard and backbreaking work. The boys now really understood it when their grandfather told them to learn their lessons well at school, as a farmer's life was not an easy one, although it was generally a healthy one.

By mid-afternoon, as they were stowing the farm equipment into the smaller barn, the first few spots of rain started to fall and it soon became apparent that it was going to be an all-nighter. No more farm work would get done today. Cabal had been out hunting but at the first rumble of thunder he tore out of the woods and into the cottage with his tail fixed firmly under his belly.

'Now whose the idiot?' Jack smirked.

Cabal did not deign to answer him. For one, he had decided long ago that he was above such sarcasm – well receiving it anyway - and, for another, he was too scared of the storm to stop, let alone make a response.

Jack smiled. He just loved that dog. They now had the rest of the afternoon and a whole evening before them to do their own thing and so it didn't take much cajoling for Jack to whisk them back to the days of myth and legend.

Arthur and his party had by now been travelling for most part of the day when Rhianne asked if they could stop and rest. Lady Elise's temperature had risen alarmingly and, so far, neither Ogwin nor any of his subjects had sent the promised dandelion medication and Rhianne was getting very worried indeed.

'I don't think she can take the shaking of the wagon any longer, Arthur. She groans as we go over each bump and, apart from that, doesn't seem to know who I am. She keeps calling me "mother" and asking me for water but when I give it to her she's sick. I am very worried. Please rest now.'

'But we are miles from Thornfalcon and could be attacked by anyone out here in the forest. It is much too dangerous to stop here for the night.'

'But mother will surely die if we move her any further today!'

'She will not die!'

'Do you want to take that responsibility, Arthur?' Rhianne was by now almost in tears.

'No,' he spoke softly and, after a few moments of considered thought, agreed. 'Let us stop here, then, and rest.' Turning to the men, he gave them instructions to make camp, build a fire, fill the water bottles and set sentry duties. Arthur was going to make sure that no man or beast would sneak up on them unawares. They hadn't passed anyone en route, but then bandits and the like would hardly show themselves, would they? They had, however, certainly heard the odd wolf's howl in the distance.

'But then, old friend,' he smiled, patting Cabal on the head, 'no-one would get past you, would they? Go, check out everywhere for me.'

And so, with Rhianne's silent request to *Try to see if you can find Percy or Merlin,'* Cabal loped off into the trees.

It was many hours later that a ravenously hungry hound trotted back into camp, tongue hanging sideways from a naturally grinning mouth. He stopped and sniffed at the air as tantalizing smells from the various cooking pots assaulted his nostrils. Having spent his time searching the surrounding area instead of hunting, he was now ready to eat whatever might be thrown his way.

Arthur called him over, laying a dish of water on the ground, and Brosc strolled over and dropped a huge beef bone onto the grass. As he lapped up the water, keeping a wary eye on the bone, he managed to convey to Rhianne the fact that he had something of extreme importance to impart to her but that they should wait until the camp had settled down for the night before they got together. As she was still ministering to her mother and was, obviously, extremely concerned about her fever, she was happy to wait a while. It would soon be Old Molly's turn to sit with Lady Elise when she had finished cooking their supper.

The stars shone down very brightly upon them and a half moon had started her weary climb into the sky before a few gentle and one or two more violent snores broke the air. Rhianne climbed down from the wagon and made her way over to the cooking fire, where a fidgety hound greeted her on her approach.

'Well, Cabby, what have you to tell me?'

'I met Merlin!'

'Eh, Merlin! But, well, where is he then? Surely he would have come back with you!'

'No, Rhianne! I didn't actually see him in the flesh! But he did speak to me.'

'Then, how? Where?'

'Hush, now, please listen; I need to get this right.'

Rhianne stroked his head and absentmindedly scratched him behind his ears as she listened to the story unfolding.

'Arthur had sent me to spy out the land and make sure that there were no brigands around. And by the way, there are none, so you may rest easy. I had made a great search of the whole area, running almost halfway to Thornfalcon which I could actually see in the distance - well, I think that's what it was as there were lights twinkling in quite a few buildings - when I came upon a spring of water. The spring started quite high up and ran down over a rock into the pool from which I,

being extremely thirsty, had stopped to drink, when the light from the setting sun as it shone upon the cascade made me look up. Now, ordinarily, I would not have thought twice about doing anything other than drink but I think it was because this spectacle had happened once before, with Percy before we set off on our pilgrimage, that my eyes were drawn upwards. Well, stone the crows, I thought - it's Merlin! And, there he was, looking down at me – slightly misshapen, I have to admit, as the water kept on distorting his features but there was no mistaking it was he.

'He spoke directly into my mind but did not take his eyes off me for a moment; well, not until he disappeared at any rate.'

'Well,' interrupted Rhianne, *'what did he say?'*

'I was getting to that! Please, Rhianne, with all due respect, do not interrupt; I will tell you everything but I need to keep it in order. I mustn't forget anything – Merlin said it was important!'

'Sorry, Cabby.'

'Now, where was I? Ah, yes! First of all he told me that when he gave that prophecy at Sir Ector's all those weeks ago, he was weakened to such a degree that he needed to go and recuperate in one of his caves. Now, I really should have asked him which one, because we may have been able to help him but I didn't think of it at the time and now I could kick myself. I hope he will be able to contact me, or one of us again, so that we can ask him. Oh, dear, what if he doesn't? Oh, he must!'

'Cabby, please don't worry about that now; go on with his message.'

He stopped, scratched and stretched before continuing. *'Sorry, Rhianne. He, er, um, oh I am so tired.'*

'Cabby!' Rhianne almost shouted in her mind, *'I know you must be and I don't think it's all physical. I reckon that mad old witch is involved here somewhere, isn't she?'*

Cabby shook himself, had another drink of water and nodded, as he pulled himself together to continue his story. *'You're right, you know! Mab is involved and that is what I expect Merlin was trying to tell me.*

'He had gone back to his - well whichever one it was – cave and had chanted the spell of sleeping – that's not just the ordinary spell of sleeping but it is the one that means mending of the mind and body. Now, he said he didn't know how long it was as, when he had performed this particular enchantment before, he had normally been up again and completely refreshed within a sennight – more usually about five nights. Imagine waking up a fortnight later and feeling that you actually needed to prise your eyes open with your fingers to try to wake up! Well, that is what he said he had been trying to do for the last month! He would stay awake for an hour or two and then be forced by exhaustion to lie down again. He said he had tried to track us by using the Glass and had managed to find Percy and I in the woods before we travelled but, because he had been unable to stay awake for long enough, could only get out a few words – and, I have to say, that he didn't actually finish what he was saying this time either!

'He told me that during the third week of his fatigue, he managed to get to the entrance of his cave but couldn't move the boulder away. It should have moved when he tapped it but he now believes that because he felt that he did not strike the stone very forcefully – well, he said that it felt like he was bouncing off a sponge rather than hitting solid stone – the rock must not have recognised his authority and thus stayed put. He said he has tried once more, almost falling backwards with the effort of using as much force as he could to strike the rock, but with the same effect as before.

'He also told me that when he tries to use one of his incantations to put this problem to rights, he gets halfway through and is then so tired, he cannot remember the rest.'

Cabal stopped and moved from his sitting position to lie down with his head upon his crossed forepaws. He lay there like that for some few moments, staring into the dying fire – almost allowing its hypnotic influence to send him to sleep - before sitting up again and continuing; Rhianne, during his rest, was itching to urge him to continue but remembered his request not to be interrupted.

'He started to ask me to find Percy or Salazar to go to him and free him. He said that Percy didn't have any dragon's droppings at the moment and so would be unable to get to him that way but that Salazar did.'

'Do you think that he is in his cave at Glastonbury? You mentioned the Glass?' asked Rhianne, interrupting.

'I don't know – he has a Glass in at least three other of his caves, possibly in all of them! Perhaps we will just have to try them all; that is if anyone knows where they are!'

'Again, I am sorry, Cabal, please go on.'

'There's not much more to tell! Apart from asking us to help him, he told me to keep watch and be on my guard. Things are afoot! However, the last thing he started to say was what he started to say when we came across him once before and didn't finish. The annoying thing is that he didn't finish it this time either.'

Rhianne waited. Cabby stared ahead. Time ticked by.

'Well, I'm sorry, Cabby, but what didn't he finish?'

'Oh, sorry,' Cabby yawned before bringing his mind back to the present, *'He said, "Sir Kay is not ..." and then his face slid off into the pool and disappeared.'*

'Sir Kay is not? Sir Kay is not what?'

'I wish I knew! That is what he said before, when he said it to Percy. We didn't find out what he meant that time either. I think that he probably fell asleep again when he got to that point and thus couldn't keep himself visible to us and just slid away again or, perhaps, that mad woman has enchanted him so he can't finish that particular sentence. I don't know!

'I've been mulling over those few words for weeks but can't come to any conclusion as to what they mean – well, I came to thousands of conclusions but none of them make any sense! It could mean absolutely anything and nothing at the same time. I reckon she obviously doesn't want us to know what Sir Kay is not!'

'What do you mean, when he said it to Percy?' Is Percy aware of all of this as well?'

'Er, no! Merlin must be getting a bit stronger as the last time he tried to communicate with us we only got those few words, "Sir Kay is not!" before he disappeared. It really is most annoying when one tries to finish that sentence. Sir Kay is not here! But we know that anyway. Sir Kay is not happy or Sir Kay is not polite when he is crossed or Sir Kay is not comfortable on his horse or Sir Kay is not very good at poetry or ...'

'Cabby – STOP! This is ridiculous and is not getting us anywhere!'

'You can say that again; it's given me quite a headache!'

Rhianne told Cabal to rest and they would continue their conversation on the morrow. She leaned down to straighten her dress before getting up to go and find Arthur and also see to her mother and it was then that she became aware of a tugging at her sleeve. Looking down she stared into the smiling face of Queen Gisele, the extremely pretty and diminutive wife of Ogwin, King of the Faerie.

'Your Majesty,' she said, rising and bobbing a curtsy. 'You've found us!'

'I didn't lose you,' she responded, all smiles. 'However, it has taken rather longer than we thought to collect the dandelions for the potion as it really was getting near the end of the season – and what with early frosts and ... but we have it now! How is your dear mother?'

'Oh, she is very ill. I am so relieved that you have come. Please let me take you quickly to her.'

'But of course you can. Pick me up and let me ride upon your arm.'

Rhianne lowered her arm and Queen Gisele perched herself upon it. They hurried to the wagon, where the Queen alighted onto Lady Elise's pillow. Drawing the tiniest phial of clear liquid from the pouch that hung at her waist, she pulled the stopper and slowly dripped the potion over her ladyship's lips. Lady Elise, still thrashing about in her delirium, managed to lick at it and, within minutes, lay still.

Poor Rhianne! She thought her mother had died. Jumping up into the wagon, she took hold of her hand and began patting and rubbing it between her own.

'Now, now, young lady,' said the Queen, 'don't take on so – there's nothing wrong. She will sleep for a day or so and then she will be in a good way again. The fever is, even now, abating. Come – touch her forehead and you will see.'

Rhianne leaned forward and touched her mother's cheek and brow. Yes, she was cooler and as she removed her hand, felt her mother's breath flutter across her arm.

'Oh, Your Majesty, I don't know how to thank you. If I can ever do anything for you, please, just ask.' Tears of relief were trembling at the end of her lashes.

Staying on with them until the morning of the third day, when Lady Elise had retained much of her usual good health, Queen Gisele took out a tiny whistle and, sending poor Cabal shooting up into the air with a sound not audible to human ears but with a high-pitched emission to canines, waited until a small cavalcade of Faerie servants arrived to escort her away. She took leave of the party, travelling north, as Arthur and his company continued on their journey east towards Hinton St. Mary.

They made good progress even though they were forced to proceed northeast once they had reached Thornfalcon, travelling over moorland areas in a continuous fog for many days, not daring to send out scouts in case they were separated and thus not strong enough to fight any brigands that may be in the area. Fortunately, they met no-one and heard nothing, not even the cry of a bird, in all the time they were on the move. No-one had any idea where they were and so it was that many days later they awoke to a watery sun that shone down upon the muddy plain of Glastonbury.

'How on earth did we get here? We are truly miles from our destination now,' groaned an increasingly despondent and agitated Arthur, 'and will be fortunate indeed if we make it for All Saints Day!'

THIRTEEN

I could feel my lip curl as I stared into that evil face, thus belying the fear that had turned me cold inside. I was still holding onto the jug and without even thinking about it hurled it straight at Mordred's head, at the same time looking around the tower for a more suitable weapon.

'Hey, hold, hold,' he yelled as, very deftly, he caught the jug without spilling a drop. Backing away from me, so as to reduce my fear of him, he spoke more softly, 'Listen to me! Please listen to me before you do another thing, I beg of you! I won't move! I promise! I'll just sit over here and won't get up unless you say it's alright - but please, just listen.'

I was, by now, standing with my back to the wall and wielding an unlit torch that I had snatched from the bracket above my head, holding it in front of me like a club and changing it from one hand to the other to hide the shaking within. I watched him lower himself to the floor but was so scared for my life that I was like a coiled spring, ready to pounce and take my chance against this demon.

We stared unblinkingly at one another, taking each other's measure for quite some time before he actually spoke.

'Percival ... Percy,' he softened his voice as he used the name more popularly used by my friends, but he wasn't going to fool me. 'Percy, I know that I don't look like me! I have seen my reflection in the water but I can assure you that I am Kay. How can I prove it to you?' He was obviously searching in his mind for the right words. 'Can you remember certain things that Sir Kay has said or done that nobody else would know about?'

'*What's this*,' I thought. '*Did he think me a traitor about to divulge the private things of my friends?*' My back stiffened at the thought and the man could see he had made an error of judgment.

101

He quickly changed tack and suggested he tell *me* some of those things.

I relaxed slightly but was still very much on my guard. 'Carry on,' I invited, forcing the words out past the lump in my throat.

For the next two or three minutes my mind reeled as Mordred told me many things that I knew about the family that only Sir Kay could possibly know. What was he trying to prove? Perhaps he had captured and tortured someone else who knew … oh I hoped he hadn't got hold of Rhianne! My heart almost stopped as my chest constricted.

He had told me that he was Sir Kay but it was evident by the monster in front of me that he could be no-one other than Mordred – even down to the missing part of his index finger that he kept waving in the air! Well, obviously he couldn't wave the missing part of the finger if it wasn't there, but was waving the hand that had lost that part of its finger.

Had that old hag somehow been able to see what we were all doing and thus tell Mordred? Had she used something similar to Merlin's Glass to spy on us? Had she been ghosting around the Hall? No! Merlin would have known! But, then, Merlin did disappear from time to time, *'like now,'* I thought and she could have done it then. My mind was reeling!

He could see how agitated I was getting and gradually stopped speaking.

I stared at him until my brain advised me that my mouth was hanging open again. Closing it and pulling myself together I merely asked him why I should believe that he was, in fact, Sir Kay when he now looked exactly like Mordred.

Taking a deep breath he stared up at the ceiling and, after letting it out he began his tale.

Now, if I hadn't believed him before, I wondered if I should start to now. The thing was, when he took in that deep breath – staring at the ceiling as he did at that moment – his

102

lips were compressed tightly together as he took the deep breath in through his nose, making his nostrils flare as he did so and then, when he let it out it was through his mouth but through clenched teeth. I had only ever seen Sir Kay do this! Could it really be him? I was extremely confused.

He continued: 'Father decided that I would be more of a liability than an asset in our battle as I had fallen from my horse and broken a bone in my foot. Not only could I hardly walk but also I couldn't get my swollen foot in the stirrup. Therefore I had started for home. He thought it best I return, as we were travelling hard and fast to battle and didn't want to delay but at the same time he didn't want me to suffer as I surely would do at the pace we were going.'

I had heard this part of the story already from the "Sir Kay" I had been transported with to the castle. Now, *whom* should I believe?

'I was exceptionally annoyed with myself for my accident but could see the sense in turning back. I would be no help to them and would just hold them up. So I took one squire with me and started for home the next morning, watching the army moving north until I could see it no more. We turned south and travelled at a leisurely pace due to the throbbing in my leg and so it was that night caught up with us before we could reach an inn. We made camp for the night in a cave by the sea and just ate cold rations. I wasn't particularly hungry, for various reasons, and Meadows was unable to start a fire due to the fact that we had no dry wood.

'That night I had terrible nightmares – perhaps I was delirious due to the wound in my foot. My whole leg was throbbing and my foot had swollen terribly. I'd got myself tied up in my sleeping bag, which had somehow added to my imaginings – or were they imaginings!

'I dreamed – at least I think it was a dream – more a nightmare - that I awoke from that place and was being crushed in a fierce rib-breaking hold. I had slept propped up against a boulder just inside the cave's entrance. There was just enough light for me to see my adversary and what I saw turned my blood to ice! I was being crushed to death by a giant octopus – well it was huge, compared to me! It must have been over fifteen feet high with two sharp and pointed pincers over its mouth each the length of a sword and thickness of a man's thigh. It made the most awful clicking sounds as though arguing with itself as it continued to pull slime from its body, adding it to the already thick casing covering me. I could feel the air thinning within this tomb and, panic rising, began trying to tear my way out only to find that the slime stuck my fingers together, making them completely ineffective in helping me escape. Hopelessness started to press upon me as the slime glued my clothing together and started to harden; my breathing became more and more laboured, there being no room for my chest to expand and contract and I eventually passed out.'

He stopped for a while either gathering his thoughts or trying to shut out the terror he was recalling – '*If it really happened,*' I told myself, though he did look uncomfortable with sweat beading on his forehead as he recounted his tale.

'When I came to, Meadows had disappeared – and so had the octopus of my dream and the slime, thank goodness - but I was alone in a sea-mist soaked, early dawn light. Drops of moisture plopped from the roof of the cave and I started shivering uncontrollably. My throat was hot and dry and it took me ages to wet it enough to speak. Dragging myself over to the side of the cave I lapped up some water that had rundown the walls and pooled in the cave until I felt I could talk. It took few attempts before I could call loudly enough for anyone to hear me but I needn't have bothered! Meadows, wherever he was, did not respond. He had gone!

'I struggled out of the cave and looked around me, trying at the same time to gather my thoughts but I could see no sign of anyone or anything that could help me in my predicament.

The horses were gone, probably with Meadows – but why? I'd always believed he was a loyal servant to my father. Where had he gone? I shuddered as a thought entered my mind – surely he and the horses hadn't been dragged into the sea and eaten by that monster! Was it a dream or could it possibly be real. I ran my hands down my clothes but if there had been any stickiness from that monster's mouth, it had now gone. My teeth were clattering together and echoing through my brain, keeping time to the shivering of my hands. I felt very miserable indeed. I tried to pull myself up, using a tree as support but as soon as I put my very sore foot to the ground the pain shot right through the whole of my body. I almost passed out again after I'd screamed. I don't know what stopped me from doing so – probably the thought of that octopus, I reckon; I didn't want him - or more likely "her" - intruding into my thoughts again.'

The man was silent for quite some time. I just stood, back against the wall, watching him. I didn't feel like saying anything, let alone urge him to continue. I was still weighing up whether I should even start to believe him or not. *'Don't be stupid, Percy – it's Mordred,'* I told myself. *'Are you trying to believe something other than what is obviously before your eyes?'* After a long time of staring into space he went through the same exercise of breathing in deeply and breathing out again through his teeth; *'Could it really be Sir Kay?'* I thought, changing my mind yet again.

'Before long, the pain in my foot seemed to deaden and I managed to pull myself up the beach to higher ground. I twisted around but in whichever direction I looked there wasn't anyone in sight. The damp and dreary plain rolled on for miles with black clouds blanketing them, shaking themselves now and then, thus enabling me to see the fact that the whole area was deserted. "I am going to die!" I said – out loud.'

'"Oh, no! You are not going to die!"

'I spun around as I heard the voice, almost falling over again as I put my damaged foot to the ground. First of all I didn't believe that I had heard a voice at all; well, I mean, I wondered if I was hallucinating again as I had just looked all around and there had been nobody there and then, when I saw what was there in front of me, I believed that I was. I didn't see or hear them approach; they seemed to have come from thin air.

'Seated in front of me and covered in what I now believe to be a cow's hide was the woman who brought me here. She didn't give her name but she seemed all compassion. She had a man with her – in fact you are now looking at that same representation – and between them they helped me onto a horse and gave me a draught to ease my pain.

'I have tried to make sense of what happened after that but all I can remember is drifting off into a dreamless – thank goodness – sleep, the slow rocking of the horse helping me to do that, I believe, and then waking up in this tower.

'I keep going over it all again and again; when they found me the man did not speak at all, although the woman clucked like an old grandmother, stroked my brow and was all kindness. Mind you, when she got a bit close to me she almost knocked me out with her breath!'

My eyebrows shot up at that! I knew who had brought me here to this tower, but it appeared that Kay – if he was Kay – did not! Hmm.

He continued, 'I don't know what has happened to me! I woke up in this tower with weird clothes on – these that you see on me – and with my foot almost completely healed and with part of a finger missing. It wasn't until yesterday that I glimpsed my reflection from the water in the bowl and saw, with shock and horror, the face of the man who had rescued me staring back at me! I stirred the water round with my hand but when it stilled it was, as now, that awful face staring back at me and not mine. What on earth is going on, Percy?'

I was now in quite a quandary. Should I believe this man or not? Oh how I wish Cabal or Merlin was here! They would surely know! And where were they? I tried mind speaking to them again but they were either cut off from my mind, as Merlin had been now for many a day, or they were still just too far away.

Just then a crow landed on the thin window-ledge and peered in, looking for all the world like a judge about to pronounce a sentence.

I jumped up and rushed over towards it, at the same time asking, in a very excited tone – completely forgetting for the moment that Sir Kay might not believe in such a thing - 'Merlin! Is that you?'

It cawed loudly, jumped up from its place and flew away, still cawing as it went.

'I don't suppose it is,' responded Sir Kay - or Mordred - quite despondently. 'It has been here every day since I've been here and I would imagine that if it was Merlin he would have done something about my plight before now. It's more than likely a spy from that woman's camp!'

I kept my thoughts to myself.

Neither of us spoke for the next half-hour or so and during that time I tried to piece together all the bits of this puzzle. I picked my brain for everything that had happened over the last couple of days, stacked all the information in a pile at the front of my head and began slowly and methodically sifting through it, discarding many bits and pieces along the way as I shuffled them about. There were so many loose ends that I found myself rummaging in the recesses of my mind to gather those elusive bits of information that keep scuttling away just when they had seemed so tantalisingly close.

And then I believed I had it! It was the way Sir Kay had been acting. Well, by Sir Kay, I mean the one that I had met on top of the mountain - the one that had travelled to the tower with Mab and me on the back of the dragon. He had definitely not acted like Sir Kay; in fact I had thought he must have fallen on his head, as he seemed quite unexciting and dull and his voice was peculiar. Also, and I was glad that Sir Kay, if it was Sir Kay slumped in front of me now, couldn't mind speak as I had always thought him a little too arrogant for his own good!

However, the man in front of me now was not at all puffed-up with his own esteem, in fact quite the opposite, whereas the one I had met on the back of the dragon was neither interesting or forthcoming; in fact I thought him quite dim-witted and one could never say that of the real Sir Kay. And besides all that, he didn't limp!

I decided that I had no other course but to grill the man who now sat in front of me until I was completely satisfied that he was who he said he was – Sir Kay.

When I started to interrogate him, he was bright enough to see where I was coming from and agreed that if it was the only way to make me believe he was who he said he was then he was ready to answer my questions.

So I started thinking of all the things that only he would know. I thought that perhaps Mordred might know some of them but not all – and Sir Kay was an intelligent man who had always had a good memory.

'What is Cabal's brother called?
'Griff.'
'Where does Lady Elise come from?'
'Wales.'
'Whereabouts in Wales?'
'Carmarthen.'
'What is her older brother's son called?
'Culhwch.'
'Where is your father?'
'Headed north to battle.'
'What is the blacksmith called?'

And so it went on, question after question until we were both quite exhausted. No-one, I believed, could have known all the answers to my questions other than the real Sir Kay and, therefore, this Mordred-figure in front of me must somehow be him! But how? Neither of us knew the answer to that one except, perhaps, a nagging thought that it could have something to do with that old hag, Mab.

Kay had never met Mab before and did not know that much about her, only what we had told him after rescuing Rhianne from her clutches. He had said that the woman's breath had been rank and that during the journey to this castle she was afraid to get herself wet, keeping herself fully covered in the leather cloak.

'Hmm, I knew the reason for that!

'She has this peculiar belief that if she washes, she will lose power,' I had explained to Kay while we searched the tower trying to find a possible way out.

I had had to take the chance that he was really Sir Kay and so, once making that decision, we agreed that the only thing we could possibly try to do was escape.

We'd had a visit from the pair of Paisley people: one had held and guarded the door while the other brought in bread, cheese and water and in the twinkling of an eye they were gone. I did wonder how they'd got past the chimera!

We'd eaten in silence, me drinking as much water as I could as my throat was still so dry, before we started our search of the walls and floor, deciding that the windows were much too narrow and high for us to be able to escape that way. There was nothing! We would have to try and plan our escape for the next time that Neg and Pos came in, believing that they must have somehow disabled the chimera each time they came into the tower.

One problem had started to niggle at my brain and the more I thought of it the more it troubled me – if Sir Kay has Mordred's appearance, it had to be that Mordred had Sir

Kay's. It must certainly be that the Sir Kay that had travelled with me on Hellion's back was definitely Mordred. What was Mab going to use him for? Was he, once more, going to get Rhianne and bring her back here? As this thought hit, I felt sick - my stomach doing cartwheels. Perhaps he was going to bring all of the party back here. I felt worse as my mind started to tell me what might be going to happen. I recalled that the witch wanted to dispose of Arthur, that Mordred had a score to settle with Rhianne and Ysbaddaden had said he was going to grind Culhwch in the flour mill. That must be it. We had to escape. It was imperative the others were warned.

'*Oh, Merlin,*' my mind screamed, '*Where are you?*'

FOURTEEN

'Granddad?' Ben queried. 'Why didn't Arthur stay and look for you? I would've been searching high and low, if it were my friend who'd disappeared. Especially as he would know there were robbers and probably wolves in the woods.'

'Well, I think he would have known that I wouldn't just go off without a reason but you must remember that I had gone off once before, for over a year, and had still come back. I expect he thought that that might've happened again. He knew that Merlin had always looked after me and I believe that's what he must have thought this time. Perhaps he thought that Merlin and I had met up again and just gone off. Anyway, he did have his pilgrimage to complete and his mother to care for and enough time had been wasted already, so I think he had little choice. Nevertheless he sent two of his men back to look for me.'

'So what happened next, granddad?' asked Danny.

Arthur and Rhianne stood and looked at the plain in front of them, despondency taking control as could be seen by their crushed expressions and the slump of their shoulders. It had obviously been raining for many days; the ground was slippery and thick with mud. Brosc and Tailor, volunteering to see what the going was like, had returned after only a few minutes, the mud threatening the ponies with at best, being stranded or at worse, with broken bones when trying to struggle out. It wasn't worth it. In any event, if the ponies couldn't get through, they would have no hope with the carts.

We'll have to go round, I'm afraid,' moaned Arthur, 'or go home. Oh, why did I bother! I thought it was such a good idea. Brother Geraint had told me about the mosaic of Christ and I really believed it was something God wanted me to do as I felt such a lift in my spirit. I did so want to make my pilgrimage to see it and give thanks to Him for looking after us so well in the past. All in all it would show my father that I could be trusted to lead an expedition – even if it wasn't to war – and all I've done is prove to him just how incompetent I am. He'll never trust me to go to battle with him now.' He started his pacing.

Rhianne knew it was not a good idea to interrupt him when he did this but thought that this might be an exception. He was obviously distraught and needed some comfort.

'Arthur,' she spoke softly.

He glowered over at her and frowned.

She took a deep breath, 'I must be allowed to speak.'

He stopped his striding and, looking over his shoulder raised an enquiring eyebrow and, pursing his lips, just stared at her without speaking.

Feeling slightly uncomfortable but being unable to stop herself, she searched for the right words.

'Arthur.' She stopped again to think how she should continue. 'I know things look bleak at the moment.'

He snorted.

'Please let me continue,' she urged.

He stopped and faced her; then, placing his hands on his hips and his head slightly to one side, waited.

Poor Rhianne – she felt so wretched but, taking the bull by the horns, launched into everything that had been building up inside her.

'First of all I believe that all the things that have been happening to us are not just coincidences or bad luck. I think that there is some sort of wickedness connected to our journey that has been attacking us from the beginning. I don't believe that Percy has just gone off on his own – I think he's been abducted. You must remember that some of us were either sick or in a bad humour while mother was ill in that inn. Percy stomped off in a bad mood and hasn't been seen since.

I sent Cabby off to find him but he returned on his own.' She obviously did not tell Arthur about their conversation or he'd think she, too, was ill and hallucinating! Continuing, 'Mother has been very unwell but, thank God, she is now on the mend. Cabby, too, you will remember, slept a lot at that time and seemed very lethargic. Even one of the men shouted at him. And,' she hesitated, 'well ...'

Arthur's expression had change slightly as Rhianne had been talking and he urged her to continue.

'Well.'

'Well what woman?' he demanded.

'Well, you have been in an absolutely foul temper, especially with me, and I won't stand for it any more!' she choked. 'You're usually so even-tempered and kind.'

They stood looking at each other for a few moments before Arthur's angry look melted and he hurried over to his sister to hug her. 'I'm so sorry, my dear,' he whispered into her hair. 'I've been awful, I know, but there didn't seem to be anything I could do about it. Quite perverse! Please forgive me. But,' he stood back and started pacing again, 'now I am aware of it, I can see you are quite right and I believe there must be something we can do about it. You said you thought something evil was the cause. What do you think it is? Or, more precisely, who do you think is the instigator of all the bad things that have been happening to us?'

'That mad witch!'

'No – it can't be. Merlin saw to it that she couldn't do anything to us any more. She was encased in that glass rock.'

'No, Arthur. She *was* entombed in that crystal rock but I believe that she has somehow got out. Cabby ...'

'Yes, go on ... Cabby what?'

Rhianne realised that she had almost told Arthur about the discussion she and the hound had had about seeing Merlin's face in the spring. She would have to keep control of voicing her thoughts; he would think she was really crazy or being

113

fanciful if she mentioned anything about that. She would have to be more careful.

'Oh, nothing,' she responded, blushing, 'I've already told you about him.'

Arthur, thank goodness, seemed not to notice.

'So, what are we going to do if that witch has managed to escape?' this a question more to himself than one desiring a response from Rhianne.

'I don't think we should go back to Kingston St. Mary as that was the evil place where everything seemed to be wrong or go wrong. However, that seems to be the only place that comes to mind – it's where Percy went missing and we left Shake Spear and Wite there. We'll need to have them with us as otherwise we are a very small party and I think we'll need all the men we can get. It seems that we are gradually being separated from one another and that is quite dangerous. Perhaps you could ask Brother Geraint to pray for us all as well?'

Arthur was still pacing up and down, clasping his hands behind his back or rubbing them together in front of him. However, he now seemed more himself than he had of late.

The rain started to fall again - a few big drops announcing the forthcoming downpour. They hurried back to the wagons and climbed aboard to await fairer weather. It rained for another full days. They awoke on the third day to a still, grey morning. The rain had stopped but dampness saturated the grey and dismal landscape as far as the eye could see. Thank goodness that most of their stores inside the two wagons were dry. They ate biscuits, which was the only ready food they had that didn't need cooking, while the men tried, with as much dry wood as they could find, to light a fire.

Shake Spear and Wite now walked into the camp some three or four days after they had been left to try and find me. Both of them were soaked to the skin, having shared the same inclement weather that had troubled the others, and Wite had the beginnings of a nasty chill. Rhianne took both of them under her wing, making sure that the other men shared their dry clothing with them, and asked Molly to provide them with plenty of hot soup, once a fire could be successfully lit.

Arthur asked Shake Spear to report to him once he had eaten but requested that this not take too long as he was impatient to hear their news.

'Sir,' Shake Spear returned some half-hour later, 'I bear no good news, I am afraid. We searched the woods, we retraced our steps but of Percival there was no sign. We found some flattened grass in a clearing where someone had obviously spent some time walking about and then footprints in the soil leading away from the clearing but, peculiarly, they just stopped, as though the person had leaped into the air and vanished. Wite got the creeps and said we should leave that place as it must be cursed but, well, you know me, I don't believe in all that stuff. However, after looking around some more we came to the conclusion that we weren't going to find him there. After leaving the wood we went back to the inn to see if he had returned but he hadn't. We stayed on there for a couple of days, looking round the countryside and waiting to see if he returned but when he didn't thought it best to catch up with all of you. I kept thinking of him, he being so young, that is, but, well, who can control his fate? At that we packed up and left. So – here we are!'

Arthur continued staring at Shake Spear, making him feel quite uncomfortable, but he wasn't to know that Arthur was just thinking hard and was not actually seeing him at all. He squared his shoulders and started his pacing. Shake Spear merely waited to see what would happen next. He felt bad that they hadn't managed to find me but one could only try.

'Come, friend,' Arthur held out his hand to Shake Spear. 'You have done your best. Percy must look after himself, I'm afraid. He has most probably gone off again with Merlin as he has done in the past. We, for our part, will continue with

115

our pilgrimage or we will not make it in time for All Saints Day. Now that mother is well, we will go on. Rest today. Come rain or shine, we will leave at daybreak tomorrow.'

Rhianne, during the whole of their conversation, had been sitting inside the cart with her mother. Lady Elise had been talking about the family she had left in Wales when she had married Sir Ector. Rhianne had heard the stories many times before but she knew how important it was to her mother to reminisce about her kin; it stopped her from becoming too homesick and so she was happy to listen. As she knew the stories so well, it was easy to tune in to another conversation at the same time and so it was she heard all of Shake Spear's news. It clutched at her heartstrings to know that I might be lost, injured or, more than likely, the way things were going, at the mercy of that witch, Mad Mab. She decided that as soon as she could take her leave of her mother she would talk to Cabal. Maybe they'd be able to mind speak to me.

Not five minutes later, Sir Niel rode into their camp accompanied by Arthur's cousin Culhwch. It was the second set of arrivals and everyone was overjoyed by it. With all that was happening, the more people that were in their party, the safer they all began to feel.

Most of them had made their way to the fire which was now blazing merrily, over which was suspended a cauldron that bubbled with a deliciously smelling beef stew. Thus it was that just before Old Molly was ready to dish up their mid-day meal, Rhianne excused herself, saying she needed to stretch her legs.

'Cabby,' she called the hound. *'Come with me. I need to talk to you.'*

They walked off together, taking care not to go too far and keeping within eyesight of the camp but at the same time far enough away from prying eyes and listening ears so as to keep their secret, not that anyone in the camp could listen in to their mind speaking – but who knew who else could?

'I need you to find Percy!' she told him. *'Something bad is happening. It's not just knowing he's gone missing but things here just don't feel right either.'*

'Well, I'm glad it's not just me! I've been very uneasy since we left home. I tried to find Percy when he went missing but he seemed to have just vanished. So, what do you want me to do?'

'Go back to where he disappeared and find him. There must be a clue as to where he's gone. I think the others have taken it much too lightly. They either don't remember or don't know just how evil that witch is. I have this awful feeling that she's at the bottom of it all.'

'Me, too.'

'OK, leave right now. You know where we left him. I'd like to say don't come back without him but that wouldn't be fair. You know, though, don't you, just how much I think of him? He's very special, Cabal, so please, please, please try your hardest to find him. I know you want to stay and protect Arthur, but now that Sir Niel is here and the other men are back, we should be quite safe.

Cabby needed no more urging. He loped off into the forest on this, his most urgent quest.

FIFTEEN

'Sir Niel! Who's he?' Both Jack's grandsons interrupted one another as he got to this point in the story. 'You've never mentioned him before! Is he a goody or a baddy? It's not Merlin in one of his disguises, is it? And how did Culhwch get there?'

'Hey, shush boys.' Jack was laughing at the consternation in their faces as their questions rushed at him. 'No!' He held up his hand as they opened their mouths with more interrogation. 'I shall most probably be able to tell you who Sir Niel is one day – when I find out who he is myself. All you need to know at the moment is that he apparently visited Sir Ector the previous year in the company of some of Arthur's friends, most of whom had travelled with their fathers on a visit. He and Arthur had got on very well, being of a similar age – well Sir Niel was about eighteen or so, I believe, and they had spent a good summer together. However, I want to get back to Percy in the tower.'

Night fell and it had started to get quite chilly. The rags that had been left on the floor were smelly and so thin that they did not so much keep out the cold as keep in the smell! Apart from that, we had seen no-one since the early morning and were by now becoming quite hungry. The water had run out hours ago as, still being so dry, I had drunk almost all of it myself.

'Are we likely to get any food or drink tonight?' I asked.

'Possibly. They sometimes forget. Does it really matter?' Mordred - or Sir Kay - was becoming downcast. 'I thought that between us we could somehow try and get out of this place. I've been here for quite a few days now and have searched it high and low, to no avail. You've tested the walls and floors as well and I hoped that you might find something I'd missed. But no!' His face fell.

'Perhaps we could rush them when they come in? There are two of us!'

'We could try, Percy, but I don't think we have a hope in succeeding.'

'Look at you, Kay? If you are Kay and are now inside Mordred's body, you are strong! Look at all your muscles! We must surely be a match for Pos and Neg!'

'Pos and Neg?'

'Oh, sorry, yes – it's just the names I've given those two painted men. But, what do you think? Shall we have a go?'

As though to put the words into action immediately, we both swivelled round as we heard movement on the other side of the door. Almost crouching down in a stance a wrestler would be proud of we made ready to charge at the men as they came in.

What went wrong?

Looking back, as we rubbed our bruised bodies, we tried to discover at what point it all started to go awry. We both agreed that that point was right at the start. First, we should have spent more time on our tactics but, on reflection, we didn't have that much time to think of that; secondly, we needed to know a bit more about our adversaries; thirdly, we should have realised that we were so much smaller than them; fourthly, we shouldn't have bothered in the first place!

Sir Kay and I had been trained in the art of armed combat with the occasional – very occasional – training in unarmed combat. Obviously we were not very good at the latter and as we didn't have any weapons wouldn't be able to see if we were any better at the former.

Pos and Neg, on the other hand, were extremely proficient in unarmed combat, as could be seen by the resultant bruising making itself shown on Kay's and my skin. However, it wasn't just that, it was as though they had been programmed to do the job they were doing, dealing with any interruptions as they occurred as if that were just bothersome things that might happen and must be put out of the way as quickly as possible, and then just continuing with what they had been programmed to do. And that is just what happened.

Looking back at that episode, we didn't have long to wait as the door swung open and the Paisley men came in. Pos carried a large flaming torch in one hand and a smaller one in the other. Kay and I lunged at him, obviously hoping not to get burned in the process and, as we did so, he threw both torches over the room into the fireplace. The dry wood in the hearth heaved a sigh of relief at this breath of life and blinking open sleepy eyes she gradually shone her warmth and light into the room. It was by this light that our tragedy was played out to the fire's delight; she clapped and cackled with glee at the farce being performed in front of her, elongated shadows mimicking our every humiliating move.

As soon as Pos had divested himself of the two torches, he leaped at both of us, grabbing us with his large hands and, with a grip of steel, lifted us up by our belts and tossed us at the far wall. We hit the wall with a crunch and slid down to land with a thump on the stone flags. The pain as our backsides hit the floor was soon replacing the soreness from our shoulders hitting the wall. All in all it was an excruciatingly painful and completely mortifying experience - and the bruising took ages to fade.

In this hapless position we watched the men continue with their tasks as though no interruption had taken place. Pos retrieved the larger torch and placed it in a sconce on the wall. The smaller one had done its job of lighting the fire and so he had no need to continue with that particular chore. Neg held a tray upon which lay a large chunk of bread, some cheese and a pitcher of water. He placed it on the floor just inside the door and then they both left, closing the door gently behind them.

There was no need to lock the door; our gaoler at the foot of the stairwell was sufficient to keep us from trying to escape that way as we had found to our cost on more than one occasion. Intermittent howls or hisses told us that he was still on guard. I couldn't understand why he didn't go for Pos and Neg. The witch had probably put a spell on the chimera, or had made them invisible to it. Who knows?

The most awful thing about being locked up in that tower was that we just didn't know what was going on anywhere else, let alone what next might be going to happen to us. The Paisley men didn't – or couldn't – speak. We couldn't see out of the window and, apart from the large black bird, which came every day, we had no other visitors; of course by then we were getting into a muddle as to what day it was. Kay had been there longer than me and it wasn't long before we began squabbling over petty things such as time and day. Boredom does silly things to the brain and it was certainly doing it to us.

However, we were fed and kept warm-ish and so, apart from our bruises, suffered no other physical hardship. The pain of the bruising eased after a day or so and, realising how petty we were becoming, we once again began thinking of ways to try and escape. It came to us on a very windy day.

Pos and Neg had just been to our tower with the morning rations and I must admit that Pos looked very peculiar – the wind had caused his shock of red hair to point quite sharply over to one side. If I weren't so fed up I would have laughed out loud. They completed their task and left.

'He looked strange,' Kay commented.

'I think it must be windy outside,' I responded. 'In fact it's getting quite blustery in here.'

We took our rations and moved over to the fire. That old witch did not allow us to have heat during the day and so the fire, coughing bronchially as it died, provided us with only a little warmth. While we were breakfasting we noticed that

121

the fading embers in the fireplace kept glowing intermittently. This happened a few times before Kay remarked upon it. I, too, had noticed it but it hadn't registered until Kay spoke.

'There's a draft – and it isn't coming from the window.'

We both jumped up and, leaning gingerly across the dying fire, tried the stone slabs behind and around the sides of it.

'It has to be coming from the fireplace! It's not coming down the chimney,' he said as he licked his finger and tried to feel some draft descending from it. The fireplace was one of those absolutely huge ones where one could almost sit inside it beside the fire and yet not get burned.

We climbed inside and spent ages tapping this, scraping that. Nothing! Everything appeared to be solid. I could have cried. Hope kept creeping in and then skipping out. I could almost hear, "na na na na na" as it did so.

Kay sat down again, head in hands.

I was now so frustrated and angry I felt like hitting out at something - even him. Marching to the other side of the tower I picked up the pitcher, crashing it to the floor. Returning, I vented my frustration on the fireplace and kicked the iron grating with such force that sparks flew everywhere.

Scrape, grind, whooshhh.

The whole of one side of the fireplace swivelled backwards to reveal a long dark tunnel to the side of it.

We couldn't believe it! Kay jumped up and stared. My mouth just hung open. (I'll have to try and overcome this obviously moronic stance!) Then, as if by mutual consent, we both moved forward into that cavernous darkness. We had no torches as Pos only brought one with him every evening and that one was spent. So, we'd have to feel our way.

'Where do you think it leads, Percy?'

'No idea! We'd best take it very slowly but time is on our side as they won't be back again with any food until tonight, so we have at least ten hours. Let's take the last of our breakfast. Stuff it in your pockets, Kay. We don't know when we'll need it.'

Everything done, we made our way over the now dead but still warm fire into we knew not what.

'Granddad,' Daniel interrupted, 'were you now sure that Sir Kay was Sir Kay or did you think he was really Mordred pretending to be Sir Kay?'

'Well, Danny,' Jack responded, 'I was about ninety nine percent sure he was Sir Kay but I was still holding back until I could be absolutely certain. I'd been caught out so much by that old witch in the past that I wasn't going to take any more chances.

'OK, so what happened next?'

SIXTEEN

The tunnel seemed to go on forever. We had to feel our way with our toes, as sometimes there would be just a gradual slope downwards, sometimes a sharp bend or, once or twice, a set of steep stairs. I'm afraid I swore a couple of times when I scuffed my hand or shin, stubbed my toe or slipped over. It was extremely dry in those passages, not like the witch's castle, but with too many hanging cobwebs for my liking – why do they always seem to go for your face?

There were small chinks in the walls in various places as could be seen by a soft glow illuminating our passageway - which lit up some more extremely suspicious-looking cobwebs - but most of them were too high for us to be able to look through. One, which was low enough allowed me to peer into a room where I noticed a fire burning in the grate but I could see no sign of activity apart from that. But, just in case, we crept along as quietly as we could and I tried not to stub any more toes. We eventually came to a dead end when we came to the bottom of a stairway into what appeared to be a small room. By now I thought I would never see again. Everything was pitch black and all we could do was feel our way. The walls were made of stone and had been stuck together with mortar or the like. We must have spent an hour trying to find some opening and were about to give up when Kay touched something and there was a faint but audible click. Holding our breath, as we knew that the sound of the opening door must surely bring the whole castle running, we stood for a good minute before feeling it safe to continue.

Pushing the door open as quietly as we could we crept through; it closed behind us with the merest whisper. Finding ourselves behind a very dusty and threadbare wall hanging, which was threatening to suffocate us, we peered around it and were rewarded by being bathed in wonderful sunshine.

We slowly let out our breath and looked around. It wasn't as good as we had initially thought as we realised we'd arrived in the great hall of the giant's castle. The back of his chair was immediately in front of us and as we could see his legs crossed on the floor on the other side of that chair, we knew he was in residence. What to do? By sign language we sorted out how we should get to the other side of the room, past the giant, who we hoped was not awake, and out of the door, which we hoped was not locked. Hope springs eternal! My main hope, though, was that Mab was not around, or the two Paisley men. If we could only get through that door, I felt sure that all our troubles would be behind us. Fat chance!

We decided the best thing to do was to move around the walls. It might be more difficult to detect us that way, than if we went straight across the floor where there was no place to hide. I had noticed that that was what mice did and it was always harder to catch them by a wall, than out in the open.

It went very well! There were one or two things we could hide behind, should he be awake – curtains, a shield, a chair or two – and so we set off around the room. It took some time as we had to keep on stopping to listen, peek at the sleeping giant and ease our pounding hearts but we eventually made it to the door. A huge door that required a tall man to reach the handle but after climbing up onto Kay's back, once balanced, I could reach it. It was well oiled and moved at my bidding, the door opening silently and quite easily. I climbed down and the two of us, gripping the edge of the door managed to pull it open and step through.

'Greetings, little men,' she crooned as we rushed into her outstretched arms.

There she stood, all grime and grin, wafting her stench about like a suffocating bog. Behind her stood the Paisley men – absolutely no expression on their faces whatsoever.

SEVENTEEN

'It appears that my tower has been unable to hold you,' she mused. 'And I thought I had been so kind to you. I'm afraid it will now have to be the dungeon. But don't fret, it will certainly not be for too long.' Off she went, then, into one of her bursts of laughter, slapping her thigh and almost falling over.

I was trying so hard to stop my knees from knocking together and I'm sure my face was as white as a sheet. However, I did find the courage to ask one question; I really needed to know the answer and be absolutely sure.

'If you put me in the dungeon could I ask one favour?'

She tried hard to stop her laughter and eventually had breath enough to speak. 'Favour? Favour?' She thought this hysterical and went off into a further fit of hysterics. We stood, shaking, while she got herself under control, Pos and Neg standing immobile and expressionless behind her. Eventually the hysterics ceased – almost!

'I don't *do* favours,' she spluttered, wiping the tears from her eyes with the hem of her skirt. 'However, I'm interested to know what it is that you want.'

I swallowed a few times to get some spit into my mouth; it had gone bone dry with my fear. 'I should like ...'. I could hardly get the words out my mouth was so parched.

Of course, being the nasty piece of work that she was, she picked up on this and started to mimic me. I must admit that she was very good at mimicry.

Swallowing again, I made a determined effort and blurted out my request in one quick burst. 'If I am to be put into a dungeon, would you put Mordred,' I pointed at Sir Kay, 'somewhere else? I don't know why you have locked him up as I thought he was your friend but I don't want him near me!'

'Oh come, come, Percy. You know as well as I that it isn't Mordred. You must know that I am the best and most powerful sorceress of all time.' She raised herself to her fullest height in her self-esteem. 'He won't do you any harm.' She turned and looked at Sir Kay. 'How do you like your new body?'

The giant had by now come fully awake and was watching the proceedings with interest. With his elbows on his knees and his head cupped in his hands he peered at the window and the witch at the same time – just who or what was he actually looking at? Was he really interested in what Mab was doing or could he see something on the wall that no-one else could? Then he spoke.

'What are you going to do with them now, Mab?'

'Ah, Ysbaddaden, you're awake! Well, let's see if they know why they're here first and then we'll see what we should do with them.'

At that moment a door opened behind the giant from the direction of the kitchens and a very pretty young woman came over and took a tray of sweetmeats and wine to the giant. She was petite, graceful and slim, with bright yellow hair, like the broom tree blossom with perfume, which occasionally drowned out the witch's stench, as sweet. Her skin was as pale as a dove and her cheeks as red as a rose. She cast just one glance at us and her eyes were bright but sad.

He looked down – at least I think he did – well, with one eye at any rate - at the young woman and I could see how his face softened as he did so.

'Who is this?' I thought.

I turned back and noticed the witch looking at me. Had she read my mind? I needed to be more careful. I looked back at the girl.

She sat down in the hearth and added a few small logs to the already blazing fire.

127

'Send Olwen away. We need to talk.' The witch had signalled to Pos and Neg to come over to her and keep guard. This they did, folding their arms as they took up their positions on either side of Kay and me.

Ysbaddaden leaned forward and, taking the girl gently by the hand, lifted her up and sent her from the room. Raising one of his extremely wild eyebrows, he stared at Mab and waited for her to continue.

'Well, Ysbaddaden, I think it only fair to let these good people know what is happening. I only want to tell them because when it *does* happen, they will know just how great I am and will have to give me all the credit, glory and praise for the amazing magician I am – so much better than Merlin! Merlin.' She howled with glee as she thought of him. Trying to talk, she looked over at me with eyes filled with tears of laughter and the words just could not come. Each time she tried to speak she fell about laughing again. Eventually her mirth came under control as she concentrated on the painful stitch that had taken hold of her stomach.

Rubbing her side, she was eventually able to say the thing that had been causing her so much enjoyment. 'I have Merlin under my spell! I knew that if I was vigilant I could eventually catch him unawares. And I did! How, you ask, did I manage it? You will have to admit that I am the absolute greatest at what I do. I cannot be bettered. Oh how wonderful I am!' Well, there was no stopping her now. Once she had got started on how brilliant she was it was hard to turn her.

But the giant had other ideas. 'Yes, yes, Mab. We know all this, but how did you do it? How did you get Merlin under your spell?'

'Eh? Oh!' She shook her head to clear it as she was still in full flow on the subject of her wonderful self. 'Yes, er Merlin ... right! Well, oh yes – that particular evening I was just going to and fro on the earth and walking back and forth in it when I came upon the clearing outside Sir Ector's hall. I could hear talking and laughter and other disgustingly merry sounds and decided to see what was going on. I hoisted myself up onto a water barrel and watched the proceedings through an archer's window. It was very interesting. I heard Merlin's songs and the prophecy he sang. That, you know, was his undoing. It weakened him so much that I knew I could capture him if I really tried and cause him loads of damage; I could even kill him off! Well, I would have to see. As soon as he left the room I decided upon my plan; and such a brilliant plan it was too.'

'How did no-one suspect you were there, Mab?' Ysbaddaden asked her.

She looked astonished at his question. 'How? HOW?' She almost screamed before forcing her temper under control. 'Because I am the most fantastic spell-maker and magician of all time! Because I can even outwit that old fox, Merlin – as you will see!' She took a few deep breaths and reined in her temper. 'You may or may not know that Merlin has only one love in his life – apart from loving himself of course!' She snorted at this. 'Nimue!' She snorted again. 'Nimue was, is, oh I can't understand him.' Mab was obviously very jealous of this woman and was finding it very hard to describe her. 'Merlin liked her very much and had, on several occasions, taught her various of his arts and craft. She was clever – too clever I thought – and was able to pick up quite a lot from him. However, she wanted to learn more and he, always wanting to hold on to his secrets and keep things close to his chest, would tell her no more. She decided to go her own way and he was devastated when she left.

'He still loves her, I know, but she hasn't been around now for some few years. She stayed with me for a while but I must admit I didn't give her much. Why should I? They are my secrets so why should I share them? Mind, she started to turn very funny – always walking about with a mask over her face! That would not help her learn anything, I'm sure. I wonder why she did that! Well, people are peculiar, aren't they? Hmm.

'To get back to my story - I knew that Merlin had drained himself of stacks of power and that in such a condition I could do almost whatever I wanted to him. And so it was that I laid my trap. He would have to go a certain way back to one of his caves and, being in the state he was in, I knew which one it would be – the nearest - and, thus, I knew which direction he would take – the shortest.

'There was a clearing about halfway between Sir Ector's hall and the cave through which ran a small stream. It forms a pool at the base of a rock. This was the place for my magic to be most effective. I set to work.

'It wasn't long before Merlin stumbled into the clearing and made his way to the pool. He was obviously exhausted and near to collapsing. It was fairly light in the clearing as a sickle moon and bright stars shone down between the branches of the trees. There was no wind and everything appeared to be peaceful and still. Merlin made his way over to the pool, knelt down and lowered his hand to take a scoop of water to bathe his face. I needed him to do more than that – I needed him to drink from this pool.

'"Merlin." A whispered voice spoke to him. "Merlin."

'"Who are you?" he asked. "Where are you?"

'"It is I, Nimue."

'"Nimue? Nimue, where are you?"

'"Look into the pool, Merlin. I am trapped within it."

'He looked down into the pool and there, sure enough, was the face of his beloved Nimue. As I said the pool was very still and her beautiful face, virtually unruffled by the water, stared longingly up at him.

'"Please release me from this watery prison."

'"But how am I to release you? How were you trapped there?"

"'I know not, Merlin, but I can only be released if you drink from this pool."

"'Then I will drink immediately."

"'No! First you must lay down your staff over there by the lightening-struck tree, or it won't work."

'Like a fool, he did it.' Mab's lips twitched as she recalled the episode.

'He walked over to the tree, laid down his staff and returned to the pool. Reaching down and disturbing that beautiful face as he did so, he scooped up a handful of the water and drank. He actually drank! Can you believe it? He never drinks from pools – too risky! He only ever drinks from springs, moving water, cascades, waterfalls – not from the pool itself and never from anything that might stagnate.

'I watched him closely as the poison took effect; I needed to know what it would do to him.

'First, he stared back into the pool to see what effect his obedience had had on Nimue's imprisonment. All he could see was a swirling of thick black-green oily water that held no promise of a face well loved.

"'Nimue," he called. No answer. He called again to no effect. Then the waters started to clear. He peered deep into the pool until he saw his own face reflected in it and then, blinking in unbelief, he saw my face over his shoulder. I can't tell you what a fantastic feeling it gave me. The incredulity on his face was a picture never to be forgotten. He stood and raised his arm, only to remember at the last moment that he did not have his staff with him. He looked over at the stricken tree but his staff was nowhere to be seen.

"'Merlin, I hope you are going to die! The poison I placed in that pool is enough to kill a legion of soldiers. How do you feel? Does your head spin? Is your body starting to lose its strength? Do you have pins and needles in your fingers? Are you now seeing double? Are you in pain? Can you speak? Am I not more wonderful than you?"

'He opened his mouth to try to speak but nothing came out. I took a few steps away from him to retrieve his staff from where I'd hidden it behind a tree and held it up before him. He made a lunge at it but was so weak that all he could do was grasp at thin air as he fell down.

'Laugh! I couldn't stop. I had him just where I wanted him. It's a shame to see a man who was once so mighty brought down to earth.

'There is only one thing that annoys me about this whole episode, though,' she grumbled as her face clouded over, 'and that is that he didn't die. Well, he didn't die in front of my eyes and I should have loved to have seen that. He should have, as there was such a huge amount of poison in that pool; I expect that it had become diluted somehow – perhaps it was too deep and had thinned out. I was going to finish him off myself but as he fell he slipped into that same pool and disappeared. He just vanished into those dark waters. I prodded it a bit with his staff but he just wasn't there. I expect he is dead! Well, all the better for me, then, although I would have enjoyed him now seeing just how powerful I have become.'

I remembered to put up the barrier to my thoughts as I digested all that the mad witch had just told me. Perhaps, because of what had happened, Merlin was caught up in water and that is why Cabal and I had only seen him in that waterfall. Maybe he was now in some half-world and might never come back. That was something too awful to contemplate. I would have to try and see what I could do to try and help him escape his watery or spectral prison, but that was going to be extremely tricky as both Sir Kay and I were in a pretty sticky situation ourselves.

'Are you going to try and ransom us? What is it that you want in exchange?'

'Ransom you? Oh my, how naive you are Percival! No, I am just going to keep you here until I decide what to do with you. Percy, somehow you just stumbled into my clutches but I am so glad you did because you know I have to take my revenge on you for what you did to me.' I had noticed that she still had a tic at the side of her mouth as a result of the naiad root poisoning. 'Sir Kay, well I just needed his body. My dear friend Mordred, within Sir Kay's body, will bring Arthur to me. He should be arriving within Arthur's camp as we speak and will put my plan into action. I think I shall keep you alive, young Percy, to show you just what I am going to do to him once I have him within my grasp again.' Her face darkened. 'This time he will not escape. Then, once I have disposed of him, it will be your turn.' Her grin was diabolical – especially with those awful teeth – and breath!

The giant had attended closely to all that had been going on and seemed enthralled by the witch's tale about Merlin. Both he and the witch continued chatting as though they were attending the vicar's tea party, talking easily about diabolical things. How they'd have disposed of Merlin had he not fallen into that pool – trying to outdo one another in their evil plans for his demise. Then, moving on to Arthur and Culhwch and agreeing and disagreeing on how they should get rid of them. At first I was shocked and extremely worried by the things they were saying but after some short while realised they were both suffering from what I had always thought of as the "my dad's bigger than your dad" syndrome, as they both tried to outdo one another in thinking up horrific plans.

Keeping my thoughts strictly to myself, and trying to block out those two schemers, I hoped that Cabal would be able to detect through any of his senses that Mordred was not the real Sir Kay. Knowing that dogs can do that, I felt slightly reassured.

However, I would not have been so comfortable had I known that Cabal would not meet up with Mordred as he had by then left the camp in search of me.

133

EIGHTEEN

Retracing his steps, Cabal covered the ground back to the inn in no time at all, arriving there late morning. Remembering the kindness of the innkeeper, he nudged open the kitchen door with his nose and was rewarded with a friendly pat on the head, some kind words and a bowl of water. The man also threw down some scraps from the huge joint of beef and, cutting off the rest of the meat, eventually gave him the shinbone. Cabal, with velvety lips, gently and politely took the bone from the man's hand and made his way outside. Knowing it was going to be some time before he would be able to eat again and also needing to rest from his long trip, he made a feast of the bone, crunching through it and licking out the marrow. Replete, he laid down to rest for a few hours. So it was, at twilight and by the light of an ever-expanding moon, he made his way into the forest.

You would have thought that I'd have learned my lessons by now. You'd think that I should know that every time I reckoned I've got one up on that old witch she'd get one up on me.

Thus it was that Kay and I were frogmarched out of the giant's hall, down a large flight of dark, dank and cold stone steps and into the dungeons. The torches spluttered continuously and made weird and frightening shapes on the walls as we were rushed along, the ghosts of previous prisoners appearing to stare at us as we passed. This time, as we were once again thrown unceremoniously into the cell, there was no window, not even an archer's slit, to look out of or to let in any light. No black bird would visit us here. The dungeon was quite large; I wondered if the giant had made it to imprison other giants, if there were any. I shivered, hoping that he would be the only one I'd come into contact with.

Kay – and after my experience with the witch, I now knew that he really was who he said he was, even though I still did a double take every time I looked at him - was the first of us to start checking our new home to see if there was any chance of escape. He disappeared into the gloom at the end of our prison.

'Keep talking to me, Kay!' I found myself speaking in a faltering voice. Fear does weird things to you, doesn't it?

'It's OK, Percy; I'm coming back. There's nothing here except wall, floor and ceiling. I can touch the ceiling if I reach up on tiptoe. Hmm, what's this?'

I had just seen him emerging from the shadow when he stopped and stared at the floor. I walked over to join him. There was a pool set into the floor. It wasn't very wide – about three feet across – more like a well but there were no sides sticking up and the water came almost to the level of the floor.

We stared at it for a little while before Kay crouched down to touch the water. It was as he did so that I saw it and my flesh began to crawl. Without thinking, I hurled myself at Kay and flung him and me right across the chamber.

'What on earth are you doing, Percy? What's the matter with you?' he yelled as he pulled himself up from the floor. 'You nearly dislocated my ankle again!'

Once more my mouth gave up on me and I couldn't speak. I pointed at the hole in a very excited fashion; I could just see the snout of one of those malevolent naiads sniffing the air.

Kay got to his feet and was dusting himself down as he looked to where my finger was pointing.

He didn't appear to be troubled by the naiad at all but went over as if to make a closer inspection of it, kneeling down by the edge of the hole.

I found my voice at last.

'KAY', I shouted. 'STOP!'

135

Thank goodness he did.

'What is it? Why are you so scared?'

'Please, Kay, come over here as far from that hole as you can and I'll tell you all about it.'

We leaned back against the furthest wall and I told him about the naiad at the witch's castle, the one on the shore of the lake before we got into the castle and the one that had bitten the witch after we'd escaped. I couldn't tell him what Cabal had told me about it, for obvious reasons. I really had to be so careful when I explained things that had happened to Cabby. If I was to say to anyone, "the dog told me …", well, they'd not believe another word I said – at best – or, believing I'd lost it completely, they'd lock me up – at worst!

He listened attentively and decided, finally, to believe me. It took a bit of explaining as he thought that if he'd never heard of these creatures before now they just couldn't exist.

'Believe me,' I assured him, 'they most certainly do!'

'If you say they are very slow on land, I reckon we stand a good chance of keeping out of their way in this dungeon, but I think we ought to keep on our guard. The only thing I think we should do is to take it in turns to keep watch. What do you say?'

'Alright, Kay.' I agreed, 'I'll take first watch. You get some sleep and when you wake up I'll rest.'

By my reckoning it was only about mid-day and so neither of us was sleepy. We spent an hour or more – or we thought it was about that length of time – for in the dark one just cannot tell – searching the rest of our prison. There was obviously no way out. We would have to try and rush the guards when they came – if they came!

Kay told me he would try and get some rest and for me to keep watch. Cold as it was in that awful place, Kay was soon snoring gently.

We managed quite well over the next couple of days. We tried to tell the time by the twice-daily arrival of our food and drink although we once ended up having a not too friendly discussion as to whether it was morning or evening.

This is getting serious, now, I thought, as my imagination started to dwell on what might be happening to Arthur and Rhianne at the hands of Mordred. We had to try to escape! But how? The Paisley men were much too strong and they didn't give us any chance to get at them. The shutter at the bottom of the iron door was used to shove a tray of food in to us and the iron grill in the top of the door allowed as much light through from the brazier on the outside wall as they thought we would need. I hoped that that light would not be allowed to go out. If that were to occur, well, goodness only knows what might happen to us. Of the witch, we saw nothing.

So it was that around the third day of our imprisonment in the dungeon, unforgivably, I dozed off to sleep on my watch.

Kay woke me by prodding me in the ribs with the finger of one hand whilst holding his other hand over my mouth to stop me from making any noise. With the spluttering light from the dying torch outside the door, we heard rather than saw that which made our blood run cold and our brains, though not our mouths, scream.

Something had crawled out of that hole and by the slithering sounds it was making was heading toward us.

NINETEEN

Cabal trotted into the forest to the place where he had last been able to smell the scent of his friend. Every trace, after all that rain, was now gone but he was almost certain that this was where I had vanished.

Now vanishing is something a dog accepts as normal. Cabal thought of those canines – and he had to admit he was rather disdainful of dogs with a lesser intelligence – that would chase a ball that the owner had pretended to throw but had held on to, hiding it, usually, under their arm. Those dogs would hunt around for a while and then return to their master to await a throw from the next ball, completely accepting that the previous ball had "vanished" and their master had a never-ending supply. Well Cabal, being of a far higher intellect, knew, with no hesitation whatsoever, that things and people *did* vanish – and this was one of those times.

Setting his mind to it, he decided that he would keep searching for the loose thread of the vanishing act until he found it and could unravel the mystery. So it was that, during this excursion, King Ogwin and Queen Gisele found him.

The tiny king, sitting high in a tree, looked down upon him and remarked to his wife, 'Isn't that the same animal that trapped me in its mouth, dear, and also took me to visit Lady Elise?'

'I believe it is.'

'What do you think he's doing? He appears to be going round and round in circles, sniffing this and sniffing that! Well, I don't fancy my chances in going down to see! At best, he looks completely demented and might grab me again and it took ages to get rid of the smell of his saliva from my best suit the last time! At worst, he might be hungry and I, for one, don't fancy becoming a snack for him.'

Cabal heard the tinkling sound of their voices in the clear night air and had stopped his activities. Wondering if they might have the gift of the Old Way, and he wasn't sure they would, as Ogwin did not seem to notice him speaking to me the last time they met, he reached out toward them with his mind.

'I wouldn't hurt you this time.'

Gisele almost fell off her branch.

'What on earth is the matter with you?' Ogwin responded as he made a grab to save her.

'The dog spoke to me!'

'I didn't hear it!'

'No, it didn't speak with its mouth, it spoke into my mind with its mind.'

'Ah yes, my dear. I forgot you had this ability. Ask it what it's doing.'

Over the next few minutes, Cabal described the mysteries that had happened to them all since they had left home. He went on to explain his instructions to find me and express his fears as to what might have happened to me. He also told them about the strange pictures of Merlin appearing in the waterfalls and his peculiar statement that "Sir Kay is not".

Gisele explained to her husband just what Cabal had said. They were both mystified and quiet for some time until Ogwin decided it best to send out messages through the webs. He clambered down the tree, gave Cabal a dubious look but then decided that he wasn't to be grabbed by those huge jaws, and went off in search of a spider.

After giving his instructions he returned to the tree and gave an explanation as to what he had just done. They now had to find the patience to wait. However, it didn't take very long.

What an amazing thing the web system is - in no time at all, all the information that was needed came humming back through its wires.

The same spider that King Ogwin had spoken to returned with the news that thousands in the insect population had witnessed me going along the enchanted road toward the flat-topped mountain; the doves had also seen me and another whisked away by the dull dragon and the frogs had made the observation that I was now in the lair of the giant.

'A giant! What giant and where is this giant? And what is the enchanted road?' Cabby asked.

'The enchanted road is the one you have been trying to find, I assume,' Ogwin replied. 'You won't find it, though, because it doesn't really exist! It's just something the Mighty Smell has conjured up in which to trap people and transport them to wherever she wants them to go. I expect she now has your friend in her grasp.'

Cabal thought for a moment and, realising he would need to find some other way of searching for me, once again asked who the giant was and how could he find his lair.

'He's the Glaston Giant,' Ogwin responded, 'and he lives in a castle in Glastonbury itself.'

'He must be awake, then,' Gisele stated, 'if they can see the castle.'

'Or him,' Ogwin added.

'What do you mean, "if they can see the castle or him?"'

'The giant can only be seen when he is awake. When he hibernates he cannot be seen and, more to the point, neither can his castle. Also, they cannot be felt – you could walk right through them and not know they were there. We know he's been starting to wake up because we've felt the rumblings. Before he wakes up he sends out his thoughts and his thoughts are quite deep and heavy – like his sleep. Because they are so heavy, when he sends them out it's as though he's walking about – sleepwalking I suppose – and some people have felt it. Sometimes, he actually does walk about; the rumblings are then much heavier.'

'I've felt it! My mistress and her mother have, too.'

140

'There you are then. The reason he does this is to check on the lie of the land. If it's a good harvest, with plenty of livestock, he'll probably want to wake up and feed, but if it's been a lean harvest, well, he might as well stay asleep that year as he's very lazy and doesn't like to go too far to find food. He steals it, you know!

'He's also been seen to take captives to the octopus' cave, miles away at Bedruthan Steps. However, if the crabs are about, they usually nibble through the ropes of most of his victims and set them free.'

'Does he eat children?'

'I don't think so,' Ogwin responded once his wife had told him what Cabal had said, 'but I wouldn't be surprised. Some of them deserve to be eaten, though,' he added. 'Especially the ones that pull off spiders' legs!'

'Now, now, dear,' scolded his wife.

'Well …'. He sulked for a moment and then remembered something else. 'The black prince is nearby.'

'The black prince?'

'Yes, you know! He was with you when the dragons fought. The spiders told us.'

'Salazar!'

'Salazar? Is that his name? Well, he and his wife are on their way to Merlin's cave.'

'How far away?'

'They arrived at the inn after dark and will be spending the night there I would assume.'

'I must see them! Thank you so much!' and to their great surprise, Cabal turned and bounded off in the direction of the inn as fast as his legs would carry him.

'If you need anything else,' they yelled after him, 'just come into the woods and let us know. If you make enough noise we will find you. Just call.'

'I will.'

141

'You must have known there was a reason we should come this way and stay at this inn,' Salazar spoke softly to his wife.

'Nothing is by chance,' she responded. 'All is as it is meant to be.'

'I shall not be long. The hound is outside and has called me to speak with him. Once I find out what it is he wants I shall return and we can then decide what we need to do.'

Salazar descended the staircase and silently let himself out of the dark and sleeping inn.

TWENTY

After spending over a day, because of the rain, shut up in the food wagon, a bored Arthur was overjoyed to greet his cousin and friend.

'Culhwch, Niel, welcome! Molly,' he turned and called to the old woman, 'something hot for my friends please – as soon as you can,' he added.

'You don't know how good it is to see you,' he sighed. 'I've been stuck here for days in this awful rain. But, tell me, how is it that you're here? And, you, Culhwch, I thought you were with my father. Is anything wrong? Is that why you're looking for me? Is my father alright? Kay?'

'No, well, yes! Sorry!' Niel responded as he saw the anxious look on his friend's face, 'Your father and Kay are well. Culhwch and I met up, purely by chance, on the road. I was looking for you but Culhwch was not – well, he was at first although he was by then headed for Glaston Castle.'

'Glaston Castle? There isn't such a place, is there? I thought it was a myth.'

'No, cousin,' he answered, 'there is such a place and I wish there wasn't.'

'I am afraid I'm lost as to your thinking, Culhwch.'

'Then let me explain.' They settled around the fire and Culhwch began his tale. 'It started many days ago. Your brother Kay hurt his foot and it was causing him so much pain that Sir Ector decided he would be more of a hindrance than a help in the forthcoming battle. Much to Kay's annoyance – and after much begging to be allowed to stay, I can assure you – Sir Ector was determined to send him home but was eventually happy to allow him to catch up with you and join your party. He went with one squire – Meadows.'

'Neither he nor Meadows has joined us. What made you uneasy enough to follow?'

'It is not quite that simple. But please, Arthur, let me tell the whole story, as I know it. Some three days after they had left us, Meadows returned riding one horse and leading the other. Of Sir Kay there was no sign. Not only that, but Meadows appeared to be in some sort of a trance. He eventually came out of it and all he could tell us was that Sir Kay had become delirious and they had taken shelter in a cave. As the night went on Sir Kay seemed to get worse, with a raging temperature; he was continually asking for water, which was hard to find. He had to collect it from condensation in the cave. When Sir Kay eventually drifted off to sleep, Meadows said he also started to doze. Without any warning, some sort of giant slimy creature had attacked them and he lost consciousness. The next thing he remembered was riding into our camp with the two horses. Everything in between is missing from his memory.

'My father and Sir Ector decided that someone had to try to find him and it was agreed that I should be the one. I must admit that I was really annoyed because this would have been my first real battle and I wanted desperately to earn the right to a warrior's queue.' His hair was, at the moment, hanging in loose waves around his face.

I remembered Arthur once telling me how he couldn't wait to be able to braid his hair, which he couldn't do until he had proved himself a warrior in battle. 'I am afraid I'm in the same position as you,' Arthur remarked with a scowl. 'Why is it that we're not allowed to join in any of the fun?'

'Be that as it may, Arthur, I reckoned mine was an extremely selfish attitude so I agreed to go. Once I had found him, which obviously I haven't, I was going to try and rescue my beautiful Olwen from her awful father's clutches.'

'Olwen?' both Rhianne and Elise, who had by now joined them, chorused.

'I thought you might have wanted to rejoin the warriors?' added Arthur.

144

'No - I didn't suppose I'd be able to find them again once I'd come this far south and as I haven't been able to find Sir Kay I don't suppose I'll now have time to rejoin them. But my poor Olwen! Oh, I know that he doesn't treat her that badly but she is a virtual prisoner to the giant.'

'Giant?' they all chorused again.

'Yes. He won't let her out of the castle without an escort and he wouldn't let her marry me. He has given me several tasks to perform before I can and they seem to be nigh on impossible. But I will tell you about that another time. I'm sure I will overcome in my quest. For the time being we need a strategy in order to find Sir Kay.'

The silence stretched out before them as each considered what awful fate might have overtaken Kay, when, miracle of miracles, he rode into their camp.

What a busy day it was turning out to be for visitors and the like.

Granddad,' Ben interrupted, 'is that really Sir Kay? Had he escaped with you and found the camp? But, then, why aren't you with him? It's Mordred isn't it?'

'Yes, Ben,' Jack replied, 'it's Mordred! And what a lot of trouble he's about to cause.'

TWENTY-ONE

Isn't it funny how one can be fast asleep one minute and then, with acute fear leaping into your brain, wide awake the next?

The flames from the spluttering torch finally died. We were in total darkness. Once again our ears twitched and the hair on the back of our necks rose as we heard something slithering toward us from the water hole and everything inside my head screamed, although at the same time I was struck dumb with fear and, of course, didn't want the thing to hear me – it would find me in no time if I made any sort of noise. I could feel the beat of my heart as it hammered through my ears and wished it would be silent, feeling sure that everyone could hear it. Walking backwards we came up against the wall. There was no-where else to go. We were locked inside a dungeon with a huge iron door and thick stone walls and, with no escape route at all, were in peril of imminent death.

Sniff, sniff, sniff. Whatever it was, was trying to locate us. I knew from what I had heard others say, that naiads were really slow on land and couldn't keep out of water for too long as they dried up and died; if they were away from water, they usually tried to keep damp by snuggling up against the roots of huge trees but, if that didn't work, ended up looking just like the exposed part of the root itself.

However - back to our current predicament. We had to try and figure out just where it was and keep moving along the walls and away from it. We had no weapons with which to whack it. Kay held on to me and we started to move along.

I could feel the animal following us and getting closer and just knew it was about to strike.

Straining my eyes was completely useless as it was pitch black in that place, now that the torch had gone out completely, but strain them I did nevertheless. Something scraped itself against my leg as it slithered over my shoe and I

146

could feel its breath against my arm as it moved its head. I almost screamed. Sweat was standing out on my forehead and running down between my shoulder blades, even though our prison was as cold as the tomb.

'Was this to be my tomb?' I thought.

'Percy! Percy, it is you! Phew, you smell bad! Didn't think it was you at first! Whose that other awful smell with you?'

'Cab? Cab, is that you?' I spoke out loud, thankfulness flooding through me.

He sneezed with joy and I almost fainted with relief.

'What's going on?' asked Kay in a whisper.

'It's Cabal, Kay.'

'Cabal? But how did he get in here?'

'I don't know,' I replied, despondency dropping into my boots, thinking that perhaps he wasn't real but was either in my imagination or was "ghosting".

'No, friend, it's really me!'

As fast as he could, Cabal explained that Salazar was outside the castle walls, he had diverted the stream that filled the pool, which at the moment was virtually dry. The naiad that had made its home in the pool had slunk off into the main river when it realised what was happening. However, Salazar could only divert the stream for so long as the banks were crumbling and once that happened the river would be out of his control and take over once again, filling the pool. We therefore had to get out as quickly as we could.

'Cabby's pulling me along, Kay, so hold on to me and we'll see where he takes us.'

I held on to his tail and one by one we dropped down through the damp and gritty water hole, which wasn't actually as deep as we had at first thought it might be and I had to disagree with Cabby's interpretation of "virtually dry". We crawled on our bellies through a lot of foul-smelling slime but were spurred on not only by the thought of freedom, but also

147

by the fact that the guards should be bringing us our meal at any moment and could even now be in hot pursuit. As Cabal moved forward I soon began to see shafts of light winking past him from the end of the tunnel. We stepped out into daylight by the side of the castle walls – on the outside, thank goodness. I was quite surprised that it was actually morning – having been kept in a dungeon, one loses track of day and night. We hurried over as we saw Salazar struggling to hold the barrier in place but he knelt down and managed to pull us over the top to safety, Cabby bounding up the bank beside us. He looked intensely at Kay for a moment or two but, because I appeared to be alright with the situation, bided his time with any questions. I had completely forgotten that no-one else knew that Kay was imprisoned in the wrong body. Cabby sat looking at me with a self-satisfied raise of one eyebrow and an uncontrollably wagging tail.

As soon as we were all out of harm's way, Salazar let go of the barricade he'd erected and the stream leapt back into place, skipping and gurgling back through the hole into the castle. I wondered if Pos and Neg might have been in pursuit; if they were, they were going to get very wet!

'Oh, Salazar, thank you, thank you.'

'Come,' he said, 'let us get away from here as quickly as we can. Jasmine is waiting for us with the horses and we must leave this place before they find you are gone. You smell terribly bad,' he added as we moved past him down between the trees.

'Sorry, but we've been locked up by that old witch for days without washing.'

'You will be able to wash soon. At the inn.'

We pushed our way through the undergrowth, well away from the giant's castle and came to where Jasmine stood holding the reins of the two horses.

'I am afraid we will have to double up on each horse,' Salazar stated. 'You two can share one and I will share

148

Jasmine's. We have a way to go to the inn, but if we rest halfway I believe the horses can make it. You must be hungry but I am afraid you will have to wait until we are well away from here.'

'We will make it,' Jasmine assured us, and I remembered that she had this special gift of being able to see up to one day ahead – sometimes! Apparently, she only did speak it out if she was absolutely sure. I was, therefore, relieved and started to relax. However, a niggling fear kept creeping into my brain – what happens if she *isn't* warned about something? Shaking my head I determined not to think negatively, not now we were out of that awful place. Seated behind Kay on the horse I was just relieved to be free.

As we rode back towards the inn, the sun rose and it became a beautiful and warm autumn day. It was so good to be outside again, to enjoy daylight and warmth.

Only one little cloud irritated our horizon, which was that as the morning progressed, the caking of the slime we had collected from the escape tunnel and the increase in its smell as the sun baked it began to make us all feel extremely sick! It didn't just smell – it stank and both Kay and I, riding together on one of the horses, started retching. Cabal was struggling to keep up, too, with the mud drying on his underbelly and chafing at his legs.

'We will have to stop,' Kay said, the smell making tears stream down his face. 'I have to get these awful clothes off. I can't stand this stench any longer.'

'A short way further, young sirs,' Jasmine urged us on, 'and there is a waterfall. You can wash yourselves and your clothes in the pool underneath it and then dry them on the rocks. In this heat they should not take too long to dry.'

'While your clothes are drying, we can talk. I will tell you what is happening and you can tell me what you know,' Salazar added.

We came to the cascade of water and dismounted.

149

TWENTY-TWO

Pos and Neg stood in front of the witch holding the tray of bread, cheese and water.

'What are you doing? Why have you brought it here? Take it to the prisoners at once;' she shouted, 'don't bring it to me!'

They just stood there.

Always on the verge of losing it completely, she stamped her foot in rage, slapping Neg a couple of times around the top of his bald head.

'Perhaps there's a problem,' suggested Ysbaddaden dryly.

'Problem, problem! What problem could there possibly be? I've dealt with everything. There is no problem! What do you take me for? I don't make problems!' She was by now almost rattling the windowpanes with her screeching.

This episode went on for quite a long time and the giant was becoming somewhat amused, something that had the inevitable effect of increasing Mab's madness.

'Don't you *dare* laugh at me!' she yelled, which, of course, had the opposite effect, though the giant either knew when to stop or had possibly remembered some of the things she had done to others when they had laughed at her. His mind recalled, especially, the story of the pretty but silly woman who'd mimicked her on the common before a small crowd of villagers. That was something, worth remembering. The woman had no idea Mab was making a rare visit to purchase some herbs and unguents and was, at that moment, staring out of the shop doorway while the shopkeeper packaged her purchases. Mab was furious! She stormed out of the shop, across the green and stood, hands on hips, behind the woman, who was acting out her mimicry to an increasingly concerned audience – they could see the witch approaching but the unfortunate woman was looking the

150

wrong way – and thinking she was having a huge impact on
her listeners was becoming very pleased at the effect she was
having upon them – she took their looks of concern as
meaning she was telling a scary tale. When finally Mab
tapped her on the shoulder, she realised, too late, the reason
for their shocked and worried faces. The giant felt sure that
to this day the poor woman had wished the wind had been in
the opposite direction so that it could at least have warned her
of Mab's imminent approach. The villagers slunk off, not
wanting to be included in what they were sure would happen.

'So, you think you're me, do you?' Mab cooed to the poor
woman.

'Er, no, ma'am,' she stammered. 'Not at all ma'am.
Sorry, ma'am.'

'But not sorry enough!' she responded, still keeping her
cool - just.

The woman turned and took off as though pursued by all
the demons in hell – in the present circumstances she was not
really far wrong, eh?

Mab's face turned stony as she watched the woman run
away. She knew who she was and where she lived and that
she'd plot her revenge. She always did.

Some six weeks later the woman was seen to start losing
her once glorious locks of jet-black hair. By the end of a
further two months she was almost completely bald. Then
her earlobes started growing downwards until they flopped
against her shoulders. It was whispered that Mab had said
she'd been kind to the woman as she could at least keep
herself warm by tying her ears on top of her now totally bald
head.

The last that was heard of her was she'd become a hermit
and lived in a cave in the rocky hillside some five miles away.
Some kind people leave food for her, which is always eaten,
proving she's still alive, but no-one had seen hide nor hair of
her – that is if she now had any - since.

151

Ysbaddaden had been ruminating on her wickedness and waiting patiently to get a word in edgeways while Mab was continuing with her ranting.

She eventually ran out of steam and Ysbaddaden decided this might be the right time to make a suggestion.

'If we see why they've brought you the food instead of taking it to the prisoners, we might get somewhere. Perhaps they're dead!'

At this, the mad woman's eyes lit up, her lips twitching with the evil thought, although, conversely, that might take away her pleasure. No, she didn't want either of them to die just yet, especially as she wanted to be the instigator of it.

'I propose we let them show us why they've brought the food to us.'

'Exactly! That's just what I was going to suggest,' she lied. Then, turning to the slaves, 'Lead on.'

She hadn't just been going to suggest that at all – she was too angry to think anything. The giant looked at the woman and wondered why he allowed her to run the show. He would be the first to agree that he was basically a very lazy person who wanted nothing better than to sit at home with his lovely daughter and just laze about in front of the fire and eat and drink. He had found that his nasty side had come to the fore when Olwen had introduced that dratted Culhwch to him and he'd had the effrontery to ask for her hand in marriage. Now why should he agree to that? He'd have no-one to wait on him hand and foot! Well, he wasn't a problem at the moment as he'd sent him off to do several impossible tasks before he'd consent. He felt very pleased with himself about this, as he knew they couldn't be done. Well, they couldn't, could they, if they were impossible? He worried, then, that perhaps they might not be impossible. He'd allowed a stream of spittle to dribble off his bottom lip whilst thinking all of this and absentmindedly slurped it and his lip back up into his mouth. Still, that problem would soon be sorted altogether as

152

Mab had agreed to dispose of him completely so long as he helped her. He was still not quite sure what it was he was supposed to do. She had explained it but he felt sure she'd left out lots of important bits. Well, it would all sort itself out in the end, he was sure, just as long as he got rid of that dratted Welshman.

'Well, come on then,' she yelled, 'let's get going.'

As the giant lumbered to his feet, the Paisley men, one still holding the tray of food, turned and led the way to the dungeons. Mab snatched the food from them and threw it on the table, crashing and spilling everything while Ysbaddaden grabbed a huge flaming log from the fire and followed them.

The rats scampered out of their way as they dropped to the lower levels of the castle, not that Mab was worried about rats. Reaching the iron door through which Percy and Kay had been shoved some three days previously, Pos retrieved the large metal key, fitted it into the lock and, with a screech of metal, opened the door.

'Now, you two, get up and come here!' Mab called.

Nothing!

'It will be the worse for you if you don't obey me immediately,' her voice rose. 'You know what I can do and, believe me, I will do it!'

Nothing!

'Right, you two,' she shoved Pos and Neg into the room, 'drag them out.'

They went in, walked round the room and came out.

Nothing!

'If I have to come in there and get you, you will be really sorry!'

Still nothing!

'Ysbaddaden, go and get them?'

'Er, no, madam - it's your problem and in any event I wouldn't be able to get through the door - but I am willing to hold my torch up inside the doorway to give you light.'

153

You could almost taste the frustration emanating from the mad woman; hot steam was whooshing down her nostrils in that cold air.

He stooped down and lifted the blazing torch as high as he could through the door.

Clamping her lips together in her anger, she stepped inside the chamber. The light didn't penetrate to the end of the dungeon. 'Hold it higher,' she whined, 'I can't see a blasted thing.' Why she didn't hold one herself, I will never know!

'Madam, that's as high as it will go.'

Straining her eyes to peer ahead and watching the light bounce off the stone walls, she realised, with a sinking heart, that the room was devoid of any human existence.

Who had helped them escape? It couldn't be the slaves - they didn't have one functioning brain between the two of them and apart from that they wouldn't dare! The giant? No. He had no interest in them. At least she didn't think he had. She would have to keep on her guard and watch him closely.

Surely Merlin hadn't regained his strength – no he was down for a long stretch this time! Percy's face appeared in her brain. How is it that this boy keeps on getting away? The next time she vowed he wouldn't be so lucky.

As these thoughts chased themselves around in her head, Mab began to get angrier and angrier. She strode up and down the cell, trying to decide what to do next.

It had taken a great deal of effort and calculating to trick Percy into thinking she was Merlin and getting him to walk the enchanted road through the forest. And now, for what? He'd got away again!

'Arrgh,' she growled and stamped her foot in fury.

Bad move! Very bad move! Very bad move indeed!

Losing her balance, which looked extremely funny from the giant's point of view, and with arms circling like windmills to try to stay upright, she disappeared down the hole and landed armpit-high in icy cold water. She started to turn blue before she reacted but when she did, all hell seemed to break loose.

'Noooo,' she screamed. 'Get me out, quick! QUICK!'

Pos and Neg ran into the room and hauled her out by her arms and immediately sat her down. Her dress clung to her in wet folds as the dirt and gunge of years coagulated within the layers.

'Years of power! Years of power!' She kept on repeating this phrase over and over again, crying and shaking as she did so. 'I'll have lost years of power! Washed away; washed away.' Holding her hands over her face and resting her elbows on her knees, she wept buckets as she rocked to and fro, but her tears of self-pity were soon to turn to tears of pain and the scream that bounced backward and forwards off those cold stone walls more than trebled the one she had cried when she fell into the water as a horror she recalled from her past once again made its acquaintance when it locked its jaws onto her ankle.

TWENTY-THREE

It felt so good to be clean again. The water in the pool was icy cold and even Cabby bathed as quickly as he could, showering us all again as he shook himself; it was so good to sit in the sun and dry. We sat with saddle blankets around us while our clothes dried, and, eating some of the late fruits picked by Jasmine, started to feel quite human again.

We needed to catch up as soon as we could with what had happened and what might be happening. Obviously something was afoot as Mad Mab was once again on the prowl and up to more than just mischief.

I started first with what had happened to me as I thought they needed to know why it looked as though I had Mordred with me; it had become obvious, by the looks he kept on getting from Salazar and Jasmine, that some explanation was needed.

I told my side of the story as quickly as I could, interrupted a few times by Kay when I hadn't got something quite right or by Salazar when he wasn't quite sure of what I'd said – or, more probably, missed out - and then waited to listen to Salazar as he told us what had been happening from his end, Cabby quickly managing to tell me that he would speak to me later.

Salazar and Jasmine had travelled the length of Britain from Carlisle to Tintagel and had visited many sites, mostly examining wells and standing stones. Many of the stones were sleeping dragons but, try as he might, he said he was unable to wake any of them. Some of the single standing stones were doorways and it was through one of these that they had been transported to the cave at Tintagel.

'The cave was the most interesting thing, young Percy, as I could see through some parts of the rockface into many chambers although I was unable to make entry into all of them. I believe I found one room that was a prison as I couldn't get into it and it was made out of some sort of see-through crystal rock.'

'It was a prison! Merlin was in there when I met him in the late summer – Mab had entombed him there but somehow I had managed to break the seal.'

'Ah, yes. Well, we made our way into the main chamber and went over to the Glass. Concentrating very hard we wanted it to locate Merlin for us. Now, this was very peculiar! We saw him – he was obviously in one of his caves - but couldn't get to him. However, we were able to talk to him. I was and still am very worried. He was lying down and looked extremely weak and, also, could hardly speak. What he did manage to say, we have done and now I shall tell you his instructions.

'We were to collect some of the naiad root and dragon droppings from his store in readiness for what we would be required to do. These we have here. He also asked me to bring a small bottle of thick green liquid for something that might happen along the way.

One of the things he kept on saying was, "Sir Kay is not" but after saying that he almost seemed to pass out or fall asleep.'

'Well, I know what that means now,' I replied. 'Sir Kay is not Sir Kay – he's Mordred. Therefore, and this is the scary thing, if we have Sir Kay here looking like Mordred, where is the real Mordred and does he look like Sir Kay? If that is the case we need to find him – and fast!'

'Right – we need to find a standing stone doorway as soon as possible. Your clothes are now dry so hurry and dress. I've collected all the potions as requested and as my next instruction was to find you, young man, it now seems as though everything is ready,' he looked up at me, 'and it is imperative you are there.'

'Where?' I asked.

'Back at Merlin's cave.'

We dressed once again in our partially dried clothes but even slightly damp they were so much better than the sticky, reeking ones they had been before. After remounting, we set out side by side and resumed our journey.

As we rode along, I described the time spent with Kay over the last few days and how I'd come to the conclusion that he was Kay and not the person he obviously looked like.

Cabby then interjected with the statement that if we were dogs we would have known who he was because of his smell. He definitely smelt of Sir Kay. If he had smelt of Mordred, well, he would have attacked him, to say the least.

As Salazar and I were the only others in our present company that had the gift of mind speaking, we were assured but felt it not necessary to advise the others of this fact. Jasmine would be OK but it would probably take forever to try and get Kay to understand just what we were talking about.

Kay then recounted his story from the time he had sprained his ankle, being attacked by a huge octopus, to waking up in the giant's tower. I had already covered our adventure from then.

'Well, it is obvious that she wanted to keep you out of the way, Sir Kay, so that she can get up to mischief with the bogus Sir Kay. I wonder what she is going to do?'

'Salazar, I think we should make haste to rejoin Merlin as quickly as possible as there is clearly evil afoot,' Kay suggested, obviously uncomfortable.

'Then let us find a doorway at once,' said Salazar.

TWENTY-FOUR

It was a very happy time seated round the campfire that evening. Lady Elise and Rhianne exchanged laughter and stories with Culhwch and Niel as they ate supper. Sir Kay was unusually quiet but then he had lost out on an important battle and also had a very swollen ankle. What had he to be jolly about?

Rhianne had chatted to him as Old Molly and one of the men provided materials for him to clean and dress his wound – something he would not allow them to do - but she felt quite aggrieved that he hardly responded to any of her questions with anything more than monosyllables or mumbles, even if he was in a bit of discomfort.

Talking to her mother later she remarked, 'He only grunted at me when I asked him to tell me how father was and whether they had managed to get news about the league of kings they were going to war against. When he did talk he didn't seem to know much and his voice was awful – gruff, as though he's got a sore throat.

'I asked him if he had a fever and he just told me to leave him alone. He's never spoken to me like that before, mother, and I was only looking after his welfare. He said he would stay in the wagon and rest and would I kindly not disturb him any more tonight. He turned his back on me then, mother, and so I came away.'

'Don't fret, my dear. I'll have a word with him in the morning. He's probably annoyed at being sent home. No-one, once going to battle, likes to lose out. It would have been his first real encounter and I expect he wanted to prove himself and show what a great warrior he was. He's probably fretting that he'll now have to wait until next time and wondering if there will be a next time. He'll come round, don't worry, and then all will be well again. He's probably

159

now feeling bad because he was unkind to you. No, my dear, it isn't your fault, so don't worry.'

Rhianne and her mother re-joined the young party round the fire. Their laughter must surely have reached the ears of Kay, but he made no attempt to rejoin them.

'Tell us what's been happening, Culhwch,' Niel prompted.

Culhwch was one of those men that all people were drawn to. He had a ready smile and a kindly disposition towards everyone. So far as his story went, he didn't need to be asked twice to relate it.

In the lilting intonation of the Welsh, he began.

'Well, I must say I am really rather glad to be here. Don't get me wrong, I was happy enough to go to war as it was taking my mind off my lovely Olwen.'

'Olwen? You mentioned her earlier. Tell us about her,' Arthur asked.

'Yes,' he sighed. 'She is the most beautiful lady I have ever seen, and so gentle.' He sat staring into the fire, lost in thought.

'Culhwch,' Arthur prompted, 'you were saying?'

'Oh, yes.' He continued, 'On our travels last year, my father decided to head for Cornwall. He was in desperate need of tin and so we travelled west. We finished our business and journeyed home via Bristol, where he wanted to see what the foreign sailing ships were bringing in to port. Mother was always going on about silks and spices so we thought this a good opportunity. Therefore, we didn't head for the North Devon coast to hire a ship for Wales, but travelled on land. We skirted the area north of Glastonbury and stayed a night or two in an inn near the tor. On our first evening she arrived at the inn.' He was once more lost in his thoughts as he stared into the fire.

'Culhwch,' Arthur poked him in the arm. 'You're dreaming again!'

160

'Oh, sorry,' he apologised and carried on. 'She came into the inn wearing a flaming-red robe and walked straight over to the fire. When her hood fell back from her head she uncovered a mass of yellow hair that cascaded down her back. The light from the fire was drawn to those bright curls, flickering over them and turning them to gold. Around her neck she wore a red-gold torc, which was studded with precious stones. Oh, man! I was mesmerised! My stomach did a somersault!

'She turned and looked at me. Her skin was as white as snow and her cheeks as red as foxgloves. Giving me a shy smile and moving to one side, she apologised for stealing all the warmth from the fire.

'I couldn't speak. Well, not immediately anyway. When I could I said she should have all the warmth she needed and pulled up a chair for her to sit down and warm herself.

'We got on very well from the start.

'She told me that her horse had thrown a shoe and her servant was having it seen to. It would probably be tomorrow before they could continue their journey and, therefore, her father would by now be very worried. He had sent her to the monastery to order wine and honey and it usually only took half a day to do this.

'As my father and I had taken the last of only two rooms at the inn I said I would willingly give up my room for her and sleep in the barn. She blushed as she thanked me.

'As it was, the night was far advanced before she retired to bed. We had talked about anything and everything and it was obvious, even to my father, that for both of us it was love at first sight.

'We had left it that I would escort her home the next day and would ask her father if he might consider me an acceptable suitor for his daughter's hand in marriage.

'She spent ages trying to dissuade me from this course, telling me that she should broach the subject first as her father

161

had a fearsome temper and, she believed, didn't want her ever to marry. In fact, due to what had happened in the past – upon which she would not elaborate– she was positively sure he didn't want her ever to marry. She added that as he was a very big man, if he hit him, he would probably kill him. No, she thought it best I didn't meet him just yet.

'Well, at that I puffed out my chest and said I wasn't afraid; that I had practised well the art of warfare, and added, hurriedly, when I saw the look of horror on her face, that I didn't think it would come to that. He should hear me out and, once done, he must surely see that we were meant for each other.

'Still looking extremely worried, she finally agreed to let me go home with her.

'Can you imagine my face when I met him? I was expecting large but he was at least ten feet tall and,' this quietly, 'as ugly as sin!'

'Culhwch, tell us, what did you do?' Arthur was in fits of laughter. 'You are a fabulous teller of tales! Almost as good as Merlin.'

'You might laugh, Arthur, but I am telling you the truth. When I first entered the castle, and I must admit I had misgivings as I rode up to it and saw its size; I began to feel very small indeed. Everything was on a gigantic scale. Well, there were some chairs and tables of a usual size but most of it was very unusual – table tops on a level with my head, chairs, each one of which would seat eight people side by side and up to four rows back, and the like. The fireplace was huge and whole trees crackled within it, rather than logs.

'Olwen ran through the room and out another door. I waited. Soon I heard voices coming toward me – one of which was extremely loud – and the first thing I saw was a massive foot turning into the room. Of course, it was followed by a leg as thick as an oak tree and the rest of him, then, really didn't come as that much of a surprise!

'I could feel the colour draining from my face.'

'"Father," Olwen spoke quietly, but I believe the giant heard everything she said, 'please keep calm and listen to what Culhwch has to say. You don't have to lose your temper; you need only say "yes" or "no."'

'He glared at me. Well, I think he glared at me; hmm at least one eye glared at me. The other eye was glaring at a point somewhere on the far wall, I think. I looked at that wall but there was nothing there that was at all interesting.'

By this time Arthur was in uncontrollable fits of laughter and the rest of them joined in.

'It's no laughing matter!' Culhwch admonished them, albeit half-heartedly as he, too, was on the verge of laughter. 'Please, just listen to what happened next.'

'I can't help it,' spluttered Arthur. 'You tell a wonderful story.'

'Story! No, young cousin, it's not a story. What I am telling you is real – it's the absolute truth!'

'Yes, of course it's real,' Arthur chuckled unconvinced. 'Pray, continue.'

'As he strode toward me, my heart almost melted. By the look on his face I thought he was going to raise his foot and stamp me out. But then, I told myself, you're made of sterner stuff than that and if that is the way you're going to die, then die like a man. At least Olwen will always remember you being brave.

'However, just before he got to that point, he took a step sideways and sat in what must be the absolutely biggest armchair in the world beside the absolutely biggest fireplace. Crossing one gigantic foot over the other, he asked me to tell him why I had come.

'Why is it that when you want to look your bravest or cleverest, all the spit dries up in your mouth or goes like glue? Not only that but your tongue tends to stick to the roof of your mouth as well and it's the devil to try and dislodge it!

163

That was the position I now found myself in. I think that Olwen must have known how I was feeling because she came over to me with a glass – a small glass, thank goodness – of wine and, after I had taken a sip from it, stood beside me and held my hand.

'Thus refreshed and encouraged, I made my request in what I considered an intelligent, adult and well thought out manner. Taking a deep breath, I blurted, "We want to get married."'

Arthur, taking a sip of his own wine, just then, almost choked as it went down the wrong way. He was crying and laughing – and choking – all at the same time. Niel bashed him on the back to dislodge the offending wine and so, finally getting himself under control, he waved at Culhwch to continue.

'I really don't know what you find amusing,' he said as everyone in the party round the fire was either holding their sides or dabbing at their eyes with laughter.

'The giant leapt up from his chair with a roared, "WHAAT?" and would have torn me limb from limb if Olwen hadn't stepped in front of me.

'She managed to calm him down and I must admit it looked weird seeing this petite young thing taking that huge monster of a man by the hand and leading him back to his chair.

'She sat, patting his hand, and talking to him for quite some time before he agreed to think about the matter. He told me that at the moment I was not welcome in his house but could sleep in the barn. He told me to call on him on the morrow promptly at mid-day when he would give his considered response to my request. So, with high hopes, I went off to bed.

'Next morning, I got up and went down to the stream to freshen up. My, that water was cold! I ran my fingers through my wet hair to get it under some sort of control and

164

tried to look as presentable as I could. Surely he would say "yes". I was considered to be quite a catch in Carmarthen.'

'And modest, too?' suggested Arthur.

'That, too,' he responded airily. 'I presented myself at the castle at mid-day precisely. I was led into the room and told to wait. I waited. After a half-hour or so I took the weight from one leg to the other – and waited. I walked up and down for a bit after one leg went to sleep – and waited.

'You know, I waited there all afternoon. I watched the sun moving round the room, lighting up this shield or that sword and this flag or that tapestry until I thought I would scream. Of him or Olwen there was no sign. Had he forgotten me or was this part of some awful plan? My mind was working overtime.

'I finally heard footsteps – but only one set! The giant walked into the room alone with his swivelly eyes and sloppy-lipped grin. He looked very pleased with himself.

'"I have made my decision," he stated.

'I waited - again.

'He waited for my response.

'Well, it wasn't a question, was it? I mean, he wasn't expecting a reply because my reply would have been a question, wouldn't it? Well, it would. I would have had to say, "Have you?" and that's a question, isn't it? So I waited.

'With a snort he eventually gave up. "I have here a list of tests for you to complete before I will give my consent. Before I hand you the list, do you give your word that you will carry out the tasks as a sign of your love for my daughter?" He looked a bit too smug for my liking but I had no option but to agree.

'I have that list on me but they are virtually impossible to complete.'

'Let me see,' Arthur requested.

'No! I am still trying to work them out but, when I do, you will be the first to see,' he promised. Then, face falling,

165

he declared, 'that was almost a year ago.' He slouched forward, staring into the fire, looking quite despondent. 'I haven't managed one yet.'

The rest of the party attempted to stifle their laughter as they began to realise that poor Culhwch was actually relating real events and that it wasn't just a tale to amuse them.

Arthur slung an arm around his cousin's shoulders and vowed to help him in his quest should he need it, suggesting that perhaps Merlin might be able to help. Culhwch gave him a lopsided grin as he thanked him.

'But now, cousin,' he said, 'tell me how you are progressing with your pilgrimage.'

Arthur's face darkened as he explained to him and Niel all the delays and troubles they had encountered since they'd left home. 'It looks as though this pilgrimage to visit the mosaic of Christ was doomed from the outset. In fact, if we don't continue our journey tomorrow, we will *never* make it for All Saints Day.

TWENTY-FIVE

Back at the inn, the ostler ran out and took the breathless horses away while we made our way inside. The innkeeper, bowing low to Salazar, also rushed off to set some food on the table for us. I was absolutely starving and hoped there was going to be plenty for all of us. There was!

We sat and ate in silence until both Kay and I leaned back in our chairs with happy, full-stomach grins on our faces. Bread and cheese is OK but not twice a day every day and both of us were sick of it. The roasted meat and vegetables had gone down a treat and the apple and blackberry pie, covered in fresh cream, was to die for. Cabby, too, was replete with what the innkeeper had given him and what we had thrown down from the table.

'There is no time to let your meal settle, Percy. We need to travel now. I have prepared everything we need in our room upstairs and so I will go and collect it, pay the innkeeper and leave. Please be ready to go as soon as I return.'

I had hoped to be able to rest for a bit but then, again, Merlin had need of me and from what I had seen of him - or his face at least - he was in a lot of trouble and it was imperative we leave as soon as we could.

The moon, a little more than three-quarters full, shone down on us through the trees as we left the hostelry and made our way south-east, lighting our path as clearly as if it were day. After walking for some half-hour, Salazar stopped and, beckoning us over to him, said we should now use the dragon's droppings and hope that we might all end up in Merlin's cave.

We huddled together and, checking that there was no wind to blow the dust away, Salazar threw it in the air; as it glittered down over us I was once again amused to think of

167

what exactly it was that was falling on our heads. My amusement, however, was short-lived; I had forgotten how quickly Merlin's magic worked.

Arriving with a flash of light, we stood blinking until our eyesight cleared. When it did, we couldn't believe our eyes. Merlin lay as still as death on a straw bed. His face was ashen and one arm, which had fallen out of the sleeve of his robe, was as thin and pale as a bleached stick. Even his eyebrows had turned from black to white. Closer inspection proved that he was breathing – just! All in all, he looked about a hundred years old and, possibly, on his deathbed.

'He couldn't die! He mustn't die,' I thought. Not only because I didn't want him to – life would be so empty without him – but I would also suffer the burden of not having said sorry to him for making fun of his singing. I know that in the whole scheme of things that my apology was the least important thing but it was something I still had to do.

'It would appear that we have arrived just in time,' Jasmine knelt down beside the sick – I hoped not dying – man. She gave many instructions to each of us and we ran about doing this and fetching that.

I had wondered why Salazar had needed to bring the bottle of green slime and the naiad root and stuff but, on inspecting the storerooms in Merlin's cave, it could be seen that something awful must have happened there. All the stoppers in the jars had crumbled and so the contents had rotted. Had that mad woman been able to get into Merlin's cave? It certainly looked as if she had.

Jasmine never left Merlin's side for a whole day and a whole night. She kept us filling bowls with as much icy water as we could manage, while she mopped his brow and neck to cool him down.

I wondered if she would remove his skullcap, as, perversely, I was dying to know if he had any hair under it, but she didn't touch it. I felt ashamed of myself but bad thoughts sometimes do intrude! Oh well! I don't suppose I shall ever know now.

Salazar left us on that first day. He told us that he needed to collect certain herbs and nuts to make a special brew to help Merlin recover. He had given instructions to Jasmine and she delegated tasks to us. We were only too happy to be busy as it took away the worry of what was happening to Merlin. Cabby had gone off with Salazar; he wasn't one to be confined for long and the out-doors always beckoned him. I can't say I was sorry, as I knew he would look after Salazar.

Poor Merlin, the first thing he saw when he finally regained his senses was the frightening face of Mordred peering into his. Growling, 'Mordred', he tried to reach up and grab him. Good job he was still so weak; a fit Merlin would have slain him in a split second.

'Merlin, Merlin,' Jasmine leaned over, laying another cool cloth on his brow, 'it's Kay! Come, now, you know what the mad woman has done. Try and think.'

He fell back down onto his bed, weak as a kitten, while his brow furrowed at the effort of remembering. He gave up; it was all too much for him and he closed his eyes again and drifted off.

Merlin was unconscious for much of that day and well into the evening, before Salazar and Cabal returned.

The African emptied the contents of all that he had collected onto the table and started to chop this and grind that, boil something else and mix it all together, softly muttering all the while as he did so.

As I had guessed it would, it smelt terrible, but then Merlin had always said that mild substances produced poor results whereas potent substances produced powerful results. In a slightly callous way, I was really eager to see what would happen when it was administered. This thought I kept strictly to myself!

Then the most amazing things started to happen.

First, Salazar took a small wooden bowl and poured the steaming, malodorous brew into it. If I didn't know that he was Merlin's friend, I would have thought that he was about to poison him. I watched intently as he put the potion in a bowl and, going over to Merlin, place it on the ground; he sat at the head of the bed and lifted the unconscious man into an upright position and, sitting behind him, propped him up and leaned him back against his chest. Once steady, he retrieved the bowl and, with Merlin's head leaning back on his shoulder, opened his mouth, poured the drink down his throat and clamped his lips together so that none was lost.

Nothing happened for a good twenty seconds and then, well you would have thought that all hell had broken loose. Merlin's eyes shot open, he arched his back, which I thought must surely break as he leaned back so far; and I thought then he must surely have been poisoned. I looked from him to Salazar and just couldn't make out what was happening. Salazar was holding on to Merlin with a grip of iron while his prisoner was thrashing about and trying to break free. He clawed at Salazar's hands, one of which was still clamped over his mouth, but to no avail. Unable to control himself, Cabal was barking like mad and running all over the place. No-one bothered to tell him to shut up as we were all concentrating on Merlin who, at that particular time was still so weak whereas Salazar was much too strong. The fight went on for about two minutes and then it was all over. Merlin collapsed and went completely limp.

Kay and I looked at each other, extremely worried, and then from Merlin to Salazar and Jasmine. Cabal was whining a little and licking Merlin's lifeless hand.

Jasmine spoke softly. 'He is not delirious any more, he is sleeping; but he's extremely weak even though his fever has now gone; also, I believe, so has whatever it was that had taken hold of him.' If he survives this night, he'll live.

I hung on to Cabby's neck for strength. *'If?'*

170

TWENTY-SIX

Rhianne was the first person to get up the following day. After having spent quite some time around the campfire the previous evening most of the party were pretty tired and not too keen to roll out of their beds. As a result, it was Sir Kay, limping from the wagon, who found her as she helped Old Molly prepare their breakfast.

'Good morning, sister,' he spoke gruffly.

'Kay, 'she turned and smiled up at him, 'how are you? Is your ankle any better?'

'Improving,' was his short reply.

He didn't appear to want to carry on with any more conversation and as the silence drew out it caused Rhianne to feel quite uncomfortable - Kay was usually a very affable young man. As the silence continued she tried desperately to think of something to say and was extremely grateful to be saved the trouble when Arthur strode up and, in greeting, clapped him on the back. Now, this would normally have done nothing more than cause an exchange of salutation, but not this time. Arthur did not see it but Rhianne was shocked when she saw a look of absolute hatred cross Sir Kay's face; it was swiftly masked but it had been there – she was certain. Was Kay ill or had he been bewitched. Whatever it was, she would make sure she would stay on her guard. Oh how she wished Percy was here. Had Cabal found him? Was he alright? Her stomach turned over as she thought of what might have happened to him. *'No,* she determined, *'I will not start to worry. I'll ask Arthur to let me pray with him and Brother Geraint for Percy's well-being and discovery.'*

During the course of the morning, as the party was breaking camp, the sun burst through the clouds; thus it was a happier band that set off again, skirting the edge of Glastonbury and onward to Hinton St. Mary, hoping that they would be able to travel on dryer ground than they had experienced so far.

They moved off at a fair pace, chatting happily to one another in the soft, warm sunshine, completely unaware of the band of small, animal-men who were hard on their heels, skipping along in the shadow of the undergrowth and trees that lined their route. Had they known this, would they have been quite so content?

'Granddad,' Ben interrupted Jack. 'Are they the, what do you call them? You know, those weird dog and cat faced dwarf-men.'

'Chimera,' Jack responded. 'Similar to the one that guarded the foot of the tower at the giant's castle. Well, that's what that type of being is called – something that's made up of two or more different types of animal. What this particular kind is actually called, I don't know.'

'But that's impossible, Daniel retorted. 'They're just a myth - unless that old witch had been experimenting!'

'Aren't all my stories myths?' Jack enquired, eyebrow raised and a small smile playing around his lips. 'Do dragon's really exist then? And what about the Faerie? Or Merlin?'

'Yes, well no, hmm I don't know,' Ben answered. 'They are stories but they seem so real! I don't know.'

'Me neither,' added Daniel. 'But carry on, granddad.'

Sir Niel and Arthur rode along at the head of the party as they continued on their way towards Hinton St. Mary. Rhianne and Culhwch rode just in front of the first wagon and Shake Spear and Brosc brought up the rear. They rode at an easy pace, knowing that in the long run they would cover more ground; travelling at speed tired horses and men alike, so apart from the sound of soft conversations drifting on the breeze, the thud and clop of horses hooves on grass and

172

stones and the crunching of wagon wheels it was, to them, peaceful and serene as they journeyed along.

Now, as everyone knows, Shake Spear has extreme shortsightedness and has had to promise, in the past, not to actually attack during any sort of confrontation with the enemy. Too many times have his own men found themselves being chased by a large maniacal warrior wielding a spear or an axe, only being saved by shouting at the top of their lungs who they were. But so it is with most people who suffer with their sight that they are blessed in other ways, like a good sense of smell or extremely acute hearing – and this was the case right now.

'Can you hear anything, Brosc?'

'Eh?'

'I can hear rustling in the trees!'

'Can't hear anything! Trees do rustle though, don't they?'

'They do, Brosc, but normally it's when they *have* leaves and not only have most of the leaves fallen off them at this time of year but there is no wind; not even a breeze.'

They rode on in silence for some ten minutes or so, all the while Shake Spear listening very acutely to every odd sound. Brosc, who used his sense of sight more than sound, found his eyes swivelling this way and that on the lookout for he knew not what but all the while feeling very uncomfortable indeed.

Even so, Shake Spear, along with all the others, were taken completely off guard when at least two dozen of those fearsome creatures came running, some barking and howling, some hissing, some snapping at the heels of the ponies and others making a grab for their legs. The ponies reared, the men shouted and panic ensued before Arthur and Niel drew their swords and rushed back into the melee to protect the ladies.

Culhwch had already drawn his sword and was valiantly defending Rhianne. He had managed to place her between himself and the side of the wagon, urging her to try and jump

173

off her horse and into it. 'It is a safer place up there, my lady, than having these little monsters biting your legs. Go on, jump; I'll hold your horse still.'

Niel shouted at the men to climb onto the wagons.

Tailor, on foot and still suffering the effects of weakness from a broken arm from his previous encounter with the Cyclops, courageously fought off the attackers using his sword in his left hand and kicking out at them with his feet. He kicked one under its neck and it ran off holding a slack and dangling lower jaw; another managed to bite right through the toe of his boot but as the boots had always been too big – they were Sir Ector's cast-offs – he was untouched and the animal was then at Tailor's mercy, not being able to dislodge his teeth from the encompassing leather. He swung his sword and the flat of it hit the chimera on the head, felling him with that one blow – this seemed to do the trick and the chimera slid off his foot. Tailor had a moment's respite and, looking round, could see that all of them had at least two, if not three, of those dwarf-animals attacking them.

The chimeras seemed to have no fear. Sir Niel, side by side with Arthur, had slain three of the beasts and was almost being drawn from Arthur's side, when he remembered that that was probably what they wanted him to do. *'No,'* he thought, *'I have to remain at his side.'.*

Then they heard the scream! It was one of those blood-curdling screams that, even with all the noise of battle, makes itself heard over and above all else, apart from making the hair stand up at the back of your head.

They, and their adversaries, suddenly stopped and those fiends that were able rushed off into the forest, dragging their dead and injured comrades with them, and within seconds were gone, as if they had never been there at all.

The party of friends might have believed that they hadn't, been there at all if it weren't for a couple of chimeras that still

174

lay on the ground, one of which was obviously dead, the other twitching violently and swivelling its head from dog to cat.

They rushed over to where the scream had come from and saw what Rhianne was pointing at. Sir Kay was riding into the forest at full tilt with Lady Elise held in front of him.

'Oh, Rhianne, what on earth are you yelling for,' asked Arthur. 'It's only Kay, and he probably wanted to take mother away from the danger. He'll be back soon when he knows it's all OK. Don't worry, Rhianne.' He held up his hand to stop her from saying any more. 'We have to sort out what is going on here and see if anyone is hurt. Please don't worry. They'll be back soon, never fear.'

Walking away, leaving Rhianne very troubled indeed, Arthur went round to all the men and wagons to make sure everything was in order. There were one or two scratches and bruises and the ponies were extremely jumpy but apart from that everything appeared to be fine.

'See if you can find out how these creatures work. Find the one that's unconscious and tie it up securely,' he instructed his men. 'What are they and where do they come from; why are they here and why have they attacked us?'

'But there aren't any here,' Brosc stated. 'They've disappeared! Magic!'

It was true! Every single one of them had gone. Vanished! After searching around for a good few minutes all they found were heel tracks in the mud where the dead or unconscious animals had been dragged away. Now, who had done that?

'We can't depart until Kay and mother return,' remarked Rhianne, once more throwing the cloak of misery over the rest of the gathering, not only for the fact that Lady Elise was still missing but also that time was now running out. It looked, to Arthur, as though they would never complete their pilgrimage.

175

TWENTY-SEVEN

'Salazar,' Merlin whispered hoarsely.

'My friend, how are you?' the African replied, lifting him gently by the shoulders and propping him up with many cushions.

'You have saved me. I don't know how to thank you. I was so weak that that mad woman tricked me. She almost had me, you know. She has become quite powerful. But I managed to get away. I was able to immerse myself in water – something that she does not like – and so she couldn't get to me. I got away. I spoke to Percival and Cabal through that same medium but I was so weak; I don't know if they understood me.' His voice became croaky and started to break up.

'Don't speak now,' Jasmine interrupted him, 'but drink this and sleep. When you awake you will be almost like your old self. It will then take merely days to regain all of your strength.'

'One thing,' he was insistent. 'You must send Percy to find Mab and retrieve my staff. If I don't have it I cannot function properly. It is part of me and I must have it.'

'Can the mad woman use it against you?' Salazar enquired.

'Good gracious, no,' Merlin replied. 'It is useless to her but she knows it is not useless to me. Do this for me, Salazar, and then I am in your debt forever.'

'I will – now drink!'

So it was, that after all my efforts to escape, I now had to put myself in the way of being captured again. Life seems extremely unfair at times. Jasmine had given me a draught that I was to drink when I came in sight of the giant's castle. It would look like I was delirious and had ridden onto his land by accident. We had discussed various ways of me getting back in – drain the pool again and get in that way, but then I would be locked in the dungeon: so that obviously was no good. Try and find a way in without being detected – the walls were too high and I couldn't open the door by myself it was too heavy. It looked hopeless.

'Why can't I do what I did before and go in through the Glass?' I asked.

'No,' Merlin replied. 'She will be ready for that one and will have put up some sort of alarm system to alert her of someone coming in through the ether. Once you are detected, you'd really be for it. We can only use something more than once if she is not involved. However, we can send you and the pony through the Glass to a place nearby, so that you don't have to travel too far.

Thus it was that Salazar came up with the plan of me being ill, barely conscious and thus not a threat; they might leave me alone if that were the case so that once the draught had worn off – and he assured me that it would leave no after effects – I could escape within the castle and try to find Merlin's staff. Like the trusting soul I was I agreed, but had completely forgotten to ask how I might get out once I had achieved my goal.

'Can I take Cabal with me? I enquired.

Merlin thought about this and said he would give me an answer on the morrow. For now, I was to study the Glass and see if I could find out where his staff was hidden. Everyone was told to be extremely quiet, first, so that I could concentrate on my task but, secondly, and more importantly, as sound might travel through it, the mad witch was not to be alerted to our presence.

Merlin, who still looked so drained of strength and appeared very old – and I made sure my mental barrier was up as I thought this terrible and discourteous thought - drifted back to sleep and Cabal, not having much else to do, wandered off to search down the many tunnels leading from the main chamber. Salazar sat cross-legged against the far wall and, to all intents and purposes, appeared to be asleep but, as he advised us later, he was not; it took a lot of concentration to put a really decent spell together. Jasmine was nowhere to be seen but appeared much later with some food.

I also sat cross-legged on a large cushion in front of the Glass and stared. Trying to concentrate on the giant's castle, I let my mind dwell on the main hall. I obviously didn't want to think of the tower or the dungeon and didn't really need to. I knew those places very well and Merlin's staff was definitely not there.

As I concentrated I saw the far door open and Olwen come into the room. She looked extremely sad as she walked over to where her father sat dozing in the large armchair. She sat down and stared into the blazing fire. Quite some time elapsed before a log, collapsing into the flames, disturbed the giant who awoke with a snort.

'Ah, my dear,' he spoke gently to the girl, 'how is our guest?'

'Mab?

He nodded.

'She is a very angry woman, father. I don't know how she managed to get away from that water sprite but she now has a very swollen ankle: I think it's infected. She managed to stop the bleeding by tearing off and wrapping some of her petticoat around it but when I offered to clean it she threw the jug of water at me and asked if I was completely insane.'

The giant almost controlled a smirk. 'I think I shall make her a visit,' he decided.

I continued to peer into the Glass as the giant pulled himself up from his chair and lumbered out of the room. I followed as he disappeared through the huge doorway, across a vestibule and then up an oversized stairway. As he turned a corner at the top of the stair, he made his way down a short corridor, through a door directly facing him and into the room where Mad Mab was ranting at Pos and Neg. They, for their part, looked blankly ahead.

'Ysbaddaden,' she yelled, 'where have you been? I've been stuck here for hours with no-one, NO-ONE, bothering to see if I'm in need of anything. How could you treat me so? You should know that I'll be the ruler of all Britain one day and will repay those who are completely and absolutely loyal to me.' She screwed up her eyes as she stared at him. 'Do you possibly think you might come into that category?' she screeched again.

'Madam,' he bowed. 'I am here now! Your wish is my command. What is it you desire?'

'Desire? DESIRE?' she bellowed. 'You know nothing about desire. We are not talking about desire here, we're talking about obedience and service to me.

There was silence for a while – well, if you can call her breathing lungsful of air in an out of her nostrils "silence". Eventually, as it became clear to her that the giant would not take the bait and retaliate to her goading, she asked him to arrange to collect and deliver to her certain herbs and the like so that she could make a poultice for her throbbing ankle.

'I have made a list,' she spluttered, trying to keep her temper under control – a very hard job at the best of times but in her sorry and painful state almost impossible. 'And, just in case you have difficulty in deciphering it, I shall read it out to you. So, if you *dare* get it wrong it will be the worse for you!'

She read it out to the giant and I wondered if I should try and remember just what it was.

Just then I became aware that Merlin stood beside me watching over my shoulder what was happening in the Glass.

'Ha!' he cried, 'she's trying that old remedy is she? Well, I think I know what we can now do!'

I looked up and almost fell off my cushion. Merlin stood there, tall and young; white eyebrows with that satirical slant to them once more marvellously restored to jet black set over sparkling eyes, and sallow completion completely gone. He was slimmer but looked the picture of health. Salazar's remedy was obviously extremely potent. 'It had to be exactly the right mixture, otherwise it would have definitely killed me,' Merlin later explained. 'That was probably why I tried to fight against it when Salazar administered it to me. I can remember that it had the most bitter and rancid taste of anything that has ever passed my lips,' he said, grimacing.

'Merlin,' I whispered, turning to face him, 'I really must apologise,' I started to say, remembering how rude I had been when he had said he was going to sing, all those many weeks ago.

'Apology accepted,' he interrupted me, flippantly.

I felt quite put out and wanted to let him know why I was apologising and needed to know that he really did forgive me; I had certainly been carrying my guilt around with me as an extremely heavy load for so long. 'But you don't know what I'm apologising for,' I started to say.

'Percy, Percy,' he cooed, 'I know everything I need to know and I know *you*! You've suffered enough just thinking about it over the past few weeks. Right?'

'Right,' I agreed.

'So come, Percy, let's eat – I'm absolutely ravenous. No, you don't have to worry any more about the staff, I know exactly where she's put it. My, I feel absolutely marvellous! Salazar, my friend, I am in your debt. You will have to tell me how you combined what it was you gave me. I was at death's door and I'm sure that the mad woman must think that I've not just reached it but have by now gone skipping through it. Well, she's in for a surprise, eh?'

We sat and ate all the wonderful food that Jasmine had prepared for us. I must admit that I, too, was famished. The

180

food I'd been given when we first escaped had only whetted my appetite and I thought I could now eat a horse. As we got near the end of our meal, Merlin outlined the plan that had been taking shape in his mind.

'Percy, you will still have to go to the giant's castle but you won't need to drug yourself now.'

I hadn't even been aware that I would need to!

'However, as you know, he has bad eyesight and once you are washed and dressed in different clothes, he won't recognise you – all servants look the same to him, just dressed differently for the jobs they are required to do. We'll dress you as a merchant and when you arrive you are to tell him that the witch had sent out a message through her secret crystal.'

'I didn't know about that,' I replied.

'Neither did I,' Merlin replied winking at me. 'Perhaps she has one; perhaps she doesn't! Anyway, the message told someone in her castle to put some ingredients together for the potion she needed for her leg. You are merely the messenger making the delivery. Hopefully, you won't have to take it to the witch but should that look likely, take some dragon's droppings with you so you can escape. I am very low on supplies of it and can only really spare enough to sprinkle once on you and my staff, but if you have to escape, well please feel free to use it. I hope you won't have to as it would mean you'd end up back here and that would set us all back but I suppose it's better to be safe than sorry. We'd then have to think up something else. I reckon that it'll all work out as the giant needs to get himself back into the witch's good books and he'd like to get all the thanks for it himself.

'Right, Percy, now to show you where my staff has been hidden.' Merlin walked over to the Glass and asked me to concentrate on the tower where Kay and I were first incarcerated. The tower slowly came into view until it was clear to both Merlin and me. Kay had wandered across and was watching the Glass over my other shoulder and asked Merlin how this magic was done.

'Kay, my man, you are seeing something here that mere man would give his eye teeth to see,' he replied. 'Make the most of it and enjoy, as once you leave my cave you will completely forget everything you saw within it!' Merlin's face screwed up in perplexity as he looked, once again, at the figure of Mordred, who was really Sir Kay. 'You will have to refresh my memory as to how you look like you do, Kay. Perhaps once we have located my staff in this Glass, eh?

'Right, Percy, set the scene in the Glass so we can see you opening the door in the tower and moving down the staircase.'

The hair on my neck stood out straight as I thought of what was lying in wait for me at the foot of the stairs.

'What's up, Percy?' Merlin asked.

'There is a guardian to the tower at the foot of the staircase, Merlin. It will attack me! Well, I know it won't attack me just viewing it in this Glass but if I am to go there to retrieve your staff, it will attack.'

'Then let us go and look, boy!'

We watched as we viewed the staircase, gliding down quite quickly over the gigantic steps. Eventually reaching the foot of the stairs, we searched the floor for the dual-headed dwarf but it was nowhere in sight. Believing it may have been taken away I heaved a sigh of relief and, at Merlin's instruction, looked for the place behind the stairwell where he was certain the staff had been hung from the low ceiling. Sure enough, it was there.

'Why can't I just travel there right now through the Glass, retrieve your staff and bring it back by throwing dragon's droppings over me?' I asked him.

'You will just bounce off the barrier that Mab has put up – you can just see it quivering around the sides of the Glass. She is bound to have put up a really strong one around the entrance point so as to protect my staff. If you hit that obstacle and bounce off, well, you might end up anywhere. Can't chance it, I'm afraid. No, you will just have to get into the tower by a more normal route.'

It was then we heard a low growling and, looking down, saw that awful apparition staring at us from the shadow of the stairwell. It knew we were there, somewhere, and looking at it but it wasn't sure where or what we were. Thank goodness it couldn't get through the Glass to us as the Glass only went one way. Somehow, it was aware of us as could be seen by the hair on its head standing out making it look twice its size, before swivelling its head round, hoping to see us more clearly using its cats eyes.

'Well, Merlin,' I stammered, 'you can now see the guardian of the tower and what I have to get past to retrieve your staff.'

'Hmm,' was all he said as he stroked his chin. Finally, 'Stop looking, Percy.'

As I did so, the picture faded and the Glass clouded over.

Turning and walking back into the centre of the chamber, Merlin called Kay over to him and they sat for a half-hour or so while Kay told him what had happened to him since he had left his father's side. Merlin did not say anything but let him tell his story uninterrupted. When he finally stopped talking, Merlin nodded and asked him to show him his right hand. As he did so, Merlin took hold of it and then whooped with laughter.

'What's so funny, Merlin? he asked him, slightly affronted at his disrespect.

'Look!' he chuckled. 'See your right index finger is missing?'

'Yes, I can see that,' he responded.

'Feel it!'

'Feel it?'

'Yes, feel it!'

183

Kay touched his right index finger and whipped his hand back as though electrocuted. 'The finger is there,' he whispered, shocked. 'Even though I can't see it, it's there! I've not noticed that before!'

'Exactly,' crowed Merlin. 'You are who you say you are. You are Kay and although we, and you apparently, see Mordred, the spell is on us and not you! When anyone looks at you they all see what that mad witch wants them to see and in this case she wants us to see Mordred. Even you see yourself reflected in a mirror as Mordred. But you are not Mordred. The proof is in your finger which we can all feel though not see.'

I was at that moment having a go myself and couldn't believe that I could feel a finger where I couldn't see one.

'But if I am Kay and look like Mordred, why has Mab done this? Unless I am mistaken,' the thought suddenly hit him, 'she's probably sent Mordred to kill Arthur and has made him look like me.'

'Yes,' Merlin responded, suddenly becoming quite sober, 'that is the worry.

'Well, the sooner I get my staff back, the better, I say. Percy, come here. Let's get you dressed up as a merchant and be ready to send you on your way. Salazar,' he called, 'please make ready the healthiest pony we have. Jasmine, do you have the ingredients for Percy to take to Mab? Good,' he said as he handed this to me.

'But you can't mean to send me back to that weird-headed monster?' I cried.

'Monster? It's no monster, Percy; it's merely a dwarf with an animal's head.'

'Not just any animal, Merlin – it's savage!'

'Oh, OK, Percy, I'll sort it out for you. Look, here's some naiad root – BUT, whatever you do, don't get it in a muddle with the dragon's droppings. Throw the root over yourself and you could end up completely mad if not dead!

'Don't worry – now that we have seen the inside of the giant's castle and some of the other rooms, we know where you'll be and I will look in on you from time to time through the Glass. However, I have lots to do, with potions to mix and spells to look up and much of this and that, so try to look after yourself, Percy; I can't keep an eye on you all the time. You must have learned something from me by now?'

I stowed the potions away on my person and put the ingredients that I had to hand over to the giant into the saddle bags. Salazar saddled the pony and Jasmine made sure I had everything I needed for the journey. They lifted me up and seated me on the saddle, fitting my feet into the stirrups. Merlin instructed me to seek the fields outside the giant's castle as he sat me on the pony before the Glass. Like a dreaded trip to the dentists, they came into view more quickly than I had hoped.

Things were definitely moving a little too fast for my liking and it was with absolutely no time to complain that I found myself riding out under a sky not only heavy with clouds but also with foreboding. *'OK Mab, here I come'*, I thought despondently with my barriers up. *And I haven't even got Cabal with me.'* Then feeling very sorry for myself, *'Merlin, how could you do this to me?'*

TWENTY-EIGHT

'Well, Kay, you can slow down now,' Lady Elise told him. 'Those creatures are nowhere to be seen.'

Kay either didn't hear or decided to ignore her as he let the horse have its head and just carry on in the direction it had been travelling for the past half-hour.

'Kay,' she spoke again, a little more forcefully. 'Please stop; I am feeling quite unwell.'

'We have only a short way to go to a hostelry I know of and then you can rest. Be patient.'

'Are you ill, Kay? Your voice sounds very tight!'

'Stop fussing and let me concentrate on my riding.'

She was taken aback by the brusqueness of his reply but nonetheless decided for the moment to hold her tongue and wait and see what happened when they stopped at the inn. She thought he must be unwell or something and just wanted to get to his destination so that he could then rest.

They rode on for a further hour and then quite suddenly turned out of a copse of trees and started to slow down as they approached a very imposing castle. Lady Elise was a little surprised at what stood in front of her but more than that felt a slight twinge of trepidation.

'Where are we, son?' she enquired.

'You will see,' he replied none too politely.

'Take me back to Arthur,' she demanded in a voice that quavered only very slightly. Then, with many legs, fear suddenly pounced upon her and began to crawl along her skin and up through her scalp.

He did not reply but rode up to the castle door and pulled a huge ring attached to the wall. Nothing could be heard from outside the castle but before long a smaller door within the main gates opened and a tattooed man stood there and stared at them. He retreated through the door and within a minute or two one of the large gates opened enough for them to pass through on the horse. It closed behind them with a clang.

Lady Elise shivered – this boded ill.

Kay dismounted and helped Lady Elise from the horse. He took her, none too gently, by the elbow and marched her toward a doorway leading, she believed, into the main hall. Once inside, her knees buckled, almost making her fall to the ground. She would have, if Kay had still not held her by her arm.

'What is this place?' she whispered. 'Everything is so big!'

Just then the tattooed man returned with a pale version of himself and they ushered their guests out of the room and up a flight of stairs. After going through a door at the end of the passageway, they found themselves before a frightful woman of dishevelled appearance who was sitting on a wooden settle with one bandaged foot resting on a stool.

The woman cooed at them, 'My love, you have returned.'

Lady Elise thought the woman must be delirious, as she had never seen her before in her life. Was she talking to her or to Kay or maybe someone behind them, she thought, turning round to look? She was about to open her mouth and say something but, looking up at Kay, was astounded to notice a sickly smile playing about his mouth, as though he thought very highly of this woman or, indeed – and this made the bile rise in her throat – even loved her! *'Not my son,'* she shivered. *'Not with her!'*

'Bring her over to me,' she demanded.

Kay took the lady's elbow, once again, and alternately pushed and dragged her over to the woman. Now, the bile did threaten as Lady Elise took her first whiff of fragrance from this sorry excuse for a woman lying there in front of her. *'What an awful smell! Does she not wash?* She noticed the grime, not only on her clothes but also on her face and arms as well – and her hair! Well, that was a sight to behold –

187

mainly stuck like glue to her head with frizz at the ends, as though she had been struck by lightening. Her dress showed, a little round the hem but mainly around the waist – what waist there was of this dumpy woman - that it had once been blue. Perhaps she had been caught in the rain and it had got wet! Altogether, she was a mess – not a lady at all.

Little did Lady Elise know, but Mad Mab had been following a little of what she had been thinking, albeit a bit sketchy. However, what did come across to her was the fact that if she were to achieve what she was planning to do, she would have to disguise her smell. *'Well, I am certainly not going to wash,'* she thought. Frowning as she did so – and thus causing Lady Elise more concern for herself – she rummaged through her brain to remember the right concoction or spell she would need to disguise it. Suddenly remembering, her expression cleared and she clicked her fingers with glee.

'It's all beginning to come together, Mordred,' she exclaimed.

Poor Elise thought that that must be the name of one of the tattooed men as apart from them, herself, Sir Kay and the woman, there was no-one else in the room.

'Go get me the special wine, Mordred, and we will drink a toast to our venture.'

You can imagine Lady Elise's surprise and shock when she saw her son leave the room at this woman's bidding, as though he knew his way.

'Mordred?' she enquired.

'Ah, yes,' she responded, 'you have no idea, have you?' Her lips twitched and then, once more unable to control herself, she went off into peals of laughter, slapping her thigh and wiping tears from her eyes, leaving the inevitable track marks down her face. Every time she was controlled enough to see the confused look on her guest's face, it sent her off into more fits of laughter so that it was relief when she was

188

able to stop – the stitch in her side causing her a lot of discomfort. However, she believed it was the best laugh she'd had since before the damage to her foot – the thought of which sobered her up very quickly.

'Oh, that's better,' she sighed when she had finally ceased that maniacal madness. 'Yes, my dear,' she continued, 'you certainly have no idea. So, being the kind person I am, I shall enlighten you. But, I am a poor hostess, you must be dry!'

Sir Kay had by then returned to the room with a silver tray holding three goblets and a jug of wine. He placed the tray onto a small table beside Mab and she poured. Holding out a goblet to Lady Elise, who did not accept it, she assured her that they would all be drinking the same wine.

'Here, take it,' she held it out to her. 'Take it and I will drink as well; yes, and so will Mor …er, Sir Kay.'

She watched as the mad woman and Sir Kay lifted their goblets in a toast to everyone's health; they drained their glasses in one go. Feeling a little assured, she raised her goblet to her lips and took a sip. After swallowing it she became aware that her companions were both looking at her very intently.

'What is the matter?' she asked.

They carried on watching her.

She put the goblet down on the tray and it was only then, as she straightened, that the first wave of wooziness hit her. She clutched at the edge of the table to steady herself as her knees buckled under her and Kay, all solicitous, helped her into a chair.

'There, my dear,' cooed the woman, 'that's better isn't it?

'Whaas hap-pening?' Lady Elise croaked; it was extremely hard to talk and difficult to move. Her limbs were heavy and didn't respond to her thoughts and it was becoming increasingly hard to stay awake.

'No, don't sleep yet, my dear,' the woman shouted at her through the cotton wool that was enveloping her head. 'You

189

need to know how ingenious I am and yes, the potion was placed only in your goblet - before the tray was brought in! But now, look at Sir Kay,' she demanded.

The lady looked up at her son and was terrified by what she saw. His body shape kept changing backwards and forwards in waves from her lovely son to a stranger – a thick and ugly, shaven-headed man with a mean and spiteful look about him.

Mab was finding it increasingly difficult to keep herself in check. Never far from the edge, she just loved it when others saw her talent; she adored bathing in their surprise.

'And now you wonder why I need you here. No, no - I can see it in your eyes, I don't want to ransom you like I tried to do with Rhianne to get Arthur to come to me. No, not at all! I want your body! Yes, like I've used Kay's body! No, your suspicions were quite correct, this isn't your son at all; it's my beloved Mordred. But now, you will sleep, and you will dream because you will know that Mordred and I, looking to everyone who meets us like you and Sir Kay, are going to meet up again with Arthur. I shall leave it to your dream's imagination as to what we will do to him – and dream you will – awful, horrendous dreams that might even send you mad – mad for the short life you have left! Oh, how great, how absolutely magnificent I am.' She had, by then, got to the point where she couldn't contain herself any longer and fell back against her cushions, gasping for air and cackling uncontrollably as poor Elise fell into the nightmarish half-world that Mab had prepared for her.

'Come, Mordred, my love,' she spoke when she had finally got herself under control, 'help me up. I must find the infusion and spells to heal this ankle of mine and exchange my looks with the lady. She had the audacity to say that I have an unpleasant odour. Be that as it may, I will need to disguise it if I do and make myself smell like her, especially if that dog is with them! You can't fool canines with their extra-sensory abilities, you know. Let us hurry; Arthur can wait for a while but he won't wait forever.'

Ysbaddaden sat in on their scheming and brewing, adding his two-pennyworth when he thought it was needed or even when he thought it was not. He had to be satisfied with Mab's word that she would bring back Culhwch with Arthur, so that he could dispose of him, too. He was still wary of the witch; he knew she could do awful things to him with her sorcery and potions but he was equally certain that, if the time came and he was able to catch her unawares, he could crush her quite speedily under just one foot.

'I will send my daughter away at that time. I don't want her to think me an ogre!' he stated.

'Hmm! Perish the thought,' Mab responded dryly.

They were all very busy.

And so it was that two days later a tired but determined Mordred and a repaired Mab, in their new guises, set off to rejoin the party of pilgrims headed for Hinton St. Mary; Pos and Neg followed but kept well out of sight.

TWENTY-NINE

How was I to know that I would arrive at the castle gates minutes after Mab and Mordred had left? Was that good planning, just luck or a bad thing? I shall never know. If I had seen them I might have gone straight up to them, thinking they were my friends, and thus giving myself away. It might have stopped them from joining Arthur's party though. Or would it? It would more than likely have confirmed their new identities if I had thought them my friends. As it is, I reckon all right things work together for good, even though it doesn't seem like it at the time. So far as I knew, Mab was still inside the castle nursing her bad ankle and I had the remedy in my saddlebags. I knew nothing about Mordred and Lady Elise arriving there nor had I any idea of the giant or the witch's evil plans.

Blissfully unaware of all these facts I turned and rode towards the castle.

Stopping just inside a copse of trees that overlooked the castle, I sat beside a stream for an hour or so, eating the food that Jasmine had prepared for me. I really didn't want to go on but was acutely aware that the minutes were ticking by and I had a very important quest - I had to retrieve Merlin's staff.

Trying not to think of where that staff lay, I took my courage in my hands and mounted the pony, all the while wishing I were somewhere else.

Meanwhile, some while later, Mab and Mordred, out of sight of Arthur and his party, doubled up on one horse; it would have looked suspicious if they arrived on more than the one they had originally left with; they tied the other to a tree for either Pos or Neg to retrieve as they followed or for an extra one for themselves if it was needed.

As it turned out, Rhianne and the others joyfully received them as they rode into their midst and they were soon sitting round a roaring campfire and eating supper. On being asked why they had ridden off and where they had been for the last couple of days, Kay merely said that he thought it was safest as those little monsters looked as though they might do a lot of damage and he couldn't take that chance with mother. They had rested up at an inn and, as could be seen, mother's health had improved no end.

It seemed to do the trick as the questions soon dried up.

It had to be said that Lady Elise looked really happy! The smile she had worn as they rode into the camp never left her face. Unfortunately, everyone was so taken up with their return, fussing around them and making sure they were well fed and comfortable, noticing only their smiles, that they never once looked into her eyes – eyes that would always be cold and calculating, evil and remorseless and completely without pity.

At Lady Elise's suggestion, they all had an early night. 'We can make a good start tomorrow to make up for lost time.'

They agreed and very soon soft snores – and a few loud ones, along with other less flattering sounds – floated on the air around the camp.

Mab lay awake in her wagon for quite a long time feeling very pleased indeed with herself. Once she was sure everyone was fast asleep she sat up and whispered a spell – it woke up the sleeping Hellion, who, at her bidding, flew silently around overhead for most of the night, breathing out smoke that turned into clinging smog. He flew for as long as Mab whispered her chant and when she considered it thick enough she stopped and rested. Hellion flew off to his lair until such time as she needed him again.

'That mist will hang around all day tomorrow,' she thought. *'Enough time to put my plan into action.'* Lying

down, she drifted off to sleep with a very satisfied smile on her lips.

'Mother, are you awake?' Arthur called from outside the wagon. 'We seem to have a terrible fog this morning and until it lifts we are stuck here.' He started his pacing up and down outside her wagon; shoulders slumped as he thought about this further interruption to their pilgrimage.

There was much rustling as faces peeped out of tents and blankets, eyes blinking at the all-encompassing mist. Old Molly had somehow managed to get a fire going and was struggling to bring a cauldron of porridge that she'd suspended over it to the boil.

'Oh how frustrating, Arthur,' his mother replied, merely sticking her head out of the wagon flap. 'Well, as there is now no immediate hurry to get going, would you ask Kay to bring me some of that porridge and then I'll get up?'

He thought it a bit weird that she wanted Kay, rather than Rhianne, to bring her the porridge but, nevertheless, did as he was bid.

Taking the bowl of steaming porridge to his mother, Kay disappeared into the wagon and stayed there until Lady Elise had apparently finished it. This was another weird thing that Arthur didn't really take on board at the time. Lady Elise alighted from her bed and joined them all some half-hour after Kay had returned with the empty bowl.

'Well, this is a to do, eh?' Lady Elise commented, as she pushed her way through to get close to the fire. Warming her hands, she asked if any of them had any idea what they should now do.

'No,' moaned Arthur, close to tears. 'We appear to have been cursed. If it's not one thing going wrong then something else goes wrong. Why?' he cried. We need to move now if we are to reach Hinton St. Mary before All

194

Saints Day. I don't know what to do. Do you have any suggestions?'

'Well, I don't suppose it will do any good crying over spilt milk. We shall just have to try and go on. But then, I do have a compass,' she smiled. 'Perhaps we can still go on our pilgrimage using it to guide us.'

'A compass, mother?' cried Arthur, his face lighting up. 'I've heard of them but never seen one. Oh, please get it and show me.'

She returned to her wagon and retrieved it, showing them all how it worked.

'It is a wonder,' Shake Spear exclaimed as he watched the arrow point in the same direction whichever way the compass was moved. 'An absolute miracle!'

'Cosmic,' Brosc agreed.

'Then we can still continue our journey,' Arthur grinned, all gloom forgotten. 'Thank you, mother; you're wonderful.'

'You are more than welcome.'

'So, then, let's get packed up and proceed. Come on men, hurry.'

Kay and the lady looked over at one another and a crafty smile twisted the corners of Elise's mouth. *This is going to be easier than I had thought. But then, of course, it would be – is there anyone as talented as me? Merlin – I bet you wish you had lived to see my triumph! Hmm, perhaps I should have kept him alive to see it! He would really have appreciated my victory.'*

Mordred smiled back at her but had no idea what was going through her mind. He did not have the gift. He wouldn't have understood even if he did; she had managed to put her barriers up as she thought it – just in case anyone in the party did have the gift.

THIRTY

As I came out of the trees and stood just above the slope, looking down at the giant's castle, all seemed serene. From here it didn't look oversized; it simply looked nearer than it actually was. How I wished I didn't have to go down there.

Swallowing a few times in order to clear the dryness in my throat, I swung the pony's head around and set him to walk, slowly, I must admit, towards those imposing gates. I wondered if Pos or Neg would answer when I pulled the ring beside the door. I believed that the giant wouldn't remember me now that I was dressed in a completely different set of clothes but I had no illusion as to those Paisley men. They definitely wouldn't forget me. If Olwen answered the door she might possibly urge me to depart; she seemed a sweet-tempered young woman. I doubted whether Mab would answer the door - she was much too lazy. It could be Mordred! Oh well, that would be something I'd need to address when and if it happened. I would just have to keep myself completely ready to kick the pony into action and gallop away as fast as I could.

As it was, I needn't have feared. I was just about to reach for the bell pull when a voice behind me - and I must admit I almost jumped out of my skin – asked if I were the new kitchen boy.

'Of course you are,' he continued, not leaving me any time to respond. 'Has your old master lent you his pony? Well, he must have thought highly of you,' be blabbered on. 'Get down and I'll take you through to the stables and then we'll go round to the kitchens.

'My name's Cornek, by the way; I'm the *old* kitchen boy now that you're here; I'll be moving up to do vegetables. That's a very important job, you know, and if I do it well enough I shall move up again if they get another new kitchen

196

boy, 'cos that's the way it works. If that happens, then you'll be on vegetables. What do you think of that then?' he puffed out his chest at his vast knowledge of the ways of a castle. 'What's your name?'

He just about gave me enough time to tell him that I was called Jack – I was certainly not going to let anyone know that Percy was here - a new name to him he told me, before he launched into the next load of data detailing the ways and workings of an important person's residence. While he talked I looked around at the castle. I needed to find a possible way of escape should it be needed in a hurry. There were quite a few places; I expect the giant didn't need to have the walls completely secured – he had enough places of confinement inside the castle that one would not readily be able to escape from to worry about every nook and cranny.

I told the boy, and boy he was – not much older than me, I thought, that I was to let my pony loose as it would find its own way home, so to take me to the kitchens direct. I tried to mind speak to the animal and tell him to move over to the copse of trees on the rise and wait for me there. He looked at me but I wasn't sure he understood. Oh well, that was something I would have to hope had happened and, if it did, I thought I might try and take it further once I escaped – if I escaped!

Cornek took me through to the kitchens but there was no-one there.

'Cook must be sorting out some meat for the master,' he said as he grabbed a cake for himself and, thrusting it in my hand, one for me. 'Eat it before she comes back,' he spluttered, almost choking on the crumbs as he rammed almost the whole cake into his mouth. Didn't they get fed?

I quickly thrust it in my pocket; I was still too nervous to even think of eating.

'Who's this,' a voice spoke from the doorway behind us. Another skin-shedding experience I thought, as I once again

197

jumped into the air. I knew who it was even before I turned around.

'It's the new kitchen boy, master,' Cornek replied as he swivelled round to face the giant. 'I was just looking for cook so she could meet him but she must be out getting meat for your pie. She wasn't here when we ...'

'Silence!' He held up his hand as he gave this order.

Cornek shut his mouth in obedience. I quaked.

The giant looked at me and I was extremely relieved that he didn't appear to recognise me.

'I'm sorry, sir,' I stammered, 'but I am not the new kitchen boy!'

I reckon Cornek must have been extremely disappointed by the news that he was now not to be elevated to the supreme position of vegetable boy but he appeared to retain his sunny disposition.

'So – are you trying to deceive us then?' he demanded.

'Oh no, sir,' I stammered, shaking my head.

'Then just who are you?'

'I've brought some ingredients for Mab,' I stuttered, rapidly starting to cower under that unsettlingly uneven gaze.

'Well, you're too late. She's gone! *And* she didn't say anything about anyone coming with ingredients.' He was now looking at me extremely suspiciously.

Oh great, Merlin, I thought. *'Didn't see this one coming, did you?'* I had to think very fast or I might end up as the main ingredient for his pie or as dinner for the chimera.

Keeping my fears under control, and thinking as quickly as I could – completely forgetting Mab's supposed secret crystal - told him that she had sent a crow to me with a sliver of paper tied to its leg, asking me to bring these ingredients, that I had come as quickly as I'd collected them all together and was sorry if she had gone but I had only done as I had been instructed.

He didn't look convinced.

Remembering that Merlin had once instructed me that attack was the surest form of defence, I took that stance. Taking the ingredients out of the saddle bag that I'd slung over my shoulder, I stood tall and asked why I was being treated so scurvily, seeing as I was just doing my duty to my mistress. Did they treat everyone so badly who had just undergone such a difficult and hurried journey? I don't know how I stood there as my legs had gone to jelly, my knees were clattering together – couldn't they hear them? - and I thought I might need the toilet at any minute! But things were starting to look slightly better than they had a minute before.

I could see that the giant was confused and I began to feel a little more confident but then a crafty look came into his eyes. It's at moments like that that your heart sinks into your boots, but this was one of those times when what was asked was something to which I knew the answer. It's brilliant when that happens, isn't it?

He asked me just what ingredients I had and what were they supposed to do.

I had seen the answer to this in the Glass as Merlin and I spied upon him and Mab.

I recounted most of the ingredients and told the giant what they were to be used for and launched into a tirade as to how I had other important tasks to do for my mistress and could better have used my time than to come careering across the countryside on a wild goose chase, to be told by ...

'Yes, yes,' he interrupted me. 'How was I to know that she didn't trust me to get all those ingredients for her; that she had sent that crow off to you to do the same? Well, I did find everything she wanted and she was not only able to mend her ankle but she was also able to block her body odour – that was a relief I can tell you! She might be welcome in my castle but man-oh-man does she smell!' He screwed up his nose and twisted down his mouth as the memory of her stench reintroduced itself to his brain.

199

Why had she blocked her body odour, I wondered.

Realising he shouldn't be talking about his friend to this stranger who might, so far as he knew, recount all he said to her and he'd thus incur her wrath, he coughed before he continued with what he had been saying.

'Let me show you something,' he suggested as he opened the door and ushered me through. 'Follow me.'

With trepidation, I followed him into the main hall where nothing had changed since the last time I had been there with Sir Kay and he preceded me through another door and up a wide staircase, all the time talking to me about Mab and her plans.

'Well now, she and Mordred, have gone off to join Arthur and his party. I don't know how you didn't bump into them! They left only minutes before you arrived!'

I was taken aback when the giant said they were joining Arthur. I knew that Mordred now looked like Kay but had no idea about Mab. She would be spotted a mile off even if, as the giant had said, she had masked her smell.

'I think Arthur will run her through with his sword, if she so much as dares to show her face in his camp,' I stated.

'Not so,' he replied. 'He wouldn't kill a stranger, would he?'

'A stranger?'

'Yes,' he laughed, 'a stranger – or maybe it's someone he knows!' he added, looking slyly at me.

My blood started turning to ice as I considered where this conversation was leading. 'But you don't mean to tell me that Mab had changed bodies with someone else – maybe someone Arthur knows?' I croaked, almost losing my voice with the awful fear that was creeping into my brain. What on earth had happened since I'd left Merlin's cave?

'But of course I do,' he crowed. 'Surely you know your mistress better than to think she wouldn't disguise herself somehow?'

'Surely she'd need to have this person here with her to be able to transform herself into them, though,' I responded, looking down at the woman on the couch in the room we had just entered.

It was, I thought, just like I had seen everything through the Glass - Mab reclining, giving her orders. However, now she didn't move but lay as still as death even though it could be seen that her eyes were moving frantically this way and that beneath her eyelids - she was obviously having some sort of bad dream. And, yes, for the first time in Mab's company I was not aware of any bad smell!

I tiptoed across to the couch upon which she lay; I certainly did not want to wake her up.

The giant watched me - well his green eye watched me – to see what reaction I would make. He was intrigued that I appeared to be scared of the witch. Feeling his acute interest in my actions, I turned and asked what was wrong with her.

'She is bewitched!' he stated.

'Nonsense,' I responded, taking my courage in my hands. 'She wouldn't allow that to happen to her – she's much too clever for that. I would have thought that you'd know that yourself.' Anyway, I thought he'd said she'd left.

My answer appeared to put him at his ease and he was then quite chatty. The hair stood up at the back of my neck as he outlined his and Mab's plans for the destruction of Arthur and Culhwch - someone who had the audacity to want to marry his daughter.

'That is not going to happen,' he confided in me. 'Mab is going to bring the party of people here. Once they're caught inside these walls, Mab will make sure that Arthur breathes his last and I will grind up Culhwch in the flour mill so that both Mab and I will be rid of them forever. Mind you, I might just let Mab have him as well. Her plan is brilliant! I thought I was evil but she is nothing less than just completely wicked. And mad! I expect that helps, eh?'

201

I hoped that my face had not lost its entire colour as I listened to the way this dreadful duo was going to dispose of two wonderful people.

'But how is Mab going to achieve all of this?' I asked, 'if she is lying here comatose?'

He looked at me as though he couldn't believe I was so dim-witted. Afterwards I couldn't believe it myself.

'You mean you don't know?' he asked. 'You haven't worked it out yet?'

I shook my head.

Laughing, he stated what should have been so obvious, 'This isn't Mab!'

I walked closer to the body lying on the couch and peered hard into her face. 'Well, who is it then?'

Hands on hips and throwing his head back to laugh – a loud and echoing pain to my ears as it bounced back from the ceiling and hit me full blast, but an even worse pain to my mind as realisation began to dawn, making me dread his reply - he eventually stopped howling enough to exclaim, 'This isn't Mab, it's Lady Elise!'

I spun round and stared at the sleeping woman. Leaning forward, I took hold of one of her hands and its feel belied its look. It was just the same as it had happened to Sir Kay. Mab's hand looked wrinkled and rough but the hand I held was as smooth as silk; Mab's hands had broken fingernails, if she had any nails at all, but the nails I touched were manicured and buffed smooth. I thought I was going to be sick. I had to get out of here quickly to warn Arthur and I had to try and save Lady Elise. But how? Looking over at the giant I got the distinct impression that he could read my mind. However, his next words showed that that thought was just in my imagination; I really shouldn't keep thinking the worst all the time should I?

'Let me show you something else,' he said in a very conspiratorial tone.

I looked around then, thinking there must be someone near listening but there was no-one about.

'He took me back down the wide staircase and out through a door at the back of the castle. We skirted the outside of the kitchens where I caught a few words from the amiable Cornek and then we were off towards the barns and stables.

Before we got there I experienced, once more, the fear that starts to creep up on you unawares. I knew that I was going to see something very nasty and didn't really want to go any further. The giant, with his huge steps, was making me run to keep up with him. Should I turn and run the other way? No! I knew I had to see what it was that was making me so apprehensive.

'Now I don't want them excited, so move slowly and don't make any sudden noises. It's the devil to get them to shut up once they get started,' he whispered gruffly as he pulled open a barn door.

What on earth was I going to see? I had checked out the lie of the land as we moved across the courtyard and had noticed a flight of stone steps leading up to the battlements. So, whatever it was that I was to be shown, I had decided that should it be necessary, those steps would have to be my escape route. Where they led to, I knew not but, well, I always had the dragon's droppings, didn't I?

The giant stooped low to enter the barn but was able to stand fully upright within. I followed as closely as I could and tried to remain behind him. What I saw made my teeth curl!

Inside a huge cage made up of iron rails on all sides were at least thirty chimeras. They rushed over to stare at us as we went in, looking as though they expected food. They all had teeth bared, with saliva dribbling from their open mouths – mouths that had too many sharp teeth in them for my liking – and they appeared to be sizing me up for consumption. Some of them watched me through canine eyes while a few were eyeing me from feline faces, occasionally swivelling their heads round but all eyes were maleficent. I noticed one couple that were preoccupied at the back of the cage: one hissing, one barking, as they fought each other.

'Come, let's leave before they start complaining,' he giant proposed softly.

I didn't need further urging. I could feel those eyes burning into my back as we moved away and I didn't feel safe until we'd got outside.

Once outside, the giant closed and secured the barn door and in a very conspiratorial tone started telling me what they were going to be used for. I reckon the giant must have thought I was one of Mab's confidants and, as such, it was OK to talk to me as freely has he was. If only Mab knew – she'd strike him dumb for life!

'Do you know what we are going to do with those little monsters?' he asked me.

I shook my head; I still didn't trust myself to speak after seeing those awful beasts.

'Well, young man, we are going to lure Arthur and his party to this castle by setting these little monsters on to them. They'll eat what they can catch! They've been locked in there for three days now without food and so will be ravenous by the time their "dinner" arrives!' He chuckled as though this was something that would cause great delight.

I shivered.

'We sent some of them out before Mab left to see if they were any good at attacking the party but, unfortunately, we didn't send enough; a few got killed but most returned. The next time we will use all of them.

Still thinking about those chimeras, I wondered if the keeper of the tower was still on duty there or whether it, too, was among those in the cage. Dare I ask?

'Do you have any more of them?'

'Why do you want to know?' He sounded suspicious. 'Don't you think we have enough?' He looked concerned.

'I just thought that if you have any more, perhaps you should put them with the others, just to make sure,' I suggested.

'Good idea,' he replied. 'I do have one or two.'

He stopped and stroked his chin. After quite while he stopped, reconsidering his decision, 'No, they're too old; I think I'll leave them where they are.'

'I just thought that perhaps you should use all of them,' I urged him again, hoping he'd move the one out of the tower.

'Are you doubting my aptitude for decision making?' he growled.

I assured him he was absolutely right and that I should have kept my thoughts to myself.

'Hmm, 'he snorted. 'Remember it.

'Come,' he said as he prodded me along. 'I am forgetting my manners and Mab will be none to pleased with me if her servants end up passing out through lack of food.'

He took me back the way we had come to the kitchens.

'Feed him,' he instructed the cook, who was organising the men to turn a huge cow on the spit over the fire. 'and hurry up and cook that beef – I'm ready for it now!'

The cook, all-aflutter, threw a loaf of bread at me and shouted for me to see to myself, stating that she didn't have time to skivvy to little boys. I can't say I was really that bothered what she might think of me and wasn't at all hungry; my stomach having tied itself into so many knots with all that I had seen and heard, considering the fact that I thought I would be discovered at any moment.

The giant disappeared through the kitchen door and I, giving up after attempting to eat something, disappeared through another.

I had a job to do.

THIRTY-ONE

I had to make a decision very soon. I felt for the cord around my neck to make sure it was still there and was relieved to fold my hand around the albeit very small pouch of dragon's droppings; if I had to, there was enough in that pouch to get me back to Merlin's cave and possibly just enough to send Lady Elise back as well; however, that still left the question of Merlin's staff. My prime concern at the moment was its retrieval. I also had some naiad root just in case the chimera was still in the stair well; that, too, was in the pouch in the tiniest phial I had ever seen. *'Root in phial; droppings in twist of parchment. Root in phial; droppings in twist of parchment.'* It had almost become a mantra as I kept on reminding myself which was in what. There was no way I wanted to throw the naiad root over my head. Wow, could you imagine it? No, it didn't bear thinking about.

I really didn't know whether I was coming or going, now that I had found the drugged Lady Elise. Should I send her back? Should I continue on my quest? I was almost sure that I should obey Merlin to the letter; on the other hand, he would be very disappointed if I didn't use my initiative when problems arose. I could almost hear him telling me that, "I should have used my brain! Why did I think I had been given one?" Oh well, I would just have to make it up as I went along! On thinking of him, I tried calling out to Merlin or Cabal in my mind but there was no response. They must be too far away. I was on my own in this.

I had made it to the foot of the stairs and was just about to ascend, when Olwen came out of the room directly opposite. She stood and looked at me for a short while and then, recognising me, turned as if to run away.

'Please don't go; please don't give me away?' I whined. *'Great start,'* I thought; *'now she'll think me a coward.'*

Turning to look at me she waited for me to continue.

'Are you aware of what's going on here?' I asked.

She just waited.

'Do you know about the lady upstairs?' I queried. 'She is not who she seems to be and I believe I must try to rescue her.'

'Are you a friend of Culhwch?' she asked me.

'I don't believe I've met him but I know that the giant and the witch intend to kill him, along with my friends,' I responded.

She went extremely pale, gripping the back of the chair she was standing beside for support. 'The giant,' she hesitated and then, taking courage, stated, 'is my father!'

Now it was I that was shocked and it must have shown pretty clearly by my expression.

However, she just shrugged and continued, 'I had a suspicion that that is what they wanted to do,' she spoke almost under her breath. 'But I didn't want to believe it. Every time I came into the room they stopped talking but I got part of a sentence here and there and it seemed that, from putting bits of them together, my father wants to kill Culhwch, whom I love, and the woman wants to kill someone called – hmm, Arthur, I think.'

'Arthur is my friend and Culhwch is his cousin.'

We were silent for some few moments before Olwen made her decision.

She straightened her back and, looking directly into my eyes, asked 'How can I help? I can't stand by and let my father kill my love. How can I exist without him now that we love one another? And, I don't want my father to become a murderer. On the other hand, I feel terrible in dishonouring him but apart from me, to whom he is very kind and loving, I've noticed he seems to be evil to everyone else.'

'It is always best to do that which is right,' I assured her. 'We must get away! If we stay here much longer, someone might see us and hand us, or at least me, over to your father. Can we go upstairs to the woman?' I asked.

She led the way and watching her I couldn't help but be amazed that the giant was her father. She was petite and elegant and he, well, I've already told you what he was like. Strange things happened in those days, all those hundreds of years ago! Or was it all a dream?

As we ascended the staircase, I told her, in a pretty rushed manner I must admit, what had happened to Sir Kay and Lady Elise. If she was surprised, she didn't show it, although she listened intently to everything I said. Reaching the end of the corridor at the top of the stairs, we entered the room and walked over to the sleeping woman.

'She is an awful woman,' she commented in an almost matter-of-fact way. 'Are you sure she is not who she seems to be? I would have thought she was and now that we have her at our mercy, well, perhaps we might, er, dispose of her?' she raised one eyebrow in query as she looked at me.

I thought, at that moment, that there was obviously a little of her father in her. I think she must have seen the absolute horror and shock on my face because she quickly looked away. People in those days were pretty ruthless – even the nice ones!

'No, madam,' I spoke through a husky throat as my spittle had once more dried up. Swallowing a couple of times, I went on, 'First, we should never attack a defenceless person and secondly we should always remember that things are not always what they seem. Come,' I urged her. 'I would just like you to do one thing for me and then, perhaps, you will believe what I am telling you. Just lean over here and stroke the woman's hair.'

'I could not,' she grimaced. 'Look at it! It's greasy and and … and it's filthy,' she stammered. 'Probably full of lice and fleas!'

'No – trust me,' I repeated.

Taking her courage in her hands, she reached out her hand but stopped short of touching the woman; she hesitated for some ten seconds or so and then, screwing up her face and eyes, leaned forward and gingerly touched her hair. She pulled her hand away quickly; then, surprised, opened her eyes and, staring at the woman before her, once again, touched her hair.

'It's soft; it's smooth,' she commented quietly as she leaned forward and touched it again. Not believing her eyes, she felt the woman's dress, which, to all intents and purposes, looked like a filthy, screwed-up rag; that, too, belied its look. 'It's silk; it isn't a rag! What on earth is going on here?'

'Witchcraft!' I stated.

'But how?'

I explained in more detail what had happened to my friend Sir Kay, and I had come to the conclusion that the same thing had happened to Lady Elise. As Mab was now obviously using the false Sir Kay to achieve her nefarious purposes, she must have used him to abduct the lady, who would have gone along with him willingly, believing that he was her son. I admitted that I did not know how she'd made the transition but I did know that if she *had* swapped their bodies, or the appearance of bodies at any rate, then she was up to no good. As she was presently masquerading as Lady Elise, I could only assume that she was on her way back to get at Arthur. I had to retrieve Merlin's staff with the utmost haste. However, before I did that I needed to transport Lady Elise to Merlin's cave and hope that he was still there to help her. Oh, I prayed that he didn't think it was Mab arriving! I sent up a silent prayer to Arthur's God and was immediately rewarded with the thought that I should write a quick note.

Olwen ran off and returned immediately with a small piece of paper, a quill and some ink. I scribbled a quick message and tied it round Elise's wrist with a strip of material from the edge of her gown. Olwen was very intrigued as, busily putting things together, I had told her nothing of what I intended to do for the lady.

Needing to be on my own for a few moments to achieve Lady Elise's transfer, I suggested that Olwen check to see if the coast was clear so that I could make my way to the tower. I had told her that I needed to retrieve something from it but didn't want to be seen either going in or coming out. I asked her to trust me and assured her that I would do all I could in helping Culhwch.

As she left the room I retrieved the pouch from around my neck and took out a pinch of dragon's droppings. *'Root in phial; droppings in twist of parchment.'* Oh, this was a difficult decision to make as there was barely enough left to transport me, should it be required. Hesitating only for a split second and mentally kicking myself for my selfish attitude, I threw the droppings into the air and watched it sparkle down over the lady until she vanished. I stood there for a good few seconds marvelling at what had just happened before turning and running out of the room. Next stop – the tower.

THIRTY-TWO

'Wooh, visitors!' exclaimed Merlin as he looked over to where the flash of light had heralded someone's entrance to his cave. 'Well this is a marvel.' he commented as he looked at the comatose form of Mad Mab lying on the floor. 'Two of my most sworn enemies in my cave at the same time!'

Salazar moved over to where the witch lay, bent down and picked her up. He was very gentle and, taking her over to a couch by the far wall, laid her down.

Sir Kay stood watching with interest. Screwing up his face, he remembered how he had been imprisoned by this awful woman and wanted to find out what they were going to do with her. He hoped they were going to turn her to stone or imprison her in the deepest dungeon they could find, never to be seen again. He told us later that he thought it was a good thing that the others were in the room, as the way he felt at the time, he reckoned he might have done her a damage that he'd obviously later regret; after a few moments that proved to be the case.

'Well, bless my soul,' Merlin laughed. 'That dear boy thinks I'm unable to see what is plainly before me!'

'What boy? See what?' Kay asked.

Merlin handed the scrap of paper over to Kay who blanched when he saw what was written on it. 'To think I could have killed her!' he whispered, tears starting to run down his face. 'But she looks dead! Merlin – is she? Oh, Mother!'

'Read it out, man; control yourself,' Merlin instructed.

'Yes, right, immediately,' he said, gulping down the lump that had grown in his throat. 'THIS IS LADY ELISE - MAB'S CHANGED BODIES WITH HER. PERCY.'

'Exactly!' Merlin stated. 'Now, all we have to do is try and find out what she's drugged her with and then go on to see if we can release her and you, Kay, into your rightful bodies.'

Kay had sat down beside his mother and was stroking her hand – a hand that was definitely a lady's hand – soft and feminine; not like the one that could be seen – gnarled with cracked and filthy nails.

'It's the smell that gives it away really,' Merlin stated.

'Smell? What smell? I can't smell anything! There is no smell!'

'Exactly! There is no smell! Mab doesn't have that joy. In fact, she'd even turn a skunk away, she smell's so awful. This lady – your mother, Kay – if she were Mab, we'd have had to evacuate my cave. I must say, though, it is extremely distracting to look at you and your mother and not feel revolted. No, we'll have to get you back to your normal selves soon, especially as I think that Mab and Mordred are up to their old tricks and if they're not with Arthur already, I reckon they're on their way. We need to move – and quickly.'

Merlin hurried over to the table and opened several scrolls. All the while he was calling out his instructions. 'Jasmine, please be kind enough to see to the lady. Do all you can for her. Don't leave her side until we return. We will try to find out what antidote to give her. Salazar, please come here and help me. Cabal, stand over by the Glass and look for Percy. I am going to send you to him. He is going to need you.'

However, before any of this could be achieved, a flash heralded yet another visitor.

THIRTY-THREE

'Mother, this fog is getting thicker than ever! Are you sure we'll be able to find our way to Hinton St. Mary?'

Don't fret, Arthur, the compass doesn't need to see; all it does is point north. We will be able to find our way quite clearly without having to see.'

That was nearly two days ago. Arthur was getting troubled, as he was certain they had passed the same tree at least twice. Trying to shake off an increasing feeling of paranoia, he nevertheless decided to start leaving a trail, if for no other reason than to see if they had already been to that place before. So, on this second day, he was not particularly surprised to find the chipped out notch on the oak tree that he'd previously etched into it the day before.

He didn't want to mention it to his mother, as she appeared to be getting quite edgy with him if he approached her about anything that was disagreeable to her, so he spoke to Rhianne.

'I can't say that I have noticed anything about where we're going to or even where we've come from but, yes, it looks as though we might be going round in circles,' she agreed with him as she ran her finger down the missing tree bark. 'I must say, though, that I am feeling quite depressed with all this fog and damp. I just can't seem to get warm and I am worried that mother is getting ill again. She certainly doesn't seem like herself and has been very sharp with me on occasion.'

'Perhaps we should tell her that we've decided to go home. This expedition appears to have been ill-fated from the start. I am sure she'll understand, especially if we agree to return next year and maybe leave a little earlier in the month so as to give us more time to get there. Perhaps we might make it for Eastertide instead. What do you think sister?'

He may as well have asked for a ladder to the moon! Lady Elise was adamant; she was determined to go on with their pilgrimage. She said that it was absolutely imperative they continue, that she would not consider abandoning their quest and for all of them to give up any idea of turning back.

They were, of course, extremely surprised by her resolve, as she was usually such an amenable person. Nevertheless, after making sure she was well enough to continue, they resumed their travels.

Keeping very close to Arthur and Culhwch, Rhianne grew silent as the mists dampened her usual sunny nature. All the while there was a growing uneasiness within each of them, a feeling none of them dared share at the time, thinking it a fancifulness all their own.

Even Shake Spear, who always appeared in better humour than most, became solitary and silent, only giving short answers when spoken to. Niel became quite concerned for him and asked him why he appeared so quiet and forlorn.

''Tis good to be sad and say nothing,' was his short reply.

'But why on earth are you so sad?' he enquired.

'I know not, sir,' was his response. ''Tis this expedition, I feel sure.' Dropping his chin on his chest and deciding he wanted to speak no more Niel rode forward to ride alongside Arthur. Rhianne, who had been watching this exchange, dropped back to enquire of Shake Spear herself but got no better response, so she moved along the line to ride alongside Culhwch.

Brosc trotted up beside Shake Spear and scolded him for the way he had spoken to their young mistress. 'I thought you treasured her!'

'I do! But 'tis better to be brief than tedious.' He pulled the bridle and moved his mount to the back of the line.

'Pathetic!' Brosc grumbled.

'The men are not happy,' Rhianne confided to Arthur. 'Shake Spear is very morose and that isn't like him.'

214

'I know,' Arthur responded, 'but what can I do? Mother insists on continuing with this journey, even though I believe we're too far away and just won't make it on time. Brother Geraint has said that there is evil afoot and hasn't stopped praying – well, I think he is at any rate, as his lips are continually moving. I don't know whether that's so or not or whether he's just being fanciful. I reckon I'll join him tonight to see what he thinks is happening.'

They continued on their journey at a slow pace. The fog was all-engulfing and hid everything but the nearest cobweb, shrub or tree from their sight; thus they did not see the two men, one of which had bright red hair, riding some hundred paces behind them, trailed by dwarf-like creatures with swivelly heads.

One or more of them would sometimes think they'd heard something when the hoof of one of those shadowy beings hit a stone but Lady Elise pooh-poohed them by saying it was a trick of the fog – their own hoof beats bouncing back from it.

'What is the matter with all of you?' she scoffed. 'Where is your backbone?'

They were surprised at her unusual attitude but, without the gift of foresight, did not even try to figure out what might be causing it.

As darkness started to close in on them, they decided to settle down and ultimately made camp when they reached a copse of thick fir trees. It was quite dry underneath those heavy branches but, even so, Brosc and Shake Spear spent a long time trying to light a fire with wood that the enveloping fog had soaked through; eventually it lit and they finally had some hot food as they warmed themselves before its smoking flames. They ate in silence; there were no jokes and no laughter.

Thus it was that a very despondent party retired that evening.

Morning came and the birds began to sing. On a light breeze, sunlight waltzed into the tents and wagons and nudged everyone awake, urging all to join in the dance. The smell of food skipped along on the air, an enticement to the nose, as was the happy sound of the morning chorus to the ear. Steam rose from damp canvasses and before long all was warm and dry.

What a difference a sunny day makes to a man. Everyone had thrown off his cloak of despair and clothed himself with a robe of happiness.

Shake Spear, one of the first to rise, was seen squinting through his myopic eyes as he bent low over a wild orchid that had peeped out through a cluster of other foliage. 'Everything that grows holds in perfection but a little moment,' he was observed to say, adding, 'All ignorant that soul that sees thee without wonder.'

'His eyesight appears to be getting worse!' Rhianne stated as she watched him.

'Nevertheless, he's still a giant of a man and many run rather than face him,' Arthur replied. 'Even if they know he's short-sighted, they'll never know that he won't actually attack them. I wouldn't take the chance if I were his enemy. It's as much as I can do taking a chance knowing he's my friend! What about you? I'm always glad he's around. I just feel safer with him there.'

It was only when several of them had risen from their beds that one of them noticed the castle.

Culhwch shouted and pointed down across the valley. 'Look, Arthur! I don't know where that compass has been pointing but we've ended up at Ysbaddaden's castle. We're at the edge of the plain overlooking Glastonbury! We've not moved anywhere at all!'

Sir Niel walked up to the pair and all three of them stood in silence as they took in the view. The castle sat in the middle of a boggy plain, with its uninviting grey walls standing impassively all around it. The sun bounced back from grey stone blocks topped by tall trees fixed together with hemp, each sharpened to a wicked point at the top.

'Not very inviting, eh?' Arthur observed.

'Wait till you see the giant, then you'll know what not very inviting really means,' commented Culhwch. 'I was only allowed to live, I think, because he would have alienated himself from Olwen if he'd decided otherwise.'

'Come, come,' purred the witch, creeping up behind. 'No-one could be that bad! I, for one, think we should go and seek the hospitality of whoever lives there. It is the civil duty of any landowner to proffer assistance to travellers in need.

'But aunt,' Culhwch put the argument, 'the giant there is not welcoming; in fact, if we were to seek his aid, we would probably never leave that place alive!'

'Nonsense!' she replied. 'If you won't go there, then I shall have to go on my own. I need proper food and a comfortable bed for at least one night before we continue our travels. Come, Rhianne, let us get packed up and depart for the castle. The servants can accompany us if the men are too scared!'

'Yes, mother,' Rhianne replied, although it could be seen by the imploring look she threw over her shoulder at the others that she was very worried. Had Lady Elise succumbed to the illness that had made her delirious so many days before? She looked over at Arthur in silent appeal for him to try to either change their mother's mind or, if that were not possible, accompany them to the castle.

As it turned out, the decision was made for them. Or, with hindsight, it was possible that the witch had had it all organised from the start.

No sooner had all the pots and pans been stowed in the wagons than Sir Niel noticed movement in the trees. At first he thought little of it as there were many woodland animals in those days, but then another movement caused him to glance quickly to his right. What he saw made the hair rise on the back of his neck. 'What on earth ….'

'Eh?' asked Arthur.

But it had gone. *'No,'* Niel thought. *'There is definitely something funny going on here,'* after which he put spurs to his pony's flanks and trotted over to where he had seen this apparition. He had hardly travelled half the distance when at least three of those weird phenomena stepped out from behind various trees and shrubbery and, baring teeth that dripped with saliva, started towards him. They were back!

Niel pulled sharply at his reins and turned the animal as quickly as he could, yelling and shouting for everyone to beware and run for it.

Arthur looked round and saw the reason for Niel's panic and, taking command, ordered everyone to draw swords and take their stand.

Positioning themselves around the wagons, they waited as, unbelievably, more and more of the chimeras came at them from all sides. Two extremely weird looking, tattooed men sat on a horse just inside the trees and appeared to do nothing, although occasionally they would point or wave their arms and the little monsters would change direction, some howling, some hissing, some barking.

Shake Spear was hit and it was only the foresight of Wite that saved him.

Rhianne screamed and Culhwch rushed to her side as two of the chimeras clawed their way up her cloak. With teeth bared, one was about to lunge at her throat before being hacked in half with one swing of Culhwch's sword. Rhianne stared in disbelief as it fell to the ground in two halves, the top half still staring at her as it slithered down her cloak. Lady Elise, on the other hand, seemed not to be unduly worried and to all intents and purposes appeared to be thoroughly enjoying herself, going so far as to tell Rhianne to pull herself together after her terrible ordeal.

They fought on bravely until it became obvious that they were not going to win. Their circle around the wagons was getting smaller and tighter and the chimeras, although not increasing in number, appeared to be making ground.

There was nothing else to be done – they had to make a run for the castle and, hopefully, sanctuary.

So, what the witch had wanted all along, but had found it hard to obtain, was now achieved by those abnormal servants.

Charging down the slight incline toward the castle, they had their work cut out to defend themselves. Although many of them had horses, the men that were on foot had to clamber up onto the two wagons. The muddy terrain also hampered their flight and wheels were continually getting stuck. Those on horseback tried to free the wagons while the men jumped down to push. All the while those horrible beings were attacking them and snapping at their legs. Rhianne kicked out at one of the chimera as it pulled at her skirts once again, almost unseating herself in the process. Her foot hit the animal in the eye and, squealing, it dropped away from her holding its head. Niel ran up to her side and defended her for the rest of the dash to the castle.

As they neared the castle's open gates more than one of them felt a chill of foreboding. They rushed through and reined in, turning to see if any of their pursuers had caught up with them; none had but Arthur and most of the others jumped out of their skins as, with a loud grating noise, the gates clanged shut behind them.

THIRTY-FOUR

Olwen took me by the hand and led me through various corridors and rooms until we came to what appeared to be a book room. There were scrolls everywhere, together with huge bottles of ink, quills and pots of sand; there were also some bound books but I didn't have time to look to see what was written on any of them.

She walked over to the wall that housed the bound books and twisted a rose on the scrollwork beside the shelves. The bookcase swung forward, making a slight grinding noise and as soon as it was wide enough to do so we sidled in behind it; Olwen pulled a lever on the inside and it ground back to its former position.

We were now in a cavity between the outer and inner walls of the castle. It was obviously not used very much but at least it was dry; it had a musty smell and many cobwebs that we had to keep brushing away from our face. Once again I wondered why cobwebs always seem to attack the face. I don't suppose they do – it's probably because we just don't feel them on our clothes! I could just about see through the half-light coming from I knew not where. The corridor sloped down gradually and, after turning many corners, we finally came to a stout wooden door. Amazingly it was not locked. After slowly and gently opening the door, Olwen cautiously peered round it. She withdrew once more into our hiding place and whispered that there was no-one about. She pointed along to where the other tower – my former prison - stood and urged me to be very careful.

'The door to the tower opens only from the outside, so when you go in, leave it slightly ajar. No-one will notice it as the door is only seen from the direction of the stables and as there are no visitors today they're not being used. Take care. I can only wait here for a half hour or so, so if you don't return within that time I can't help you any more. My father is always asking where I am and sending for me; he'll turn this place upside down if I go missing. If that happens, you will be found anyway, so you will have to find your own way out of the castle if you take too long.'

'Go back now,' I urged her. 'I know how I will get away, so you don't need to stay. It will be safer in any event, if you return to your father now. Agreed?'

She nodded and after wishing me well, went back in and closed the door. Amazing! As soon as it was shut it looked just like the rest of the wall; it was only because I'd come out of it that I knew there was a door there; however, I also noticed there was no handle on it. *No way back that way then,'* I thought.

Looking quickly around the grounds, I made my way along to the tower. I felt the cord round my neck to check that I had the dragon's droppings handy, just in case that awful thing was waiting for me inside. Holding my breath and trying to still my thumping heart, I quietly turned the iron door handle. Why are those things never quiet? Going as gently as I could, it still sounded as though it was warning villagers at least two miles away. *'Well,'* I thought, *'in for a penny ... '.* I turned the handle, wincing at that awful grinding noise and rushed in, heading as fast as I could for the stairs, knowing that the chimera could not climb up. It was dark!

Why oh why am I such a coward? I climbed up two of the stairs and sighed with relief, knowing that that beast could not now get at me. I was mentally clapping myself on the back at how clever I had been when my congratulations to myself stopped in their tracks, the thought rushing in at me like a thunderbolt that Merlin's staff was not up the stairs - it was suspended above the chimera's head. Brilliant! Aren't I just? Now what was I supposed to do?

Then, there it was! The snuffling and shuffling as the thing woke up; but more awful were the sounds it started to make as it became wider awake, and the grinding of its teeth petrified me as it peered around the corner and made its way towards me. I went cold! The none too comforting thought nagging away in my head was that if I had not been so scared I could have run over to where the chimera slept – and yes I believe he would have been sleeping – grabbed the staff and left. Hindsight is really the most annoying thing, isn't it? The times someone has made me look a fool and I could have come back with the most cutting and wittiest of remarks but, unfortunately, I only ever thought of them a couple of hours later or, at the earliest, when they'd walked away and it was too late. You know, I could write a book!

But, as I said, I didn't have the comfort of that particular foresight and was now trapped – just as I had been when Sir Kay and I were imprisoned there before. I waited on that huge stair sitting with my knees drawn under my chin, hugging my legs to my chest and wondering what was going to happen next.

Of course, the thing that turned the corner was no surprise and the fear was still as big inside me.

It stood up in front of me and stared; its arms were folded in front of it and its cat-like head, held slightly to one side, considered me, while its whiskers twitched and waved. What was it thinking? That I would make a good meal? That if we were out in the field it would enjoy the chase, like Cabal after hare or more than likely the cat after the mouse?

'Oh no,' I thought, *'it's drooling! It really does want to eat me!'* I watched as strings of saliva began to slide down from the side of its mouth, which it opened slightly as it ran its tongue over its lips to catch up any loose dribble; its nose twitched, sniffing at me as it leaned forward. Then its head swivelled round to that of the mad dog.

I found myself moving as far back on the stair as I could.

After what seemed an eternity it began to move towards me. I couldn't go any further back on that stair – the back of my legs were already stuck to the next step - and so I had to climb higher, even though I just knew it couldn't climb the stairs. Well it couldn't, could it?

As it moved to the foot of the stairs its hands gripped the top of the first step; its face was level with it. I watched as it heaved one leg up sideways only to slip back down again. This happened four or five times until, with one almighty pull, it managed to get that first leg high enough until its heel was over the edge. With a gigantic pull of his arms, he got onto that first step.

My eyes were bulging! I turned and made my way up onto another stair. Looking back quickly, I saw that this awful being was now getting the hang of climbing and had almost managed the second stair. This was getting scary! At this rate it would become a race as to who would get to the top first; but that was not the reason for this race! I needed to get to safety but he was just out for lunch – and I was lunch!

In my panic, reason fled. All I was thinking of was getting away from the chimera. I did *not* want to finish my life here and now. My mother and father would miss me. I was only a boy and had a whole life in front of me. Whole life! It was beginning to flash before me. They said that happened when you were about to die! Was this it?

By the time I reached the top of the stairs, the dog-headed dwarf was almost on top of me. I judged that I had about thirty seconds left to live. I ran around in the room that Kay and I had shared looking like a demented imbecile as I searched for a place to hide. The walls were sheer and the window's sill sloped inward and downward – well, it was too low in any event – he'd still be able to grab me. There was nowhere! I couldn't remember what I had kicked to make the fireplace move and, as I tried it a couple of times and failed, looked for somewhere else to conceal myself. Nowhere!

Naiad root! The thought shot into my head like a bullet and without more ado, with shaking hands I took the pouch from around my neck and removed the contents; now I was ready for the beast. Not before time! I stood panting and waited.

It was the cat head with those evil yellow eyes that looked round the door and victory could be seen written clearly on its face. There was more than enough dribble sliding out of its mouth and down its whiskers as it contemplated the meal set before it. The rest of the animal entered the room, pushed the door firmly back until it clicked and very slowly began to make its way over to me, its head swivelling round and round as though arguing with itself as to which face was to have the pleasure of biting into my flesh first; eventually the dog countenance won. It knew it didn't need to rush – where was there that I could go? How was he planning to get me, I wondered. Was he going to grab me with his long-fingered hands first so that he could hold me while his fangs tore chunks out of my body or was he just going to lunge at me with those huge teeth? Would I watch in horror as bits of me disappeared into his mouth or would he tear the head off my body first so that I was put out of my misery and thus not feel myself being riven to pieces as I was eaten? Would he toss any bits of me over his head to the cat so that they could both enjoy the meal? There goes my over-active imagination again – quite a morbid part this time – especially when I wondered which part of me had he decided to eat first? Well that, thank goodness, is something I would never find out – not this day anyway.

As it stood within arms reach looking at me I moved at such lightening speed that I shocked even myself as I threw the contents of Merlin's brew over it, waiting to see what effect the naiad root would have upon this weird creature.

Merlin had told me of many of the effects – some quite awful and some very funny. When it was used on people, they would sometimes completely lose their memories or, and this was more usual, they would imagine they were someone or something else. One lord of the manor who refused to let his daughter marry a neighbouring lord of the manor – and it must be advised that this neighbouring lord was as ugly as sin, much to the dissatisfaction of the daughter – was doused with naiad root whilst supping a pint in the local inn. He was incapacitated for a twelvemonth, thinking that he was a prize boar. He walked, sometimes on all fours, all the way back to his manor instead of riding his horse which, being an obedient mount, followed him all the way home, but the man, instead of striding in through the front doors as usual, walked round the back, climbed over the pigsty and started eating the slops that had been thrown into the trough. His daughter and the servants tried to get him out and clean him up but he pushed them off, cabbage leaves, carrot tops and mushy waste sliding out of his mouth and down his chin as he grunted at them. Usually so gentle and polite, he had now become quite violent when accosted, especially when eating with the pigs. So, he spent twelve months and one day – it being a leap year – in grunting and swilling about in the pigpens. When he came round he only had partial memory; he somehow knew he was the lord of the manor but believed he was only about ten years old and that his daughter, who was only twenty at the time, was his mother who should never re-marry – that would dishonour her late husband, his father's name - even though the girl had never been married let alone widowed! Thus it was that she lived forever as an old maid and had to look after her father who insisted on calling her "mother". He never ever regained his memory sufficiently and his daughter eventually became an unattractive and bitter old spinster. And obviously, much to his chagrin and after all his scheming, the other lord never married the daughter either. Sad for all, I thought.

However, back to the present. After dousing the chimera with the potion, I stood expectantly waiting to see what the naiad root would do to it.

You can imagine my surprise, therefore, when it disappeared! Whoosh – gone! Just like that! I stood for a good few seconds before the awful truth crept into my brain and tapped at my temple before politely coughing behind its hand and advising me that, 'You've used the wrong stuff, idiot - dragon's droppings! You've thrown the wrong thing over him. He's probably right at this moment attacking Merlin and, worse, you, let alone Merlin's staff, now can't get back!'

'Oh, what a completely idiotic dolt! What a moron! I can get the staff now, but I can't get back with it'! I railed at myself as I jumped down those huge stairs. Going round to the back of the stairwell, I reached up and retrieved the staff before slipping out of the door. I would now have to make my way back to Merlin's cave over land. I found my horse, which had not moved too far - in fact, amazingly, he had obeyed my instruction to wait by the trees - mounted with some difficulty, as he now had no saddle, and headed west. This was going to take days.

I was still berating myself when, as I looked up, I saw, a stream of people, horses and wagons making haste towards the castle. *'It's Arthur,'* I thought. I was just about to hail him when I saw the reason for their haste. There were at least twenty of those awful dual-headed dwarfs chasing them. So the giant had sent them out after all, had he? No, he didn't have the time! Another awful thought interrupted my swirling brain – were there more of those beings? If so, how many? Now what was I supposed to do? Help Arthur? Find Merlin?

I stood and hid in the copse of trees and watched as the party sped off over the muddy terrain towards the giant's castle doors. I saw Sir Kay riding beside a wagon upon which was seated Lady Elise.

I almost growled as I thought of those two charlatans riding along with my friends. I saw Rhianne sitting beside

226

Elise and was very concerned for her but then I had to trust the others to keep her safe. I didn't know who the other two men were but hoped that they were friends. Shake Spear and the rest of the men brought up the rear but they, too, were careering towards the castle. I was surprised to see the gates open wide and watched as they disappeared through them; they closed immediately behind them as the last one entered. *'This is very suspicious,'* I thought. I needed to get into that place again. It looked like they were all in serious and imminent danger, remembering what Ysbaddaden had said they would do to them.

The chimera didn't enter through the gates, however, but merely ran round the other side of the castle and disappeared, like expectant puppies – or kittens - going back to their kennels for supper.

THIRTY-FIVE

'Looks like they know where they're going,' I thought.

'I believe they do!'

'Cabby!' I exclaimed, swirling round on my horse and nearly slipping off backwards. 'Where did you come from? Oh I am so glad to see you!' I jumped down from my mount and hugged the hound, noticing, because it made a slightly bloody and wet mark on my face, a small bite, which was still weeping, on his ear. 'How did you get this?' I asked.

'I believe you sent something back to Merlin's cave,' he commented dryly.

'One of those chimeras?' I answered shamefacedly. 'Are you alright?'

'Yes, but what a carry on that was.'

'Tell me,' I ordered.

He raised one eyebrow and launched into his story. *'We were just preparing to go our separate ways – Merlin and Salazar were going off somewhere and I was to find you. He was about to place me in front of the Glass when there was a flash and an uninvited guest arrived. Chimera, did you call it? Well, it looked quite surprised for a moment as it had its hands reaching forward as if to grab something.'*

'Me! It was about to grab me!' I said.

'Well, be that as it may, it suddenly caught sight of Jasmine and started towards her. Merlin shouted for me to attack so that is was I did. He was a dirty fighter, Percy, and it took all my cunning to get the better of him. Every time I thought I had the upper hand he was there, facing me again with those massive teeth. I tried to get behind him but every time I did I came into contact with another face and his body just swivelled round to join it – weird! I thought my teeth were big but his, well, I wouldn't want to come face to face with him on a dark night! Mind, now I come to think of it, I

was face to face with him and it was pretty dark in Merlin's cave, seeing as we were all just about to go off somewhere and you know what he's like, making sure everything is safe, turning off all the candles and wall torches, just in case there's a fire. You know, once he ...'

'Cabal,' I said his name sternly, getting exasperated at his meanderings, reminding him that he was supposed to be telling me what happened.

Er, yes, um, where was I? Oh yes. He managed, at one point, to make a grab for me and got my ear; it was only the tip of it and his teeth just ripped the edge, hence the blood, and ears, you know, are terrible for bleeding. Once it started it was a job to get it to stop. Merlin has some ointment, though ...'

'Cabby, you're doing it again! Please get back to the point.'

'Right. Yes. Even if you aren't concerned about my poor ear! Well, once he'd managed to get that one tiny piece of flesh from my ear he was probably testing it to see if the rest of me was going to be as tasty; he must have been taken completely by surprise as Merlin threw something over him - he just turned to dust! Poof! Small flash and then he disappeared completely – little pile left in the middle of the floor!'

'Naiad root, probably. I wish I'd thrown some of that over it when I was face to face with it; I've never been so scared in my life! Well, I did have some but in my panic used the wrong stuff.

'Oh, that reminds me. There's something in a pouch round my neck.'

I got quite excited at that, thinking that we could go back to Merlin's cave now. It must be dragon's droppings. The relief I felt was amazing.

'Sorry, things are still a bit tight - it's just enough dragon's droppings to send Merlin's staff back to him. He

229

asked that you do it as soon as possible as he is waiting to leave the cave immediately.'

My heart sank into my boots. 'But what are we supposed to do? I thought we'd go back to the cave!'

'Oh no, Percival, we have to save Arthur. Hurry now, send the staff back; the longer we wait, the longer it'll take to save them all.

Obedient to the last, I sprinkled the dust over the staff and watched it disappear. *'Now what,'* I thought as I waited to hear the rest of Merlin's instructions.

'Now we use the green stuff to go ghosting,' Cabal replied.

'Green stuff? I asked.

'Yes,' Cabal replied. *'Don't you remember when you used it the last time? When he took you and Arthur to the lake to rescue me? Merlin put that small bottle in the pouch as well. He knows that you don't have the Glass to look into but he said that if you closed your eyes and looked inside your head for a particular place inside the castle and held on to me tightly, we might both end up in the same place.*

'You'll just have to make sure that you concentrate on our destination as intently as possible otherwise we could end up somewhere completely different. I'll leave my mind blank.'

'That shouldn't be too difficult for you.' I responded, immediately wishing it unsaid as I saw the hurt expression in Cabal's eyes. 'I'm sorry Cab; shouldn't have said that – it's just that you do wander from the subject sometimes. No, I really am sorry.'

He stared at me for a little longer and, making me feel worse by not responding at all, decided to just continue with what Merlin had told him. *'Once we arrive - if we arrive together - we will stay together,'* he said. I noticed the slight dig. *'He said we would have to trust him on this one, as he was sure it worked with people but he wasn't sure it would work with me. We would need to lick the green stuff at the*

230

same time, though. He's also given me an antidote; it's in the pouch as well, so that when we need to, we can throw it over ourselves and become visible again. We would need to be somewhere safe when we do this as once it has been thrown over us we will be seen by all and sundry. Not a good idea if that mad witch is about, eh?' He started sneezing at the thought. *'There's no way we're going to end up back in Merlin's cave this time.'*

Yes, I now recalled the time we'd done this before when Merlin had sent Moon Song to save Cabal from being drowned in the naiad lake.

'OK. What I will do is put a drop of green blob on both my index fingers and then, when I am ready, I'll put my arm around your neck and put the potion on your tongue and mine at the same time so you'd better make sure your tongue is hanging out.'

After some thought and preparation, I eventually decided to go to the room with the books and scrolls in it; it was on the ground floor and might possibly be a good starting point.

Holding on to Cabby as tightly as I could, I counted three and then applied the sticky green blob to our respective tongues; once again it felt as though we were flying through the air at great speed and then as suddenly we were standing still, both panting, in the book room of the giant's castle.

'Well, we made it,' Cabal said, sounding miles away and speaking in slow motion.

We both turned, in unison, and made our way out of the book room and through into the main hall where Arthur and his party stood talking to the giant.

Amazingly, we saw that Lady Elise and Sir Kay were not among their party until the reason for this hit me like a thunderbolt. In our present state we saw them as they really were – Mad Mab and Mordred. Even though their shapes kept hazing between who they were and who they were pretending to be, it was clear who they really were. She knew

231

we were there though – as could be seen by her crafty eyes searching for us throughout the room: she couldn't see us even though she knew we were there; she was also aware that she could not give herself away by saying anything. The thought entered my mind as to whether the giant saw her as she really was as well, whether he saw her keep changing shape or whether he, too, was duped. The answer to that became clear as the day wore on.

I looked at the others in the party. There was a man – a knight - who was introduced to the giant as Sir Niel. I had not met this man before but had heard of him when Arthur had told me some of the adventures they had had during the summer that I'd been away; I expect that was why he looked vaguely familiar and there was Arthur's cousin, Culhwch whom the giant eyed disdainfully. Brother Geraint was also with them but was, as usual, calm and serene, albeit alert.

I suppose Arthur had already introduced himself and his family. Rhianne was clearly scared as could be seen by the way she held her hands together – her knuckles were white, but she was managing to put a brave face on it. She kept very close to Mab and I could have screamed. *Didn't she have any idea who that woman was?* I wanted to try to mind-speak to her that it wasn't her mother but I dare not; it would give the whole game away. Mab might hear and then who knows what would happen to them!

Arthur, after getting over the shock of the size of the giant, had explained why they had had to take refuge in his castle. The giant put them at their ease by explaining that they had had much trouble from these little monsters but his men were out, even now, hunting them down. By tomorrow the roads would be clear of them and they should be able to leave quite safely and continue on their journey.

I didn't believe him for one moment; he was just playing with them. I knew he wanted Culhwch dead as much as Mab wanted Arthur dead and now that they had the two men in the same place it looked as though it was going to happen here and soon. What could I possibly do?

My fears were still not allayed when Mab asked if they could possibly freshen up.

'Phew, that'll be the day,' I heard Cabal mind-whisper.

It was enough for the witch; she turned and looked directly at us. I could have throttled him for thinking it without putting up his barriers – even though I was thinking the same thing. I glided over the floor to stand somewhere near the giant. Cabal, of course moved with me. Keeping my eyes on the witch I noticed that although she followed us, her gaze was intermittent so it was obvious that she couldn't see us, she must just be able to sense us; she certainly wouldn't be able to smell us! A small relief!

As I watched her I saw a crafty expression come into those evil eyes.

'Perhaps you have somewhere where the men could go and where my daughter and I could go?' she asked the giant sweetly.

'Of course, madam.' He bowed exaggeratedly to her. Clapping his hands, it wasn't long before two young men came hurrying in. I was extremely relieved as I thought it might be some more of those awful beasts. One of the men was Cornek and another looked very like him – a relative, I thought. *'How could such ordinary people work for such a beast?'* I thought with my barriers in place. *'Perhaps they didn't know.'*

But what was I to do now? Cabal and I were joined together by the potion. We needed to follow both groups but would only be able to follow one; my heart told me to follow Rhianne and the witch but my head told me I had to follow Arthur.

I couldn't do anything to help them unless I became visible and I felt in my bones it was best for me to stay the way I was for the moment. At least I might be able to leave and find Merlin if that was required. So, with dragging feet, we floated after Arthur's party.

I wondered where the other men and the wagons were but supposed they had been sent to the servants' quarters or the barns. Perhaps, if I got the opportunity, I would go and search for them; it would be best to know exactly where everyone was - just in case. *'Just in case,'* I thought. *Just in case of what?'* I shivered.

I had no idea where Rhianne was being taken but became more and more alarmed as I followed the other party. The young man chatted quite amiably as he guided them through many corridors towards the far side of the castle.

Culhwch, feeling slightly uneasy, asked where he was taking them.

'To the west wing, sir. Where the master directed.'

They followed and were led through a huge door, but, then, everything in this place was huge. As they entered, the boy bowed himself out and clanged the door shut behind him. Sir Niel and Arthur lunged back towards the door as they heard the lock turning; too late, they realised they were trapped.

'Open this door at once,' Arthur cried furiously. 'Come back now.'

'It's no good, cousin. Look around you. We're imprisoned. I know that Ysbaddaden doesn't want me to marry his daughter but I didn't know he hated me this much. And why he should take it out on you and the others, I do not know.'

With clenched teeth, Arthur paced about for a few minutes before getting all of them to check out the room. It was not quite a dungeon. Although they had not gone down any stairs they believed that all the walls of this room must have been built almost entirely of stone, giving the impression that they were below ground. There were two small windows set high with metal grilles in them, which let in some air but little daylight. There was no other lighting in the room – no sconces in the walls for torches, no brazier for a fire and no chimney. Just stone walls and a stone floor with a beamed ceiling some thirty feet above them, nothing to sit on and nothing to eat or drink.

'Where's Kay?' Niel asked. 'He was with us when we left the hall but I can't remember seeing him since.'

They all looked around at one another and the room but Kay was nowhere to be seen.

'Oh, no,' Arthur groaned. 'What are they going to do to him?' He was beside himself with worry. 'This is all my fault! If only I hadn't taken it into my head to go on this pilgrimage. I only did it because they wouldn't let me go to war! Well that's not quite true, as I did want to go and properly thank the Lord for all the good things He has done for me and mine. Oh,' he thought suddenly, 'what on earth are they going to do with mother and Rhianne?' He flopped down against the wall, put his head in his hands and, moaning, continued to berate himself.

Cabal and I would have to investigate soon.

We turned and stared open-mouthed – well I was open-mouthed at any rate as Neil started to speak. It appeared to the others that he might be losing his mind when he stood in the middle of the room and, speaking slowly and clearly, said, 'If anyone is listening, then first go and see what is happening to Rhianne and Lady Elise, after which find out what has happened to the men. If possible, come back and let us out.'

Brother Geraint walked over to Sir Niel and put his arm around the man's shoulders. 'Now, now, young sir,' he whispered, 'don't take on so. All is well and all will be well and all will be sorted out in the Lord's good time.'

Niel turned and looked at the monk and smiled. 'Yes, of course!'

Meantime, I had those chills creeping up and down my spine again. Did he know I was there and was giving me instructions? If so, how? And should I obey? Well, I couldn't do anything here could I? Remembering the last time that Merlin, Arthur and I were ghosting at Mad Mab's castle, I recalled that I could actually pass through walls and doors and so, turning – Cabal with me – I glided through the door, getting that peculiar dragging, suction feeling as I did so, and started my search through the building as I popped out on the other side of the wall.

I found the men before I found Rhianne; well, actually I heard them first and went to investigate. They were all locked in one of the barns and were being guarded by, guess what? Yes, chimeras – about four of them. Cabal later told me they were quite old and so had been left to guard them. A job not given to some of the younger ones, who were not averse to running off and getting into trouble – they were generally kept under lock and key until such time as they could be trained up to be obedient. Shake Spear was being bandaged by Wite. He must have tried to attack the dwarfs and had received a bite on his arm for his troubles. Oh how I wish that man could see better. He'd make a fantastic warrior if only he could discern which was friend and which was foe!

'That is a nasty bite, my friend. It'll take a bit of mending,' Wite commented.

'What wound did ever heal but by degrees?'

The chimeras looked over at Cabal and me and sniffed a bit but did not leave their posts.

The men and Old Molly were in a better position than those I had just left as they had the wagons with them. Molly, helped by Brosc, was putting a cold meal together.

'We're in a sorry state,' Tailor observed.

'Catastrophic!' answered Brosc.

'Where are the others? What should we do?'

'For tonight, I suggest we rest and regain our strength and then, tomorrow, wait and see!' Shake Spear replied.

'Fantastic!' Brosc responded sarcastically.

'Well,' barked Shake Spear, 'have you any better ideas?'

'Perhaps we should not fight each other,' suggested Old Molly. 'Perhaps we will feel better once we have eaten something and had a rest. Let us try to be alert but also get some sleep so as to be ready for the morrow.'

'Sleep seldom visits sorrow; when it doth, it is a comforter,' Shake Spear answered, agreeing with her. 'Perhaps a plan might appear to one of us in our dreams!'

They finally surrendered to the pull of sleep.

Cabal and I had long since glided out of the barn and headed back into the main hall of the castle.

I saw Mab enter the main hall from a direction I had not visited up to now. I waited until she had seated herself next to Ysbaddaden and exited where she had entered. We slid up the staircase and came to a poorly lit corridor, which seemed to melt off into an endless void in both directions. Glancing this way and that we saw a glimmer of light creeping out from under a door. Locked doors now no barrier, we glided through it and came across Rhianne lying fast asleep in the middle of a massive bed. We leant across and could just about hear her shallow breathing.

'Look at her cheeks, Percy,' Cabal whispered. *'She's either been drugged or poisoned.'*

I got that awful feeling in the pit of my stomach and my heart leapt into my throat when I looked at that beautiful face. Her cheeks were pale and she was hardly breathing. I was even then struggling to reach the pouch around my neck so that I could throw the powder over me and help her.

'No, Percy! If you do that we all die!

'But look at her, Cabal. If I don't help her ... '. My words trailed off. I knew that what he said was right and it was with much mental struggling that I eventually tucked the pouch back inside my jerkin, almost weeping as I did so.

'Come, Percy. Let's see what the witch is up to.'

237

THIRTY-SIX

'Granddad,' Ben turned to Jack the following morning as they set off to plough the south field. 'Why do most of the stories you tell us happen in late autumn or winter?'

'Well, there's a question! I've no idea, Ben! Most of them have only come about because of that mad witch, Mab. So, it's probably something to do with her. Perhaps it's too hot for her to work in the summer – perhaps even *she* gets overcome by her own fumes and becomes too weak to do anything when she gets heated up by the sun!' Jack grimaced. 'It could be that the heat from the sun cakes all the grime on her and it bakes so hard she finds it hard to walk or move in any way.'

Both boys burst out laughing as they considered Mab in that state.

'Or it could be that she thinks she can't be detected if she does her evil deeds when it's dark. That might be it; have you noticed how evil people nearly always do wicked things when they can't be seen? So, the nights being longer in the autumn and winter, it gives her more time to do her dark and evil deeds.

'Maybe the potions she makes require herbs and the like which are only ready at that time of year. Who knows? All I do know is that as soon as the season of mists arrives and the sun starts to rise later and set earlier I need to be on my guard.' He looked at them with a barely disguised twinkle in his eye. 'I'd suggest you do the same!'

'Oh come on, granddad,' Ben laughed. 'They're only stories. You can't frighten us as much now as when we were younger!'

Jack made a very stern face and, looking unwaveringly into first one boy's eyes and then the other's, asked, 'But are they?' The question hung long and heavy in the morning air

238

as they stared at each other before Jack, with a laugh, added, 'but of course they are!'

Daniel, after a short while, joined in with the laughter although it seemed, even to him, rather brittle; however, the seed had been sown and the thought was now there, niggling at the edge of his brain, *'But are they?'*

The field had been harvested and all that was left were stalks. *'Still a great hiding place for warm, fresh food,'* thought Cabal as he shadowed the plough. *'This was going to be a good eating day!'* He always enjoyed the chase at this time of year.

'Don't forget to stop off at the Post Office, Danny, just in case your mother has written,' Jack called after the boy as he headed towards the village.

Danny turned and waved as he called back that he would.

That evening Jack and his grandsons busied themselves as usual – lighting the fire, preparing and eating supper and settling down for an evening where they were carried back to the age of heroes.

'I would have thought that these two growing lads should have had enough of my stories by now,' Jack spoke to Cabal as they did the rounds of his smallholding, making sure everything was locked or made secure.

'Ah, but they were great times, even if they did scare the wits out of us!' Cabal responded. *'Any true and exciting adventure is always worth the telling – and the listening to. I reckon you'll get fed up with telling your stories before they get tired of listening to them,'* he added.

'No way,' Jack said. *'Although I'm always worried that just speaking her name might be just enough to bring that mad woman back again. Remember what happened last time?'*

'Hmm. Perhaps you're right. Well, we'll just have to keep our eyes and ears open, eh?'

'And our noses?' Jack suggested, tongue in cheek.

239

'Yeuk! Did you have to mention that?' he answered, sneezing at the thought.

Sitting down and staring for a long moment at flames in the fire that had inexplicably turned into a troupe of maniacal actors pirouetting and whirling along the logs as they bounced back and forth from the sides of the chimney, Jack's thoughts flew back to that other fire - much larger and more menacing than this one - before which sat the mad witch and her colossal companion.

He shuddered at the remembered scene and recalled how the dastardly duo had sat planning their diabolical deeds as though they were normal people planning a dinner party. *'Normal people,'* he grimaced. Blinking, he attempted to remove the actors within the flames; it would be no good if they were really there and actually leapt out at them. *'Am I ready for them?'* he thought. *'Would I be fit enough to meet their challenge or their spells? I doubt it,'* he answered himself; *'seeing as I am without Merlin or any of his potions. I need to start getting myself prepared; who knows if and when she might try to get back – like before.'* he shuddered. *'Am I, like my mother always told me, merely letting my imagination get the better of me or am I going mad. Or is a long lost friend from the past whispering down through the ages into my brain and warning me?'*

Not realising how long he had been staring at the scene within the fire, he was taken aback when Daniel interrupted his reverie. Shaking off his dark thoughts he turned to the boys and without further ado lay back in his rocking chair and continued his tale, only vaguely aware – unless he was still being fanciful - that eyes, other than theirs, were watching him.

THIRTY-SEVEN

Now I don't know whether Mab knew that we'd returned and was putting on a show for our benefit or whether she thought she was alone with the giant and laying out her wicked plans to him but I was riveted to the spot as I listened to what she had prepared for all of the prisoners within her grasp. The giant was salivating as she spoke, obviously enjoying everything she suggested, nodding in agreement and adding ideas and evil extras to her plans, most of which she sneered at. To her mind, her planning and expertise were perfect. This oaf had no idea; he was merely the brawn to her brain.

They had attained this almost amicable stance some hour or so ago. Cabal and I had arrived at the end of an extremely violent argument between the two and I was, therefore, beginning to think that things might eventually go our way. Their discussion was getting decidedly nasty so it couldn't be long before the witch hammered him with some spell or other – her face was suffused with colour as her anger mounted. But I believe the giant knew just how far he could push her and, as things mostly work out for her, they eventually called a truce. Well, to be more precise Ysbaddaden was defending himself against the wrath of this almost uncontrollable witch. She had flown down the stairs, eyes blazing and talons out, after finding that her "body", the Lady Elise, was missing. Even though she still saw the reflection of Lady Elise in the mirror over the fireplace, she didn't know how long the spell would last if she weren't in complete control. A thought nudged away at the corner of her brain, *'If Merlin had got hold of her, he could, if he knew the spell, reverse our roles and everyone would see her as she really is and then they'd see me as I really am. Oh, well, so be it!'* she shrugged. *'I have my captives now so it doesn't really matter. Besides, Merlin's dead!'* However, as she continued to dwell on her situation she wondered what would happen if she could not turn herself back into her real self. She would definitely need Lady Elise here if she were to achieve this. It was just not good enough. She must be herself again – a cuddly and slightly plumpish, all-woman person who was not too bad looking! Not like that skinny weak-looking woman now staring back at her from the mirror. She needed to be her real self - it was the only way she could work effectively.

She had finally calmed down once she realised that for the moment she was stuck in this form and so let her temper return to normal – whatever normal is for her. There was no need to incense this supposed ally too much – not while he could be useful, she had concluded. Time enough to deal with him when she had what she wanted. Shrugging off her wrath she turned to him.

'Our plan has come together beautifully,' she gloated as she spoke to Ysbaddaden.

'Even better than you thought!' he grinned.

'No!' she frowned. 'It is as good as I thought it would be. And I don't *think*,' she spluttered, almost completely losing it again, 'I *know* for sure! I don't leave anything to chance. How could it be better than I thought it would be? It is as I *knew* it would be.' She was getting quite close to the edge again, her voice beginning to screech as it rose higher and higher. Gripping the arms of her chair she took a few deep breaths and made herself remember that this huge lout sprawled in the chair opposite was, for the time being anyway, useful to her and had to be assured of her friendship. *'Friendship, hah,'* she thought. *Still, he was of some use - for the moment.'*

Forcing a smile to her lips – if you could call that grimace a smile even on Lady Elise's face - she calmed the man who was by now starting to turn ugly again. Well, he was ugly to

242

start with, of course, but now he was beginning to look mean. 'Of course, you are right,' she struggled to say these words. 'Let's get back to our plan of action.' Looking what she believed to be coquettishly up at him she was relieved to see his darkening mood lighten. *'I really must take care to keep it together,'* she thought.

He had been staring at her and had allowed his mouth to hang open; now slurping a large amount of spittle back up his floppy lip and swallowing it – the spittle, not the lip - he spoke, spluttering the majority of it back at the witch as he did so, 'You can do whatever you want with your prisoners just as long as Culhwch is mine to do with as I will. But – and this is important – Olwen must never know it was me who ordered it. My daughter is the only thing of any importance to me and I don't want to lose her. If she was to find out about it I know she would run away. The only reason I want him done in is because I want to keep her with me. I don't want him, or anyone for that matter, taking her away. I hate it when these suitors keep coming here.'

'You mean there have been others?' Mab asked.

'Scores of them: she's so beautiful, you see,' he replied. 'I have to keep travelling about at night to take them away. I usually travel to the sea carrying them on my shoulders; it takes me days to do this, travelling east to west and then back again. Before that it took me months to find the perfect place to despatch them. I always take them to an old smuggler's cave I've found and leave them for the sea creatures. They are usually alive when I take them so if I was ever accused I could honestly say that I had not killed them; but I don't suppose they survive - tales are that there's a giant octopus that frequents the cave and has a taste for young flesh. Still, if I haven't actually exterminated them myself I don't feel quite so guilty.'

Mab, by this time, had fallen into a fit of hysterics. Slapping her thighs as she listen to his story and almost

243

falling out of her chair in her mirth, she just kept pointing at the giant, unable to speak. Enjoying herself for some few minutes, she was finally exhausted and explained to her extremely annoyed host why she had found his discourse so funny.

'You can't consider yourself innocent for one moment,' she stated. 'If you've taken these young men somewhere and left them to die, well, you're as guilty as sin, but, tell me,' she asked between fits of laughter, 'why did you take them so far away?'

'She'd know,' he answered.

'Who'd know?'

'Olwen would know,' he replied. 'I got rid of the first one, leaving him unconscious about a day's walk away and she found him. I thought I'd managed to cover my tracks sufficiently by choosing nighttime to do the deed but she was clever. She'd woken up early after the night I'd slung him over my shoulder and was on my way to dispose of him - I suppose that must have been after midnight – and followed me. I'm a fairly heavy man' he commented ingenuously.

Mab snorted at this.

'Well, yes, I suppose it's obvious,' he responded. 'It had been raining all day the day before and my footprints were clear to be seen in the ground, so it was easy for her to follow my trail in the bright moonlight. Olwen arose and after discovering that her suitor had disappeared, started to search for him. She finally left the castle and discovered the first of my footprints heading west. Thinking I might help her find her love, she followed my trail in the hope that she might find me soon; it was then she discovered him lying at the foot of a hill and at the mercy of wild beasts. I, of course, had left the scene and was on my way back by a roundabout route.

When I arrived home the servants told me that she had gone looking for me. Overcome by a fear of what she might find, I returned to the place where I had left him and found

244

that she was taking care of him, staying with him until he was recovered, lighting a huge fire and chasing away any beast that came near. I couldn't deny it was me who'd taken him there, as I was the only person in the neighbourhood with size 99 feet! As it turned out, he was a youth with absolutely no backbone and as soon as he was able to, legged it. Olwen was devastated! She obviously blamed it all on me. I'm afraid I had no defence at all.

'I suffered for months after that as she wouldn't speak to me; however, she finally relented when I promised faithfully never to do the same thing again.'

'But you have done the same thing again!' Mab interrupted him.

'No, I haven't,' he replied defensively. 'I have never taken any of them back to the same place!'

'That's splitting hairs!' she responded, trying to hold on to her bubbling laughter.

'Be that as it may,' he defended himself superciliously, 'she cannot walk as far as me and, therefore, if she has her suspicions, she has to prove them. I'm making sure this time that she doesn't have anything to hold against me.'

Mab kept her laughter in check – just.

While this interaction was going on I came to the conclusion that the rumblings that Rhianne and her mother had heard ….

'And me,' interrupted Cabal.

'Barriers up!' I ordered him, realising I must have let mine slip as well, putting us and thus everyone else in jeopardy.

Looking back at Mab I saw her searching in my direction. Moving extremely slowly across to the other side of the room I was relieved to see that she didn't follow me with her eyes; it must, therefore, just be the sound that she tracks, even though I remembered being able to just about see Cabal when he saved me from those two bullies some years ago.

However, it was a relief to know that she, at least, could not detect us by sight – well not very well at any rate and she couldn't possibly smell us – not past her smell I would have thought. I didn't know, at that point, that she'd used a potion to disguise it; I just thought that in my present state I couldn't smell anything. Not so, as I would soon find out.

Getting back to my thoughts, I reckoned it must have been the giant travelling over the land with one of Olwen's suitors that had caused the vibrations Rhianne, Elise and Cabal had experienced. I also wondered whether Olwen even suspected that her father was going further afield to dispose of the men; surely she must, as all of them kept disappearing.

I was brought back to the present by Mab telling the giant that she was returning to her room to rest; she would be back for supper, after which she would start to put her plan into action. 'Make sure you have that room ready for me; my men will be bringing all my paraphernalia in during the next few hours and on the last day of the month my greatest desire will be realised. It has to be then – all the signs confirm it. *And* you'd better make sure that I don't lose any of my prisoners in the meantime!' she added.

The giant heaved himself up from his chair and lumbered out of the room towards the kitchens. Mab, meanwhile, started to ascend the gigantic staircase, puffing and panting as she did so. *'So,'* I thought, *she might look like Lady Elise, but by the way she lumbers up that staircase, she still has the same difficulty Mab has!'* Cabal and I followed her.

Walking through the door she moved over to where the comatose young woman lay. She leaned forward and listened to her breathing. Satisfied that she would not wake up for quite some time yet, she flopped down into a chair and, with head eventually dropping onto her chest, began to snore. One of my questions was answered: I thought the witch never slept but here it was shown that she, like the rest of us, was only human.

246

'Human?' Cabal responded with a snort.

'Yes, well, you know what I mean Cab.'

We moved over to where Rhianne lay sleeping and, silently promising to do everything possible for her, left the room and made our way to where Arthur was imprisoned. The witch would sleep for a while yet. The cell in which Arthur and the others lay was almost dark - evening was now fast approaching. I listened intently but reckoned that their conversations had dried up some time ago. I made out Niel slumped against one wall fast asleep. I had wanted to try and mind speak with him as I thought he might have the gift; that would now have to wait. Culhwch was walking round checking all the stone slabs by tapping them to see if any of them might move while Arthur and Brother Geraint were talking quietly or praying in the far corner.

Cabal and I left to see what the giant might be up to. We travelled back down the staircase and passing Olwen, who not surprisingly didn't appear to see us, carried on in the direction we had last seen the giant leaving the hall, finding him in the book room organising his servants to clear the floor space completely, apart from the large table in the middle and several large floor candelabra which Cornek was fitting with scores of new wax candles.

Apart from this, nothing seemed to be happening at the moment so Cabal and I decided it best to relax - we might need all our strength for later. The only thing that bothered me about our present state was the fact that we couldn't come back to solid form until we needed to and, more importantly, we couldn't eat and I for one was getting awfully hungry. We made for the cavity wall behind the book room and, not needing the switch that Olwen had used to enable us to do so, floated through the secret door into the musty area beyond. Drifting towards the floor, we settled down to rest for however long we had to wait.

THIRTY-EIGHT

I'd shifted about trying to relax, annoying Cabal as I did so because as I moved, he moved, so not only could I not sleep but I was also preventing him from doing so. It was no good; I had to do something – and now! Where on earth was Merlin? Why was he taking so long?

I got up from my "rest" inside the cavity corridor at the giant's home and, nudging Cabal, we arose and floated back through the walls into the room beyond. We hadn't heard a thing, but what met our eyes was amazing. Two huge candelabra, each of which must have contained at least a hundred candles, lit the room. They were positioned at each end of the large table and illuminated an array of dusty bottles, bubbling phials over flickering flames, one or two books and many scrolls.

Looking quickly this way and that we found that the room was currently empty. Gliding over to the table I looked to see what it contained.

'What's going on?' Cabal asked.

'Shh, I'm trying to read what's written on the scrolls and bottles.'

I could smell some disgusting brew as belches of smoke erupted from the bubbling phials. 'So I can smell in my present state,' I thought and, remembering what Merlin had once said, shivered as I thought about powerful smells producing powerful results and wondered just who was going to get whatever this foul smell was. Somewhere in the back of my mind was a niggling worry about something I should know about smelling things in my present state. However, it wouldn't come to the fore so I shoved the worry to the back of my mind and concentrated on what was before me.

The scrolls didn't give anything away as they were rolled up and unless I made myself solid I couldn't unroll them.

However, I saw that there was one book lying face up on the far side of the table and so I glided through the middle of it to the other side to see what it said. I wished I hadn't! I shuddered!

"Potions to bring forth Agonising Death." Straight and to the point – no fancy words there. I wonder how many copies of that have been sold!

'What's does it say?' Cabal asked as he experienced my trembling.

I repeated what the book was entitled. He said nothing for a while and then ordered me to do something quick.

'But what?'

'I don't know,' he prevaricated, *'I'm just a dog! You can't expect me to be able to make decisions like that! But I'll do what you want me to,'* he added graciously.

I looked down at him with disgust. He was as able as I to make decisions.

Taking a deep breath I realised that we were both in the same boat – seeing a huge problem before us and unable to come up with a solution.

My thoughts went back to Merlin and I called out to him in my mind.

As if from a great distance, I got a response. Both Cabal and I jumped as his words penetrated our thoughts. *'Carry on just as you are! If you are able – if it is safe, speak to me in your mind and let me know what is happening. I might not respond but I believe I will hear. Don't do anything hasty. I'll come just as soon as I can.'*

Oh it was so good to hear him. It is such a relief to know that you're not on your own – even when you are on your own or appear to be on your own, if you understand what I mean.

Merlin and Salazar, meanwhile, were at that moment rounding a copse of trees and had come face to face with Pos and Neg who were leading a very lame horse and thus, after a long walk, were on their way back to the castle and were more than a little weary. It was, therefore, that the two Paisley men were taken so completed by surprise that in a split second Merlin was able to overcome them. Muttering one quick word, which caused the falcons' eyes on his staff to light up, the two strange men had no chance. The beams took charge of one man each, shining into their eyes and mesmerising them – they couldn't move. Whistling, Merlin summoned the Faerie folk who'd been keeping track of them; they skipped out of the trees or flew down to him on the backs of birds. Ogwin and Gisele, grinning, each leapt down from the backs of doves and strode up to the wizard.

'Merlin, my old friend from ancient days,' he cried in welcome as many little folk congregated around him. 'What can we do for you?'

Merlin and Salazar made their obeisance to the king and queen who responded in kind, and made introductions before sitting down with them to talk about why they were here. The light from Merlin's staff, which he'd stuck in the ground behind him, continued to hold Pos and Neg prisoner. The Faerie folk eyed them cautiously as they made their way past.

'It's alright,' Merlin assured them. 'Just so long as the lights don't go out!'

The two Druids and the Faerie King and Queen, together with their nobles, spent the next few moments in polite conversation as is expected; it is always necessary to observe the correct formalities. However, after all the official procedures had been completed, Merlin began to speak seriously to the king.

'I am so glad you were near,' he said to him. 'There is devilment afoot with that evil witch.'

'Ah, the Mighty Smell has returned!'

'Yes. She has paired up with the giant in the castle on Glastonbury Plain.'

'My people had told me it had become visible again and we've been keeping watch on it. It only becomes visible, you know, when the giant awakes.' He clapped his hands and a senior soldier from his army stepped forward, back ramrod straight, he clicked his heels together and quickly bobbed his head. 'Tell Lord Merlin what has been going on,' he instructed the Faerie.

For the next ten minutes or so the soldier read from a small book extracted from the turned-back cuff of his sleeve. In a very well-documented fashion he spoke about all the comings and goings at the castle, including the giant's many trips to the coast with drugged men. He spoke scathingly of the Paisley men, at which point all eyes swivelled to look at them – some folk moving further away - and described the chimeras and how the giant and the witch were using them – how they had chased Arthur and his party toward and into the castle.

'There were many people in the party,' he added. 'I saw a lady and her daughter in a wagon, surrounded by many lords on horseback and another wagon escorted by servants. They had no option but to make for what they thought was the sanctuary of the castle. The chimeras, once they had chased them all through the gates, continued around the side of the castle and into their quarters.'

'Please be kind enough to describe the chimeras to me,' asked Salazar.

'Certainly, sir,' he responded. 'They have the body of a dwarf and a large head with a cat's face on one side and a dog's face on the other, although their feet are rather too large in order to counterbalance themselves.'

'Ah! Same as the one sent to us by Percy - not your usual chimera,' added Merlin nodding. 'Possibly something whipped up by the witch, I would imagine.'

The soldier went on to describe the others in the party, giving names where they knew the individual or where he had

251

heard the person's name when he had been listening in on their conversations.

'We are always interested to know what you humans get up to, as you know,' the king added, 'so my subjects are often sitting up in the trees or hidden in shrubbery or on top of a door lintel, or somewhere, listening to you. That way, we are always aware of when we need to take action. Ah, I know you are wise and true, Merlin, but as I have told you on many occasions, not all humans are! My poor legions of spiders, especially my Daddy Long Legs who are my fastest runners, are quite depleted due in the main to cruel children.'

He looked about him but as there were no children around – and I recall that he always seemed to search me out and look at me in a decidedly pointed fashion when speaking about them, even though I can't remember ever having pulled the legs off a Daddy Long Legs in my life – continued, 'However, I am training all species to run faster and to find the most convenient hiding places; they are also learning to send quicker messages along their web lines when necessary.'

It seemed that the soldier had come to the end of his discourse. His book was closed and replaced in the cuff of his jacket sleeve, which he then buttoned down securely. After standing to attention and bowing his head at his king, he stepped back and sat with the other subjects.

They discussed what the tiny soldier had said and how they could best use the information. Although Merlin had decided upon most of his plan, it would be some few hours yet before a complete solution would show itself.

Merlin turned to the king, a mischievous grin playing about the corners of his mouth, enquiring, 'Perhaps your spiders could help me?'

'Of course! But in what way could they assist you? Do you want them to send a message? Frighten someone? Run up and down someone's spine?' The last offer rather tongue in cheek!

252

Turning, Merlin pointed at the two peculiar men held still by the beams of his staff. 'Would your spiders be able to wrap them up securely for me so that I can continue on my way?'

'It would give them much pleasure, I am sure,' he grinned.

The next twenty minutes or so were very interesting. Some of the largest spiders Merlin had seen in his life were summoned and even he had to admit to me later that they more than frightened him.

Pulling out long silken threads, it seemed to take no time at all before they had tied both men's ankles together and their arms to their sides. Running up the rough bark of a large oak tree, they dropped down over the other side of a tough branch and hundreds, if not thousands, of the arachnids hauled each man up until he was dangling by his feet from the tree. Without more ado many of them seemed to swim across the air until they had latched onto the men, cocooning them in multi-layers of silken thread, leaving merely their faces and chests free – well they had to be allowed to breathe!

Merlin, after watching one of the most amazing spectacles of his life, turned and thanked the Faerie King, asking him to extend his thanks to his subjects. Then a few whispered words and the lights in his staff dimmed and then went out.

Goodbyes were said and both he and Salazar watched as Faerie and spiders skipped or flew off through the trees.

'Now, Salazar, this is what we will do!'

THIRTY-NINE

'Bring Arthur to me now,' Mab ordered as, still in the guise of Elise, she turned from mixing an extremely offensive brew.

My eyes flew open. I must have dozed. How could that have been? Both Cabal and I turned and floated across the room to the other side of the table. Whether Mab knew we were there or not, it appeared that she was determined to make no sign; I expect she didn't care if we were – she always liked an audience when she was doing something really bad. However, I reckoned she did know as she was taking great delight in making clear to whoever might be listening just what she was mixing, who she was going to use it on and what effect it would have on them. I could feel that my hair, even in my ghostly state, was sticking straight up!

'One hundred dried warts from the giant ugly toad – ground down and mixed with the slime of the blackberry slug. There – a lovely soft pink colour shot through with shiny sequins of green!' She added it to a fairly large bulbous phial and left it to one side while she looked around for something else. I could see her face starting to swell as it went red - she obviously thought what she wanted wasn't there, but then she saw it. I almost felt the air losing its pressure as her temper lightened.

'Ah – just the thing!' she sighed as she reached across the table to retrieve a small jug. Holding it up to her face she very slowly and deliberately read the label attached to it, '"Complete memory loss"'.

Remembering to put up my barriers, I was relieved to think that she would use that – bad as it was – as opposed to the title I had read on the book earlier that evening.

'But no,' she turned her head to one side considering. 'Just losing his memory is not good enough. Too kind of me – much too kind!' – and after some deliberation – 'But I

254

could use it as well as,' she decided. She stood for a few moments trying to hold herself in check - but it had to happen. She was so off the planet she couldn't help herself. Her lips went first – closed but moving uncontrollably until they parted and let forth the most heinous laughter. Slapping her thigh and then holding onto her grossly wobbling stomach, she rocked backwards and forwards with glee; it was some few minutes before she was able to contain herself. Wiping her eyes with and blowing her nose into the hem of her skirt – and she should have blown it properly so as not to leave a long slimy tendril hanging from one nostril which swung about as she moved - she eventually stopped cackling. It took another minute or so before she was able to catch her breath. Wiping her nose again with the back of hand, the sliver of slime now attached itself along her top lip and onto her cheek, drying and puckering her face as it did so. This looked disgusting on the witch but, as she was still, to me, drifting backwards and forwards between her real self and Lady Elise, it looked very out of place on the lady.

'Come, come, Mab,' she told herself as she spun around, 'Get yourself under control! You've got your man at last and now you can dispose of him at your leisure. A nice, long, slow demise is the order of the day, I think. It's been too long, my girl – this waiting. But now he's yours. There's no way he'll get away this time!'

She started scrabbling around among the equipment on the table, singing a tuneless song – well, more of a la la la than a song - as she did so. I must admit that I did wonder, in the back of my mind, whether all magical people couldn't sing - until, with a whoop of triumph, she held a tiny phial aloft.

'Swamp dragon fire!'

I waited for her to elucidate but she did not. What was that stuff? What did it do? From the sound of her triumph it would appear that it would do awful things.

Shoving as much as she could off the table with a sweep of her arm, she cleared a space in the centre of it. Pulling a candle out of the candelabrum, she angled it to enable a few drips of wax to fall on the table; after securing the candle in the wax she was now able to see more clearly that which she was about to do. Setting a bulbous phial into an iron bracket, she placed it over the flame and, when it started to bubble, carefully removed the stopper from the swamp dragon fire bottle. As soon as the stopper came out there was an almighty belch before a stream of purple smoke erupted from it. Mab grinned before, with great precision, she measured one tiny drop into the slowly bubbling mass of pinkish glue.

Cabal and I were mesmerised as we watched the performance being played out in front of us. First of all nothing happened – the brew continued slowly to bubble and burp. We watched – we had to - I don't think we could have turned away even if we'd had the option.

So it was that Mab, Cabal and I were almost thrown off our feet as a mighty blast suddenly crashed throughout the room. The force lifted Mab off her feet and almost straightened her frizzy hair as it shot back from her head. There was the sound of bottles breaking and candelabra crashing as well as the candlelight whooshing round the room like rippled lightening. This took mere seconds and was a complete shock to the system.

I thought that she had managed to blow up everything in the room and was just starting to congratulate her on her stupidity and feel relieved when all stood still. There was now a quietness that was so unreal, I wondered if, even in my spectral state, I had been blown up along with everything else and was now in that silent space between earth and heaven. But no, not only did I suddenly hear movement but also felt pain in my eyes, which I had screwed up much too tightly. I must have had them closed like that for a few seconds and was expecting to see complete devastation when I opened

256

them. You can imagine my shock and surprise when I did – nothing had changed; all was still in the same order.

The candles stood in their holders and all were still alight. The bottles, scrolls and books, etc, were in their place on the table – not one was broken, blown away or burned, except the ones she'd already shoved onto the floor - and Mab's hair was still glued to her head. Just what, then, had taken place?

'Hee, hee, hee! Brilliant! Just look at that!' Was she talking to herself or did she know that Cabal and I were in the room? I was still not sure but became more careful – just in case.

We floated over to the table and looked at what Mab had achieved. At first it didn't appear to be any different to the pale pink mixture she had made earlier. Then I saw it! There was a flame bouncing around within the mixture and there was also an eye – an angry eye - exactly like the eye of a dragon burning within the flame itself – staring at me!

'I know you can see it, little man,' she cooed as she looked around the edge of the table. I almost jumped out of my skin and then moved slowly away. She didn't follow me with her eyes and so I felt slightly better. 'But let me enlighten you as to the delights of my exceedingly brilliant concoction. Even you will have to admit how great I am once you know what it will do.'

I stared once more at the eye bouncing around within the flame and was quite unnerved by the fact that every time I looked at it, it was looking straight back at me. I had to mentally shake my head and tell myself that I was imagining it. It's a bit like some paintings you look at on a wall where the eyes of the subject appear to follow you round the room wherever you might be in it.

Still thinking about the swamp dragon and being mesmerised by its evil eye as it continued to follow me about the room, I was brought back to the present by the witch continuing to talk to me.

257

'You won't be able to do anything about it, you know. I have your friend in my clutches and this time he won't get away. In fact, in a very short time indeed, he won't be anywhere that he could get away from – as he'll no longer exist. Then I shall be safe,' she sighed, 'at last.'

We all turned as the door opened and Arthur was pushed unceremoniously into the room. We didn't see who did the pushing as the door was closed immediately.

'Mother!' he cried as he rushed over to the witch and flung his arms around her.

Mab looked exceedingly pleased at this.

I could have screamed. In my preoccupation with watching what Mab was doing and, of course, seeing her in my present ghostly state as she really was – her body continuing to fluctuate backwards and forwards between her real self and Lady Elise - I had completely forgotten that everyone else only saw her as the Lady. What should I do?

'What's happening? Oh Mother, let me wipe your face,' he asked as he took out his handkerchief, eyeing the very unpleasant paste stuck to her cheek.

Pushing him away, she proceeded to wipe it, quite unsuccessfully, herself.

'Why are we here and,' turning and looking at the table with all its paraphernalia, 'what is all this?'

'I'm not sure, Arthur; it was here when I, too, was pushed into this room. Perhaps the giant is up to some sort of devilry?' She looked shocked but turned her back on him to hide the glee that was threatening to engulf her.

Arthur must have thought that she was about to cry and, all sympathy, hugged her and replied, 'I don't know. Come; let's get out of here. Do you know where Rhianne is? Is Kay with her? We must save her and try to escape. If you can get her, I'll go back and get the men and we can meet back here. There must be a way out of here apart from those gates. Perhaps Culhwch can find Olwen – she might know a way.'

'Now, now, Arthur, there's plenty of time and Rhianne and I have been treated very well. Sit down and tell me more of your plan. I'll pour us some refreshment.' She turned towards the table and, with her back to him and shielding his view, poured the contents of the bulbous phial into a goblet.

My blood went cold. What was she now going to do? I watched her as Arthur looked for somewhere to sit.

'What a peculiar room this is, mother - there are no chairs!

'Come, let's leave at once. We can sort out our plans as we go along. Culhwch and the others need to be freed and they can help us to fight, if necessary, now that we know the people here aren't friendly. Yes, there is definitely something evil about this place and I, for one, don't want to stay in it one minute more than I have to.'

Mab tut-tutted, putting on a motherly smile, 'Now I'm sure you're imagining things. Here, son, take this and you will feel much better. If you are anything like me, you'll be thirsty; I haven't been given anything since I arrived.' She held the goblet towards him, taking the other one for herself.

Arthur took the goblet from her and held it between both hands. Mab raised her glass in salute and put it to her lips.

I was almost screaming. What should I do? Should I throw the powder over Cabal and myself and become visible. I had to warn him somehow. If he drank that brew he would surely die – and die an awful death at that. On the other hand, if I became visible the game would well and truly be up. Goodness knows what that witch would then do. Whatever the cost, Arthur had to be saved. So, as I was scrabbling about to retrieve the powder from my neck and make myself visible, I was at the same time screaming in my mind to Merlin and asking him to help.

FORTY

The door opened with a mighty crash as Pos and Neg rushed into the room. Arthur jumped out of his skin as he spun around, slopping some of his wine onto the floor. Mab watched helplessly as the swamp dragon flame skipped out of his goblet and into the fireplace setting fire to the logs as it did so; dancing and frolicking among the now kindled flames its eye mocked Mab as she rushed towards it. Screaming, she made a grab at it but missed the flame by centimetres, burning a couple of fingers in the process. Not wishing to damage herself further, she stood stonelike for a few moments, staring helplessly into the hearth before succumbing to her madness.

Screeching at the top of her lungs, she flew about the room pulling at her hair and stamping her feet. The language that came out of her mouth is completely unprintable and would even curl the toes of a fish.

Arthur stood there, mouth agape, as all this was played out before him. Not knowing what had happened or why, he attempted to go to his mother to calm her down, thinking she'd had a brain storm or some other form of madness had attacked her, but, of course, the witch would not let him anywhere near. Mab's fury was exacerbated further when she saw the goblet fall after Arthur, attempting to put it down to go to her aid, misjudged the edge of the table.

Now, not only had the swamp dragon fire now hidden itself among the other flames – and thus could not be retrieved until the fire went out – but the concoction to make him suffer agonies and then lose his memory forever was even now soaking itself into the floorboards – and steaming as it did so. *And* it was those two fools that had caused this.

She turned, mouth distorted by fury and with outstretched arms moved forward to attack the two Paisley men; she'd had just about got a hand round each of their necks, when her madness seemed to leave her. She must have realised she needed those two idiots to carry out her wishes; releasing them, she ordered them to take Arthur to the tower.

'And manacle him,' she snapped as they took hold of him.

'Mother, what on earth is happening?' roared Arthur as he struggled with the men. 'Call them off!' He looked completely bemused by his present circumstances and extremely frightened as to what was happening to Lady Elise. 'Mother!' he cried out as they pulled him backwards through the door.

'And don't "mother" me,' she screamed, slobbering spittle all down herself, which was the last sight he had of her as they dragged him from the room.

Left on her own, she sat down by the fire and could have wept as she thought about what had almost happened but then had not – again! 'I nearly did it this time. Now I'll have to wait. Don't worry, Arthur - it will be soon. You don't stand a chance with me,' she whispered to herself – or was it to me?

While this was going on I re-twisted the parchment containing the dust that I had been about to throw over Cabal and myself and tucked it back inside my shirt; it could wait for another time. I then left Mab as Cabal and I followed Pos and Neg to the tower. If Arthur were manacled, he would certainly not be able to get out through the fireplace as Kay and I had done some few days ago, even if he knew of it. With a mighty sense of relief that Arthur was still in one piece, we floated through the walls and followed the trio to the tower, up the stairs and into the room at the top. We didn't see a sign of any chimeras this time. I wondered if perhaps they'd decided not to replace the one I'd sent packing, that is, if they'd missed it at all.

Pos and Neg pushed Arthur into the room and took him over to the far wall where they pulled down the manacle and attached it to one of his arms. What an awful sound it made

261

as it clunked into place. The Paisley men left without one last look around.

Arthur yanked at the manacle but he was not going to be able to pull his hand through that hole. He slumped down to the floor looking not only beaten but also angry and confused. I couldn't blame him. It would take him a long time to work out what had just happened even when someone took the trouble to try and explain it to him. So far as he was concerned – his mother had lost her senses, he had been taken prisoner and the world or he had gone completely mad.

Well, I couldn't do anything here even if I became visible, but at least Arthur was safe for the time being.

Cabal and I turned and headed for somewhere quiet to think. I wondered if it might be worthwhile trying to contact Merlin again or whether I should keep quiet in case that witch might tune in. Concentrating, I reached out to him in my mind.

'Don't keep on for too long, Percy, in case she hears you.'

'Don't worry, Cab, I won't and you, too, had better not try to talk to me again.'

It was no good, though. He either couldn't or wouldn't respond at that time.

'Let's go, Cab.'

FORTY-ONE

On our way back down the staircase, Cabal and I discussed our next move.

'I'm in favour of becoming visible again, Percy. For one thing I am extremely hungry and I think we'd do much better if we were able to attack physically rather than just float through things and if we don't eat something soon I for one will be too weak to physically attack anything – even a mouse – hmm, a mouse! Sorry, I'll not mention that again. And another thing, all this going through walls and doors is making me feel sick. It's the stone walls that do it for me! They're a bit like those standing stones and you know what I'm like with them! They scare the whiskers off me!'

'For goodness' sake Cab, get a grip! I'm hungry too but I don't keep on about it. Some of the others are in a worse state than us! And travelling through walls is an adventure! Just try and do it when you're not invisible!'

'Hrrmph.'

'Come on; let's see what the others are up to.'

Spending the next half hour floating round the castle, we found that Shake Spear was improving. His wounded arm had been well dressed and there appeared to be no infection. He, like most of the others, was asleep. The remains of supper sat on a bench in the middle of the room – Molly had obviously done a good job of putting something together – and I could feel the saliva filling my mouth as I thought of the hole that that food could fill.

'Don't!'

'Sorry Cab!'

We turned around and went to look at the chimeras who were guarding them. Of course, they knew we were there and I felt very uncomfortable indeed as every eye watched us float through the room. I, for one, was extremely glad to leave.

'Let's go and see what's happening to Niel and Culhwch,' I suggested as we turned and headed towards their prison.

As we entered that room we found that they were in exactly the same situation as before, except, of course, that Arthur was not with them. They had been supplied with food and drink as I could smell something or other – and I must admit that that subject was now starting to take over most of my thinking; I could hear my stomach rumbling even though, in my present state I didn't really have one. And it was extremely dark in that room now that the sun had gone down.

I could hear the even breathing of people who had gone to sleep. Thinking that I could not do anything for them at the moment I turned to leave the room and search for the witch or the giant. Maybe I needed to know what they were getting up to right now.

'Don't leave yet!'

My ears flipped. I heard in my mind a voice that I didn't recognise. It wasn't Cabby and it certainly wasn't Merlin.

I waited.

All was quiet for a long half minute. I suppose I had frozen and was rooted to the spot. I knew that Cabal was still with me; well in our present state he wouldn't be able to extricate himself – we were joined until we released ourselves from our present ghosting state. So I waited.

'Please listen to me.'

I still waited.

'It is I, Niel. Like you, I have the gift. Like you, Merlin has summoned me. Like you, I am to protect Arthur. However, unlike you, at the moment I am confined to this cell and cannot help him. But you can help me and then together we can help him.'

I didn't know whether to believe him or not. It could be a trick. He might be working for Mab. Well, I mean, look at Mordred and Mab! They could also have done something with Sir Niel. I needed to speak with Cabby first.

We floated out of the cell and far enough away to be able to converse secretly.

'*What do you think, Cab?*'

'*About what?*'

'*Now don't ...*'

'*OK, just trying to lighten things up a bit. He is Sir Niel. I'd know if he wasn't. I think it's worth listening to what he has to say. You talk to him and if I think there is something funny going on, I'll let you know.*'

So we went back into the cell. Still seeing absolutely nothing in the pitch black room, I spoke in my mind to Niel.

'*Sorry, Niel. I had to make sure you were who you said you were as so many strange things are going on here at the moment.*'

'*I'm glad you did. If we know for sure we are who we say we are we can work together without any fear. Now, please listen to what I've planned.*'

Over the next few minutes he outlined what we could do. Merlin had given me a task and had also given him a task. They were not too dissimilar and together we could hopefully free Arthur, Rhianne and all the others.

'*Culhwch and the priest do not have the gift and so we will have to leave them here for the moment but once we are free we can come back and get them. I have some of the green potion to send us ghosting again but we will all need to use it together. Merlin told me you have the dust to make yourselves visible again and for me to be able to use the green potion to enable us all to go off together, you will need to make yourselves visible first; we can then decide where we want to be and then lick the mixture together.*'

I did wonder, for one moment, if he might be lying. What if Cabal and I became visible and he didn't have the green potion. I certainly didn't have any more. All I had on me was a little bit of naiad root, which I could throw over him if he was proving to be false. Should we take the chance? If he were lying, we, too, would be locked up in this cell. What good would we be to anyone then? He might be working for the witch but saying he's a friend so that we'd end up imprisoned; then, when the witch comes to our cell, we'd be caught and he'd be set free. No, if Cabby said he was alright, it must be so.

He waited patiently as I tossed the arguments to and fro in my head. Finally making a decision, I felt rather than saw him smile as he sensed us appearing.

Working in the pitch dark and speaking in our minds so as not to wake up the other two sleeping men, we eventually decided to make our appearance outside the barn where Shake Spear and the other men were being held. Once more I held a blob of green potion on each forefinger and put one arm around Cabal's neck in readiness to place the blob onto his tongue. Niel counted up to three and we all applied it together. Well, it took a little time to come to that decision as Cabby wanted to know if he should be ready to get blobbed on the count of three or whether it would be one, two, three and then get blobbed. After much confusion, we eventually decided on the count of three.

Wow – once again I felt the rush of air as we flew through the atmosphere before arriving outside the large barn. Niel appeared to be the leader of our little group this time and if he turned, we turned. We floated over to where Shake Spear lay and were relieved to see that he appeared to be recovering. His arm must be healing well. Wite was obviously dreaming as his eyelids were moving about at a terrific rate – more than likely a nightmare, though, looking at their present circumstances.

Old Molly was still awake – trying to prepare something for the following morning. She was a tough old woman but, as could be seen by us at that moment, had a heart of gold.

We looked over at the chimeras. Our arrival had woken up most of them and holding on to the bars they stared at us as though they could see us clearly. However, they didn't give us away as they made no sound and we eventually decided to search for the others in our party.

We drifted into the castle through the main door – literally, as it was locked for the night; though who would want to break into that place at any time of day or night, goodness only knows.

Gliding across the floor we flew past the stairs until we came to the book room. Making sure we were as silent as the grave, we made our way into the room to find Mab mixing and sifting potions, muttering away to herself as she did so. If she noticed us, she gave no indication that she had done so.

Leaving her to her schemes, we went in search of Rhianne. She was exactly as she had been the last time I saw her – lying as still as death on the huge bed. I tried to speak into her mind but there was no response. My heart reached out to her. What could I do? I had no dragon's droppings left so it was stupid to try and make myself visible; complete waste of time. Even so, I didn't have any of the other dust left to make us visible – Niel had it and he obviously had different plans to mine – well, they were probably the same plans but at this moment mine only dealt with Rhianne.

'*Come, Percy,*' Niel spoke gently into my mind. '*We will come back for her soon. The witch will not harm her!*'

'*How do you know?*' I almost wept. *You're not a wizard, are you? You couldn't possibly know what is going to happen!*'

'*Trust me.*'

So we left her as we turned to make our way to the tower.

Pushing our way through the door of the tower, we looked around for its weird guardian and were satisfied to see it staring at us from the turn in the stair well; they must have decided to place another one there after all, just in case Arthur managed somehow to escape. It just glared at us with curled canine lips and made one or two pathetic attempts at howling.

267

Ignoring it, we made our way up the giant spiral staircase until we reached the top. Upon entering the room we were satisfied to see that Arthur was still there and had not been attacked in any way by Mad Mab or those two weird men. He was fast asleep. While we had been ghosting around I got Niel up-to-date with what had recently happened to Arthur.

'I think it would be best if we now made ourselves visible,' Niel stated. *'We can then free Arthur – the key to the manacle is on the wall just outside the door. Once we've freed him we'll go and get Rhianne and then, somehow, we'll try and escape from this place.'*

'Haven't you got any dragon's droppings then? I asked.

'No. Only the green potion and the dust to release us.'

'Great!'

'Well, you've got the naiad root, should those two Paisley men attack us – or Mad Mab.'

'You'd better get on with it then,' said Cabal as his ghostly stomach rumbled, *'the sooner we get out of this place, the better!'*

'Right. Are you both ready?'

We said we were and he'd better do it while Arthur was asleep otherwise he'd think he was going mad if he saw us materialising in front of him. So, he threw the dust over us.

Cabal shook himself from his nose to his tail and snorted to clear his nose. He trotted over to Arthur and started to lick his face. Once the licking had had the desired effect he moved over to Niel and licked his hand, all the while wagging his tail.

'Niel! Percy! Where have you come from?

'Arthur,' Niel responded as he stuck the retrieved key into the lock, thus releasing Arthur from the manacle's confinement, 'we don't have much time. We can talk about this later but for now we need to go to Rhianne and escape. If we can, we should also try and get to Culhwch and Geraint and see if we can get them out - the more of us the better.'

268

'But what about mother? She's gone mad, you know. I don't know if it's a return of her fever but she's certainly not herself!'

'She's certainly not that,' Cabal agreed on a sneeze.

'Yes, er well, we'll see what we can do,' Niel replied.

Niel turned to leave the tower by the door but stopped as he considered the chimera at the foot of the stairs, airing his concern as he did so.

'I've been here before,' I said as I walked over to the fireplace. Kicking the grating for a few minutes, my foot eventually found the knob that released the lock in the wall at the rear of the fireplace, but not before Niel and Arthur thought I'd completely lost my wits. However, once discovered, and without more ado as the corridor behind the fireplace came into view, we all disappeared through it.

FORTY-TWO

On our way back down the staircase, Cabal, Niel and I discussed our next move.

'I've seen where everyone is, Niel, and I think we should try and set them all free. The more men we have, the better our chances of getting out of this awful place. Though how we're going to get past those little monsters is a problem.'

'Percy, let us speak properly – for Arthur's sake.'

'Oh right, yes – sorry!'

Arthur had by then already started to ask questions. Where had we come from? How had Niel escaped? Where had I been all this time?

I told him as much as he needed to know at that time, promising to give him the whole story when we'd got out of our current predicament. Asking him to whisper, I managed to explain to him where we were, how we might get out and just who might hear us.

Understanding the situation completely, he, once more took the lead, preceding us down the gloomy stairway. Reaching the small opening through which I had seen the fire burning on my last excursion there, we all froze at the sounds of voices rising and falling as they made their way through that gap and into our ears. Arthur peered out through the opening and we crept up behind him. One voice was that of the giant who intermittently blocked our light as he paced up and down as he passed our hiding place; we had to listen intently to half of what he said as, big as he was, his words kept fading as he moved away from us.

'That mad woman … going to be sorry … not my fault that Lady Elise has … still got the daughter …'

It was quiet for a few moments and then he turned and our ears twitched when we heard a door open and then slam shut.

'Well, Ysbaddaden, I'm ready once again.'

'Yes, ma'am,' he replied and then merely stood looking at her. He was standing still and we could only see him through the narrow hole, one eye looking straight at us. However, at that time, we believed, he was not using that eye but staring, with his other one at the witch. At least we hoped that was the case.

She, though, thankfully, was out of our line of vision.

'Well, don't just stand there like a moron! Go get Arthur. The potion is ready – again! I eventually caught the swamp dragon flame,' she added, blowing on two of her fingers. 'How many times do I have to do this before I seal his fate? Why do I have to be surrounded by so many incompetents? Hurry man,' she screeched at him, 'before it becomes useless.'

The giant turned and gave his instructions to the Paisley men, who rushed past him at terrific speed out through the same doorway from which Mab had entered.

'Well,' sighed the witch, 'at least someone in this place sees the need for urgency. Now, while I'm having fun with my nemesis, you can go and fetch Culhwch. You can do what you like with him but if you need help, well, just wait until I'm finished and then I can give you a hand.'

It was probably just as well that we could only hear her; I dread to think what would have happened if Arthur had seen her! Up to now she had tried her hardest to play the part of Lady Elise but had now, in the presence of the giant, reverted to her usual vile self. Yes, if Arthur had seen her as his mother and heard those same awful things, he would most surely have thought her mad at best and possessed at worst, even if he didn't think it was he that had lost his wits.

'We'd better move on,' Niel prompted me. *'Once those two men find Arthur gone, this place will be in uproar!'*

'Arthur,' I whispered. 'Let's go; we need to hurry now before they find you're gone.'

271

We moved on then, down the rest of the stairway until we found our way out behind the tapestry. Without wasting any time I led them over to the huge door, climbed up onto Niel's back and lifted the latch. Once outside, we pulled the door to behind us, crept along close to the castle walls and headed towards the barns. I knew that most of the chimeras were locked inside a cage, while four or five of the older ones were left to guard the rest of our party who were locked in the barn.

Arthur was all for going back into the castle so as to release his mother and sister and it was all we could do to persuade him otherwise. He finally agreed to let the men out of the barns when he realised that it would quadruple our number.

Cabal was sent ahead of us to sniff out the land. We weren't particularly worried about being caught in the next few minutes as both Pos and Neg and the giant had been sent off in the other direction but we knew that as soon as we entered the barn those chimeras would set up a deafening noise. I'd heard the odd wild dog howl and cat screech as I lay in my bed back at Sir Ector's home – at least I think they were wild, but now that I'd met these things I could be mistaken –so what would a couple of dozen sound like. Still, there was no help for it - it had to be done.

We must have looked extremely suspicious as, keeping as close together as we could, we tiptoed across the grounds towards the barns and with heads twisting this way and that, searched for danger whilst moving forward.

True to form, those weird little monsters set up a hissing and a howling fit to shake the ground as we pushed our way through the barn door. Making a grab for a pitchfork, and just in time, Niel spiked one of the chimeras as it leaped at him. It let out a pathetic yelp as it flew through the air, before landing on the far side of the barn with the pitchfork sticking in the air. The others closed ranks, keeping their eyes on us but moving backwards towards the gigantic cage where the rest of the hoard, heads swivelling round and round, were baying and banging the bars in their craving to get out.

'Don't let them release the others,' I yelled, looking around for a weapon to defend and attack with.

Cabal had managed to move around the inside walls of the barn and was, even now, out of eyesight of one face of the chimera guards. The backs of their heads saw him too late; they realised their peril as, like lightening, he pounced upon them, virtually cutting off most of their yowled warnings. We all rushed in, then, and in no time at all they were overcome. The other men, led by Brosc, had come rushing up to assist but it was by then all over - apart from the terrific din the imprisoned chimeras were still making.

'Quick, men, let's go as quickly as we can. Tailor. Brosc. You men take the wagons and the others out of this place and make camp behind that copse of trees over there,' Arthur ordered, pointing at the horizon about a half a mile away. Wite. Shake Spear. You two come with us. Bring a couple of men. We need to save the ladies.' Arthur was, by now, shouting as he gave directions, trying to get his voice heard above the terrible din that was going on.

At the same time we were all keeping watch as we hitched the horses to the wagons, saddled the ponies and, that done, pulled open those gigantic gates and put our shoulders to them, before, finally, watching them escape.

Arthur stood for a few seconds and watched the party ascend the hill before turning to re-enter the castle and so it was that we were taken completely off our guard as two large horses shot past us and through the gates. Almost being felled by the draught they caused as they rushed by, we watched in consternation as they raced off in the opposite direction to our wagons.

'It's mother! Stop; STOP!' cried Arthur impotently as Lady Elise, screeching at the top of her lungs, was attempting to thump the life out of her red-headed abductor. Racing after the two horses, Arthur came to a sudden halt, stamping his feet in fury as he realised the futility of chasing after them on foot.

I wanted to laugh but was caught up in a bevy of emotions. I couldn't laugh because Arthur would think me extremely insensitive to the fact that his mother had been carried off by those two men. I was, apart from Cabby, of course, probably the only person that knew that that wasn't Lady Elise. Had Niel understood all I'd told him?

I wondered why the Paisley men should take her away. Perhaps she had gone completely mad or, on the other hand, perhaps they had. Maybe she'd hit them round the head one time too many. Also, if she was now not in residence, it would be much safer to save Rhianne; that was a relief! Then again, Arthur didn't know that that was Mab and so might waste time looking for the witch instead of trying to rescue Culhwch.

All these emotions and thoughts went through my brain in double-quick time and so I was able to keep up with what Arthur was now saying.

'We'll have to chase after them,' he cried.

'What with?' I asked watching both sets of equestrians disappearing over the horizon. 'We have no more horses.'

'I think we should try and see if we can find Rhianne and then get out of this place,' Sir Niel suggested.

'And Culhwch and Brother Geraint,' I added. 'The giant was headed towards your cousin and might, even now, be doing something awful to him.'

That made up Arthur's mind. 'Let's get to Culhwch first. I was going to suggest we split up but I think it would be best if we all stayed together.'

I didn't have any qualms whatsoever, now that I knew the witch was not around to do any serious harm to Rhianne or Arthur. However, she might be back at any minute, thus time was of the essence. So we set off in search of Culhwch.

274

I'd remembered everyone else, but how on earth could I have forgotten about Mordred?

The howling of the chimeras receded a little as we made our way around the courtyards of the giant's castle. Keeping a lookout for trouble, we were surprised to see Olwen beckoning us over to the keep. Mostly hidden behind the great oak door we could see that she, with eyes darting this way and that, was expecting discovery at any moment. 'You must come quickly,' she whispered.

Arthur, leading our party over to her, asked who she was but I, knowing that a lot of time would be wasted in interrogation if she told him she was Ysbaddaden's daughter, quite rudely interrupted, telling him she was trustworthy and had freed me once already. That being so, Arthur was happy, so we all followed her into the room.

'Terrible things are happening,' she choked on a sob. 'My father has gone completely mad and has left the castle. I don't know why or where he's gone but it can't be far as he's taken nothing with him. That witch told him to do something; so he's gone to do it.'

'Do what?' Niel asked.

'I don't know but it must be something awful. He was chuckling all the way out of the castle and up the hill.'

'Who, pray, is your father?' asked Arthur.

'Ysbaddaden,' she replied.

I held my breath thinking that Arthur would now explode with anger as he thought of the giant but he either hadn't been told his name or didn't remember. Slowly exhaling I waited to see what would happen next. However, thinking about them, I hoped he hadn't gone after the men.

'Is Culhwch still here,' Niel asked her.

'Oh, yes, he is still imprisoned over there,' she answered, pointing towards the furthest part of the castle situated by the wall.

275

'Well, let's get him out.'

After rummaging around the lintels and frames, we finally located the key, unlocked the door and let out Culhwch and Brother Geraint. Olwen ran into the arms of the young man while the older one blessed the rest of us.

'Yes, yes,' said Arthur, a little ungraciously, 'but come; there's no time to be lost - we must now go and rescue Rhianne and mother. Oh, I hope that witch hasn't got hold of them. Keep your eyes out for her,' he warned, completely unaware that she wasn't still there and I obviously couldn't enlighten him. 'Come, men, grab hold of whatever weapons you can find; Percy, show us the way.'

Most of our conversations over the last few minutes had been conducted through the medium of the loudest whispers you have ever heard. The chimeras had not ceased their howling since we'd released their prisoners from the barn. It was hardly surprising, therefore, that we didn't notice that the sound was escalating; I suppose in the back of our minds we must have thought that they'd just increased their volume.

'Run,' yelled Wite, the first to turn the corner, as he spun round and rushed back at us. Tripping, as he bumped into Shake Spear, they both fell over and wasted precious seconds getting to their feet. I had been walking almost side by side with Wite as we made our way back to the castle and saw, just a split second after him, the reason for his horror and panic.

Helping Niel get the two fallen men to their feet we turned and ran as fast as our feet would carry us away from those baying monsters. The one relief we had was that they were smaller than us and, like us, only had two legs; therefore, we should be able to outrun them – but where could we go? The other side of the coin was that they were starving and appetite would give them wings. I shivered as I thought of what might happen if they caught us. They might have shorter legs than us but they certainly had bigger mouths!

Olwen had grabbed Culhwch's hand and was pulling him towards the bulbous-roofed tower at the eastern side of the castle.

Cabby was our rearguard as we ran, continually turning to face the chimeras with curled back lips and teeth almost the same size as theirs. They would stop for a second or two but, because of the sheer weight of their numbers pushing from behind, it could be seen that they would not be deterred from their course. Besides, they'd looked forward to this meal for a very long time by now.

'Thank God,' sighed Arthur, catching his breath, as we ran inside and slammed the door behind us. Not before time, for as soon as the bolts were rammed into place, the first scratches could be heard on the other side of the door along with extremely angry squealing and baying – the chimeras would go without their meal for a little while yet.

'Did you see him?' Cabal enquired.

Both Niel and I turned and looked at one another as Cabby's voice penetrated our minds.

'Who?' asked Niel.

'Mordred! Well, Mordred looking like Sir Kay!'

He looked up at Niel and then over at me, noticing our blank expressions.

'Tell me, Cab,' I demanded. *'What about him? Where did you see him?'*

'When we turned the corner, before Wite told us to run, I saw him holding the barn door open. He's the one who let the chimeras out of their cage.'

Niel and I looked at one another and it dawned on us, if on no-one else, that not only did we have those monsters prowling around outside but that Mordred was also on the loose. Now, what might he get up to next?

277

FORTY-THREE

'You'd better put me down at once, if you know what's best for you,' screeched the witch. 'Put me down!' She was wriggling, fit to burst and it was becoming exceedingly difficult to keep a hold of her. 'If you don't obey me at once, right now, I'll turn you into dung beetles; yes, dung beetles – you'd enjoy that, wouldn't you, you pathetic, ungrateful wretches. No more of my delicious meals for you – dung from now on – dung. That's all you'd be able to eat! And, because I am so kind, as much of it as you like! Ha!' She almost laughed but, then, being jolted to bits by the horse and being crushed in a vice-like grip by Pos, it was difficult to keep her face still, let alone contort it into a grin. 'I'm warning you! Put me down – RIGHT NOW!'

Neg, pulling alongside, leaned over, lifted up and opened his hand and blew a grey powder into her face. Within two seconds she slumped over, slack jawed and dribbling, and so, thankfully, the rest of the trip was conducted in silence.

It took some three hours to complete the journey and thus it was that two tired but satisfied men arrived at the cave, struggling down the stairway with the heavy and cumbersome woman slung between them.

'We'll take her over to the large table; she shouldn't wake for another hour or so, so there's plenty of time to do what's necessary.'

'We'll need to be quick though; we can't give her any more of that powder or it'll kill her. Well, it wouldn't be much of a loss so far as I'm concerned and after all the things she's done to me I'm sure that no-one would blame me, but I don't want to become a murderer, even of her! I couldn't live with myself!'

Pos dropped the woman onto the table and stood back looking at her for a long minute. Shrugging his shoulders, he walked over to a wall covered in shelves and poked around until he found what he was looking for. Lifting it up to the light, he swirled the contents around until they had formed a uniform yellow.

'*Cover your nose,*' he ordered the other man. '*I'm going to take the stopper off this bottle; smoke will come out and fill the room for about ten seconds. Everything in this room that breathes it in will sleep for several hours, leaving us more than enough time to complete our plans.*'

True enough. As soon as the stopper was removed, a dirty yellow smoke filled the room. The two men stood and looked around, holding thick rags over their noses; ten seconds later the fog cleared, they removed the rags from their noses and gingerly sniffed the air. Apart from a slight tang of sulphur, the room held no fears for them.

The black cats that had been roaming around the room had curled up where they'd stood and slept; so, too, had the spider, previously busily knitting his web, as he now sat suspended in mid-row.

The two men checked everywhere to make sure they could get on with their work without any interruption, especially checking the witch, before settling down to read through several scrolls set out on a well-lit bench. Not finding it Pos told Neg, '*It's entitled "Transformation" and if you find it before me I'll treat you to something amazing.*'

'*And if you find it before me, then I shall finally believe that what they say about you is true! There is none better!*'

'*So, then, what can we lose?*' he chuckled. *We will both be winners. Let's get started.*'

FORTY-FOUR

We looked down at the unconscious Rhianne. My heart went out to her. She was as pale as death and we could hardly feel any breath coming out of her.

'We need to get her out of here,' Arthur cried. 'Let's take her somewhere where there's some fresh air.'

'We can't go outside,' Olwen reminded us. 'It's much too dangerous with those creatures running about.'

'Oh, Merlin, what can we do? We need you! Rhianne is so ill – it looks like she's close to death. Merlin, please help her.' I didn't care if Niel or Cabby heard my plea. Rhianne was much too important to me for me to consider myself.

'She will be well, Percy,' I heard him speak to me. *She is entranced and will be released quite easily when I come to you. Do not worry. Help the others.'*

What a relief! Niel and Cabby drew close and I was encouraged by their friendship.

Meanwhile, Arthur was instructing us all as to what we should try and do next.

'It's going to be extremely hard to get away with Rhianne being unconscious but, nevertheless, we must try. Mistress Olwen, do you know a way out of this place? Do you know of any secret stairways or passages?'

'I do, sir, but I'm afraid they all lead out into the castle grounds.'

'There is one place, Arthur,' I added, chewing on my lip. 'It's in the dungeons; there's a sort of well set into the floor but there's a problem - it's full of water for a start and it's also guarded by a naiad. Salazar managed to divert the stream that fills the well when Kay and I were imprisoned and we got out by crawling on our bellies till we reached the other side. No, I don't think we can go that way! How would we get Rhianne out? She'd drown. Sorry, stupid idea.'

'Maybe not! Perhaps we could lure the guardian of the well out of it and disable it in some way.'

'There's still the well to overcome,' I moaned.

'How far is the tunnel? Could someone swim it?'

I thought about it for a moment and realised that it might be possible. It had taken Kay and I some little time to drag ourselves out by our elbows but full of water it might just be possible to swim it fairly quickly.

Arthur was watching me intently and could follow my thoughts as they travelled across my face. 'Yes, it can be done can't it? Can you swim Percy?'

My heart sank. Why me? Why is it always me? I looked from one to the other and it could be seen by all their faces that I was the chosen one. Big deal! Still, they might not be able to overcome the naiad. That thought satisfied me for a short while but only for a short while as, turning, I looked once again into the comatose face of my lovely Rhianne. No, we had to do everything we possibly could.

With Arthur urging Olwen to show the way, he followed as she and Culhwch made their way out of the tower and into the castle. We passed the kitchen doorway and were greeted with a wave from Cornek and in the back of my mind I wondered why he and the others were not surprised or alarmed at the party of strangers passing by. This was a peculiar place.

In the main hall I ran over to the huge entrance door and with my ear pressed against it listened intently. The sniffs, grunts and occasional howl told me that our guardians were still on the prowl. Sighing, I followed the others down into the lower regions of the castle.

Shake Spear grabbed a couple of torches and he and Wite held them aloft as we stepped, cautiously, ever downwards towards the dungeon, my heart also dropping ever downwards with each step. It wasn't that I minded being the one to swim along that tunnel but I wasn't that strong a swimmer, and,

281

say, what if there was a Mrs Naiad down there waiting for her mate to come home? It's common knowledge that the female of the species is much more dangerous than the male! It would also be extremely difficult to make a turn in that tunnel and, as one already knows, naiads are extremely fast in water; even if I did manage to turn, I would never get back to the dungeon before at least one leg went missing! How would I be able to swim with only one leg? You might have realised by this time that my biggest fear at my age was being eaten bit by bit by whatever weird and hungry creature I might bump into.

'Percy, get a grip!' Cabal was pushing me along with his nose; I hadn't realised I stopped. I also hadn't realised I'd let my mental barrier down. Niel would certainly have been following my train of thought and must think me a complete coward! Thank goodness, Rhianne in her current state, at least, wouldn't know. Well, I hoped she wouldn't. Pulling myself together and catching up with the two last men as they carried Rhianne almost fireman fashion between them, I pushed past them to speak to Arthur.

'Wait,' I called. Arthur turned round and let me catch up with him.

'Well, what is it?' he asked.

'I'm going to need someone else to come with me. I won't be strong enough to hold back the stream by myself. Salazar held it back the last time, when he helped Kay and I escape, and even though he is huge he was struggling to hold back the flow of water; what chance would I have on my own?'

'You're right!' Turning round, he asked, 'OK men, who else can swim?'

'I can,' Shake Spear stated as he stepped forward.

'No,' Arthur shook his head. 'I'll need you to pull Rhianne through the tunnel. That reminds me – we'll need to make some sort of pallet to lay her on. Perhaps you could get

282

to work on that,' he said to the man. 'Anyone else able to swim?'

'I can a bit,' Fisher admitted, 'though I'm not very good at holding my breath.'

'It's not far, Fisher,' I told him. 'It didn't take much more than a couple of minutes to drag ourselves along it when there was no water in it, so it should only take thirty seconds or so to swim.'

'Well, there's no-one else, so it will have to be you, Fisher,' Arthur decided.

'I'll go, too,' said Niel. 'There'll then be three of us – a cord of three strands is not easily broken! I'm quite a strong swimmer so, if we tie ourselves together, I can pull the others through once I reach the outside. There was a pile of hemp at the entrance to these cells which we could use to make a rope.'

'Well, done, Niel, a great idea – the three of you it is, then.'

I'd watched Fisher's face lighten up when Niel volunteered and then look resigned when he realised he still hadn't been let off the hook.

Turning to the rest of the party Arthur started giving orders on how the naiad might be lured out of his lair and what to do with him once that had been achieved.

We had by now reached the door to the cell.

'Better hold the torches high,' I suggested. 'You never can tell if the naiad is here or where he might be.'

Shake Spear would have gone blundering in first, if we'd let him.

'Stand aside, Shake Spear,' Arthur ordered him. 'I think it would be far better if someone went in who could actually see at least their nose in front of their face!'

Shake Spear looked crushed but gave a wry grin when Arthur punched him gently on the shoulder.

'It's not enough to speak, but to speak true,' he agreed.

I looked up at him again in wonder. Surely he *must* be an ancestor of that great bard.

Returning to the present, Wite stepped past him and, holding his torch high, peered round the door. 'It's very dark over by the far wall, but there appears to be nothing near the door.'

Arthur moved forward and the rest of us followed. Cabal, all his senses on high alert, walked gingerly across the floor, sniffing as he went. *'Can't smell anything,'* he advised me, leaning over the well. *'Wonder if it's at home!'*

Whoosh! A mighty explosion of water!

Olwen screamed as she saw, for the very first time, the ugly head of the naiad as, jaws wide, it made a lunge at the wolfhound's neck. Blood spurted as sharp teeth bit into Cabal's throat.

Pandemonium reigned. Wite rushed forward and, putting his torch out as he did so, whacked the naiad on the head. The sprite let go of Cabal's neck and slid back into the well.

I was close behind Wite when I saw what was happening and hurried over to Cab. Well 'hurried' was hardly the word. My legs had turned to jelly when I saw what had happened and I felt like I was flip-flopping across the room on barely-felt feet. With my heart in my mouth after seeing that fountain of blood springing from him, I expected to see him dying, if not already dead. However, relief flooded through me as I saw him standing there, head bowed and with the blood, which now merely trickled, matting his hair.

'It was only a blood vessel, not an artery' Niel told us as he examined the hound. 'Not too serious,' he added. 'Someone give me a cloth or scarf; I need to tie it round his neck. It should stop bleeding soon.'

I watched as Niel ministered to my friend; my emotions were raw but relief was uppermost in my mind as I considered just what might have happened had he been half an inch nearer to that hole.

284

'Don't even think about it!' Cabal whispered into my mind. *'It didn't, so please let your imagination stop there!'*

Trying my hardest to stop shaking I looked around at the others. The men were hardier than me but I noticed that Culhwch was finding it hard to comfort Olwen, who was still trembling.

I finally let my eyes wander around the dungeon. It obviously hadn't changed at all since I'd shared it with Kay.

Kay! My mind did a backflip. What on earth had happened to him? Was he still with Merlin? Did he still look like Mordred? And what was Merlin up to? I knew he was alive, as he'd been answering me when I called but as to what he was doing, I didn't have a clue. Added to that, what was Mordred up to? Cabal had seen him let the chimeras out to attack us; but what was he now up to? Perhaps they'd turned on him and had him as their lunch. The thought wasn't unattractive and I indulged myself for a few moments, wondering just what parts of him they'd dine on first. Shaking my head, I turned from that thought; it would make me as bad as them, thinking that way! No, he was too evil to perish like that. They'd choke on him anyway!

By now Arthur had organised almost everything: Wite and Fisher had broken up two chairs and roped their backs together to make a pallet on which to carry the still unconscious Rhianne; Shake Spear had raided the kitchens and the ever-pleasant Cornek and a couple of his workmates had aided him in carrying a whole side of beef down to the dungeon. He didn't appear to think that what they were doing was anything out of the ordinary and, once the job was completed, wished them a happy day and departed.

We had all helped in setting the carcass up against the wall, hoping that the tantalising smell of meat would lure the naiad out of his hole. Some of us hungrier ones had hacked off some of the food for ourselves!

But now, all we had to do was wait.

FORTY-FIVE

'Got it,' he cried, jumping up and running over to the shelves on the opposite wall.

'Congratulations,' his companion applauded as he, too, moved over to observe. *'What is it that we're going to use it for?'*

'She has used the most poisonous of all the umbelliferous plants.'

'Hemlock?'

'Yes, hemlock.'

'So what is it that you are now looking for? Is there something that can counterbalance it?'

'Yes! Yes, there most definitely is! But I am afraid, my friend, it is something that is entirely my own. I cannot share it, even with you! However, please assist me with the main ingredients – here's a list – and I shall add the rest.'

There was a flurry of activity as the two men boiled, grated, sieved and mixed the concoction. Finally satisfied that all was now ready, the secret ingredients were, secretly of course, added.

'You can come back now,' he called and the other man returned. *'Let us collect the women and lay them on the table.'* After clearing the large table of everything, they walked over to the bed in the far corner. To all intents and purposes Mad Mab lay there in a stupor. Very gently, they lifted her up and lay her on one side of the table. Then, taking a deep breath to help with the struggle ahead, they hoisted up the other woman, ostensibly Lady Elise, and lay her beside the first.

'I shall stand at their heads and apply the mixture to their temples. It should work first time but, if not, it will definitely work if I apply it again. They shouldn't awake for at least an hour afterwards.'

286

It did work first time and when I heard about it I was amazed. The man dabbed a small amount of the mixture on both women's temples at the same time. The room zipped with such luminosity that the men had to cover their eyes for the time it took to work. What they did see, however, was incredible. The women seemed to move between being sound and being wraithlike, changing from the colours of a rainbow to becoming ashen and grey; at the same time changing places with one another until, with a final whoosh, all was still.

The men moved over and looked at the two women, who had, by now, changed places. The man with the shock of red hair put his hand on the head of the Lady Elise and stroked her hair.

'Back to normal now,' he confirmed as he felt the silken threads of her pretty locks. *'Come, friend, let us lay the Lady back on her bed. We'll need to set a herbal candle on the table as a remedy to restore her – and all - once we've gone.*

'In the meantime, let's get this witch off the table.'

Leaving a note to say just who she now really was, they carried the Lady Elise back to her bed and lay her gently upon it; pinning another note to the wall with further instructions.

Returning to the table it was extremely tempting to just pull the witch off the table and allow her to thump onto the floor but, not being that sort of a person, he instructed the other man to help him lift her off the table.

'Help me carry her over there; just in front of the Glass,' he added.

They struggled across the room with the unwieldy woman and sat her down on the floor. With each of them holding her up by a shoulder, the one with the red hair commanded the other to look deep into the Glass and find the place where the two men had been mesmerised by the ruby eyes of the merlin-headed staff.

As soon as the picture appeared, in a flash, they were gone.

287

Brosc and Tailor had got very fidgety. It had been almost the whole day since Arthur had sent them up the hill to wait for them.

'Where do you think they've got to,' Tailor asked. 'And I don't like the sound of that howling,' he added, as the light winds wafted the odd noises across to them. 'Do you think we should go back?'

'You've got to be joking!' was the tart reply. 'We daresn't disobey Arthur. I don't know how you could think such a thing.'

'Well, I think it's a good idea. What if things are going wrong down there and they need our help? I certainly don't like the sound of that howling!' added Tailor.

'No! We should wait here like he told us.'

'Let's ask the others? If they say we go, we go!'

'No!

With the air turning electric, the two men stood looking at one another to see what other arguments they might have for or against, all the time thinking up answers to questions that might be asked, when they were both taken off their guard by a small – in fact it was so tiny it should not have been noticed at all, but it was – puff of smoke over the other side of the copse of trees in which they were standing.

They saw it out of the corners of their eyes and, with both heads swivelling round in the same direction, wondered what it was.

'Did you see that?' asked Tailor.

'Yes. But what was it?'

'Dunno. Let's go see.

Without more ado, and without telling anyone where they were going, the two men made their way, very cautiously, to where they had seen this phenomenon. With Brosc in front and Tailor close behind, they almost fell over one another as Brosc suddenly and without warning came to a complete stop.

'What on earth did you …?' Brosc clamped his hand over Tailor's mouth as, horror of horrors, they saw what was happening beyond the trees. Once he was sure that Tailor could see what he could see, he took his hand away and placed it over his own at the shock of what he was witnessing.

The two Paisley men were assisting the mad witch to her feet; this was quite a job in itself as, apart from the fact that she appeared extremely drunk, she was not the smallest woman on the planet. This would have been very funny in different circumstances; the situation here, though, was as far from comedy as it could be – just beyond the acrobatic trio, and propped up against the trunk of a tree, sat Merlin and Salazar, both asleep or unconscious and tied up with such a mountain of string that it would be impossible to break free.

Tailor and Brosc looked at one another, mouths open and shock written plainly on their faces, for the moment unable to move. Brosc indicated by pointing that they should move back from the scene. 'What are we going to do now?'

'We'd better go back and get some men and try and rescue Merlin,' Tailor replied.

'Come on then, quick!' he responded and the two of them had started back when it grew suddenly dark. Stopping in their tracks and wondering what was happening, the ground began shaking under them and they were thrown to one side as the giant, with Merlin and Salazar now slung over his shoulder, strode past them, leaving them to watch helplessly as he strode back towards the castle with Pos and Neg following behind dragging the witch between them.

'Now what are we going to do?'

'I think you were probably right the first time. We'll have to go back to the castle and help them. Now that Merlin and Salazar are in the clutches of that witch, they're going to need all the help they can get.

FORTY-SEVEN

The witch was howling with laughter. She clapped Pos and Neg on the back as she circled the pathetic bundles slumped on the floor before her. The giant stood against the wall with a huge – well it would be huge wouldn't it – grin on his face, his floppy bottom lip all-aquiver. He watched what was going on with great satisfaction – well, one eye watched what was going on with great satisfaction at any rate!

'I forgive you,' she said to the two Paisley men as she passed them for the third or fourth time. 'I promise I will never, never turn you into dung beetles; I promise,' she vowed. 'It was just a joke! Really, it was,' although she always broke every promise she had ever made without compunction, never giving it a second thought; so they showed absolutely no gratitude toward her as she said this; but, then again, they'd shown no emotions whatsoever at any time - no change there, then.

'Now, I know I was making many spells in your book room, Ysbaddaden, but how on earth did I manage to get Merlin all wrapped up like a parcel? I must be more powerful than I thought; my spells are working even when I don't know I'd made one!' she crowed. Smirking, she continued, 'I expect that, being as weak as he must have been when I last dealt with him, he was more than ready to be gift-wrapped!'

This was all too much for the mad woman; throwing back her head she dissolved into uncontrollable cackling and it was a good two minutes before she managed to stop and this due solely to the fact that her sides were aching so much that her back felt like it was about to break. Wiping away the tears of laughter from her eyes and the tendrils of mucus from her nose onto the sleeve of her dress, she finally managed to stop.

'Now,' she continued, her breath still rasping as she tried to catch it, 'how did I do it and how can I bring him and the

290

other one round? It's no good just me seeing him all tied up like that! He's got to see it too. That's the most important part! That's the bit that gives me the most enjoyment of all. He has got to see just how clever I am and just how stupid and powerless he is!' She stood, hand holding her chin, as she delved into her mind to find the solution. She started to get irritated when, on trying to find out how she'd captured him – and no part of her twisted brain shed any light on this – not only had she no idea but also couldn't find out how she'd knocked him out or, more importantly, how she could bring him round. She looked between him and Salazar and, after clicking her tongue and stamping her foot, decided it best to return to the room and check her herbs, spells and potions.

'Stay with them,' she ordered the Paisley men. 'See who's still here,' she instructed the giant. 'And for pity's sake, lock up those beasts; I can't hear myself think - they're giving me a headache with all that squealing and howling!'

The giant pushed himself away from the wall and departed, leaving the witch to wonder if he would, in fact, do as he was told. 'He'd better!' she muttered under her breath as she, also leaving, headed for the book room.

Pos and Neg took up their positions on either side of the still unconscious Merlin and Salazar.

Not two seconds after each of the wicked duo had left the room, Mordred walked in. Still looking extremely innocuous and elegant as Sir Kay, a look belied by the fact that he came straight over to the trussed men and kicked the unconscious Merlin quite ferociously in the kidneys, he stared down at the two of them with such unveiled hatred in his eyes that it was unnerving.

'You will now have to obey Mab,' he said to the comatose man. 'You will have to help her now, whether you like it or not and I hope it will be you who has to kill Arthur.' He sneered at Merlin, adding, 'that would give her enormous pleasure, even more than killing him herself! Making you do it while we watch would be the ultimate satisfaction anyone could have – complete bliss. Just wait until she brings you round – you'll see.'

He walked over to the fireplace and kicked a log, sending hundreds of tiny sparks scurrying up the chimney. Laughing at the glittering display, he called over his shoulder at the two uninterested magicians, 'Or how would you like to be placed on top of a huge stack of logs, watching and waiting for the pretty flames to start crawling up them before they licked at your toes? Well, whether you'd like it or not, I'd love to see it. Then, once you've gone; well, there's no-one left to help Arthur, is there? And that is the main thing, isn't it? Mab wants him dead for her own reasons, but so do I for mine.'

He spun around and strode over to the bound men; raising his foot once more he sent a vicious kick into Merlin's back. There was obviously no reaction from the unconscious man but there was from another quite unexpected source.

Mordred, without being able to do anything about it, was grabbed hold of first by the tattooed man with the shock of red hair and then by the black one with the white tattoos. They frogmarched him at great speed over to the fireplace where, with much fear on his face, thinking they were going to throw him into the fire, they shoved him into the huge, warm, grey stone that held up one side of the mantel. With a faint flash he was gone.

Wiping their hands as if to get rid of something dirty, they took up their places once again beside their captives.

Another flash, this time in Merlin's cave, where Jasmine, Lady Elise and Sir Kay were waiting in readiness and with great expectancy for their visitor.

Mordred blinked rapidly a few times, wondering what on earth was happening. He was being manhandled in the giant's castle one minute, fearing for his life, and then was standing in a cave with three angry-looking people about to pounce on him the next. 'One of whom looks very much like me,' he thought. He turned to run away – but where to? He was in a strange place and there was no way he would know where the door lay – but, thinking he must have come in through a door, he turned around to run out through it and crashed straight into the wall. Almost knocking himself out – and that would have saved a lot of bother - he was grabbed from behind and, with a hand holding a cloth shoved over his mouth, lost consciousness.

'Come,' said Sir Kay. 'Let's get him on the table and follow the instructions so that I can, once again, regain my own body.'

They took up the potions and read the words left for them and, watching almost the same play that had occurred the day before, but with different performers, Jasmine and Elise were relieved when Sir Kay finally awoke and left the table as his own self. They turned Mordred over, trussed him up in very strong twine and locked him in one of the side caves. Merlin would deal with him when he returned.

'Now,' asked Sir Kay, 'what are the rest of those instructions?

FORTY-EIGHT

The torches were beginning to splutter before there was any sign of the naiad. We were about to give up hope when Cabal, whose ears hear things a million times louder than ours, nudged my elbow and spoke into my mind that the waters were stirring. Why didn't he hear before, I wondered.

'I think it's coming,' I whispered to Arthur.

We sat quietly and as still as possible as, eyes and ears straining, we stared at the hole in the floor. Sure enough, within the next minute a snout poked out of the well, followed by two beady eyes. It sniffed around and stared but didn't or couldn't see us; perhaps, like some other animals, it couldn't see very well and only noticed us if we moved. Mind you, that carcass stank to high heaven and it would be hard to smell anything else – even Mab, I thought – which almost set Cabal off sneezing (I held my hand over his nose). We watched as it decided that there was no danger and saw it slither across to the meat. Then pandemonium reigned for a good few moments as, according to plan, Shake Spear used one of the chair backs to cover the well in order to cut off the naiad's retreat, while Wite and Niel attacked it from both sides with the largest of the torches.

'It worked! Thank the Lord,' Arthur cried as he watched the comatose form of the naiad being dragged out of the dungeon and placed in the adjacent cell. Making sure it was locked, Wite returned with the rope to help carry out the next part of our plan for escape.

Niel tied the hempen rope around his waist, making sure it was secure before running out several arms' lengths to tie it around Fisher; finally the same process followed and I was tied securely on the end of the rope.

'I'll try and get to the other side before you follow Fisher, but if it is too far, and the rope pulls taut, you will just have to make the best of it and follow me. Percy, you'll follow straight after him. Once I get to the other side I'll pull you along as fast as I can. Remember – take a deep breath before going under. Wish me well,' said Niel as lowering himself into the pool of water he disappeared.

We watched the rope vanishing into the hole, becoming concerned when it stopped and there was no signal that Niel had reached the other side; we held our breath and it was with relief and a collective exhalation of breath that we saw it start moving again. I started to worry again, even though the rope was still moving down – surely no-one could hold their breath for that length of time? And then it happened – with barely an arm's length of rope left – two tugs. He'd made it! We all cheered, albeit quietly, and Fisher dropped down into the well, quickly followed by me. We moved along at a cracking pace, with our lungs barely warming up or even getting near bursting before we, too, were out in the open air. It had been quite airless, albeit cold in the dungeon but out here, even though still cold and raining, we could at least breathe easier.

Sitting down on the banks of the river for only a few minutes to catch our breath, we set to, looking for some heavy logs and timber to make a dam. It was difficult work; the rain had made everything slippery and had also raised the level of the river - when I had crawled out the last time it had only been a stream! Fisher and Niel, both strong adults, managed to find some fallen trees and so, some hour and a half later, we were ready to divert the river. While they were busy lashing the logs together, using the best part of the rope we'd used on our way out, I had been trying to dig a trench with the hollowed out side of a tree trunk. It worked pretty well, I thought and, once the water started to make its way along it, it would widen and deepen, helping to take the stream in a new direction.

Once we'd manage to divert the river, it was another hour before the water in the tunnel had fallen down to a trickle.

'Hello! Its Percy, can you hear me?' I called, holding my hands around my mouth to project my voice along the tunnel.

A very faint 'yes,' from I know not who answered me.

'Tie one end of some rope to Rhianne's pallet and then send someone down with the other end. We can then try to pull it through,' I yelled. 'But hurry; we don't know how long we can divert the water.

'We'll send Cabal down with the rope.'

Two minutes later, Cabby trotted out of the tunnel with the end of the rope held firmly in his jaws. Shaking off the mud and slime he loped over to us and up the bank, letting go of the rope as Niel took it from him.

I was still worried about him but on looking at the bandage around his neck could see that the bleeding had stopped. I gave him a hug to show just how pleased I was that he was OK.

Niel and Fisher had somehow managed to wedge the logs that were holding back the river between two stout trees; some water was still trickling through but it looked like it would hold for a while yet.

The two men were now peering into the tunnel and listening for instructions from that end. They heard the men at the other end lowering the pallet and getting it into position before laying Rhianne upon it.

'Pull, men,' called a voice from the other end and, with muscles bulging and one foot flat against each side of the tunnel walls, Niel and Fisher pulled with all their might.

It took a while to accomplish this feat, as the pallet kept snagging on the sides of the tunnel, but eventually we all gave a sigh of relief as it came into view. Lifting it onto their shoulders, the two men carried Rhianne high enough above the bank to be out of danger once the river flowed back along its normal route.

'You could have warned me that you were going to pull quite so fast,' Shake Spear complained as he tumbled out of the tunnel. 'I was holding on to push the pallet along from my end but then you went and moved so quickly with that first pull that I fell flat on my face!'

We turned and looked at the huge man covered from head to foot in stinking black and green slime. In fact, if we hadn't heard his voice we wouldn't even have known it was him!

A small respite from the grave situation we had been in for so long, as we laughed at him.

'Never mind, Shake Spear. The rain will soon make you clean again,' chuckled Fisher as he pulled him up the bank.

Wite and Culhwch, who was pulling a distraught Olwen along with them, soon followed.

'What's up? What's the matter?' cried Niel as he looked at the trio.

'The giant's got Arthur,' Culhwch answered him, causing Olwen to burst into torrents of tears. 'We were just about congratulating ourselves – too soon as it turned out – as we lowered Olwen through the hole, when the giant crashed down the stairs and stuck his hand through the doorway grabbing him before he could manage to lower himself down into the tunnel. He shouted for us all to get away and save ourselves. We need to find Merlin – and quick.

'Arthur had already told me that he'd sent the rest of the men and the wagons into the woods. Let's go find them and plan our next move. Arthur, dear lady,' he said gently to Olwen, 'will be saved.' After placing her into the hands of Brother Geraint, he easily took up Arthur's role of leader ordering each one of us to our different tasks.

Busily pulling the fallen trees away from the bank, we watched as the water cascaded back down through its usual course, splashing mischievously and gurgling happily as it bounced back once the dam had been dismantled. We headed up through the trees to find the other half of our party and were surprise to find the men headed our way with the astonishing and awful news about Merlin and Salazar.

FORTY-NINE

'Where is that blasted Mordred?' screeched Mab as she strode into the hall. 'He's never here when he's needed!'

The giant, sprawling back in his chair with his feet resting on the hearth, threw a lazy look in her direction and, with mouth turned down, merely shrugged. He was getting increasingly irritated by this poor excuse for a woman. He had thought it a great idea in the beginning to join forces with her so that they could both do away with irritating people but the whole thing was now beginning to pall. At best, all he wanted to do was sleep or laze around and spend time with Olwen; at worst, all he wanted to do was make his way to the dining hall and eat. Now what more could a man want? The only reason he was doing anything at all was because he didn't want to lose his daughter. *'Well, I suppose I'll just have to put up with her for a little while longer; I mean, we're almost at the end of our plans. Then everything will get back to normal again,'* he sighed.

Tuning in once again to the woman's twitterings, he heard her saying, 'I'll give him what for when he comes back. Give someone a simple thing to do and it takes him forever to do it. Still, I can manage without him. I never rely on anyone – I am the only one I can rely on because I am perfect!' she gradually lapsed into mumbles and mutterings until she espied Arthur sitting tied to the chair opposite the giant.

'Another prisoner?' she asked him, lumbering over to stare at the young man and getting more and more excited as she realised just who was now in her grasp.

'Yes, Mab, another prisoner. This is the cousin of the one my daughter had the audacity to think of wanting to marry but, as you can see, I now have him at my mercy.'

'No, Ysbaddaden, you mistake the situation - he is now at *my* mercy! So, young Arthur,' she turned back to him grinning like a Cheshire cat, it must be my lucky day! I now have you, that annoying wretch Merlin and that other druid. Three down - and one to go if you consider that irritating nuisance, Percy.'

She stood staring down at Arthur for some long minute, though, unknown to him, she didn't see him at all – her thoughts were miles away. Even so, he felt very uncomfortable at her unblinking stare. Not only that, but she had an unusual aroma which seemed to be getting stronger by the minute! He wished she wouldn't stand quite so close.

'Come, Ysbaddaden, I shall call my dragon. Now that I have Merlin and his side-kick and you have very kindly provided me with Arthur here, let us go to the place prepared for us. We can then dispose of these three wretches in one go. The time is right. Oh, don't look like that,' she grimaced looking at the giant. 'We'll get Culhwch as well – later.'

Then an awful grin spread slowly across her face. *'She really shouldn't smile,'* Arthur thought, as he looked at her ghastly yellow, through brown and then green teeth - well the few that were still hanging in there!

'Ysbaddaden,' she smirked, slapping her thigh, 'am I not just fantastically brilliant? Once Merlin is out of the way, all the kings of this land - why stop there! – of the whole world - will be completely at my mercy! They will have no-one to protect them any more! Oh, what a clever, clever woman I am.' She started dancing around the room until, almost tripping over the cocoon in the middle of the floor she stopped and was completely overcome by hysterics.

'Why didn't I think of it before?' she wheezed as she got herself under control. 'I've been trying to do too much at one time – trying to steal Rhianne or provide the correct potion to make a man kill his relation or even try to steal Merlin's spells, when all along all I needed to do, primarily to get Arthur, was get Merlin. Well, I have him now – *and* I have Arthur!'

Her face suddenly turned stony as she looked down at the man who'd been the bane of her life for as long as she could remember.

Right! I'll call my dragon and those men,' she pointed at Pos and Neg, 'can go with me. They can take Arthur up on his back and we'll all head towards that special bay due west. You can carry the parcels,' her lips twitched involuntarily as she looked down at each chrysalis enveloping the two unconscious men, 'and meet me there. We can be there by evening and we'll then have all day to prepare. Tomorrow is All Hallowes – it has to be tomorrow or it will become extremely difficult to incorporate all the power we need. The most evil day on earth is the best day for wickedness. And I am the queen of mean!' she screeched.

Returning to the book room, she started filling her sack with all sorts of paraphernalia – scrolls, potions, herbs, phials, pots. Finally slinging it over her shoulder and tying the string in front of her she returned to the giant, shouting instructions as she went around until before long they were all standing on the parapet to await the arrival of Hellion.

Eventually the sky turned dark as he flew overhead.

FIFTY

'What was that?' cried Brosc ducking, although the creature was quite some way above us.

'Hellion,' I said through gritted teeth. 'She's summoned the dragon! What on earth is she going to do?'

Tailor and Brosc's words had tumbled over one another in their attempt to tell us, some half hour earlier, about what they'd seen in the copse of trees on the other side of the fields. Niel had finally held up his hand to silence them and, advising the men that he could only listen to one at a time, asked Brosc to tell us what had happened.

It took minutes to tell, one of us interrupting him now and then to ask the man to clarify a point.

Culhwch's face turned dark with anger as the story progressed and the seriousness of the situation made itself evident. He asked Tailor if there was anything he wanted to add; it then fell silent as we all tried to digest what had happened.

'Oh what are we going to do?' cried Olwen. 'Is there any hope?'

'There is always hope, my child,' responded the monk, as he comforted the young woman, finally handing her up into one of the wagons where Old Molly took over from him with a, 'There, there, dear; don't take on so. Stop crying - it'll be alright.'

The rest of us were all sitting around under the dripping trees, mostly covered in mud and feeling as miserable as the weather.

Thus it was that the dragon's arrival had made us jump to our feet with astonishment.

'Now we've got to do something!' said Niel.

'Like what?' asked Culhwch.

'I don't know,' he answered. 'Perhaps we should storm the castle and try and rescue them.'

'How are we going to get in? Do you think we should try and go back through the tunnel? I think it more than likely that the giant will have locked that door! What about the gates? Do you think we could get through or even over them? Does Olwen know of any other doorways? I don't think so, as she would have told us about them when we were trying to get out!' Culhwch's face was becoming more and more downcast as he listened to our suggestions until the futility of them made us finally dry up.

All this despondency, planning and questioning was about to become inconsequential as, with a mighty roar, Hellion took off from inside the castle walls, rising higher and higher with his human load – the last things we saw as he flapped away were the Paisley men holding Arthur between them and Mab – and I was sure it was her and not Lady Elise - staring down at us with a look of complete triumph on her face.

We'd hardly had time to wonder where Merlin and Salazar were before, with hearts sinking, we saw Ysbaddaden striding out through the castle gates, the cocoons holding Merlin and Salazar slung over his shoulder, leaving the gateway open as he did so.

We all must have wondered why he'd done that when, with horror written on all our faces, we heard the baying of those unearthly creatures as they ran round the corner and straight at us. The giant looked back and laughed as we, spurred on by panic, loaded ourselves onto whatever pony or wagon we could in order to make our escape.

We had one thing in our favour - although it was hard, in all that mud, to pull the wagons along or for the horses to move – and that was, that it was much easier for us than it was for the chimeras. Their little short legs became stuck much quicker than ours and so it was, with relief that we at last, albeit slowly, pulled away from them.

But what should we do now? Where should we go? We must save Merlin!

The rain was still lashing down and we were now really struggling to make any headway. Headway to where? You have never seen such a miserable band of people in your life.

Brosc and Wite were behind the main wagon and pushing it along, Old Molly and the still unconscious Rhianne were inside with Olwen, while Shake Spear sat at the front with the reins, trying to urge the horses forward; Tailor held the reins of the second wagon, which carried Brother Geraint, and the other men pushed from behind, while Culhwch and the rest of us sat astride the ponies. We, in our turn, were trying to pull or push the wagons along from the sides. Cabal was struggling along although, having nothing to look after but himself, was making a better job of it than the ponies.

It was in this mode that we were found.

The sky had lightened quite considerably and very quickly - even though the rain still poured from an unrelenting sky, - when, turning in the saddle, my heart leapt. Gaining brightness by the second, I saw once again that most beautiful sight as Moon Song swooped around us, flashing past and soaring back into the sky as she danced around the heavens. Finally, when she came to rest, we were amazed to see Sir Kay, Lady Elise and Jasmine beckoning us over.

My first reaction was to jump up and pull Sir Kay off the dragon before he did something awful to any of us. Jasmine was quick enough to see the look on my face and called down that all was now well – Sir Kay and Lady Elise were back to normal. Just as well – I'd nearly got him!

'We've come for Arthur, Niel, Culhwch and Percy and, of course, Cabal. I'm afraid the rest of you will have to try and make it on your own. The rain will stop very soon and when it does, head west,' ordered Lady Elise as she looked around at our party.

303

'Take me to my daughter, Culhwch. I shall look after her now. Merlin has left this potion that I am to give to her but not before you have gone. She will quickly recover once she has swallowed it but I don't want her going with you. This has all been much too much for me and it's bad enough thinking that you and Arthur might not come back, without thinking I might lose her as well. But,' she looked around, 'where is Arthur?'

The poor lady almost collapsed when she heard our story but, being made of sterner stuff than we'd given her credit for, she pulled herself up to her full height, telling us to, 'Go! Do what you have to, but bring Arthur back to me safely; all of you come back safely,' she almost choked on a sob as she was lifted into the wagon where, once she saw her daughter, was determined not to worry any more but to minister to her.

'Come,' urged Jasmine. 'There's not much time.'

We started to climb onto Moon Song's back when we were surprised by Olwen who, looking defiant, scrambled up beside Culhwch.

'I must be where Culhwch is. We cannot be separated ever again,' she explained. 'In any event, I might have some influence over my father.'

We were in too much of a hurry to argue and so getting settled and allowing her to stay, we set off at a rapid pace.

Even though were in extremely dire straights, that flight will forever be treasured in my memory. Evening was upon us as we climbed up into the folds of Moon Song's back, just behind her neck – soft, silken scales whose iridescence shimmered as she moved, the colours of her mainly red body glistening as they changed through every colour of the rainbow. What a difference to my flight on Hellion.

I luxuriated in our flight looking up at bright stars that twinkled merrily down at us as we flew above the clouds. We were all in awe at this experience; all except Cabal, I believe, as he squashed himself between Kay and me, making himself as small as possible until such time as he might safely be able to jump down.

Feeling the absolute power of the animal beneath us, we became increasingly aware that she was flying at an extremely rapid pace; she obviously had to get where she was going fast. It didn't take us long to find out why.

As the clouds became more and more intermittent, we were able to look down at the ground beneath us and make out certain shapes. Dusk was falling fast as Moon Song made her descent and as soon as she had landed and we had disembarked, she curled up to rest.

Why was she doing that? Was she really tired after her flight?

We looked around. It was a cool evening and the rain clouds had flown off to the north leaving a bright and clean full moon that bounced slowly off the rivers as they made their way to the sea and made our going easy as it shed it's light before us.

Jasmine and Sir Kay made us walk as far away from the dragon as they thought safe and it was from this distance we watched as electricity fizzed and zipped through her as she metamorphosed once more into a circle of standing stones. As I recalled from the last time I'd seen this phenomenon, it was with no surprise that I noticed the occasional glitter or zip of colour emanating from various rock faces or felt the deep vibration from the warmer stones along or the occasional droning sound travelling throughout them.

'Now what are we to do?' Culhwch asked.

'Now, we wait,' Jasmine answered him as she walked back inside the outer ring of standing stones, beckoning the others to follow. Cabal stayed outside! 'We must not be seen until the right time,' she cautioned us.

'When will that be?' Niel asked her.

305

'We will know when it is right,' she answered him, 'but at the moment, even I don't know. We have to trust in what Merlin has told us to do.

'What has he told us to do?' Culhwch asked, getting a little exasperated.

'Nothing! Just be here! That's all he's told us to do. All will be revealed.'

Shrugging his shoulders, he started fidgeting until Jasmine told him to stop. 'It is vital no-one knows we are here until the right time, so please be still and quiet.'

FIFTY-ONE

Once again covering herself in the cowhide to keep dry she peered out from under it and stared straight ahead while Hellion made his way to that special place.

She was not in the least worried that Arthur and the Paisley men were getting soaked and it didn't enter her head for one minute to get Hellion to fly above the clouds; she probably thought it would take longer to go up and then have to come down rather than go straight there, not considering at all that the higher she was able to climb in the atmosphere, the faster she would be able to fly.

Still, be that as it may, it was still some twenty minutes after Moon Song had landed that Hellion made his appearance, flying round the stones a few times before eventually landing just along the beach from them.

We watched her as she alighted, ordering Pos and Neg to stay where they were and guard the prisoner. 'And don't move until I tell you to or you'll be sorry!'

Scratching her head to alleviate the irritation from whatever was obviously making its nest within its greasy folds, she waddled over to the block of stone that stood in the centre of the stone circle. Raising her arms and looking up into the sky she shouted something but none of us understood what it was. We needed Merlin here to help us understand all that was going on but, I realised with my heart sinking, he was now under the control of the witch. I wondered what she'd asked the giant to do with him. Perhaps, even now, he might be dead!

'No,' Cabal spoke clearly into my mind. *'Have you tried to communicate with him lately? I believe we'd know if he was – something would happen to us! We're so closely linked with him in mind that we'd feel it. I haven't felt anything. Have you?'*

'No, Cab. You're right! I need to have more faith in him. Let's try and speak to him again. Perhaps he'll be able to tell us what we can do. But no! Because on the other hand, if we do, that witch will pick up on it and know we're here. Perhaps she's even now heard us. Better stop straight away!'

I don't know whether she ever did know or even heard Cab and I; I think she was so wrapped up in herself that she considered everything else of no consequence.

Peering round the stones, we all watched as she set out the phials, potions and scrolls she'd brought with her, mumbling all the while as she did so.

Hellion, who had by now regained his breath, was still puffing out smoke, tinged every now and then with sparks of fire.

A misty dawn was almost upon us and it was with a curious eye that I espied the many hundreds of spiders' webs that were strung everywhere, shimmering with moisture and many colours as the sun shone upon them. I wondered if King Ogwin was aware of what was going on; I reckoned he must be – the spiders would tell him.

My ears twitched suddenly and, swivelling around, I watched as the giant made his way across the plain towards the stones. I moved back a bit so he wouldn't see me.

'And about time, too,' Mab screeched as she watched him approach. 'Throw them down there,' she pointed at the altar stone. 'No, no – throw them, I said. You don't have to be careful with them – they're nothing now,' she crowed. 'A few bruises is nothing to what I have in store for them.'

The giant rolled them forward off his shoulder and they landed, none too gently but not as brutally as the witch would have liked, onto the ground in front of the stone table.

'Now you have to help me,' she ordered. 'I've set out all the potions in order and I've decided upon the best incantation. All you have to do is hand me what I want, when I want it. You'll just love what is about to happen,' she smirked. 'I am going to dispose of all these three,' she stated, waving her arms in the direction of the cocoons and then at Arthur, 'and then we'll go get Culhwch. So you'd better do it right or you won't get what you want! Also,' she added, 'I've come up with a very potent brew for Olwen; once she's swallowed it she will never look at another suitor and will only want to stay with you.'

The giant grinned at her. 'Just say whatever you want me to do, Mab, and I'll do it.'

'Right! We have today to get everything done that needs to be done. It has to be tonight – All Hallows Eve – tomorrow will be too late!

'First of all I've mixed up this concoction which has to be poured down the throats of those two wizards; it has two effects: first it will make them conscious once more and, secondly, although able to see and hear they will not be able to move or speak! Brilliant, eh? If they can't speak, they can't make any spells and if they can't make any spells, they are powerless and doomed and I am all powerful; also they will only be able to listen to me as I tell them how they are going to die! And die they will! Ooh, that will be lovely – looking at the panic and fear on their faces as they come face to face with an awful death. Although,' her lips started to twitch but she kept herself under control, 'I could send them to the netherworld – the place of the living dead – not dead but not alive. They will spend forever like wraiths – not dead but wishing, nonetheless, that they were. Ooh yes!' She stood staring into space for a very long time, salivating as she contemplated this particular end to her enemy. But then, screwing up her face, she realised that she hadn't brought the right potions to achieve that particular end. Still, she had organised the former.

Shaking her head to clear it from these delicious thoughts, she continued, 'That's the easy bit.' 'The hard bit is what I have to do with regard to Arthur. That has to be done tonight

309

– and at the right time! Not only is he to die but he is also to be given as an offering; that way I attain so much power that I will become forever invincible! What I can do with such power is something that hasn't been achieved by anyone before me and nor will by anyone after me. I shall be great! The greatest! I shall rule the earth! Everyone shall be subservient to me – they will learn to fear and obey me - or else!

Did I hear a distant rumble of thunder as she spoke; I certainly felt that she had angered someone by her remarks!

FIFTY-TWO

'Granddad,' Ben interrupted Jack. 'Why was it so important that the witch dealt with Arthur on Hallowe'en? I thought that that was just a fun night.'

'Not at all, Ben. That is the most evil night of the year and should never be taken lightly. Mab knew it and so did Arthur. Because so many sorcerers, wizards and the like get together on that night, evil abounds – it creeps about in the dark waiting to pounce on the unwary, especially on a misty or foggy evening. It takes up residence in the grinning heads of pumpkins – have you ever looked at one; I mean really looked at its face? It's grotesque – not quite a smile, more a grimace, as if it's trying to pull you into its fire. Wickedness starts to crawl up your legs and along your spine as you stand outside someone's door, and who knows who will answer that door! Is it really a person or could it be a ghoul or another witch or wizard waiting to get you or, maybe, it's one of its wicked servants? How would you know? Most of them look so normal! And then, look at what it makes you do if someone doesn't give you a treat! It starts turning you into an evil person – albeit in a small way at first, but who knows where that first bad step will take you? It has already taken root in your soul by taking you by the hand to make you do a nasty trick and I, for one, don't think it will easily let go of you once it has taken a hold; you're like a staircase and once wickedness has climbed onto that first step, I tell you, it will be a long time before it climbs off, if it ever does!

No, I tell you, Hallowe'en is a night when I always stay in to keep safe, especially after what happened that night at the standing stones.'

'Go on, granddad; what did happen?'

Jasmine had already told all of us to keep absolutely still. We were not to move or do anything to help or hinder; it was absolutely essential to stay where we were. Merlin said so.

It was very hard not to intervene as things were going horribly wrong, so far as I could see. Niel gripped my shoulder as I leaned forward, stopping any move I might make within the circle and so give us all away.

The afternoon moved on and we all got quite tired and fidgety. Jasmine handed out some dried biscuits and we shared a water bottle. It wasn't a lot but it stopped the hunger pangs. Watching the witch got quite boring after a while and my mind starting to wander. What was I going to do if Merlin was allowed to die? How could I save Arthur? Was Rhianne recovered? Would she forgive me if I let anything happen to Arthur? These thoughts seemed not to take any time at all as they rolled around in my head and it was with complete surprise that I found that darkness had fallen.

Kay had fallen asleep and was being shaken awake by Culhwch, Jasmine appeared to be either in a trance or praying and Niel still sat beside me secretly watching the witch. Of Cabal there was no sign - probably hiding some way away from the stones. I thought it best not to try to reach him with my mind.

Now that it was dark, there seemed to be more activity in the centre of the standing stones. The giant was arranging the lighting around the stone table; huge stakes had been hammered into the ground with torches attached to their tops; thus it was that the central area was very well lit and provided much light for Mab to be able to see what she was doing and also a good light for us to be able to watch and, being in the shadows, remain undetected.

'Fetch that scroll, Ysbaddaden,' she ordered. 'I am going to start mixing the brew required to deal with those two pests; I have everything ready, here in front of me, so I want you to start reading the instructions while I mix. And don't you dare get it wrong,' she shouted at him, 'or it will be the worse for you!'

'Trust me,' he growled back at her.

'I trust no-one,' she snorted. 'Just do as I say. You seem to forget that I am going to be mighty and supreme soon. Therefore, I can make you the most important person after me or,' and she glowered at him, 'the least thing on this planet. Just don't forget who you are and, more importantly, who I am. The choice is yours.'

'Ma'am,' he bowed, 'I'm at your command.

She glared at him for a few moments before turning back to her work. 'Begin,' she commanded.

'2 gills of water.'

'Yeuk, water,' she mumbled, pouring the required amount into the large pot that had been suspended over the, as yet, unlit fire.

'Ten large crow feathers.'

'Ten large crow feathers,' she echoed.

'Six roasted and shredded toads.'

'Six roasted and shredded toads,' she repeated as she added this ingredient to the pot.

'A large pinch of dried and sieved frog spawn; half a pint of owls' spit; the powdered residue of bats' fleas …'.

And so it went on with the giant reading it out and Mab repeating everything he said as she measured and weighed, sifted and counted everything into the pot.

All the while the two wizards, who had been given the first part of her evil brew, were watching wide-eyed and with sweat pouring down their faces as their fate approached. Whatever was going to happen to them, they had no defence in either speech or action; the witch had made sure that they couldn't speak and the spiders had made sure that they couldn't move.

'Perfect,' Mab had observed more than once as she looked over at them. 'It is now *my* time,' she'd crowed.

313

'Right, I am now ready,' she stated as, mixing the contents of the cauldron one last time, she clicked her fingers for the giant to light the fire beneath it. Taking a taper and lighting it from one of the torches he soon had the sticks alight, adding more wood as the flames took hold.

The two bound men looked petrified as, with the minutes racing by, they now realised they had no hope and were absolutely terrified as to what was going to happen to them.

Not only they, but we, too, were mesmerised by the cauldron and what was happening within it. The smell was awful – as usual - but that wasn't the worst of all that was happening. We watched as smoke rose, quite lazily at first – black, purple, green, twisting, intertwining, dancing – but then, as it became more active, shapes began to form within its mists, skeletal arms beckoning, legs stamping out a maniacal dance, grotesque faces leering, skulls grinning until suddenly, after a loud belch, all was quiet apart from a soft bubbling from within the pot.

Mab moved over and dipped a phial into the pot. As she lifted it out we couldn't keep our eyes off the contents – green, yellow and red slime that swirled about and burped, letting off a pungent sulphurous smell that burned the hairs inside your nose.

She turned and walked towards the two men who were sweating, with eyes bulging fit to burst. The look on her face was awful, determined. I wanted to run and grab the phial from her and fling it in her face but couldn't move as Niel, understanding my thoughts, held a grip on my shoulder that I couldn't easily escape from.

'Ysbaddaden, get hold of Merlin's second-in-command - we'll deal with him first. I'm sure Merlin would like to see what's going to happen to him before it actually does! And I want to watch his face while he watches his friend!'

He knelt down behind Salazar and gripped him each side of his head. Forcing his mouth open with his thumbs, he pulled his head back and watched as Mab moved forward with the brew.

'Merlin, watch now - this is going to happen to you next. You'd like to know what effect it's going to have before it happens to you, wouldn't you?' she grinned at him. 'Ready? OK, Ysbaddaden, keep him still,' she ordered as she poured the mixture down Salazar's throat. 'Watch, Merlin,' she snarled. Merlin wouldn't have been able to keep his eyes off Salazar if he'd wanted to. Both men's eyes were bulging out of their sockets and sweat running down their faces as they watched what neither of them could do anything about.

Ysbaddaden had pressed the man's lips together and held his hand securely over his mouth to make sure nothing escaped. Not a lot happened at first and then, amazingly, the man started to disappear. He came and went a bit at first but then, over the next few seconds, just faded away. But it was awful to look at his face, which, even when he had nearly completely disappeared, was racked with silent agony.

We all looked at Merlin. Rivers of sweat were now pouring down his face with fear. It certainly wasn't anything to do with the weather as it was starting to get very cold; my feet were freezing.

Mab walked back to the cauldron, dipped the phial back into it and returned to face the other man.

'Well, Merlin, this is one of the greatest pleasures I have had of all time. Just to see you there all trussed up like a chicken waiting for the oven is passionately exciting but to know that you know what is going to happen to you next surpasses even that emotion. I am so extremely content; so deliriously happy – you have absolutely no idea at the way I feel having you at my mercy. To know that you now know that I am greater than you! But now, you are going to join your friend – oh, how kind I am letting you do that – you will not even be lonely,' she started shaking with glee, 'You must have known there was some goodness in me!'

315

'There she goes again,' I thought as I watched her rocking backwards and forwards as she cackled, almost falling over with delight. She finally stopped and the immediate change in her expression made my blood chill.

'Come, Ysbaddaden,' take hold of him.'

I watched with horror, completely impotent but fascinated nonetheless as the witch went through the whole procedure again but this time with Merlin. I felt the scream climbing up my throat but wouldn't hear it leave as Niel, anticipating my action, clamped his hand over my mouth.

Once again, the man's visibility ebbed and flowed until, finally he, too, disappeared with the same awful look of horror etched into that beloved face. The cocoons that had held them were now deflated and fell flat to the ground.

'Well, that was very satisfying,' she cooed as, dusting her hands together, she moved back to the fallen stone that she was using as a table. 'I'll miss him, though,' she added. 'It was always very challenging to see who would come out on top. It was usually him,' she grunted. Then, face lightening, she declared, 'but this time it was me! And from now on it will always be me!' She danced around the altar stone, clapping her hands and grinning. 'Now it's time for Arthur,' she chuckled, returning to the table. 'Come, Ysbaddaden, let's get his potion ready.'

FIFTY-THREE

I was sobbing silently into my hands. How had this all come about? Merlin was the greatest magician, the most true and loyal friend, not only to Arthur but to me as well. The loss was unbearable. And now that awful witch was going to do something to Arthur. I couldn't let that happen. He was going to be king one day – and not only king but high king – High King of all the Britons. Perhaps it was up to me to save him. But how? How would I be able to look Lady Elise and, more to the point, Rhianne in the face knowing that I was here but did nothing? No, it was all too much, that was why there were so many tears. Staring at the others, I could see Culhwch and Kay looking very pale and stony faced; Niel was beside me but his expression was inscrutable. Cabal, who had now crept up to the stones but still stood outside them, had his tail between his legs and his head hung low. Jasmine was still sitting in a trance-like posture.

Mab and Ysbaddaden had cleaned out the cauldron and allowed the fire almost to go out. Replacing the pot over the glowing embers, they once again went through the ritual of cutting, weighing, counting and mixing various potions before placing them into the cauldron.

Lighting the fire, Ysbaddaden was instructed to go and fetch Arthur.

We had to do something now! It would soon be too late! These thoughts were screaming their way round and round in my head as I lumbered to my feet.

Niel gripped my shoulder again and forced me down, clamping his hand over my mouth as he did so. Turning me round to face the others, I saw that Jasmine was beckoning us over to her.

'We are to be ready just before midnight. That is the time the mad woman considers the witching hour and that is the time she intends to sacrifice Arthur on the centre stone. It is the first All Hallows Eve that possesses a full moon in many a year and she intends to call all the forces of evil to her at that time in order to have her wicked way.

This was something that must not happen!'

Continuing to whisper, she gave us all different instructions and made us creep around the stones to our allotted place in readiness for what was about to take place.

I was still so upset that it took all my resolve to do as I was bid. Fortunately, my designated place was just outside the largest stone in the outer circle. I say "fortunately" because Cabal felt bold enough to join me there; it was so good to have him nudge me - I flung my arms around his neck and cried silently into his fur and we got comfort from one another.

We had no idea of the time but watched as the moon, sharp and bright in her fullness, started to rise over the distant hillside. She climbed higher and higher until she could shine benignly and bright upon all that were gathered before her, in and outside that circle of megalithic stones.

Watching Mab as she finalised her mixing, we started to put Jasmine's plan into action. Not wishing her to pick up on Cabal and I mind speaking, I had whispered to him earlier just what we were supposed to do as midnight approached; Jasmine would give us a signal. He understood what was expected and said he would do his part.

Keeping one eye on the scene in the middle of the stones and one on Jasmine – almost like the giant, I thought – we waited. Jasmine did it first! Making sure she was behind the witch, with a deep breath she ran so fast that it was almost impossible to see her – and *I* was actually looking at her - from behind one stone to another. Mab heard the sound and spun round but it was too late – she saw nothing. While her back was turned Kay did the same; we all took our turn until she was spinning about uncontrollably.

'Who's out there?' she called out. 'Come on, I know someone's there and if you don't come out I'll find you and then you'll be sorry.' She spun round again as Niel took his turn.

And so it went on - as she called out, so someone else behind her ran.

The giant had been seated beside the altar stone, where he had tied Arthur to the table, before the witch had begun spinning around and calling out.

'Get up, get up,' she yelled at the giant. 'Go and find what's happening out there. Bring them back here. Quick,' she shouted at him as she looked with concern at the sky, 'there isn't much time!'

The moon shone down benevolently, completely unaware of the malevolence crawling about in that place. As she climbed majestically into the heavens, how was she to know it was down to her timing that much evil was intended that evening?

The giant lumbered to his feet and stood staring down at the witch. He was becoming more and more irritated by her behaviour. If it wasn't bad enough that she kept on ordering him around, as though he hadn't ever been in charge of his own life, her screeching voice was now grating on his nerves. He'd almost decided that all this carrying on was not worth it and had got to the point of opening his hands to make a grab at the woman and crush her when out of one of his eyes he espied Culhwch who had, unfortunately, not completely hidden himself. Stretching himself to his full height and going through the motions of a mighty yawn, he suddenly, and very swiftly for one of his size, made a lunge and grabbed the unfortunate man by the seat of his leggings.

This caused a series of things to happen.

First, Culhwch let out a mighty roar as he tried to fend off the giant – a pretty useless waste of time and energy as it turned out – well it would, wouldn't it, against someone so

319

big. Niel and Kay, who'd climbed one of those great megaliths, launched themselves onto his back, hanging on by grabbing – and pulling – his hair. He spun around and tried to grab them with his free hand; he almost made it, too, but at the same moment Culhwch bit into the soft area of his hand between the thumb and forefinger, thus forcing Ysbaddaden to abandon that task and go to the aid of his other hand.

'Aaarghh,' he cried, opening his hand and letting go of his prisoner; but, as Culhwch turned, he ran straight into the arms of the witch who, blowing some fine dust into his face, watched him as he dropped like a stone to the ground. Niel and Kay ran down his back, jumped down and rushed off in different directions.

'Pick him up you imbecile,' she screeched at the giant who abandoned the chase and turned back to her. 'Tie him to Arthur. Come on, come on,' she yelled. 'It will be too late in a few minutes.' Once again looking up at the moon, she started twitching as she realised that the day was nearly spent.

While Ysbaddaden busied himself tying the two prisoners together, Mab went back over to the table and checked that the ingredients were all there in order to make the brew for the sacrifice of Arthur – *'and also Culhwch,'* she mused.

She counted off the final potion before thrusting her hand deep into the pockets of her skirt. Rummaging around she grinned as she brought out a very small bottle. Holding it up to the light she swirled it around until she saw the eye staring back at her. 'Swamp dragon fire,' she muttered.

'What?' asked the giant.

'It's swamp dragon fire,' she chuckled as she looked over at him.

He trudged over to her and looked down at the bottle. 'What does it do?' he asked.

'What doesn't it do, more like,' she snorted. 'It all comes down to what I mix it with,' she informed him. 'I could mix it with wormwood; that would make him a mindless moron.

He would walk the earth not knowing anyone or hearing anything; he'd be stony-faced and dumb until the day he dies! Or, I could add this,' she held up a jar of wriggling things, 'and he'd spend his whole life throwing up – and throwing down!' She went into hysterics at this one until the pain in her side made her stop. 'No-one would want to go anywhere near him then,' she wheezed, wiping the tears from her eyes. 'He'd stink!'

'*He'd stink!*' thought the giant. '*How could she tell?*'

'But I think I'll mix it with this one,' she grinned, 'hemlock! He'll surely die with this one,' she said, hugging the pot to her chest like a beloved child. 'Or at least be like the living dead!'

'But you've left it too late!'

She spun around looking for the owner of that voice.

'Nooooo,' she cried looking at the moon and then around to see what couldn't possibly be.

Standing high upon the largest stone and with arms upraised stood Pos. She looked from one to the other as she espied Neg standing on the stone next to him.

'Come down here at once,' she ordered, but there was a quaver of uncertainty in her voice as she looked up.

Ysbaddaden took one step forward to grab the two men but his move had been anticipated by the Paisley man with the shock of red hair. Whipping the belt from his trousers and holding it aloft, it turned, in a flash, into a long, black staff topped by the head of a hunting bird, with ruby eyes set in a silver mount. The giant stopped in his tracks; he'd heard what could happen to someone struck by a beam from those eyes.

The witch screamed. Realising, in a split second that she had wasted all of her time and effort in disposing of what she thought were Merlin and Salazar when it had been the Paisley men all the time and now that her immediate plans were in jeopardy she swirled around to see what she could possibly retrieve from this wretched situation. 'Grab those men,' she shouted at the giant, pointing at Arthur and Culhwch, 'and follow me.'

He bent down and grabbed them and, stuffing one under each arm, ambled after the witch.

Scooping up the contents from the other table, she ran through the stone archways and out onto the plain where the white dragon lay resting and puffing out the odd wisp of steam. Thrusting their two captives into his clammy folds, Mab climbed up onto Hellion's back and urged him into flight. It took a little longer for the giant to manage to climb aboard and they all had to wriggle around a bit to enable his great length and width to do so, and so it was that with just a little delay the dragon was soon airborne.

But it was not enough for the witch to just try and escape; as she circled the ring of stones before heading west she cried out in an angry but defiant voice that they would never see Arthur or Culhwch again. She might be angry that she would not attain all the power she was expecting with a sacrifice, but she had to be thankful for small mercies; once they had got far enough away, she would make sure that Arthur met his maker and then she would be safe from ever again being in a position to be destroyed by him – as the prophesies had foretold.

As she flew over their heads for the final time, Mab threw a very small pot containing an unblinking eye high into the heavens. 'That's for you Percy,' she shouted triumphantly. 'Thought I hadn't seen you, eh? And thought you'd get away with it did you? No, I always repay debts! Just wait – you'll get yours!'

My head swivelled round and I screwed up my eyes to see where the pot fell but I never saw it land. Another of life's little mysteries, eh?

FIFTY-FOUR

'What did she mean, granddad?' Danny asked. 'You'll get yours?'

'Mab was always threatening people and she'd never forgiven me for helping Arthur escape that last time when she held us both captive in her dungeons. I'll always have to keep my eyes open, so far as she's concerned. I'm sure she'd try to reach through into the future to get her revenge,' Jack explained. *'Like she did some few years ago,'* he thought.

The boys looked closely at him to see if he was serious or not but, catching sight of a twinkle in his eyes, decided it was all part of the story, although Jack mentally kicked himself when he noticed Danny nodding at his unveiled thought.

Laughing, albeit rather weakly so far as Ben was concerned, they asked him to continue with the story.

Watching Mab disappear into the west, the rest of us rushed into the centre of the circle of stones, all but Cabal, that is.

The red-headed man still stood high on the standing stone and looked down at us, as did his companion.

Kay called up to him, 'what's happening? Who are you?'

It must have been close on midnight of All Hallowes, when fabulous and scary things started to happen. We were caught up in a fireworks display, the like of which I had never seen – before or since. Catherine wheels and rockets twisted all over the place, crackers snapped as the rockets burst in myriad colours and shapes. Ducking down behind the stones again, we watched as this exhibition ran its course. I could vaguely hear Cabal howling somewhere outside the circle.

It suddenly went quiet and was worryingly dark until the smoke cleared.

The moon was still high in the sky and carried on shining down munificently as if everything was completely normal and right in the world, and looking very pleased as though we'd put on the show just for her.

It was then I noticed him. Still standing on top of the high stone with staff held above his head, my heart did a flip as, rubbing my eyes to make sure I wasn't dreaming, I looked up into the smiling face of Merlin.

'You're alive!' I shouted up at him, tears of relief starting to overflow my lids. 'But I saw you die – and Salazar!' I added. 'And where are the Paisley men? What's happening Merlin?'

He floated down to earth along with Salazar, who was also now as he should be, beside him.

'There's no time for explanations right now, young Percy,' he answered, gathering us all to him. 'Come, we must pursue them and rescue our friends – before it is too late.'

Ushering us out of the stone circle and standing us all together, Cabal included, at a safe distance, he raised his staff and sang the song of being. I knew better this time than to even think of the awful noise he was making.

We watched as, like before, the stones started to hum and buzz, flicker with light and colour before, eventually, crashing and clicking and fusing together.

A head unfurled and rose high in the night sky while yellow-green cat-like eyes blinked away sleep before peering down at us; the song that it started to sing along with Merlin was mesmerising and just so beautiful that it made you want to weep. As our eyes searched the length and breadth of this beautiful creature, we couldn't help but notice the difference between it and the one the witch flew. Where one was flat, clammy and lifeless, this other was sleek, silken and vibrant. I had hated my flight upon Hellion's back but was now extremely excited and couldn't wait to take to the air once again with Moon Song.

It was as though Merlin must have read my thoughts for almost immediately he was shaking us out of our reverie and giving orders. 'Quick! There's no time to waste! We must be after them as soon as possible. Climb up now; you, too, Cabal,' he ushered the dog onto Moon Song's back, finally leaping up himself and urging the dragon to fly.

Within ten minutes after the witch had left, we followed. I looked from one to the next and could see the determination on all their faces. Merlin, Salazar, Kay, Niel, Olwen and Jasmine knew just how urgent was our quest. I knew in my heart how Cabby felt; but, obviously, his expression couldn't change.

Moon Song increased in speed as she galloped rapidly along the ground until I thought we'd run right into the trees but she finally gained enough momentum and rose gracefully into the sky; I don't think I was the only one to let my breath go as we gained height.

The moon, brighter and seemingly bigger than I could ever remember seeing her before, lit the landscape below us and it was therefore not only a swift flight but also an extremely interesting one. Merlin pointed out a few places we may have heard of as we flew westwards; I was amazed at how few there were. Most of the land was covered in trees, with a few fields dotted here and there and if I saw any roads at all they were all dead straight. *Not like in my day,'* I thought, although it was amazing to think that those straight roads, which were more than likely laid down by the Romans, are still in existence today – well by that I mean the roads follow the same path as those laid down by the Romans and I also mean the twentieth century.

'How do you know which way to go?' I asked Merlin.

'I'm following the thermals left by Mab's dragon,' he replied. 'You can't see them but they can be felt; they're just slightly warmer than the rest of the air around them. The dragon has definitely gone this way. In fact I'm almost sure where they're headed.'

'Where?'

'Bedruthan Steps.'

'Bedruthan? Where's that?'

'Cornwall. It's a magical place and it's also the place where the giant octopus resides.'

'She's not going to feed Arthur and Culhwch to the octopus, is she?' I asked, shocked.

'Not if I can help it,' he replied but I noticed how grim he looked. I was not at all reassured and flung my arms around Cabby's neck for comfort. I looked towards Jasmine, who would always let us know if everything was going to be alright, but right now she wasn't saying a word. My heart sank; it didn't bode well.

'Right,' Merlin said abruptly. 'Let's climb higher, we must see if we can get there before her. We can hopefully find the cave and hide there, while Moon Song can go foraging across the cliff tops; with some luck,' he added, 'she might leave us a nice mound of droppings for future use – my present supply is getting very sparse! By the way, Percy, have you still got that pinch of naiad root I gave you?'

I pulled out the pouch from around my neck and, lifting it over my head, gave it to him.

He gave a small grin and asked me to hide it again. 'We might just need it! Now,' he added, 'let's hurry.' And stroking the dragon behind the splayed fan on her head he started, once more to hum. Moon Song joined in.

As we accelerated into the higher atmosphere, I hoped we wouldn't be too late.

FIFTY-FIVE

The witch didn't look behind her once, but peered ahead until she saw what she had been straining her neck to see. 'The sea, Ysbaddaden!' she cried at last. 'We're nearly there! Then you two will get what's coming to you,' she growled at Arthur and Culhwch.

The giant grinned. 'No-one's going to run off with *my* daughter and think they can get away with it,' he crowed. 'You'd think it would be common knowledge by now that anyone who tries dies! Oh, I like that,' he chuckled. 'I'm becoming a poet! Tries! Dies!' He peered at the witch for approval but she didn't even deign to look at him. Shrugging his shoulders he thought that it wouldn't be long now before they'd disposed of those two troublesome men and then he'd also be free of Mab. *'Perhaps he might be able to dispose of her as well,'* he thought, staring angrily at the back of her head as they flew along.

She turned and glared at him until he had to turn his eyes away. *'Surely she couldn't read his mind,'* he wondered.

'Am I not the greatest?' she cooed. 'Can I not do anything?'

The giant was now not so sure at all. Perhaps he should stop thinking altogether!

Flying over the cliff tops, they headed out to sea for a half-mile or so before turning and heading back towards the sandy beach. They flew in along the shoreline and, within seconds of landing, the witch had jumped down from Hellion's back and was shouting orders to the giant.

'Bring them over here; tie them securely; light a fire and find the cave; get my bag – I must start mixing the potion before morning comes.'

'So just what do you want me to do first?' the giant asked in an extremely sarcastic manner, standing over of her with

327

hands on hips and legs astride; he was by now getting very fed up with her indeed.

'Now, now, Ysbaddaden,' she tutted at him, trying to look coquettish in order to alleviate the tension but without any success – her effort at doing so merely made her appear stunned. 'There's no need to take offence; there's just no-one else to do anything. Come, now. You want them killed off as much as me! You help me now, while I mix the ingredients. We'll soon be ready.'

Ysbaddaden glared at her – and the moon at the same time – and, after staring thus for a good few seconds, decided it was best to just get on with it. It would soon be all over.

'I'll do as I think fit but don't give me any more orders or you'll just have to do it yourself. I can quite easily feed Culhwch to the octopus now and leave you to your devices,' he growled as he turned to find some driftwood for the fire.

Mab curled her lip at him as he walked away, wishing that she hadn't bothered with him in the first place. 'Although he's wicked and, surprisingly, thinks he's almost as evil as me – as if - he's too boorish and stupid,' she mumbled as she laid out her equipment. 'Can't wait till its all over and I can get rid of him too. Hmm, I might just prepare enough for him as well!' A small grin spread across her face. Humming to herself, she continued with her mixing and stirring, looking for all the world like a farmer's wife - albeit an extremely dirty one – mixing the ingredients for a cake.

We watched all this from the safety of our hiding place and hoped that neither of them would have any inkling that we were so close.

FIFTY-SIX

Shortly before the witch had arrived we had landed, by the light of a very bright moon, on the cliff top some few hundred yards or so inland from the sandy beach at Bedruthen Steps. Merlin, urging us all to alight quickly – and it didn't take much for Cabal to be first off - turned and whispered something into Moon Song's ear, before he, too, climbed down.

Moving as swiftly and quietly as we could, we made our way toward the top of the cliff and watched Moon Song, graceful and beautiful, flying towards the north, keeping frighteningly close to the sea in case Mab caught sight of her.

'She's not gone too far, young Percy,' Merlin assured me as he turned me round to catch up with the others. Salazar who was holding Jasmine's hand, was leading us all along the cliff and setting a cracking pace; even Cabal was having to trot quite fast in order to keep up.

'We've not long,' he explained. That was all the urging we needed. We must have looked a strange band of people as we felt our way down the face of the cliff – Salazar and Jasmine in the lead, closely followed by Kay, with Cabal and me behind them – all being urged along by Merlin.

Thank goodness it was still a bright night; the extremely full moon preening herself as she watched her reflection in the calm waters of the Atlantic providing a carpet of moons that stretched towards us on the rippling waves of the sea. The stars applauded her, winking and twinkling all around, as they showed their appreciation of her glory.

Running along the sand, our lungs were bursting when we finally reached the cave, with more than one of us was mopping an extremely wet brow as we cautiously made our way inside. Even Cabal, who was used to running for miles, was panting heavily. Kay, however, started to shake uncontrollably as he peered into the depths of that place of remembered horror.

'Oh, dear,' he quaked, pulling back from the entrance to the cave. 'It's all coming back to me now! Merlin, I don't think I can go in! If that octopus is in there now and waiting for me, well ...'.

'Now, now, Kay, don't carry on so. It isn't in there I can assure you; you can trust me, you know! That was then and this is now! Completely different story!' Merlin assured him; though Kay didn't look entirely convinced.

'But it must be waiting for me! It had me all trussed up like a chicken before, ready to eat! I'm sure it's there!'

'Trust me, Kay, I can deal with it if it is, but it isn't there!' He watched while Kay digested this information and waited until he was sure he understood that he was safe, before turning to the others. 'Right! Quickly now! Everyone get inside! You too, Cabal!' Taking Kay by the shoulder he kept close beside him until he was sure the man could cope and then was only satisfied when Salazar took over from him. It took a moment or two longer to make sure everyone was secure inside the cave before we all watched, mesmerised, as Merlin started to craft an enchantment.

What an amazing experience that was. We were all quite far back in the cave when the moon, slipping into view along with her reflection, shone full into the cave. She made a great display, once she'd decided to give her full attention to it, of beaming down upon Merlin so that all we could see was his dark shape, black and bat like, with the moon's bright and glistening aura caressing him all around.

He lifted his arms and, with staff raised, started to whisper. We couldn't hear what he said but now that we had all recovered sufficiently to do so, held our breath as we watched him, not wishing to miss a thing.

The ruby eyes in the staff's head glowed until all that Merlin wished was achieved.

Then – silence. Merlin said no more, we were still holding our breath, the moon still shone as she began to dip towards the horizon – though not quite so brightly as before, and the sea was quiet! The sea! I could still see it but couldn't hear it at all.

Merlin turned and started to make his way to the back of the cave where we all still stood.

'Something bad has happened; I can't hear the sea, Merlin!' I whispered.

'No? Oh dear, I'd better remedy that. We don't want them to hear us but we need to hear them. I must have put that bit the wrong way round. Well noticed Percy.' He muttered something and then we could hear it again.

'I don't understand what you've done,' I said to him.

'Sorry, Percival, I should explain.' Sitting us all down he continued. 'I have cast a spell. We can see out through this cave and, when the time is right, we will be able to walk out through its entrance. However, there is an invisible veil over the opening that inhibits anyone from the outside seeing in! In fact, from the outside it merely looks like the continuation of the rock face, so no-one will be at all curious to investigate within because they cannot see the cave entrance. When it is time to leave I will tell you. For now – rest; you will need all your strength for later.'

'Ahhh,' cried Kay. 'Look!' He pointed a quivering finger at the cave's entrance. We all jumped to our feet and backed towards the rear of the cave. As the thing heaved itself up and forward, the moon, now very low on the horizon, shone through its legs, making it look as though bars had been placed across the cave's opening.

Merlin and Salazar walked forward and stood watching the thing swaying outside. We were frozen to the spot, with bug eyes watching everything that was happening, trying not to imagine what might take place should the worst come to pass – another breath-catching experience for our little band.

331

Poor Kay – what must have been going through his mind must have been a thousand times worse than for the rest of us.

The giant octopus weaved and slithered around for many minutes, obviously sniffing about and searching for something it knew must be there but had for some unknown reason disappeared, before lumbering back down the beach and slithering back into the sea.

The moon, about to disappear completely, gave us a final wink as yawning she pulled the sea's shimmering covers over herself before retiring for the rest of the night under its rolling blankets. We watched the glow fading on the horizon.

It soon became very dark. Why does darkness play games – usually nasty or frightening ones? I got the odd flash, or, more likely, thought I'd got the odd flash of light in my vision as I tried to see. My imagination, though, was worse! How many monsters, small and large, are there all around you when you can't see them? There was something bad crawling up my leg and I wanted to scream; then I felt Cabby's nose on my hand. It was his fur that had touched me! Something had now landed on my head! Was it a huge spider with pincers about to pluck out my eyes? I shut my eyes and screwed them up as hard as I could. Merlin's hand patted my head and told me to be brave! I felt terrible. How much longer was it going to be before I grew up? I was still acting like a child! Cabby licked my hand in sympathy.

Our eyes gradually became accustomed to the dim light. Although the moon had now gone, the stars still twinkled down and were giving a moderate glow. We could see where the sand met the sea, the many little bays, the horizon – just – some large boulders and rocks and the curve of the cliffs as they rose right-angled to our place of hiding. And we waited.

Thus it was, some ten minutes or so since the octopus had slipped back into the sea, that Hellion arrived with his sweet and sour passengers.

What on earth was going to happen now?

FIFTY-SEVEN

Once she had arranged everything as she wanted it, the witch strode into the middle of the sandy beach and, with hands on hips and looking this way and that, finally spun round to face the giant. 'OK then, where's the cave?'

Ysbaddaden had been walking alongside and close to the cliff face. He had stared into our hiding place on more than one occasion, causing a few of us step back involuntarily.

'I was sure it was here!' he uttered, perplexed. Scratching his wild mane of hair with one hand and screwing his mouth up with the other, he continued with his search.

Mab, shifting her weight from one leg to the other and shaking her head at the man, told him to stop. 'We might just as well get on with things; what's the point in searching for it – we don't need anything from it. I was just interested. That's all!' she yelled. 'Come here and help me set up.'

We were relieved that they had no inkling of our existence in that place and watched curiously as the two of them, making several trips to and from the dragon's back, filled the top of a flat rock with her equipment.

She was all the while muttering this and whispering that, along with ordering the giant here and there until, finally satisfied, she stood back content that all was now ready. 'Make sure those two stakes are firmly stuck in the ground,' she commanded as she looked up at the giant. 'I don't want them upping sticks and running away in the middle of my spell. It's bad enough were too late for Hallowe'en – we've lost loads of power missing that; we don't want to lose those two as well!' she grumbled.

'They're firmly wedged in,' he snapped at her. By now his patience, like hers, was beginning to wear thin. *'Come, come, man,'* he said to himself, *'Keep calm – not much longer now.'* He took several deep breaths to control himself.

333

Mab looked over at him, thinking once again that it might be a good idea to dispose of this mountainous moron. Yes, she'd mix up some extra brew! With that thought in mind she made her way over to the flat rock and, humming away to herself, started working. 'I could use some more driftwood for this fire,' she called over her shoulder to the giant in as friendly a manner as she could muster.

Shrugging his shoulders, he walked along the beach to see what he could find. *'Once she's disposed of Culhwch, I'm going to crush her underfoot.'*

Mab, unable to discern all that he was thinking, got the gist of most of it. *'I'm going to have to be subtle here,'* she thought. *'And quick!'* she added. Could she manage either of those things?

We were all held as if spellbound by what was going on outside the cave. It was vital that none of us spoke: we didn't want the witch to even *think* that we might be anywhere near her. Also, Merlin was watching what she was mixing and pouring, cutting and measuring; so we needed to allow him to concentrate without any distractions. I held on to Cabal, and, without thinking aloud, was almost wishing him to keep quiet; I was relieved that he seemed to understand - dogs appear to have this sixth sense, don't they?

It took a long time but eventually it was done. The witch stood back, satisfied that all was now in readiness for the time she had been waiting for since she knew not when. She could only remember that on a day long ago, whilst delving deep into the black crystal, she had seen a play acted out within its depths: a man – no, a king - was riding towards a woman. His sword was held high above his head and although she couldn't hear his words she knew that he was riding in triumph. The woman stood up and was throwing everything she had at the king: fire, arrows, evil faces, ghoulish masks, swirls of mixed red and green gasses. But he still charged towards her. As this was being played out, Mab had stared at the woman – she looked familiar. She was certainly a sorceress as could be seen by the clever way in which she used the evil at her command but it took a good while before she realised who that woman was! "It's me!" she had exclaimed, dumbstruck. "The king is attacking me! But this can't be so! Not me!"

Unable to take her eyes from the crystal, Mab had stared, mesmerised, as the king rode her down. She finally held up her hands to defend herself as she realised that her best spells and curses had had no effect in stopping the man. He was now upon her and Mab stared horrified as she witnessed her own crushing beneath the huge hooves of the king's horse. The horse reared high before plunging down upon her and the last thing Mab saw was the name written on the side of the sword as it was lifted high before being plunged into her heart. That name – Excalibur!

After the shock of this revelation, it had taken Mab many weeks, first to get over her disbelief that anything could ever happen to her and, secondly to find out who that king was and thus deal with him. During this time she met an itinerant witch who, like her, leaned more to the evil than to the good. The witch stayed with her many days and during that time one evening went into a trance. Whilst under the influence of this trance she explained the story of the crystal to Mab, telling her about Arthur – that he was really the son of Uther Pendragon, that he would be High King of all the Britons one day and that his chief minister, albeit in name only, was Merlinus Ambrosius – a power to be reckoned with. All this was interesting but the thing that startled her the most was the fact that it was this Arthur who would one day kill her; there was only one thing that could change everything and that was, "If I kill him first," she'd said out loud.

The travelling witch came out of her trance and couldn't remember anything she'd said. This suited Mab because the less people that knew what she now knew the better.

It had now all paid off. She was at last in the position she had been striving for all these years. Arthur was in her grasp, would soon be dead and all power would now be hers. She couldn't help the grin that spread across her face as she clicked her fingers and ordered the giant to bring their two prisoners to her.

Arthur, if he was afraid, didn't show it. Holding his head high, he demanded the witch let him go. 'Why do you keep after me?' he demanded. 'I've done nothing to you! I'm not even considered a man, and yet you appear to fear me.'

'Fear you! *Fear* you!' she screeched. He'd obviously touched a nerve.

'I fear no-one – *no-one* I tell you!'

At this point I was standing quite close to Merlin as we watched this interchange between Mab and Arthur and I was surprised, if not a little shocked, to feel his shoulders shaking in silent mirth. How could he think that what was happening out there was at all funny? It was dire! Arthur was in the clutches of that odorous, evil woman and Merlin thought it funny! I was learning, though! He wouldn't be able to tell what I was thinking this time, as I'd put up my mental barrier!

The witch was standing very stiffly as she attempted to get herself back under control. It took quite a long time but she finally managed to unclench her hands and relax sufficiently to enable herself to move, albeit awkwardly, towards her table.

'Tie them tighter to the stakes, Ysbaddaden,' she spoke to the giant through rigid lips, her voice hardly more than a croak. 'Tighter!' she screamed, more like her old self. 'Don't want them getting away now, do we?'

While he did as he was bid, Mab threw more driftwood onto the fire, watching as flames jumped up around the suspended cauldron. She started adding her ingredients to the pot and, now that she had herself completely under control, looked once again like a normal, albeit fat, cook preparing

336

dinner. She added this, sprinkled that, gave it a stir and took the occasional sniff. How looks can deceive!

The mixture was bubbling away quite merrily in the pot, only giving off the odd burp or foul acidic rectal thundering along with sulphurous smoke, when Mab, finally content with the way things were now going, strolled over to her two captives. She wiped her greasy and very dirty hands down her dress – more for her sake than for anyone else's – before running them over Arthur and Culhwch's faces.

They winced.

'Just making sure you are who look like,' she smiled. 'Didn't want Merlin changing someone else into you, did I? Merlin,' she spat as she remembered him. 'Well, he won't find me here! I'm sure of that at any rate,' she said with just a small quaver in her voice. 'Even if he does,' she murmured, 'he'll be too late! Much too late!' Shaking her head to clear it of any unpleasant thoughts about him, she returned to her brew. 'Make no mistake about it. This time,' she shouted back at them over her shoulder, 'you really *are* going to die! And,' she added for effect, 'in the foulest way possible. Time to get scared, Arthur! Time to fear!'

FIFTY-EIGHT

As we were watching all of this going on, whilst hiding behind Merlin's invisible cliff face, I was aware that I wasn't the only one quaking in my boots – surely Merlin must be able to do something!

Looking down at me I could see amusement and resolve playing over his features. Not wishing to talk to me or even speak in his mind, he merely gripped my shoulder in a reassuring and friendly fashion. Unsurprisingly, I felt only slightly better.

The rest of our party were crowded behind us, equally silent, equally grave.

'Ready! I'm finally ready,' she squealed. Dancing up and down and swirling about, she pranced up to Arthur and poked him in the chest as she laughed into his face. He, although trying hard not to look scared, couldn't help but screw up his face at the stench of her breath.

'Frightened are we?' observing the grimace on his face she grinned at him, completely misunderstanding the reason for his expression. 'And you should be! I have such a wonderful experience in store for you and your cousin! But,' she stopped dancing as she considered her next move, 'they're both the same! No,' she stamped her foot and looked slightly put out, but then craftily from one to the other of them. 'Ysbaddaden, come here! We must mix a different one for Culhwch; can't have them both dying the same way – that'd be too boring! Let's use the wolfsbane on him instead of the hemlock.'

She strode over to the cauldron, scooped out some potion and took it to the table and, humming again, it wasn't long before a second phial of liquid stood beside the first.

'Now,' she stood back looking at her workmanship before turning to the two men. 'Who would like to be first?'

'I would,' said a familiar voice, causing her to stiffen in shock. Then swirling round she glared - there, on the other side of the cove, standing at the foot of the cliff, stood her perpetual nemesis, Merlin.

'Sooooo, you've found me!' she scowled at him. 'But it's too late! You see,' her scowl turning to a grin, 'I have placed an invisible barrier round my little camp and so whatever you do, it will bounce off! You won't be able to do anything to help Arthur. So, you'll just have to accept that he is already dead!'

Merlin merely smiled at her.

It had been fascinating, minutes previously, to watch him leave the cave. He'd tested the strength of the invisible shield by pushing his hand through; it was like pushing it through jelly, with the merest trembling of movement experienced on contact. We all stared spellbound as his hand appeared on the other side of the rippling wall. Once tried, he made up his mind and, after patting me on the head with a "wait here", strode through, closely followed by Salazar and Olwen. I, too, was moving forward, when Jasmine stopped me.

'Not just yet, young man. You heard what he said,' she admonished, before our attention was turned, once again toward the witch.

'What are you smiling at?' she snarled. 'You always think you have the upper hand, don't you? Well, not this time, Myrddin; not this time!'

Turning back to her table she retrieved the two phials of bubbling liquid and strode determinedly toward Arthur and Culhwch. The giant watched, waiting to see what would happen next.

Well, what happened next was not what he or the witch expected.

'Nor me!' I thought.

Merlin had raised his staff, roared two or three unintelligible words and looked completely unsurprised as the ruby eyes in it glowed. Now, I'd seen those eyes glow before but this time, even inside the cave I had to screw my eyes tight shut; the light from them was blinding.

The witch started screeching and I could hear her retaliating with one of her incantations. Peeping out between my lashes, I was surprised to see that, although the blaze from the staff shone like a rainbow over the area that Mab had made her own, she had somehow created an umbrella under which they were now sheltering. The giant still stood watching, although he had moved closer to the two bound men.

'Your move!' she grinned at Merlin. 'But I think you need to know that I am now more of a match for you and also, if you make one wrong move I shall make sure Arthur dies first. My spell is already in motion and even if you disable me, it will still happen. There is now no turning back. This potion,' she held up the phial, 'is merely the icing on the cake. Look at him,' she screamed. 'He's a dead man in all but name!'

'Ah Mab,' Merlin cooed back at her. 'You mistake it! All might have worked if you had got your timing right but you've missed it! It's now almost dawn of All Saints' Day. What you've forgotten to consider is that it was yesterday – and more specifically yesterday near midnight – when the evil ones were at your beck and call; not today!'

We all watched her as she digested this information. She still couldn't hide her feelings very well and it was interesting to see her look of defiance gradually start fading to one of disbelief, then through anger to despair until she seemed to crumble. She would not receive the power at the offering of her sacrifices; she'd made the mistake of taking herself out of that time – missing the deadline for herself and her small troupe - thus taking her into tomorrow and away from

Hallowe'en. Then an artful look crept into her eyes when, standing, she squared her shoulders and looked triumphantly across at Merlin.

'No, Merlin, not that old chestnut! You can't make me believe something that is not! Maybe All Hallows has now gone but I am still here and so are my captives. I shall just have to extend the day of evil. The power will still be mine!' She swished her skirts as she turned to face the giant. 'Come here, Ysbaddaden. I want you to get Culhwch for me. Arthur can watch him die first! It'll give him some idea of how he will have to suffer before death releases him. And Merlin,' she shouted over at him, 'you can watch too!'

The giant strode past her and took the two steps it required for him to reach the stakes.

He looked, as did we, goggle-eyed! The stakes were there, the ropes were there, but they hung loosely, binding no captives. He hesitated before turning round to see what he should do next.

'Well, hurry up man,' she shouted up at him.

'He's not here,' he answered.

'Of course he is,' she growled as she looked up at her two prisoners. Amazingly she could see them, where the rest of us could not. 'Don't start playing the fool now,' she shouted at him again.

'I think I've just about had enough of you,' he responded as he curled one hand into a fist and the other ready to grab as he took a step towards Mab.

'Can't you see the seriousness of the situation, you buffoon,' she yelled. 'Just do as I say and bring him to me.' By now her face had darkened to the colour you get just short of crimson; an overripe tomato that was obviously about to burst, with spittle cooling it as it spluttered out of her mouth and ran down her chin.

'They're not there Mab,' Merlin explained to the maddened woman. 'You think you see them but I have

341

whisked them off to somewhere that's safe from you. Ysbaddaden is right when he says they aren't there.'

'You couldn't have done that!' she cried. I had them – I have them,' she corrected looking again at the stakes but seeing, to her consternation, the gradual vanishing of Arthur and Culhwch. Turning to the giant, in her madness she kicked him in the ankle before storming off to the table where she replaced the phials of cooling potions.

'That's it, woman,' yelled Ysbaddaden in fury. 'I've had enough of you. Not only have you forgotten who I am but you've also lost me my captive. You now have to pay for both of those mistakes.' With teeth bared and one eye staring at the witch, he was about to reach down with open hand to grab her and was at the point of doing so when he espied, with his other eye, his beloved daughter standing in the bay alongside Salazar and facing him and Merlin. Rather sheepishly closing his hand, he stopped short beside the witch and almost looked ashamed of himself.

None of this had been lost on Mab. While the giant had been making a grab at her she had pulled a small draw-string bag out of her pocket and had thrown the contents at him. 'It'll hold him for a while,' she thought as he creaked to a stiff halt, unable to move. Turning towards the sea she lifted her hands, started clicking her fingers and began cooing. What on earth was the mad woman doing now? To the clicking she added what can only be called the weirdest dance in the world. Her arms were raised and her hips were swaying to the sound of the bizarre song she was singing. Some people aren't made to do any of those things and she certainly was one of those people! She looked completely demented. But she continued and we soon saw why.

The waves, which as dawn rapidly approached were becoming more noticeable, suddenly parted and one large tentacle dragged itself forward as it felt its way over the sand. I believe we stood like the proverbial mouse before the snake

– mesmerised as we watched its slow and swaying progress –
and so were taken completely by surprise as the giant octopus
leaped high out of the sea and, curling itself around Olwen's
waist, grabbed the young woman.

Salazar was quick but not quick enough as the sea
monster started to drag her towards its watery lair. Just
before it would have been too late, he made a grab for her
hand; we watched helplessly as they were both pulled closer
to the sea, Salazar's heels leaving two deep track marks in the
sand. Olwen's screams were terrible but it was those sounds
that spurred everyone into action.

Cabal tore out of the cave and was the next to give aid to
the sea monster's captive. Clamping his teeth onto the sash
around Salazar waist, he dug his heels into the sand and
pulled. Kay, who was still terrified of the monster, and I were
fast behind him and we, too, started to pull. A great tug of
war then ensued with the creature sometimes pulling us one
way into the waves before we managed to drag it back ashore
and then it would get the upper hand again. This went on for
what seemed to be an endless time; the worst part being that
the octopus, having so many limbs, was able to attack from a
different angle every time – just when we thought we'd
managed to deal with one tentacle, another took over. The
battle wasn't going our way; Olwen was being dragged inch
by inch into the sea, which was by now up to her shoulders.

Mab was still making her weird noises and swaying on
the beach. She continued clicking her fingers with sparks of
fire cracking from them and electricity building up all around.
The frizzy part of her hair was standing out all around her
head whilst the ends glowed. Shame she didn't set herself
alight.

Merlin, who had somehow moved from the beach and
was now standing high up on the edge of the cliff; was still
holding his staff aloft, the light blazed all around and was
bouncing off the umbrella shield that Mab had created; soon

cracks started to appear on one side of her screen; even struggling to help Olwen, I watched as Merlin concentrated on that area.

By now Salazar, who had a firm grip around Olwen's waist, had, with his other hand, withdrawn the sabre from his sash and was hacking away at the octopus. Two severed tentacles twitched on the beach and bled into the sand as the rest of it desperately tried to wrestle Olwen from our grasp.

Completely out of the blue and with a loud cry Culhwch soared into the air, fell upon the monster's back and, holding his sword high, plunged it down into one staring eye. The scream it made was terrible to hear; crying out it let go of its prey as it tried unsuccessfully to stem the fountain of black ink that sprayed high into the air, all the while dragging itself back into the safety of the now murky depths.

A still very shocked and tearful Olwen threw herself into the arms of the man she loved and who had now utterly proved himself to her by saving her from a certain and terrible death, without even considering his own life in the process.

Whilst this reunion was taking place, Jasmine and I had, at Merlin's beckoning, climbed up the ridge to the cliff edge and waited for his instructions. Still holding his staff aloft, we looked down at a woman so demented that she had obviously by now completely lost the plot. She was screeching fit to burst as she watched the widening inky patch on the sea gradually being dispersed by the waves. 'You've lost your octopus as well,' she kept shouting over at the giant, as her arms twitched and waved at him and her feet stamped or kicked at his still form. 'Do something you dolt!'

The giant, creaking as he became released from the powder Mab had used on him, ignored her and merely stood staring at Culhwch and Olwen as they embraced on the sand. The rage that he felt towards the witch was even more potent than that which he now felt towards the man; it was starting to build up inside him but it would be minutes yet before it

344

reached its climax. Mab, with her taunting, was helping to fire this wrath.

Meanwhile Jasmine, whom Merlin had now finished talking to, nodded and walked off along the cliff face towards the north, where a sleeping Moon Song would be waiting to take her to do Merlin's bidding. He turned to me and I waited as he gave me my instructions and so it was, frightened but determined at what I was about to do, I made my way back down the cliff face.

FIFTY-NINE

I walked across the sand towards the breach that Merlin's staff had been making in Mab's defences, trying very hard not to let my knees knock together; my teeth were already playing a tune as they clattered together uncontrollably.

Standing outside Mab's crumbling barricade I waited for her to notice me. She had been stomping around in her fury and so it was that a good minute passed before she looked my way. Coming to a frigid halt she stared at me – for ages. Well, I could have melted on the spot – or wet myself! Her face was terrible and my imagination was perched upon my shoulder and gleefully whispering into my ear all the awful things she was thinking of doing to me. I would have turned and run if I didn't know how important this was to Arthur and to Merlin. Let's face it, I would have turned and run if I could have moved! However, as it was, my fear had me rooted to the spot and my legs belonged to someone else.

She was the one that finally moved first. Stepping towards me she mumbled something and a door space appeared in her defence wall at the exact spot that Merlin had told me to stand; that was all he needed. The witch reached through to grab me but as this opening appeared, along with the crack Merlin had been working on, with a mighty crash Mab's whole defence system collapsed, falling all around us like invisible shattered glass.

She spun around like a trapped rat, dragging me with her as her suffocatingly putrid armpit smothered my face; I couldn't breathe – but then, again, would I really want to? She is surprisingly strong and as we backed off towards the table I found it impossible to break free from her grasp and was almost passing out from the fumes coming from her unhygienic body. I was screaming in my mind for Merlin to do something but he either couldn't or wouldn't answer me; I heard other voices but they became more and more indistinct as I slipped gradually into unconsciousness. When I awoke I found that I had now been bound to the stake that Culhwch had once been tied to.

'Try not to be afraid,' said a voice to my right.

I turned and felt my ears twitch with fear. 'Arthur! I thought Merlin had taken you away!'

'No. I don't know how he did it but he managed to free Culhwch. That witch has done something else to me, or at least she had done something to breach time over me. I watched as an invisible hand or something loosed the cords that bound my cousin; once that had happened they seemed just to vanish. I know you can now see me as can the witch – and Merlin, more than likely – but I don't think anyone else can.'

'They most probably can see you as clearly as I, as Merlin has shattered her defences.'

'Shut up you two,' she yelled from a few feet away. 'I'm trying to concentrate.'

I had noticed that Merlin's staff had gone out. Where was he? I looked for him at the place I had last seen him but he wasn't there. Dawn was just breaking as I looked above me and saw paleness in the heavens, which now separated cliff top from sky.

Mab was moving about feverishly as she tried to erect another barrier. The language she was using was unprintable as she failed in one attempt after another until, finally, she had to be content with a force field around us. It had one drawback – it had no roof! Had she got it wrong, had Merlin involved himself in it or had she been in too much of a hurry?

'Now,' she sighed contentedly, 'I can deal with you at my leisure.'

The morning light, growing stronger, enabled me to look through the invisible barrier into the faces of my friends, Salazar, Culhwch, Olwen, Kay and Niel. By the set of their shoulders it would seem they were at a loss as to how they could help us. Cabal was at the edge of the obstruction and was digging furiously to try to get under it. I tried to talk to him to get him to save his strength; that Merlin had it all in hand and that he would save both me and Arthur, but he either had his barriers up or was ignoring me. But, then again, where was Merlin?

In my fear I'd obviously let down my mental barrier; I was brought back to my present circumstances with a bang as the witch, listening in to bits of my thoughts, burst into mad laughter. 'You always think he's going to save you, don't you?' she wheezed. 'Well, he won't get through in time to do that this time,' she gasped, trying hard to stem her hysterics. 'This is my day! This is my triumph! This time I will win!'

I swivelled my head as far as it would go as I searched unsuccessfully along the cliff top. *'Merlin, where are you?'*

'Merlin, where are you?' she mimicked, shoving her face into mine as she did so. I must admit she was getting more proficient at reading my thoughts, although, thinking about it – and it's weird how one thinks of stupid things at serious times, isn't it? – I have never been able to read hers. Be that as it may, I almost threw up, then and there, at the terrible stench of her breath; it would just have to be that it was at that same time that I happened to be breathing in as she spoke into my face – and I had my mouth open! Have you ever swallowed a midge? They always seem to get stuck at the back of your throat and it doesn't matter how you try to cough or choke it up. You can feel its body stuck to the inside of your throat - it just doesn't budge. In the end you have to swallow it and then the thought of it stays with you for ages – you think it is still there!

Well, Mab's breath is just like that! I couldn't breathe it out and I couldn't choke it up and I was so scared that as my mouth had dried up there wasn't even enough spittle to try and spit it out; it was there, almost suffocating me and I was

348

scared to swallow it; what might it do? How on earth could people like Mordred or Ysbaddaden put up with her? They must have no sense of smell whatsoever.

While these thoughts were going through my head - and, I should add that Merlin did not respond - the witch was busying herself at the flat rock she was using as a table. Her back was to me and as I watched her sifting and stirring I became more and more agitated. Arthur and I looked at one another but could give no comfort; we stared round-eyed and pale faced as the morning increased her light.

'Ah, just right!' We held our breath as we stared at the witch. She had turned and was approaching us with a phial of bubbling liquid held high in each hand. 'One for each of you,' she chuckled. 'Now, whose first?'

As she stood looking from one to the other of us, I had that weird experience of seeing everything happening at once. They say that happens to you when you are about to die. I saw my mother and father looking for me at Tintagel Bay and I tried to shout to them; as I twisted my head I saw Rhianne reaching out towards me with both arms, trying to draw me away from where I stood, sobbing all the while; I heard Cabal barking wildly and digging frantically at the same time as he tried to get under the barrier; I saw Niel and Salazar hurrying towards me, with Olwen and Culhwch racing after them, I saw the giant's face as he leaned over from behind me, opening my mouth as he pulled my head back and, and the witch as she poured the steaming, bubbling, pungent liquid into my mouth. I saw nothing more as a huge darkness descended upon me.

SIXTY

'Granddad, what happened when you swallowed the poison?' Ben asked.

'Yes,' added Danny. 'What sort of effect did it have on you? You obviously didn't die, as you wouldn't be sitting here now telling us about it.

Jack laughed at his grandsons' questions. 'You have macabre minds,' he chuckled. 'Do you want all the details? They could be embarrassing to me, you know.'

It became very quiet in the cottage; the wind, which had been howling for most part of the day, died down as Jack got up to place a few logs on the fire before going across the room to close the curtains. A last puff of the dying breeze pushed a few leaves under the door before he placed the draught excluder up against it.

Cabal moved away from the fire, which was unusual for him, but what caused Jack concern was when he noticed the hackles that had raised themselves on the hound's back.

They'd been too long together for either of them not to notice when something was amiss or, perhaps, about to happen. Before he had a chance to ask him what was wrong, there was an almighty whoosh and a thunderous amount of soot crashed down the chimney and into the room, dislodging logs from the fire and covering them all in black grit, which not only blinded them for a while but got up their noses and into their mouths, choking them. Coughing and spluttering, they struggled across the room and made their way out through the door into fresh air.

Still choking, they helped one another by thumping each other's backs until they could all breathe again.

As soon as he could see and breathe properly again, Jack rushed back into the house to make sure all was secure. Apart from the black dust that covered everything and still swirled in the air, all seemed well. The fire was still alight; although most of it now resided in the hearth it still had a healthy glow.

'*Too healthy,*' Cabal noted. '*What is that dancing flame?*'

'*What dancing flame,*' Jack asked, a bit bewildered.

'*The one with an eye in it?*' he replied.

A cold fear with many feet crawled up Jack's spine as his eyes searched among the flames, hoping not to find what Cabal had seen; hoping he'd been mistaken.

'Water. Quick,' he shouted to the boys and they hurried off to the trough to scoop some out. As each of them handed their half-full buckets to Jack he quickly threw the contents over the fire and watched as it hissed and steamed back at him. 'More,' he called over his shoulder, not daring to take his eyes off the smouldering mass. They rushed back for more and were back in a trice. A second dousing had more effect than the first and the fire spluttered, sizzled and coughed as it died. That is, apart from one flame. Jumping out of the fireplace it bounced onto the ragweave rug in front of it, setting light to one corner; Jack rushed over and stamped on the flames as they bit into it. Putting those flames out he watched, horrified, as it set off towards the cottage's open door.

Cabal was running after the flame, trying to jump on it to put it out but it was always one leap ahead - it didn't have an eye for nothing!

'More water boys – and hurry!' Jack shouted as he rushed after the flame and the hound, both of whom were headed towards the barn, muttering to himself that he really should stop telling his stories – they always seemed to bring disaster to his door.

Cabal skidded to a halt in front of the closed barn doors and then took off to his right, running round the corner of the barn and out of sight. Jack rushed after him, noticing that the flame had bounced around the corner in front of the hound. The flame had ignited a few bits of fallen straw here and there

351

as it leapt along and Jack had his work cut out, stamping on any potential fires as he rushed along.

His mind working overtime - he tried to remember if he'd left any windows open or whether he'd properly repaired the breach in the barn wall. Speeding along the sides of the barn, Jack could only guess at where Cabal and the flame were, by hearing the odd bark as he rushed after them; he didn't catch up with them until he reached the front of the barn again, only to see the flame creeping through a crack under the bottom of the door.

Danny and Ben were standing staring at him as though he'd gone completely mad.

'What on earth's the matter, granddad?' Ben asked worriedly.

Gasping for breath, he forced out the words, 'Water, quickly. Get the door open. Swamp dragon fire!'

The boys rushed to do his bidding as Jack, pulling back the huge bolt, rushed inside. Now was that sensible or not? The rush of air swooshed into the barn, helping the flame to do its worst; dry hay began to smoulder and glow, with one or two tongues of flame beginning to light the otherwise gloomy interior of the barn.

Danny rushed forward to throw his bucket of water over the nearest flames, closely followed by Ben.

As they hurried back for more water Jack, with a look of resignation, joined in. After five minutes or so it became apparent that they were losing the battle.

Still covered in soot from the chimney and with runnels of sweat cleaning their otherwise filthy faces and arms, they eventually stood back and watched despondently as the fire took hold.

Crash! Craaasssh! Whoooosh!

They all turned into the wind. A mighty wind! A wind so sudden and swift that it didn't fan the flames but put them out completely. Turning back, they couldn't believe their eyes.

The fire had not only gone out but they had lost no more than a few bales of hay.

The boys whooped for joy and Cabal ran around them wagging his tail and barking dementedly.

Jack, however, was still on his guard. Searching high and low for the flame, he moved into the barn, at the same time calling Cabal to heel. They stepped cautiously over the blackened stubble and watched for any movement, flare or glow. So engrossed were they in their mission that they were taken completely by surprise and almost jumped out of their skin as a familiar voice asked them, 'Is everything alright?'

Jack spun round and just stared, mouth hanging open.

'Close your mouth Jack. It really doesn't do anything for your looks, you know! I thought you'd have controlled that particular mannerism by now! Especially at your age.'

'Granddad, it's Mrs Ambrose,' Ben explained to his grandfather, now worried that he might have gone a little crazy.

Pulling himself together – and shutting his mouth – he rushed over to the old woman standing in front of him and, remembering in time to call her by her present name instead of the real one, gripped both of her hands in greeting. Almost in tears at the pleasure of seeing her once again and forgetting what his living room now looked like, he asked her to come into the house so that she could refresh herself with some tea and tell them where she had come from.

Both boys gave the old lady a welcome hug while Cabal, unable to control himself, pounced on her and licked her face.

As they turned through the cottage door, Mrs Ambrose stopped dead. 'Phew! What's happened here?' she asked, looking around at the blackened surfaces.

'Oh no!' Jack remembered as he turned again to leave the cottage and rush back toward the barn. 'The flame is still out there! I must try and find it.'

'You mean this flame?' asked Mrs Ambrose, holding a jar aloft. An eye encased in a flame stared out angrily at them all.

Jack just looked at the old lady and nodded. He should have known that everything would be under control when she was around.

'Boys, will you do me a favour please?' Jack asked.

They had been grinning at the old lady who'd started fussing on how much they'd grown and filled out and how Danny now looked so much like his grandfather and Ben had his mother's eyes, but they all turned as Jack spoke.

'Please go home and make up a bed for Mrs Ambrose. As she's come to visit it would be nice for her to sleep in her old home. Set a fire to take the chill off the house and, here, take some milk and bread back with you, oh, and some eggs. It's a pity Kate's not here,' he said to the old woman. 'She would have loved to have seen you.'

'Now don't fuss,' said the old woman. 'I can stay at the pub.'

'No,' the boys chorused. 'Stay in our house. Mum won't mind.'

'Well,' she replied pushing up her sleeves and tut-tutting as she stared around her. 'If that's OK with you, the least I can do is help tidy up this mess.' At which they rushed out of the cottage and down the lane.

True to her word, and in less time than it takes to say "broom", Mrs Ambrose miraculously turned the blackened interior of Jack's cottage into a gleaming miniature palace.

'Now, Percy. You did say tea didn't you?'

And so it was that Mrs Ambrose made herself comfortable in Jack's rocking chair with Cabal settled on the floor beside her furiously wagging his tail at her presence, while Jack, setting the kettle on the hob and a placing a huge slice of the wizards's favourite cherry fruit cake on the table, asked, 'How do you come to be here at this moment Merlin?'

'Well, you can't say you didn't need me, can you?' he responded, one white eyebrow raised. It didn't matter whether he was now Mrs Ambrose or the wizened old man of the forest or anyone else – even himself, come to that - he still had some mannerisms that gave him away, and raising one eyebrow was one of them, whether it be white or black.

'No, that's true,' Jack agreed. 'And thanks. How did you do it?'

'Ah, you now expect me to give away all my trade secrets as well, eh?'

Jack looked over at the old woman and saw the challenge in her eyes but also the twinkle of fun that could only belong to Merlin.

Laughing, he told Merlin how pleased he was to see him and how grateful he was that he'd saved a year's hay – a year's hard work.

'Ah, well,' he responded matter-of-factly, 'isn't that what friends are for?'

And Jack, once again, thought how wonderful it was that Merlin was – is – his friend.

'Now,' he said, 'let's talk while the boys aren't here. I must admit that it was really just an excuse to visit, you know! One of the things I needed to know was whether I could still travel in time – I hadn't done it for such a long time, you see! Another reason was that about a month ago I ran out of this delicious tea; I'd managed to take some back with me the last time I came here and miraculously it didn't disintegrate or change its taste as I travelled back through time. I just had to come and get some more. No, nothing is wrong but, on looking at what was happening here, it seems that I must have been sent. Just in time, eh? Well, there isn't much to tell but we need to tie up some loose ends before the boys return.'

So it was, that, as Jack poured the tea and waited while Mrs Ambrose stirred in some sugar and watched the glow of

355

satisfaction sweep over her face as she took her first sip, that she told him why she had come to see him.

Both Jack and Cabal hung on every word Merlin spoke over the next thirty minutes, Jack sitting with his back against the side of the fireplace alongside a log fire that now behaved itself, while Cabby sat on a slightly singed rug. Neither interrupted.

He'd just finished when the boys returned.

SIXTY-ONE

Panting for breath, Ben strode over to the sink and poured them both a glass of water. They'd obviously run all the way there and all the way back.

'I hope you've done everything I asked you to,' Jack asked them.

'Oh yes,' they chuckled looking around and exclaiming at the amazingly clean room. 'But we had to get back as soon as we could to see Mrs Ambrose before she goes back to our house. Where have you been? It's been so long since we saw you. Mum would have been so pleased to see you. She's back on Friday; will you still be here?'

And so the questions ran on until she held up her hand. 'Whoa,' she laughed at them. 'One thing at a time, young men. I'm afraid I won't be able to see your mother as I have to leave in the morning before dawn but I'm happy to spend the rest of the afternoon with you all; I shall go there after supper and so will say my goodbyes to you all this evening.'

'Oh,' they responded, looking extremely disappointed.

'Still,' Mrs Ambrose interjected, 'I believe your grandfather was telling you one of his tales. Perhaps, when we're all settled, he can continue? I love a good story.'

Jack continued.
I awoke with a burning sensation in my throat. For a few moments I couldn't work out why my tongue felt as though it should hang right out of my mouth. Then, with eyes bulging – everything seemed to be standing out of my face - all that had previously happened rushed up into my head like a mini-tornado, threatening to burst through my cranium. I was poisoned, probably half dead and petrified as to what might happen next. Why had I put myself into the witch's clutches? Why had I listened to Merlin? Why hadn't he saved me?

Had she done the same to Arthur? Where was Cabal? All these thoughts were swirling around in my head in a matter of seconds before I realised that I could move. My hands were not strapped down at my sides any more, I realised, as I held them in front of my face. I was extremely grateful to the wind that had suddenly sprung up; as it flew into my face it gradually cooled my tongue until I felt almost normal again. But what had caused all this fog and why did I feel so tight around my middle? Perhaps it was the effect of the poison. I was terribly tired – another effect? Closing my eyes I allowed the wind to continue to cool me as I drifted off into a sort of sleepy trance.

It's amazing how the brain keeps working, even when we're asleep! My eyes suddenly flew open and I was completely wide-awake in a split second. What had awakened me? One question! How could it be so windy and foggy at the same time? That couldn't be! The wind always blew the fog away! What was happening? Where was I? I reached out to Merlin and Cabal and was rewarded with a sigh of relief from Cabal and a word from Merlin, 'Patience!'

My stomach still felt tight and so, bringing my dangling hand up to rub it, I almost jumped – well, if I could have jumped I almost would have – out of my skin. An enormous girdle encircled my waist. It was like nothing I had felt before; it was thick and made up of three coils. I followed the line of it around my waist until I encountered another coil enfolding the other three and coming from the other direction; this one had a huge talon protruding from it. I moved my legs but could feel no ground; I stared about me but could see only fog, fog that was finally getting lighter. I twisted one arm behind me and could feel what could only be a huge leg. Was my bladder now going to let me down? I hoped that I would be able to control myself.

The dragon had got me! But which one? I must be in the sky; I eventually realised that it wasn't fog but clouds! Was it

358

going to drop me into the sea? I could swim, but how far had yet to be discovered. And how far would I fall? Too far, I thought. If I'm in the clouds and now drop – I'd burst on impact on land or sea!

Then we came out of the clouds and looked down upon an amazing scene.

From up here I could see for miles. To the south Hellion lay dozing on a huge rock that jutted out into the sea. That was a mighty relief, I can tell you. Once I had seen him I knew, even before I looked - and look then I did - that it was Moon Song that had me in her grip and she would not let me fall. She would also not let Arthur fall. I could see him slumped over like a child's discarded rag doll as, like me, he was held in the grip of Moon Song's other talons. I called to him but there was no response. Was he dead? I couldn't tell. I tried to reach over to him to shake him or even feel if he breathed but he was too far away. I sent up a silent prayer to Arthur's God; he always said that he knew God loved us all, so I had to trust that if He loved him he'd be OK.

As I couldn't do anything right now, I determined not to worry about Arthur but to see what was happening and be ready for my part in all of this when the time came. Feeling better, I watched the story unfolding before me.

Camped some two miles away towards the east was a party of travellers. I felt sure I knew who they must be and called out to Rhianne in my mind. She answered immediately and I watched as they struck camp and started to make their way towards the beach. I warned her what was happening and to make sure they took care because the witch was now completely mentally unstable.

My eye was drawn back to the sea where a small sailboat, manned by two sailors, tacked southwards towards our bay.

Then I looked north and there, standing high on the cliff top, stood Merlin. He was holding his hands high and the fall of the sleeves from his robe made him look magnificent and powerful. Even at that distance I could see the steely glitter of his eyes as he stared towards the beach and the witch. As the daylight grew, the light from the staff that he still held high faded but its potency did not diminish.

The witch was still screeching and jumping up and down as she stamped her feet in frustration. Her plan had gone completely awry; she had watched helplessly as Moon Song, diving out of the morning sky, had snatched her captives from her grasp and had soared back into the clouds, leaving her momentarily dumbstruck and fuming.

Cabal had stopped his digging and had run back to Salazar and the others on the beach who had by now fanned out around the witch's enclosure.

'I will not be outdone this time,' screamed Mad Mab as she spun to face Merlin. 'They are mine. By now they must be dead anyway,' she screeched as she turned towards the sea. 'Hellion. Hellion.' The cry she made echoed and re-echoed around the bay as she called the leonine dragon to her.

I turned to where I had last seen the dragon dozing, only to watch, petrified as it rose from the outcrop of rocks and soared into the sky.

'Get them,' she cried to Hellion as he climbed before turning and swooping down toward us.

Still held securely in Moon Song's great claws, we were now in the most invidious position anyone could possibly find himself. Moon Song, turning to face the ever-nearing white dragon, readied herself for battle.

I looked round to see if Arthur had yet shown any sign of life – he had not. I still didn't know if he was alive or whether the witch had actually killed him with her deadly potion. Thinking about it I licked my lips and moved my tongue about in my mouth; apart from a slight tingling, the awful burning sensation had now worn off. I must have spat the brew out of my mouth, or had it squeezed out of my body when Moon Song had grabbed me from the witch's stake.

I needn't have worried about licking my lips or tongue. As I turned back to look in front of me my mouth went completely dry with fear. The two dragons were almost head on into collision, Moon Song diving at the last minute to slide under Hellion's belly and make a stab at it with her huge jaws. Hellion, however, rose swiftly into the sky and missed having his belly ripped open by a whisker. They were moving at such great speed that it took some while before they turned and attacked once more.

Every time we were almost head-on I screamed at the top of my lungs; I couldn't help it, it was petrifying. Looking back I remembered afterwards that I couldn't hear myself scream; I think the sound of it was whipped away by the wind or roar of the dragons, but, nonetheless, scream I did. And wet myself!

'You would too,' Jack chuckled as he watched his grandsons crack up laughing.

The white dragon had an advantage over the red dragon in that he was free to use his claws, whereas Moon Song couldn't unless she dropped both Arthur and me. We were extremely high in the sky – sometimes over land and sometimes over the sea. If she was going to drop us at all I hoped upon hope that it would be over the sea; I dared not think what might happen if it was over those steep and jagged rocks.

So we were back once again on a head-on collision course with Hellion, only this time I noticed steam coming out of his nostrils. 'Oh no. *Merlin, save us,*' I cried. *'We are going to be fried by Hellion.'*

By now the steam had turned to a very pretty pink colour, rapidly turning orange and then crimson before a huge jet of flame poured forth, advancing on us with such rapidity that I just knew I was going to die.

This time Moon Song rose above the other dragon and I watched bug-eyed as the jet of flame shot past just underneath

361

us. I can still feel the heat as it rose to tickle my feet. Then we were travelling away from each other before tacking round and facing our adversary once again.

I felt something different this time; Moon Song had tensed herself, gripping us a little tighter as she did so, and lowering her head as she moved determinedly through the sky towards Hellion.

I tried hard to close my eyes so that I wouldn't see the awful things that were about to happen, but it's like watching a scary film on the TV – even if you hold your hands over your face, you always manage to peek through a crack in your fingers. It was like that now; first I'd open one eye just a crack to look through my eyelashes, then close it and then do the same with the other. It was no good – I just had to know what was happening and we were getting nearer and nearer.

Crunch! Thump! The two dragons hit one another with such a force that I thought every bone in my body must surely be knocked out of joint; my brain rattled in my skull and stars and whorls of coloured light swam before my eyes. I could only get glimpses of what was happening; being under the belly of the dragon all I could see, apart from Hellion, were Moon Song's giant wings and her head when she reached forwards. Soon, even this view was obscured as she drew her legs close up under her belly to protect us.

The dragons fought craftily and shrewdly, Hellion being the more cunning of the two who used as many dirty tricks as he could to try and bring us down. Moon Song was tiring rapidly, I realised, her chest heaving against me.

By now both dragons were using their firepower and after several hits the stench of burning scales made the gorge rise in my throat. I watched as Moon Song's head thrust forward, her jaws making a sudden grab at Hellion's throat; he pulled away but, blood spurting, I noticed he'd lost a chunk of neck.

Screaming he leapt high into the sky before flying away. We watched as he landed on an outcrop of rock while he

362

caught his breath and tended to his neck, lowering his wing into the sea and rubbing water onto the sore; screaming as the salt bit into the wound. Before long he appeared recovered enough to continue the fight.

'*Merlin,*' I called. '*Can you get Moon Song to fly above Hellion?*'

'*Ah, yes. Why not? Yes, we'll do it that way,*' he answered me. '*Clever boy!*'

By now Hellion had risen high in the sky and was swooping down upon us, all nostrils blazing. Before we had time to climb, Hellion had dropped down upon us and dug his claws deep into Moon Song's back. She screamed in agony as she thrashed about, trying to dislodge the white dragon's talons from her body, scales dropping past me like roof slates.

'*What's happening Merlin,*' I cried. There was no answer and I found myself being shaken violently as Hellion continued his attack. I could feel myself losing consciousness as my head cracked from side to side before, suddenly, all seemed to change. Merlin was singing.

Then, as though we were suspended in time as well as in the sky, all was still. Nothing moved at all. No wings flapped; no clouds moved; there was absolute silence. For about five seconds. Then everything happened at once. Merlin resumed his singing; Hellion, who had apparently not been able to move for double that time, lost his purchase on Moon Song's back and the tables turned.

She rose majestically into the air and hovered above the white dragon who, momentarily confused, was falling towards the edge of the sea.

'*Well, come on then Percy – move!*' an exasperated Merlin called.

I scrabbled about round my neck until I found the small phial. Hands cold and shaking, I carefully removed the stopper and, praying it would find its mark, sprinkled the powder from its container down over the spiralling dragon.

363

'Please don't let there be any wind to blow it away,' I whispered to anyone that might be listening.

I couldn't drag my eyes away from the dragon. He, realising the danger he was in as he spun towards the earth, spread his wings to catch the thermals and take flight. He moved away and my heart sank. I watched as he flew across the sea towards the beach where Mab, who had been watching the fight, screamed at him to attack.

Then it happened! Just as he reached the shoreline he dropped – literally like a stone – onto the beach. The sand rose up like a storm cloud as the wind of his landing thumped it into the air. Nothing could be seen of him until the sand settled back onto the land.

I looked across at Merlin who, with arms still raised, was grinning from ear to ear. Looking further inland I could see Rhianne and her party getting closer as they headed towards the cliff top – she would be here in less than half an hour, I reckoned. The little sailboat had turned round the point and was headed into the bay. The giant looked as though he'd been buried up to his waist as the sand began to settle around him; of the witch and the rest of our party on the beach there was no sign.

'Cabby, are you alright?' I called out to him.

After a short interval he called back, *Almost choked to death in this sand, but it's getting better.'* I watched him struggling out of the sand.

Then everything cleared.

The landscape had changed somewhat. The witch was howling like a banshee as she scrabbled around trying to find her paraphernalia, which had been buried under the settling sand. The giant hauled himself up and out onto more solid ground looking utterly confused. Salazar, Cabby and the others were dusting or shaking themselves down and making towards the water's edge.

Where an amazing sight met them.

364

I also stared as the dragon – or what was left of him – was metamorphosed before our eyes. Part of his spine stuck up out of the sand while his neck appeared to be buried; further along his head and snub nose rose up through the sand, while his eyes stared, albeit lifelessly, at the place where the witch still thundered around; one wing was thrown some good few feet away and had broken into two pieces but of the other wing or tail there was no sign. The dragon's life-sound hummed and dimmed until it faded away completely and, as it did so, its visible body parts turned to stone.

My friends stood for quite some time staring at this astonishing transmutation from animal to mineral and from life to death, before moving away from the phenomenon and making their way back along the beach.

I became aware, as the figures on the beach were growing larger, that Moon Song was now descending. It soon became apparent that there was to be no soft landing for Arthur and me. She flew as low as she could and as near to the beach as she could before, opening one set of claws, she dropped me unceremoniously into the shallow waters. I still had the wind knocked out of me by the shock of cold water but was almost immediately hauled out of it by a hand seizing my collar. Nell's son grinned down at me as his other hand, grabbing me by my pants, dragging me roughly over the side of the boat. We went through the same process with Arthur who, still unconscious but not dead, thank goodness, needed both of us to haul him into the boat.

One quick thought ran through my head – now that I was wet all over, no-one would be able to notice the lack of control I'd had over my bladder!

Then I turned and noticed who the other sailor was – Jasmine. As soon as we were both aboard, she started ministering to Arthur, while I assisted Nell's son to steer the boat towards the shore.

SIXTY-TWO

I watched the sky dim as Moon Song flew out to sea and disappear around the headland. Staring back at the land I started to become alarmed as the witch, turning this way and that, endeavoured to search us out.

'Don't fear, young Percy,' Jasmine, without leaving her ministrations to Arthur, spoke softly to me. Turning to Nell's son she asked him to hoist the other sail. Now I'm not the greatest sailor at the best of times and I have to admit that my stomach started to contract at the thought of going out to sea on this very small boat but imagine my surprise when the sail was none other than Rhianne's cloak of invisibility. We would be able to stay at the water's edge and watch all the fun – if fun it be - without being detected.

The witch's eyes fell upon Ysbaddaden and her fury exploded. 'It's all your fault,' she screamed at him.

'Me?' he questioned, shocked, as he held his hand to his heart. 'How on earth do you work that one out?'

'If it hadn't been for you and your wretched daughter, none of this would have happened! Look at my poor Hellion! Broken in pieces! It will take me forever to find all the bits and try to get him back together again. How am I supposed to travel now? Who is going to fight in the sky for me? Aarrghhh,' she screamed, shaking her fist at the sky, where, through streaming and slitted eyes she espied her archenemy, still standing with arms outstretched.

'You!' she mouthed the word. Turning back to the giant she screamed, 'Get him! Go on – you can reach him. Pull him down off his mighty perch and crush him against the rocks. Grab him by both hands and twist him into two. Break him pieces across your knee! Go on, go on.' She was by now so completely lost in her fury that all she could see was Merlin; all the hate she had for the man emanated from every part of her being – from the weird set of her hair which stuck out almost as though shot through with electricity, to that which was greasily plastered to her head, through grabbing, talon-like hands at the end of windmilling arms, to her feet which flailed at the end of stamping and kicking legs. Froth had started to build up at the corners of her mouth and the whites of her bulging eyes were by now becoming bloodshot with the strain of staring at him.

Without turning, she screeched at him to grab the man.

'*You* get your man,' he roared back at her. He had by now had enough of the ridiculous woman. As much as it might have been considered fun at one time to fall in with her nefarious plans, even he had now had his fill. All he wanted to do was rid himself of the stupid woman, crush the obviously unsuitable Culhwch underfoot – somehow without his daughter being aware of what he was up to – gather her up and be off. 'I'm just going to get Olwen and take her home. I've had enough. *You* do what you want.'

Well, you could have cut the atmosphere then like a hot knife through butter. Everything seemed to stand still. Even the sea breaking on the shore stopped in mid-roll, held its breath and was silent as it waited with bated breath to see what she would do next. The giant, unfortunately, was completely unaware of anything except the fact of his daughter and didn't see or feel the signs.

My eyes were glued to Mad Mab and she really stood up to the name she had been given as she turned slowly and stared across at the retreating form of the giant.

'No one! No-one does that to me! No-one disobeys me and no-one walks away from me.' Her voice was more or less non-existent as she started to speak but by the time she had finished the volume control button had been turned to maximum and the ground was shaking.

Ysbaddaden hunched his shoulders almost up to his ears to try and drown out her noise but was determined to go after his daughter. Culhwch had taken Olwen's hand and the party were running along the beach as fast as their legs would carry them. They didn't stand a chance - Ysbaddaden would obviously reach them in less than a dozen strides.

Well, that would have been the case but for the witch!

She is absolutely witless at times, you know. And this was one of them. A house divided against itself will fall. Everyone knows that. Well, almost everyone – the witch was an exception.

Her madness and lack of self-control came to the fore; she just couldn't stand being baulked and it sent a red mist of madness through her brain. Without thinking, but did she ever think rationally anyway, she rushed over to the bottles and packs she'd managed to dig out of the sand, opened the nearest one and threw it at him.

Another breath holding moment! The waves stopped once again in mid roll and watched with myriad sparkling eyes at the curious pantomime being acted out before them; the clouds, embellished at the edges with pink from the rising sun, stared down with many weird and wonderful shapes, while all of us, goggled-eyed, gawked as the container smashed against his shoulders and spread down his back.

Ysbaddaden, that great, frightening, mountain of a man was stopped in his tracks. He creaked to a halt as he half turned to find out what had hit him and ended up facing out to sea. As his body stopped moving, he, like the dragon before him began to crack and shift until he collapsed down upon himself – a huge rock formation settling onto the beach. The sea started moving again and tentatively at first but then with more bravado and vigour began to lap around the edges of the former Tormentor of the Downs.

Culhwch, Niel and the rest of the party were drawn irresistibly back along the beach to see what had happened to him and, knowing what a tender young woman his daughter was, gave her comfort on his loss – even for one such as he.

However, there was hardly time to do much more than wipe away a tear or two as all eyes were, once more, drawn back to the witch who had, by now, realised the error of her ways. Not one to dwell on those errors for too long, she determined that this had to be the time to rid herself of her adversary now that he was in her sights. Once he was out of the way, then there would be no one to stop her from getting Arthur. He might have been snatched from her for now, but soon – yes soon – she would get him!

'Be ready Salazar,' I heard the whisper that Merlin sent to the African Druid and watched as he separated himself from the rest of the group, sending them to take cover on the other side of what had previously been Olwen's father – he'd become useful for something then!

Our boat had by now half beached itself at the end of the bay but we stayed within it, being only slightly buffeted by each strengthening wave. Jasmine sat with her back to the inside of the boat with Arthur's head nestled into the crook of her shoulder; he was still unconscious.

'I'll go and help the others,' I whispered as I climbed out of the boat, only to be pulled back abruptly by Nell's son.

'No, young man - you stay here,' he responded, as I fell backwards onto the floor of his boat. 'Miss Jasmine here has already told me we are all to stay here out of the way until it's all over.'

'Until all what's over?' I wheezed, then started coughing after having the stuffing knocked out of me by my fall.

'Merlin told me to keep you and Arthur here until he had put all of his plans into action. All will be well, Percy,' Jasmine advised me as the first flash of light blazed all around us.

Like a mini explosion, masses of things were lifted and thrown, striking the cliffs or falling onto the sand or into the

369

sea causing it to broil all around us. One such missile thumped into the middle of Arthur's back and no-one was more surprised than me when the force of it caused his mouth to open and what I can only describe as green slime mixed with yellow pus shot out of it. I grimaced as I watched it coagulate; it landed on the seat and then appeared to hop onto the edge of the boat and then into the sea. I looked over the side quickly but it had gone; I was sure it was some sort of toad and shuddered as I thought of it inside my friend.

'Percy, you're alright,' a croaky voice whispered as I leaned over the boat looking for that warty creature.

'Arthur. Thank God!' I turned and rushed to his side. 'I thought at one point you were dead!'

'Yes, thank God indeed! I thought you were dead too - after that witch poured that poison down your throat. But we're alive somehow. But how did we get here?'

We'd have to do our catching-up later. Another huge flash and all eyes swivelled towards the centre of the beach. Mab's madness appeared to be in full flow as she ranted and screeched within her set boundary. Standing as high as she could on a stone shelf, she was throwing burning missiles at anything that moved, especially at Merlin who still stood with arms upraised. She was swearing and cursing at the top of her lungs as she spun around hurling fireballs here and there until the much louder voice of Merlin penetrated her brain.

'Mab, Mab, calm down. You've lost – again. Why keep trying?'

'Lost! Lost! No, I never lose,' she screeched at him. 'A minor setback, perhaps, but you know, Myrddin, that in the end I will win! I have to win!'

'You've lost your collaborator,' he changed the subject as he pointed across at the huge outcrop of rock that was once the giant.

She fumed for a short while before pretending it was all alright. 'He was a moron,' she cried out. 'I'm better on my own. At least I know I can rely on me! You just can't get the right help these days!' the last muttered under the breath.

'Then why has it all gone wrong?'

We all watched as the ever-simmering rage started to take hold of her again. Just as her face had attained that wonderful crimson hue before it turns to burgundy, she managed – and how she found that ability I shall never know – to compose herself. Her chest was rising and falling and her hands were stretched out in front of her with fingers curling, a mad pianist waiting to crash the keys in a thunderous crescendo.

And then, almost immediately, a crafty look took over her features; her eyes closed to slits and her mouth grimaced, while her back straightened with resolve.

Without another word she turned and made her way down from her rocky dais, across the sand and over to the few bits and pieces she had been able to salvage from their burial place under the sand. She only looked over her shoulder once, checking to see if all the players were still in their correct places. Yes, Merlin was still on top of the cliff; Salazar stood in front of Ysbaddaden's rock; I believe she managed to espy our little party in the boat as she looked in our direction for quite some time. I tried to stand in front of Arthur but I'm certain she was looking at him, even if she was staring straight through me.

'What are you up to now, Mab?' Merlin asked. 'Do you need my help?' He chuckled as he watched the effects of his questions; her shoulders scrunched up and then tried to relax – a hard job indeed – as she, trying hard not to listen to him, started to "la la la" very loudly.

Merlin burst out laughing and was rewarded with an increase in noisy "la-la-ing" from the witch. But she couldn't keep it up for long – it only made her start coughing.

'Mab, why don't just you and I have a showdown?'

'You and me? No. No way. I am stronger than you now. I know it! I shall finish you and him,' she cried, pointing at

371

Salazar, 'and then him,' she crooned, pointing at us. Did she mean me or Arthur? Probably both! Well, she'd tried once, and failed. Let's hope she fails again. Oops, my barrier was down. I looked up at Merlin, hoping he hadn't heard my impertinent thought – as if *she* could ever win!

'I shall give you no quarter,' she called over her shoulder at the Druid.

'No quarter, eh? So be it!' His face turned stony.

'Ah ha,' she cried in triumph as she rushed back onto her platform. Without more ado and before she could be stopped, she raised her arm high and, with lighted taper in one hand, lit the touch paper on what could only be described as a huge firework and we all watched with foreboding to see what was going to happen next.

We didn't have to wait long.

There was an almighty bang before the most beautifully painted display of flames ballooned around us – an umbrella of colours unmatched by any produced by the fireworks companies I had bought from. We were mesmerised – and, of course, that is what she wanted.

The flashes, whiz-bangs and whirrings went on for a considerable time, blues turning to reds turning to purples, and so on, until the very last flashes blasted off in a multitude of colours, shapes and bangs. We were still staring into the ever-lightening morning sky, waiting to see what would happen next, when we were brought back to the present by maniacal laughter. As though a hypnotist had clicked his fingers to bring us out of our trance, her laughter brought us back to the present with a bang.

The smoke cleared; we strained our eyes to see what was happening.

How had she done that?

Trapped inside her invisible boundary were my friends – Niel, Kay, Culhwch, Olwen and Cabal. How had she captured them? Not only that, but there were also at least a score of those awful chimeras, snapping at their heels. Cabal, bigger and braver than they could ever be, kept them at bay; his lips curled back over massive teeth as he snarled at them whenever they got too close. My heart went out to all of them.

'I've got to go and help,' I cried as I flung one leg over the side of the boat. Nell's son dragged me back again. I could have wept.

'We are not to cause any distractions. He has enough to do with that wicked woman without having to see to you too. You have done your part. Now let Merlin do his.'

He sat down opposite me, took up the oars and, setting them in the rowlocks, rowed us out a fair distance from the beach. If I had to, I'd jump overboard and swim. Arthur, I noticed, was locked in prayer.

From our vantage point out at sea, we had an excellent view. At the cliff top, some three-quarters of a mile away, Rhianne arrived with a small band of people. I reached out to her to find out if she was alright and who was with her.

'Mother is with me and Brother Geraint is also here with Shake Spear and Brosc. But what is happening?'

I explained the situation as quickly as I could and she soon got the gist of what was taking place. I told her that Arthur was praying and asked her to get Brother Geraint to do the same. She said that she would.

'Stay where you are, though,' I cautioned her. *'Merlin is working out how to defeat the witch. She's captured some of our men and I don't want that happening to you. Don't let the witch know you're here.'*

'We'll do as you say.'

Then I turned back to see what was happening at the beach.

SIXTY-THREE

Merlin removed the ruby eye from the left side of his staff by twisting it out of its socket. He blew upon it until even I, at my distance, could see it start to expand and glow. It turned from red to gold and its brilliance rivalled the sun; the larger it got, the less I could look at it without shading my eyes and trying to squint through my eyelashes.

'Don't look at it,' I heard Merlin speak to me. *'Look away or look past it but don't look directly at it. Tell the others.'*

I told the others in the boat; Merlin had told Niel to do the same.

I stared past it but could see it out of the corner of my eye. It grew in size until it was almost as big as a football and the intensity of its luminosity multiplied Now, I don't know if I imagined it, but I am almost sure that I could see figures within the ball; it is hard to say, as I wasn't looking directly at it but I was soon to find out.

Meanwhile, Mab was making her way across her compound towards Sir Kay. Her arms were outstretched to grab him when Cabal, stupid, brave hound, rushed at her. Without even slowing her pace she turned, threw something at him and didn't even watch as he creaked to a halt, turning white as he slumped to the ground – another stone edifice decorating that beach.

'Noooo,' I screamed from the sea as I watched my friend turn to stone. I called out to him in my mind but there was nothing – my mind thoughts bouncing back into my head with a mighty crash. Tears were coursing down my cheeks as I, once again, tried to get out of that boat to see if I could do anything for him.

Once again, but more gently this time, I was pulled back into the boat. 'Now, now, young sir,' Nell's son tried to comfort me. 'Leave it to Merlin. If anyone can do anything, he can. 'No,' he pulled at me as once again I tried to get out. 'You will only make it worse.' He was gentle but he kept hold of me. I eventually collapsed in a heap at the bottom of the boat. When the thought came into my mind, I looked up at Jasmine in the hope that she would give me some good news but her face was impassive. I couldn't then stop the sobs that took hold of me as hot, salty tears coursed down my face.

My poor, poor friend.

'Granddad,' Ben interrupted, 'he got turned back again, didn't he? Did the giant also get turned back and Hellion?' he added.

'Do you want to tell this story or shall I? Jack laughed.

'Sorry, but I really wanted to know if Cabal was really alright or whether he's still a rock on the beach at Bedruthan Steps.'

'I'm sure you do,' Jack replied. 'Shall I continue?'

'Yes please. Sorry.'

Grabbing hold of Kay – and she must have done something to him to make him go with her because he wouldn't have gone willingly and he was much stronger than her anyway – she pulled him up to the stake and tied him to it. She then went back and did the same to Niel, tying him back to back with Kay at the same stake; then, using the other stake, she did the same with Olwen and Culhwch.

'Now,' she beamed, 'I'm going to make them my slaves. They will drink this brew and fall so completely in love with me that they will then do anything I command. It's irreversible, you know! I've already done it to Ysbaddaden's chimera and they now obey my every wish. Watch this!' and turning to the animal-headed dwarfs, she commanded, 'Dance. Dance a jig.'

Have you ever seen anything so ridiculous in your life?

Those diminutive dwarfs with their outsize, swivelling heads and feet were jigging up and down like deformed jesters, heads swivelling this way and that like toy windmills. If I hadn't been so stricken with grief I would have roared with laughter. What was that ridiculous witch trying to do - laugh us all to death?

'Mab. Catch!'

She turned as Merlin threw the glistening ball of light at her. She jumped to one side, narrowly missing one of the dancers as she did so; the flaming ball bounced off the sand and was caught on the other side of her barrier by Salazar who threw it back up to Merlin. A blazing shadow of smoke was left behind filled with grimacing faces, long-haired ladies swimming along in gossamer dresses that trailed for yards in their wake on the thermals left by the flaming ball gradually turning to skeletons as they floated up to her; and elongated imps and dragons and, worst of all, skulls, whose faces stretched out and thrust themselves into Mab's face and contorted as they swam past her. Screaming, she ran backwards, falling over as she tried to run away from them.

'Mab. Catch!'

Without turning, she ran behind her captives to take shelter from that which was scaring the living daylights out of her. The flaming ball followed her and bounced once again in front of her, the mist creating those frightening grins and distorted sneers that left her screaming in terror and fearing for her life.

She realised she had to do something about this – and quickly. But what? Grabbing another one of her fireworks, she lit it and waited as, once again, the air fizzed and popped as it went off, showering us all with its colourful show – a little less bright than the previous one due to the fact that it was, with the rising sun, by now almost full daylight. However, we were once more mesmerised by the display and thus it was that the witch had a moment's respite to catch her breath and plan her next move.

'Stop,' she screamed at the jigging dancers. They did, and flopped onto the ground exhausted. Curling her lip at them she turned back to her potions. Rummaging through them as quickly as she could, she finally came to the one she was looking for and with an almost silent 'aha', pulled off the stopper, lifted it to her lips and drank.

Zap! She disappeared.

'Ha! Now throw your wretched ball at me Myrddin,' she called up at him. 'Now I can put my plan into action without any interference from you!'

'Er, how are you going to do that, Mab?' he called down at her. 'Fly?' And at that he hurled the ball once more, barely missing her again.

With a high-pitched yelp, she ran behind her captives for safety.

Salazar, catching the ball, hurled it back up the cliff to Merlin, who, pitching it like an experienced test cricketer, managed to hit the hem of her invisible dress, causing it to smoke.

'Now I can see you - instead of just your footprints in the sand,' he called down to her as he retrieved the glowing orb once more from Salazar and hurled it back down towards her.

Screaming, she banged her hands against the smoking dress to put it out, noticing the footprints that Merlin had been talking about. Quieting herself, she stood still and waited. Nothing would happen for as long as she didn't move. She looked up at Merlin who was holding his arm aloft ready to strike; she could see him looking this way and that.

No-one had noticed, but Niel had been working loose his bonds. The witch was now standing in front of her captives and so was unaware that he had got to the point of bending down to untie the rope around his legs. He had no weapons but was very strong. He might just be able to overpower her.

Looking up towards Merlin, I saw him nod. Did they communicate? Were they mind-speaking without me hearing? I didn't have more time to pursue these thoughts as Niel, launching himself – more by smell than by sight – landed on top of the witch and wrestled her to the ground. It looked really weird – as though Niel were floating about two feet from the ground. That was all Merlin needed. Tossing the ball down at the speed of light, it hit Mab in the centre of her forehead, setting light to some of her hair and knocking her senseless – not that she ever had much sense to start with; she also now became visible again. But, a split second before she received that blow, she had managed a half turn and blasted some sort of spell at Niel. He flew up into the air and landed with a mighty splash in the sea some fifty feet away.

We turned in our boat and with sail hoisted headed to where he had landed. The wind had suddenly whipped up and the sea was now becoming quite rough. It was a day that was turning out very bad indeed. We struggled through huge waves as we sailed around for a very long time calling his name and peering into the water but of Niel there was no sign.

Hours later I would still be found looking out to sea and along the beach in the hope that I would see him swimming towards us or dragging himself up the beach, and I was not the only one, but of him there was no sign. My heart was getting heavier by the minute: first Cabal and now Niel.

Who might be next?

I don't know what the witch had used on Niel, but it had had a terrible effect on him. Not only that, but it had an alarming effect on the sea; as he splashed into it, it broiled and bubbled to such an extent that a mini-tidal wave began to grow and make its way towards the shore.

Salazar moved along a crevice in the cliff face that led up to where Merlin stood and surveyed the scene, noticing Lady Elise and her party travelling towards them along the edge of the cliff top. But all stood motionless as the wave, gathering momentum and height, pushed its way relentlessly towards the shore.

Kay, having been tied to Neil, had by now also struggled free of his ropes and both he and Culhwch were hurrying to untie Olwen; there was no way that they would be able to get through Mab's barrier but they would stand more chance of living if they were not tied up. 'Hold on to the stakes,' Kay shouted at the others through the deafening noise the sea and winds were making. They did so and, holding on to one another, braced themselves ready for the onslaught of water.

The wave rolled in.

Nell's son, Jasmine, Arthur and I were safe on the sea; the wave merely lifted us as it passed underneath. We couldn't really see anything until it broke on the shore as it was hiding everything from our view. It wasn't that big a wave but it did some damage. As it hit the land it rushed up the beach, over several large rocks – one being Ysbaddaden – up and almost to the top of the cliffs before it fell back down onto the beach and then back into the sea. That was it, but what it left behind was devastating – for the witch!

Kay and Culhwch were helping Olwen over the lip of the witch's barrier and down the other side. She had to drop about six feet once she'd let go of their hands but she landed fairly well on the soft, wet sand. The two men dropped down after her and ran as fast as their wet clothes would allow them to the foot of the cliffs.

When they looked back, what a sight met their eyes. Mab, who had regained consciousness just as the wave was about to strike, was swimming about in the murky sea water within what looked like her own personal see-through swimming pool. It was obvious she couldn't swim as she kept sinking to the bottom, where she would push herself up, take a quick gulp of air before falling back down to the bottom and going over the whole process again; until she managed to reach the side and cling on.

She was weeping fit to burst. All those years of power washed off her by the salty attack of the sea! It was going to take years for her to recover.

A hard realisation for her but a relief for the rest of us.

We could see that she now had no heart to continue with any attack on Arthur, or Merlin for that matter. She realised that whatever power she had accumulated over the years had, with one fell swoop, been completely washed away. I don't think she even considered anyone else from that moment; she was just, as always, thinking about herself.

But I just thought that, at least for a while, she'd smell a bit better.

SIXTY-FOUR

We all eventually, except Cabal and Niel of course, sat around on the grass at the top of the cliffs while Merlin, as ever, took charge.

'We have much to do and a very little time in which to do it,' he stated. 'Each of you must do his part without any questioning; otherwise it will not all get done in time.

'First, come Salazar; come Percy,' he beckoned us. 'Let's see if anything can be done for Cabal.' My heart leapt!

We hurried down the cliff face and onto the wet sand. The barrier had started to crack quite seriously now and water was seeping out in many places. Very soon the witch would once more be on solid ground and I, for one, wondered what she might do when she was able to walk about again.

'Don't fret, Percy,' Merlin broke into my thoughts. 'She won't be doing anything for a long time to come. There! There he is!' he shouted as he pointed at the rock that was once my wonderful friend.

Merlin lifted his arms and shouted an unintelligible command, causing the rest of the fast-cracking barrier to split in many places and crash apart completely. We were on high enough ground to stay almost completely dry as water cascaded out of it, rushing back towards the sea, carrying a screeching woman with it. I wanted to laugh, even though I was still mourning Cabal, and almost did so as I watched Mad Mab pulling herself out of the waves, plastered hair elongated with seaweed and arms and face running with dirt and sand. She was almost so clean I might not have recognised her if I hadn't known who she was in the first place and yes her dress was blue.

I was wrenched back to the present by Merlin as he strode across the sand towards the rock that was Cabal. He ran his hands over the rock, shaking his head or nodding as he did so.

'What?' I cried. 'What?' I asked again, even louder, panic rising up in me again.

'I thought we might be in time,' he whispered.

'No!' I cried. 'Don't tell me it's too late.'

'Salazar. Find the tip of his tail. I'll touch the tip of his nose. Now, do you remember the Spell of Reclaiming?'

The African Druid nodded.

'Fine. We have to say it together. Ready?'

He nodded again.

They started together – a language unknown to me that sounded so old, it didn't seem possible that two people could say the same things at once. The air buzzed around us as they spoke on, crackling and fizzing as magic filled the air. The rock that had been Cabal glowed, the fire within it strengthening and weakening as the vibrating sound within it ebbed and flowed. Then all was still. No voices, no humming, no magic in the air – just silence.

We all looked at the stone that had been Cabal until tears started to fall from my eyes. He wasn't coming back! My beautiful friend wasn't coming back to me. The tears ran unchecked down my face, dripping off my chin onto the rock as I knelt down beside him. Tears fizzed as they dripped onto the rock. I leaned down and touched the very warm rock and flung my arms around my poor Cabal's neck, my tears running unchecked down his cooling and solid ruff; and then he moved – head raising up, limbs turning, lungs breathing – and then he was there, lifting his head and with his beautiful brown eyes once again looking at me. I just couldn't contain myself; the tears flowed again, this time with joy as my Cabal was back. He got up on very unsteady feet and then came over and licked the tears off my face. I just flung my arms around him and hugged him for joy.

'The magic was good, but it couldn't soften this body of stone,' he spoke into my mind. *'It was the tears of love that revived me!'*

I couldn't speak past the lump in my throat as I hugged him.

Merlin and Salazar just stood grinning down at us.

'Right,' he said after he'd given us enough time to recover during which time he screwed the ruby back into its rightful place. 'Now, we have to sort out Culhwch and Olwen.' Climbing back up the rockface, he strode over to the monk and, after very few words, made his way back to talk to Culhwch and Olwen.

'The monk is happy to conduct your marriage ceremony if you really want him to. However, time is short and if you agree, then it will have to happen now. I am prepared to give you away, seeing as you have no-one else to do the job,' he added, looking at the rock that had once been Ysbaddaden.

The look on their faces was something to behold. They were very happy to be wed; now was as good a time as any.

Jasmine and Rhianne rushed around on the cliff top collecting as many wild flowers as they could to make her a posy to carry and a garland to wear in her hair. Within no time at all the happy pair had been given to each other and were setting off on their honeymoon. Nell's son led them to his boat and with everyone waving, we shouted our blessings to them, as they set off on their new lives together. We didn't stop until they'd disappeared around the headland, headed north.

I looked more than once at the rock that had been Ysbaddaden and wondered if it was the sea still held in pockets within his rockface or whether it could have been tears in his eyes that glistened as he was forced to watch his daughter sail away. Cabal told me later that he was more than likely crying; he said that even though he'd been converted to rock, he was still aware of everything around him. *'Quite scary really when I was stuck at the bottom of all that water; I thought I must drown but couldn't as I wasn't able to breath! Weird! No, I reckon he could see her alright.'*

'And now, Arthur,' Merlin beamed as he turned towards him. 'Hinton St. Mary! The day of evil is now behind us and it's finally All Saints' Day and, if I remember correctly, you wanted to be there today, eh?'

Arthur's face looked grim as he merely shook his head in despair.

'I've sent the wagons and the rest of the men on to meet us there, so that we'll have some transport when we go home. In the meantime, we merely need some sort of conveyance to get us there, eh?'

Arthur looked perplexed, wondering if Merlin had overtaxed himself whilst sparring with the witch.

Laughing, Merlin turned and looked north. Humming – and I wasn't going to make any comments this time – we all watched Moon Song rising high into the sky, dipping gracefully around as she made ready to land alongside us all.

'We'll be there in less than an hour,' he grinned at the astonished assembly.

And so it was that we all, even though rather cramped, climbed up and, settled ourselves between her wings and watched as the world sped by beneath us. We'd already waved goodbye to a witch who didn't even have the strength left to scowl at us as we took off. The last we saw of her, she was wringing the seawater out of her sodden skirts and keening like a banshee as she dragged herself from the sea.

For the main part Moon Song flew high but now and then dipped quite low when something of interest caught her eye – had Merlin told her to do that? We skimmed the ground where the giant's castle once stood; it had completely disappeared and as it had been raining for quite some time all that was left was a huge, muddy bog – no brick, no gate, no chimera or Cornek - nothing remained to show to even the most keen eye that anything other than sheep resided there.

Turning, we flew back up into the sunshine until all the clouds had disappeared; then flying low over our wagons and men as they neared Hinton St. Mary, more than one of the men ducked as we roared overhead.

So it was, that mid-afternoon we landed beside the shrine that held the mosaic of Christ. We'd made it!

Arthur was glowing. He couldn't stop thanking Merlin and Salazar or hugging his mother and sister. Jasmine and Kay also basked in the sunshine of his happiness, while I, well I was still being thumped on the back! One day, I thought, one day!

Cabal was his usual happy self, even more so now that he'd been able to extricate himself from the dragon's back.

As soon as we had all alighted, Moon Song took flight - back to her rest as that mysterious circle of stones; sleeping the long sleep until Merlin or Arthur had need of her once again.

Arthur knelt down outside the shrine alongside Brother Geraint. Praising God, they shone as they thanked Him for bringing them safely to their destination and asked His forgiveness for not trusting all along that He would do so.

Once they rose to their feet we turned and followed him inside; each one of us ducking through the low doorway, we couldn't wipe the grins from our faces as we completed our pilgrimage, thanking the Lord not only for Rhianne's rescue all those many months ago, but also for all of ours this time. We'd made it, as Arthur had so desired.

We stayed a few days and then set out to make our way home - a happy band of people, satisfied on the outcome of their amazing adventure.

There was, however, one blight on our happiness - the loss of a dear, dear friend. He had been included in our prayers and, as had already been proved, most of our prayers had been answered. Perhaps this one would be too; perhaps one day we would meet up again with Sir Niel.

SIXTY-FIVE

'Well boys,' Jack said as he stretched. That's about it. You can clear up and get to bed while I walk Mrs Ambrose down to your mum's house. I won't be long. Cabby, you stay here!

'Sorry we won't be seeing you any more this time Mrs Ambrose, but you will come back and see us again, won't you? Come back again when mum's here.'

'Oh, we'll be meeting up again, never fear,' she responded with a grin as she and Jack swept through the doorway and into the starry night.

He waited until they were well out of earshot of the boys before Jack launched into a great list of questions that had been building up inside him since Merlin had arrived but had been unable to ask because of the boys.

'Whoa, whoa!' Merlin laughed. 'One at a time, please! Or should I just explain a few things to you?'

'Go on, then.'

'Well, looking back at those days, first of all, you'll be pleased to know, Culhwch and Olwen are very happy and living not too many miles away from Lady Elise's family in Carmarthen.

'Secondly, that mad witch has disappeared for some few years now – more than likely licking her wounds after her drenching at Bedruthan Steps. But, 'he sighed, 'I expect that once she gets angry enough – and she's had lots of time to do that – she'll be back. I'd just like to know where she's hidden herself.' He chewed at his lower lip a while as he considered this but, being the pragmatic person that he is, shrugged his shoulders and carried on.

'Arthur continues much as before, although he still worries about you, going off like you did.'

'What do you mean, going off like I did?' Jack asked.

Merlin turned and looked at Jack. 'You mean you don't remember?'

'Remember what?'

'Remember how you got back here; to the now.'

Jack stopped walking. Suddenly the vacuum that had eluded him for years danced before his eyes. 'No,' he mused as something he should always have known began to tap at his brain. He turned to face the wizard. 'No!' he exclaimed more loudly. 'There was always something missing from my mind; always something that eluded me. You've just hit it on the head! I don't recall how I returned to my own time. Tell me. You do know, don't you?' he asked worriedly.

Merlin laughed. 'Of course. I watched you mostly from the Glass after we went our separate ways but, even as I tell you, it will all come back to you. You will remember.

'When halfway home from the journey to Hinton St. Mary, you and I suddenly told Arthur that we needed to return to Bedruthan Steps. He tried hard to dissuade us, as he felt sure the witch would still be there and we might suffer much as a consequence. However, he couldn't turn us from our course and we almost had a falling out when we refused to listen to him.

'You said, "No. We have to do this. We must find out what has happened to Sir Niel. There was something about that man and I feel sure he still lives. We shall just head west and then follow the coastline until we get there. We might find him along the way."

'It took us over a week to get to that beach, by which time we'd used up almost all of the provisions we'd taken with us. I went in one direction and you scoured the beach in the other but there was no sign of a living being – no witch, no Sir Niel. I orchestrated your return from the cliff top before I returned to my cave watched you through the Glass. I was amused as I watched you walk around the rock that was Ysbaddaden and the broken pieces of Hellion. It's really hard

387

to imagine that they once lived and breathed, isn't it? I expect that they can be restored – like Cabal – like Moon Song! That witch will one day do something, I'm sure.

'Well, on the evening of the second day you saw, out of the corner of your eye, something bright clinging to one of the almost submerged rocks just a few yards out to sea. I could almost see the cogs moving in your brain as you realised it was the same colour as the jacket worn by Niel the last time you'd seen him.

'Stripping off your jerkin, shoes and shirt, you waded into the water and swam the last few feet, only to find that although it was Niel's jacket, Niel was not in it.

'Then the wave struck. You were washed halfway to the shore before being sucked back out to sea; no matter how you struggled, the currents were taking you further and further from the beach. It had now got very dark and, realising that you would most probably swim the wrong way and drown, you turned onto your back and allowed the sea to take you where it would, as you set your body to float.'

'The next thing was my father pulling me from the sea at Tintagel! I remember now!

'They all thought I had a fever. I was shouting for you and hoping Arthur would understand when I didn't return.

'After a while I believed I'd dreamed it, as only one night had gone by from visiting the cave to being saved from it.'

'Yes, well, sorry about that but I couldn't really have you spilling the beans. I needed to keep myself a myth in your day and age. I knew I could call you whenever I needed you but I didn't want everyone knowing that I am real for real! Real for real! That's a good one, eh?' he repeated it again as he doubled up laughing.

Jack stood shaking his head as Merlin tried to get himself under control.

'OK, Merlin, what happened to Niel. I have wondered all these years about him. I'm sure you know what happened so please let me know that he lived. He was such a great fellow. He didn't die, did he?'

'No, Percy, he is still alive. Like you, I bring him back from the future to help me from time to time. It just seems that he disappears. He is back now where he belongs.'

'And where is that?' Jack enquired.

'Well, it's somewhere you haven't got to yet. A brilliant place of invention and beauty; alongside destruction and ugliness – pretty much like today, I suppose – just different.'

Jack stood looking at Mrs Ambrose, hands on hips, not to be put off by inconsequential chatter.

'Hrrmph,' he cleared his throat. 'I brought him back that time from the year 2010.'

'2010!' Jack exclaimed. 'You've been to 2010?'

'Yes, well, once I'd been able to travel to you in the 20th Century, I wondered if I could venture further and so was quite surprised when I came back to my old house – old Mr Fellowes' house – in the 21st Century and found the family still there. I decided, then, that I might be able to use …'.

'Well, go on,' Jack urged, becoming increasingly uncomfortable at what he believed he was about to hear. 'You might be able to use what - who?'

'I think you know,' he said, rather sheepishly.

Jack waited.

'I might be able to use Daniel, who had become extremely receptive to the Old Way's way of communicating.'

'Daniel? Daniel?' Jack had started to walk on but stopped and turned so suddenly that Merlin almost walked into him.

'Daniel! Yes, Sir Niel. He was Daniel, wasn't he? I knew he looked familiar but he was always my grandson – so much younger; I didn't even stop to consider it might be him then – he was about seven or eight years older than me – or me as I was then! Can you believe it? It *is* him, isn't it?'

Merlin merely nodded.

389

'Why didn't you tell me? Did he know who I was?'

'Sorry Percy, it would have been too complicated for you to understand at your young age. Yes, he knew who you were. As it was, he was tempted on more than one occasion to tell you but I had made him promise he wouldn't.'

'I can't believe that I had an adventure with a grandson who was older than me. Who would believe it?' Jack moved on, shaking his head. 'Did anyone else know?'

'Er, yes – just one other.'

'Cabby! It had to be Cabby – he'd know.'

'Yes.'

'Why didn't he let me know?'

'Don't ask! I'm not going to give away all my secrets you know.' Becoming all businesslike again, he invited Jack to share a delicious cup of hot chocolate with him. 'If there's something I like as much as tea, it's hot chocolate. Had nothing like that in my day,' he grinned.

'Come in, come in; while I'm boiling the milk, ask me what you will. I think I've covered all the important bits.'

'Does Danny – my Danny sleeping in my home now – know about any of this?'

'No, of course not – and you are not to tell him either. As I reached out to you with no-one else involved, so you should leave me to do the same for him. Don't even try to mind speak to him – that will come when I've made him good and ready. You probably already believe he knows what you're thinking from time to time. Well, it will come to him naturally all in good time. So, leave well alone!' She looked over the rim of her glasses at Jack and frowned.

He nodded, and then grinned. 'Do you think you could take those glasses back with you and give them to Shake Spear?' he asked.

Merlin grinned back. 'Good idea! I'll do that. I'm pleased to see that my training of you has not been wasted!'

390

'There were one or two other things that puzzled me. I hope you can enlighten me?'

'Go on.'

'What happened to the chimeras at the beach? I didn't see them any more after all the shenanigans. Did they drown?'

'I couldn't really say. There was such a lot going on. But I believe that after the giant turned to stone, they eventually did too. It's really weird, but when the giant slept – I mean properly slept for weeks, months or years on end – everything disappeared: there was no castle, no servants, no chimeras and definitely no giant – they just disappeared. Olwen is the only one who appears to have stayed solid – thank goodness.'

'It's a shame, you know, because I met a very friendly youth called Cornek, who worked in the giant's kitchens. It would have been nice to have met him again.'

'These things happen, Percy,' Merlin answered with not too much compassion. 'That's life!'

'Oh, by the way, I've always meant to ask you! What is Nell's son's name? I never did find out!'

'Me neither! Everyone always just called him Nell's son! Didn't seem to need another name. Everyone knew who he was without needing to know it!'

'Oh, and did Sir Ector and Lady Elise's brothers return?'

'Yes, they managed to sort out all that trouble for the time being and arrived home safely late in the summer.'

Sitting comfortably each side of the roaring fire, they sat for some time in companionable silence before Jack, looking up and still being amazed at Merlin's transformation, asked, 'One last thing. Why could I not see it was you and Salazar when you looked like Pos and Neg?'

'Now that is something I am not going to tell you, young man. You don't know who might be listening in,' he replied with a wink. 'Besides, I must be allowed to keep some secrets, you know!'

Also by Jenny Hall

On the Dragon's Breath – a tale of Merlin

The first book in this series which tells a tale about the greatest sorcerer of all time – Merlin the Magician – that embraces mystery, magic, mayhem and madness alongside dragons, druids and a dreadful witch.

Jack, our 20th Century hero, is taken back through the mists on the Dragon's Breath to a time of adventure in the Dark Ages of King Arthur, son of Uther Pendragon. He shares those adventures with the future king's wolfhound, Cabal, who, you will discover, is more than just a dog!

For anyone who has ever told all their troubles to their dog, this tale is a must to read.

Ranging from the nail-bitingly frightening to the hysterically funny – this is a fantasy to please both young and old alike.

Enchanting!